She had no idea how long he had been there, silently watching her. But rather than trying to cover her naked body with her hands, she found that she was paralyzed, and could do nothing but look into his eyes, which were locked on hers.

Without taking his eyes from hers, slowly he began to undress. Wordlessly, he waded into the water and came toward her.

He stopped only inches away.

His hands were under the water now, lightly touching her forearms. She felt his fingers gliding up to her shoulders, sending shivers through her limbs. She was mesmerized by his eyes. She wanted to climb inside him, to fall endlessly into those green, green eyes.

"Jessie," he whispered, enfolding her in his arms.

As his kisses became longer and more insistent, her lips parted. Just when she thought she could stand no more, he pulled away, and began to lower her deeper into the water, kissing his way up her throat until her face was level with his. . . .

HEARTFIRE ROMANCES

SWEET TEXAS NIGHTS (2610, $3.75)
by Vivian Vaughan

Meg Britton grew up on the railroads, working proudly at her father's side. Nothing was going to stop them from setting the rails clear to Silver Creek, Texas—certainly not some crazy prospector. As Meg set out to confront the old coot, she planned her strategy with cool precision. But soon she was speechless with shock. For instead of a harmless geezer, she found a boldly handsome stranger whose determination matched her own.

CAPTIVE DESIRE (2612, $3.75)
by Jane Archer

Victoria Malone fancied herself a great adventuress, but being kidnapped was too much excitement for even Victoria! Especially when her arrogant kidnapper thought she was part of Red Duke's outlaw gang. Trying to convince the overbearing, handsome stranger that she had been an innocent bystander when the stagecoach was robbed, proved futile. But when he thought he could maker her confess by crushing her to his warm, broad chest, by caressing her with his strong, capable hands, Victoria was willing to admit to anything. . . .

LAWLESS ECSTASY (2613, $3.75)
by Susan Sackett

Abra Beaumont could spot a thief a mile away. After all, her father was once one of the best. But he'd been on the right side of the law for years now, and she wasn't about to let a man like Dash Thorne lead him astray with some wild plan for stealing the Tear of Allah, the world's most fabulous ruby. Dash was just the sort of man she most distrusted—sophisticated, handsome, and altogether too sure of his considerable charm. Abra shivered at the devilish gleam in his blue eyes and swore he would need more than smooth kisses and skilled caresses to rob her of her virtue . . . and much more than sweet promises to steal her heart!

Available wherever paperbacks are sold, or order direct from the Publisher. Send cover price plus 50¢ per copy for mailing and handling to Zebra Books, Dept. 3352, 475 Park Avenue South, New York, N.Y. 10016. Residents of New York, New Jersey and Pennsylvania must include sales tax. DO NOT SEND CASH.

WILD CAPTIVE FIRE

Caitlin Adams Bryan

ZEBRA BOOKS
KENSINGTON PUBLISHING CORP.

This book is for Murphy,
who never left my side.

ZEBRA BOOKS

are published by

Kensington Publishing Corp.
475 Park Avenue South
New York, NY 10016

Copyright © 1991 by Caitlin Adams Bryan

First printing: March, 1991

Printed in the United States of America

AUTHOR'S NOTE

In 1850, when Scottish immigrant Allan Pinkerton founded his Chicago-based detective agency, rural law enforcement in America was loosely comprised of overworked marshals, sheriffs aided by occasional and amateur deputies, and bounty hunters. In the larger cities, political control and corruption of law enforcement were often the norm. Because there was no centralized federal policing agency, criminals most often escaped by simply stepping over jealously guarded lines of jurisdiction into the next county or state.

The Pinkerton National Detective Agency took up the slack. A private police force, they could cross these lines with impunity in pursuit of their quarry.

The agency thrived. By the 1880's, when our story is set, Allan Pinkerton and his sons, William and Robert, were household names in America and most parts of Europe. The nineteenth century prototype of the yet to be created FBI and a forerunner of Interpol, the Agency had connections not only to our own Department of State and Secret Service, but to numerous foreign governments as well as Scotland Yard and la Sûreté.

Allan Pinkerton's agents tracked down train robbers, murderers, thieves, and rogues of all varieties. They battled the Mafia, already well entrenched in North America. They broke strikes, retrieved stolen jewels and art treasures, quelled riots and ferreted out embezzlers. The American Banker's Association subscribed to their services, and so imposing was the Pinkerton's reputation that, on more than one occasion, thieves (learning too late that they'd robbed a bank thus protected) returned their booty anonymously.

Operatives were recruited from all walks of life. Their ranks included former salesmen, lumberjacks, clerks, sailors, storekeepers, farmers, and policemen; near illiterates and college graduates; and all ages, types, and sizes of both men and women—the first female detective in America was a Pinkerton agent. But this diverse group had a few common characteristics that fitted them to be Pinkertons: they were highly secretive, resourceful, and perceptive; they were capable of assuming completely convincing undercover identities; and they were absolutely tireless.

The Agency's logo was an engraving of a watchful eye, beneath which was printed the slogan, "We Never Sleep." It is from their motto and insignia that we derive our term for the modern investigator: "private eye."

The Pinkertons had their failures. They made mistakes. They were human. But they cracked countless important national and international cases and brought innumerable criminals to justice. They brought order to a time when, in many parts of the United States and the world, chaos was the norm.

The series of events described in this novel are completely fictional. Jessica's father, the very proper (and very shady) Samuel LaCroix, as well as his brutal nemesis, Nathaniel Kane, never existed. Nor did Clay

McCallister or his friend, Charles Allen Brewster. But LaCroix and Kane are representatives of the sorts of underworld kingpins who operated during those strangely anachronistic Victorian times, and McCallister and Brewster typical of the talented and dedicated agents which would have been deployed by the Agency. The operation itself is as complex and far flung as many investigated by the Pinkertons.

Caitlin Adams Bryan
Phoenix, 1991

ACKNOWLEDGMENTS

My thanks to Ray, whose generous loan of the Kaypro greatly facilitated the birthing of this book; to Margaret, who kept demanding new chapters; to Tom, who provided the box; and especially to Mom and Dad, who had faith.

My beloved spake, and said unto me,
Rise up, my love, my fair one, and come away.
For, lo, the winter is past, the rain is over
   and gone;
The flowers appear on the earth; the time of
   the singing of birds is come, and the
   voice of the turtle is heard in our land . . .
                     Song of Solomon 2:10-12

1

San Francisco
Late May, 1885

The Gull Tavern was hazy with cheap tobacco smoke and stank of sweat and salt and stale beer. Gaslights mounted at irregular intervals along the peeling walls cast a greasy, halfhearted light upon the inhabitants' faces as they moved slowly through eddying currents of yellow smoke.

They were rough and dangerous men, most of them. A few seamen gathered around the front tables, their enthusiastic drinking and loud talk frequently punctuated by bursts of raucous laughter. Elements of the lower echelon of San Francisco's underworld crowded around other tables and leaned against the cracked and filthy bar. Some were bunched in tight little groups, talking quietly with heads bent. Others stood alone and apart; watching, listening, waiting.

Two women, attired in an abbreviated form of what might, in very poor light, pass for a parody of fancy dress, floated from table to table serving drinks, sizing up the men.

A third woman, blond and stuffed into a well-worn,

red-sequined gown, was perched on a drunken sailor's lap.

"Rosie's my girl, ain' she?" he slobbered with a lopsided grin.

"As long as you've got a dollar in your pocket and you can still dock that schooner of yours, she is, honey," she answered, and smacked his stubbly cheek with a damp kiss.

He laughed with a bellow of sour whiskey breath and roughly clamped a meaty paw over her breast. "Tha's right, Rosie, jus' you 'n' me."

With a smile of encouragement, she extracted herself and managed to haul him up—a surprising feat, for he was a big man. But then, she'd had plenty of practice.

She aimed him toward the rear exit that led to the Gull's tiny private rooms. "C'mon, sugar, you just come along with Rosie and show her how much you love her." They staggered away as the seaman's mates roared, then fell once again to their stories.

As Rosie passed the little table in the back corner, she was too busy piloting her besotted client to notice the three men who sat around it, engrossed in conversation.

Clay McCallister, tall, broad-shouldered (and at the moment, more than a little apprehensive), sat with his back to the room. It was something he would have avoided instinctively even if it hadn't been drummed into him over and over, but this time he hadn't any choice in the matter. The two men with whom he sat had chosen the tavern, the table, and the seating arrangements, and he had to play by their rules if he wanted to avoid suspicion.

Fletch and Loco had subjected him to this sideways audition for more than two hours now. Well, Fletch had, anyway. Young Ed "Loco" Wheeler mostly just sat there fidgeting in his chair, sucking at his beer, and giggling every once in a while. The way the wiry thug constantly twisted and squirmed, and his tittering, in-the-wrong-places laugh were bad enough, but what really made Clay's skin crawl were the boy's eyes. Set in a pasty-complexioned, hatchetlike face crowned by a shock of prematurely white hair, they were watery, large, and protruding. The left orb wandered so that the eyes never quite focused, but seemed to dart at random around the room, independent of each other. Strangest of all was the color of the irises: a pale, dirty yellow speckled with darker flecks of gold, so that he resembled nothing so much as a deranged and hungry bird of prey.

Clay thought he looked quite mad.

Fletch was a different story. He was muscular and robust, and at just better than six feet tall, he was nearly Clay's height. In his middle thirties, he was also roughly Clay's age, and he was Loco's senior by at least fifteen years. His skin, leathered by wind and sun, was tanned to almost the color of his sandy hair, and his clear blue eyes were alert, penetrating. Although his patterns of speech were rural and uneducated, he was, Clay suspected, much brighter than he was letting on: a man of whom to be wary.

Fletch had been doing most of the talking, asking questions, waiting for a slip. So far, Clay seemed to be providing the responses he wanted. Clay was careful, very careful. The operation was too important and too far along for him to slip up now. His normally calm, even speech and strong, passive features stood him in good stead. Like the outlaw across the table, whose casual questions and diffident manner masked a subtle scrutiny of every reaction, Clay, too, was holding back, playing the game.

The seeds of his infamy had been sown quietly, planted discreetly over the past months, so that Clay

13

had been preceded by a full-grown reputation as a man who could do a job and keep his mouth shut—a good man with a gun.

The first kernel had been pressed to fertile ground last fall, when Fletch got to talking with a ranch hand in an El Paso cantina. The cowboy made a fleeting reference to a tall, silent gunman named McCallister in connection with a shooting "somewhere up north." A month or so later, he overheard a snatch of conversation in an Arizona border town, something about a big man, a shootist-for-hire named Clay McCallister with a poker face and a fast hand. Then a rumor came around—floated past him—about a gringo called McCallister who had been drawn on by two pistoleros in some dusty Chihuahuan town; been drawn on by two men and dropped them both before they could get off a shot. They said his expression never changed.

Three weeks ago, Fletch had been having a beer in a saloon on the outskirts of some dying little town not far from Sacramento. It wasn't a busy night. There were less than half a dozen men scattered at the tables, and only two at the bar, himself and a big, stony-faced cowboy down at the other end, minding his own business. Fletch had a habit, born from years of necessity, of sizing up nearly every man who crossed his path. He was good at it. And after watching the stranger for a few minutes in the cracked mirror over the bar, he decided that this was not a man he'd choose to tangle with. He ordered another whiskey.

As the bartender poured, a new arrival stepped up to the rail and ordered a beer. Fletch gave him a cursory glance and dismissed him. *Farmer,* he'd thought, taking inventory. *A little jittery. A lot tired. Been riding a ways. Blond, big, maybe a Swede. Dull through the eyes, not too bright. Wearing an old Army-issue Colt. Not the type to use it well. Harmless.* All this he gathered in the second or two it took him to sweep a glance in the farmer's direction. He was turning his attention back to the shot glass in front of him when he noticed that the big Swede had suddenly stiffened. He was staring at the solitary cowboy at the other end of the bar.

"McCallister," he said under his breath, then louder, this time to the cowboy. "Clay McCallister."

The cowboy looked up. His eyes were intense, unblinking, their gaze absolutely unwavering, but his body seemed relaxed, his posture casual. His face was expressionless, unreadable.

Fletch made the connection immediately. This was interesting. It broke up the day. He had a feeling something significant was about to take place. Leaning on his elbow, he turned to get a clearer view of the proceedings.

The Swede had stepped away from the bar and out onto the floor. He looked scared, but determined. "McCallister!" he repeated. "My name's Thorson. I come from Kincaid County."

No response from the cowboy, not even a shift in position. Just the same flat, silent stare.

"Don't that mean nothin' to you, McCallister? It should, by God. It should make you weep for the shame of it!" The Swede was really agitated now. Fletch could see his fingertips twitching where they poked from his tattered cuffs.

The cowboy spoke. His voice was as flat and controlled as his gaze. "Get out of here, Thorson. Go home."

"Ain't goin' nowhere until you're dead. You're a bad man." His voice was getting higher, louder. "A very bad man."

C'mon, you chickenshit sodbuster, Fletch thought, *do something stupid. Hurry home to God.* Maybe the

15

farmer was just dumb enough and scared enough to try it. Interesting.

"Go home, Thorson," the gunman repeated quietly, evenly. His eyes narrowed just a little. "I don't want to kill you. No money in it."

"Trash!" the Swede shouted shrilly. "Filthy murdering trash!" His trembling hand went for the Colt.

Fletch didn't look quick enough to see McCallister draw. He only heard the shot. Saw the flash as the bullet struck metal. Saw Thorson's pistol fly into the air. Heard Thorson scream in pain and rage and surprise.

The farmer clutched his gun hand to his chest, cradling it. "My hand, you broke my hand!" he cried. Agony and frustration twisted his features.

McCallister had already reholstered his gun. "Go home, mister," he said. If there was any emotion in his voice, it was annoyance. "Any business you had here is done."

Thorson slunk toward the door, cowed. Just before he stepped out into the dark street, he looked back toward McCallister, who was just reaching for the glass in front of him. "Why . . . why didn't you kill me?"

"Told you," he said, tossing back the whiskey. "No money in it."

Fletch had waited a while, weighing the possibilities. Then he approached McCallister with a proposition. A money-making proposition.

In that decaying, half-deserted saloon, he had given Clay a rough outline of what the job might entail—no details—and had arranged tonight's meeting at the Gull. Clay wondered when Fletch would trust him enough to let him in on the particulars. The file they had on Fletch was accurate in its descriptions of the criminal's background, habits, and known associates, and had made note of his cunning, but it hadn't

16

prepared Clay for the sheer doggedness of this inquisition.

Loco, on the other hand, was just about what he had expected, except that the kid was even more bizarre than his dossier indicated. Even now, two hours into the meeting, the hair on Clay's forearms stood on end every time the boy started that crazy tittering laugh. The two were second cousins, or so the report said, and there were no indications that he ever worked with anyone except Fletch. In fact, in the intervals between his infrequent criminal surfacings, he did not seem to exist at all. Clay wondered where they locked him up between jobs.

The sailor passed out before he could get his money's worth, and Rosie rolled him cheerfully. She found three dollars, a pouch of tobacco, a pocket knife, a whale's tooth scrimshawed with the torso of a naked woman, and a nickel-plated pocket watch with the initial "H" on the inside lid. She took the money and stuffed the rest back into his trousers, then, on second thought, she exhumed the whale's tooth, jamming it and the silver cartwheels down the front of her dress. *Souvenir,* she thought, stepping over his snoring bulk.

She walked back into the tavern, and, leaning her elbows on the bar behind her, signaled to one of the other seamen. "Your mate's ready to go home now, sugar," she smiled, "but I think he's gonna need a hand."

The four remaining sailors, still in high spirits, rose in one boisterous unit and retrieved their luckless companion, jovially dragging him through the bar and out the front door, waving to Rosie. "See ya next time you're in port," she called.

Another of the girls, a petite, bedraggled brunette, joined her. They exchanged weary, understanding

17

looks. Rosie twisted her head around toward the bartender. "Coupla bourbons, Harry. Real ones, this time."

"Slow night," the other girl said as Harry placed two glasses on the grimy bar behind them. She indicated the door through which the sailors had departed. "Pass out on you?"

Rosie lifted the chipped glass to her lips. "Never got an oar in the water." She downed the whiskey in one gulp, then made a face and craned her head back toward the bartender. "Dammit, Harry, you water this stuff down any more, I ain't gonna be able to tell it from that crappy tea I been drinkin' all night."

Harry shrugged and went on about his business.

Rosie's attention wandered back to the customers. Nance was right about it being a slow night. There was no more money to be made from this group. She knew most of the men by sight, some of them by name. If any of them wanted a little female companionship, he would have had it by now. Her eye came to rest on the little group in the corner.

The sandy-haired guy seemed to be doing most of the talking. She thought she knew him. Not by name, but she'd seen him in the tavern a time or two before. Not a bad-looking fellow, almost handsome. Why didn't the good-looking ones ever want to pay for it? Then the little guy next to him leaned out of the shadows and started to giggle. Rosie shuddered and unconsciously rubbed at the gooseflesh sprouting on her arms.

"Spooky one, ain't he?" Nance said, having much the same reaction. "Hope he ain't in the market for a good time. It's guys like that make me want to take up honest livin'."

Rosie nodded and turned her attention to the third man at the table. His back was toward her, but she could catch fleeting glimpses of his profile as he spoke.

He seemed familiar. She wished she could see his face.

He reminded her of something. Some*where,* maybe. She watched his broad shoulders as he slouched in his chair. His hat was on the table, and she could see his hand thoughtfully fingering the brim. The band on the Stetson was silver, unusual in its design. Four strips of thin flat metal, plaited together and joined by a cartwheel in the front. That, too, struck a chord.

I know this fella, she thought. *I* know *I know him.* Just then the little guy laughed again. She jerked involuntarily, then snatched her empty glass off the bar. "Harry!" she snapped, "Do me again!"

Harry leaned over and poured her another shot. "You're gettin' awful pushy for somebody who ain't doin' squat business. O'Hanlan says—"

"Screw O'Hanlan," she snapped. Harry shrugged and went back to washing glasses, or at least pretending to. Rosie swallowed the whiskey thoughtfully, and got back to the business at hand. Where, when, had she seen this guy before? Not in here, that was for sure. A long time ago—Texas maybe. Dallas? Fort Worth? Galveston?

Galveston. That was when she worked at Bessie Bodine's big gaming house. She worked for Miss Bessie for almost six months and might still be there today except that Pinkerton men had come in and closed them down. Something about a smuggling ring. The agents had been real nice to her, treated her like a genuine lady. Those were better days, when she was younger and prettier, and when the pleasure of her company had cost more than a few dollars and a chunk of scrimshaw. Could it have been only three years ago?

The thought was depressing, and she was about to yell at Harry to pour her another watery bourbon when the three men stood up. The tall man with the broad shoulders rocked the silver-banded hat down on his head and turned into the light.

She knew him, all right.

"OK, then," Fletch was saying. "I think it's time we go talk to Mr. Kane."

Clay nodded, relieved that this part of the ordeal was over. Now, on to Nathaniel Kane. If he could pass through the next interview unscathed, he was in. The three men rose, Loco's eyes dancing separately around the dim room as he stifled a new outburst of giggles with a pale, narrow hand.

Clay put on his hat.

"Clay? Clay McCallister?" A frowsy, overrouged, once-pretty blonde stepped toward him. He did a mental scramble, trying to place her.

"It's me! Rosie! From Galveston? You know, the time you—"

Galveston, that was it. Damn, was there any worse timing? "Hello, Rosie!" he said, interrupting her. "It's been awhile."

She beamed, delighted he had recognized her. He was even more handsome than she remembered. "I'll never forget how nice to me you was when you 'n Mr. Brewster—"

Damn. He reached out and grabbed her, halting her in midsentence, and did the best thing he knew to keep her from saying more.

Rosie never knew what hit her.

With a quick twist that took her slightly off her feet and hid her body from Nance and the others, Clay gathered Rosie in his arms and kissed her, kissed her hard. One hand, flat against the small of her back, pressed her to him tightly, and the other stroked the side of her neck. But the fingers at her throat were not the bearers of a lover's caress, for as he deepened the

20

kiss, distracting the enthusiastic Rosie (as well as Fletch and Loco and the other barmaid, who he knew would be watching), his fingertips searched the side of her once-beautiful neck until he found just the right spot.

As he felt her knee slide hopefully up the outside of his thigh, he said a silent prayer and gently but firmly pressed his thumb into the column of her throat.

Nance said later that it started out like a regular kiss, but somehow it got to be, well, something entirely different. The cowboy's back was to her, she said, so she couldn't see much. All she knew was that it must have been one hell of a kiss.

"It was like she had the catatonics or somethin'," Nance recalled. "She didn't even know the rest of us was in the room." Rosie started to pant then, Nance said, "like a scrod pulled up on the dock." Then all of a sudden, her head jerked back, all the cords standing out in her neck, her eyes wide. Her mouth opened up and she took in air with a hiss that sounded like a scream going the wrong way. One of her arms uncurled from the cowboy's neck and extended, rigid, over his shoulders, the palm at a right angle and the fingers outstretched "like a Bible thumper at a prayer meetin'." Then she went limp.

It took far less than a minute, and it was the damnedest thing little Nance had ever seen.

Clay carried Rosie to the bar and laid her down, neatly arranging her skirt. He put a bar towel under her neck, and draped it against her throat to cover the faint red mark his thumb had left. *Sorry, Rosie,* he thought. *But at least there shouldn't be a bruise. . . .*

He looked up. The tavern had gone dead silent. To his left stood Nance, open-mouthed and clutching a glass, her knuckles white.

"Is she—she ain't dead, is she?" she half-whispered,

21

as if she wasn't quite certain it was such a bad way to go.

Clay shook his head. "Passed out," he said. "Better let her sleep it off." Nance nodded dumbly.

Fletch and Loco stood off to one side. Loco was giggling wildly, both hands covering his mouth, his feet tapping an odd little dance. Fletch leaned with one hand on a chair back. He was slowly shaking his head in disbelief.

"Shit," he grinned.

Clay shrugged noncommittally. "Old friend."

"Musta been glad to see you."

"Looks that way." Clay turned toward the door, closing the subject. "Let's get on with it."

They entered the dark world of the Barbary Coast back streets, redolent with the odors of raw sewage and fresh manure, and, detouring around the occasional sprawled drunkard, made their way up the hill. It was not yet midnight, and there was still some traffic. The sounds of echoing hoofbeats and frequent murmurs of laughter or raised, angry voices drifted between the buildings.

Neither Fletch nor Loco were aware of the figure pressed into the shadows of the alley across the way, so they assumed nothing out of the ordinary when Clay paused in the gloom to light a cigarette. The match flared briefly, brightly in his palm, and the man in the shadows, seeing it, retreated into the darkness.

A few blocks later, Fletch stopped in front of a dilapidated storefront. After double-checking the address against a slip of paper he pulled from his vest pocket, he motioned them inside.

Loco hesitated, suddenly more terror-ridden than manic. He gripped the door frame with trembling fingers. "Don't make me go in there, Fletch," he whined. "I'll stay right out here. I won't go nowhere, I

22

promise." His eyes, already wild things, were now frightened, his face distorted by fear. *"Please,* Fletch," he begged.

But Fletch took him by the shoulder and dragged his limp, quaking body through the doorway. "You got to go in, kid," Clay heard him whisper. "He said he wanted to see you, specific like."

"Oh, God, Fletch," Loco whimpered. "I seen what he had 'em do to Drago—he was . . . he was . . . all over the place. Pieces of him! What if—"

"You *gotta* go in, kid. He told me he'd give you another chance, honest. But you gotta go in there and face up to him, or you *will* end up gutted on the dock."

The boy shivered under Fletch's hand, but at last got himself enough under control that he could stand unassisted.

"You gonna be OK, boy?" Fletch asked, not unkindly.

Loco nodded somewhat uncertainly, and Fletch motion to Clay. "C'mon," he murmured. "Let's get this over with."

They walked through the night-filled room toward a dimly lit, bead-curtained doorway. Fletch parted the beads, and they came into a narrow hall. They passed several doors before Fletch, consulting his paper again, led them into a room small enough to be garishly illuminated by the single kerosene lamp hanging on one wall. At the far end of the chamber was another door, over which was mounted a small brass store-keeper's bell.

The room contained no couch or chair, only that glaring lamp and a battered wall clock bearing the flaking legend, "Dr. Blossom's Indian Tonic! A Miracle Restorative From Our Red Brothers." Dr. Blossom's pendulum swung inexorably back and forth, filling the cubicle with its monotonous and somehow

23

ominous sound.

They stopped here, and Clay looked at Fletch questioningly.

Fletch understood. "We wait," he said, and leaned resignedly against the peeling wall.

And wait they did. The time stretched out: five, then ten minutes went by. They did not talk among themselves. Somehow the atmosphere of the stark, windowless chamber robbed them of words or the energy to speak them.

Fifteen, sixteen minutes passed. Fletch slid down to the floor and sat with his arms wrapped around one knee. His face was tilted down, hidden from view, but Clay could see the outlaw's fingers clenching and unclenching in time to the relentless rhythm of the ticking clock.

His back pressed tight against the wall's flaked paint, Loco stood opposite them, twisting his hat into an unrecognizable rag. The boy's face, normally pale and wan, was now frighteningly bloodless, whiter than new parchment. His feet had stopped their nervous shuffling, and he seemed rooted to the dirty floor like a deformed and ghostly sapling, a prime candidate (if ever there was one, Clay thought) for Dr. Blossom's Miracle Restorative. His only movements were the unconscious wringing of the sodden felt in his fingers and the darting of his yellow eyes—now, it seemed, in time to that all-pervasive ticking.

Twenty minutes. Twenty-five. It was all Clay could do to keep himself from ripping the damned clock from the wall. He wanted to smash it, to shut it up, and then to get out and never come back. But now he, like the mad boy, seemed rooted to the spot, hypnotized by the pendulum's meter. For the fiftieth time in the last half-hour, he wondered what the hell he was doing here. *I should be home,* he berated himself. *Home, safe at*

24

Turtle Creek. Why didn't I listen to the Captain? Why am I so goddamned bullheaded?

A slither, a slide of wood against wood, snapped him back to attention, and he looked up just in time to see a tiny, heretofore hidden panel in the door snap shut. Loco jerked forward, a shrill wail escaping his pursed white lips, and Clay saw a wet stain spreading darkly on the boy's trousers.

Fletch, too, had started at the sound and scrambled to his feet. Now he stood expectantly, if somewhat hesitantly, before the door. Clay could see that he, too, had gone pale—pale enough that his tan seemed translucent, almost painted on. And it seemed to Clay that none of them were breathing.

Then the tiny bell over the door tinkled, the macabre jingle of a shopkeeper's bell. Loco shied backwards, bounding off the wall and into the center of the room. As Fletch put out a hand to steady him, he glanced down at the stain blossoming on the boy's pants, then back into Loco's eyes. The boy was terrified and humiliated beyond speech, and began to cry soundlessly.

But Fletch turned away from him, twisted the knob, and entered the next room, leaving Clay and Loco to the ticking of the clock and the rising smell of urine.

A few moments later he reappeared and, with a gesture, beckoned them inside. Clay reluctantly took Loco's arm and helped the trembling boy through the door.

The cubicle was deep in shadow. Clay stood between the other two men. Their backs to the door, they faced a heavy, worm-holed desk which appeared to be the only piece of furniture in the room. A small, tin-shaded oil lamp on the desk was turned down to a feeble glow, and it cast a yellow pool of light on the dull wooden surface. They waited silently, hats in their hands. Loco stood to one side, weeping quietly.

As Clay's eyes grew accustomed to the dimness, he was able to discern someone behind the desk. A shadowy figure before a clasped pair of manicured hands appeared in the circle of lamplight. The right hand bore a heavy gold ring set with a large piece of carved jade, a bas-relief dragon's head.

Nathaniel Kane.

"Yes, Mr. Fletcher," Kane said, breaking the silence at last. The voice was quiet, cultured, effete. "I believe he will do."

Next to Clay, Fletch nodded solemnly. "Yessir."

"Mr. McCallister, Mr. Fletcher recommends you to me. I trust his judgement. Therefore, I trust that you will not disappoint either of us. Mr. Fletcher informs me that he has already apprised you of the terms of your payment, correct? And these terms are satisfactory?"

Clay nodded.

"Good." Kane paused briefly. Clay could hear Loco's feet shuffling nervously on the floorboards.

"I want you to, shall we say, *detain* a woman. A certain Mrs. Jessica Lawrence. You will remove her from a stagecoach in the Arizona Territory. As to the exact time and place of the abduction, Mr. Fletcher will provide you with the pertinent details as he deems necessary.

"This is how you will know her. She is a young woman of twenty-four years, slightly taller than average, slender, dark haired. They tell me she is rather attractive. Once she is in your possession, one of you will take her to a location chosen by Mr. Fletcher. This person will have to be either Mr. Fletcher or Mr. McCallister." The voice grew even more ominous. "Under no circumstances will this person be Mr. Wheeler, as we all, with the exception of Mr. McCallister, remember what happened the last time he

26

was placed in a similar situation."

Loco raised his hat so that the crumpled brim covered his mouth, and stifled a nervous, frightened giggle. The stench of his urine grew heavier by the minute in the confines of the tiny, airless room. *Any second,* Clay thought, *this kid is going to ricochet off the walls.*

"The remaining two," Kane's disembodied voice continued, "will lay down a trail to divert the rescue party which is sure to follow."

Clay raised an eyebrow.

"Perceptive, Mr. McCallister. You are wondering why a posse would follow the trail of two horses, especially two horses bearing single riders, when three were used in the abduction. I am not in the habit of offering explanations, but since you are new to our organization, I shall put your mind at rest.

"Only two of you will actually approach and detain the stage," Kane continued, rather smugly. "The third will stay behind, well out of sight. He is to fill two sacks—which Mr. Fletcher will provide—with stones and gravel to a weight of approximately one hundred-twenty pounds. These he will attach to his saddle. Thus, the tracks made by the decoy riders will appear to have been made by one horse carrying a single rider and a second horse carrying two."

Clay straightened, as much as to lean a little further away from Loco as to indicate satisfaction with Kane's explanation.

"I see I have your approval, Mr. McCallister. However, keep in mind that I do not need it. I require only your loyalty and your silence, for both of which you will be well paid." The index fingers of the hands clasped in that desktop pool of light extended to form a little steeple. The tips tapped together twice before Kane's voice continued. "As to you, Mr. Wheeler—"

A whimper escaped Loco's lips, muffled by the hat he still pressed over them. The smell of damp trousers grew suddenly more pungent, and Clay realized that the boy's bladder had voided for (he hoped) the last time.

"—you are aware that this is your final opportunity for redemption. Had it not been for Mr. Fletcher's intercession on your behalf, you would be . . . no longer with us. He assures me that the incident in question was isolated, and will not occur again. I hope he is correct, Mr. Wheeler. It was very messy. All that blood on the draperies . . . This time you will exercise more self-control."

Loco's fingers twitched. "Yessir, Mr. Kane," he croaked. "You can count on me, sir." The boy was still squirming, but Clay sensed the tension in the tiny room easing appreciably.

"Very good. By the way, I would prefer that you avoid bloodshed altogether when you detain Mrs. Lawrence's coach. If, however, circumstances should compel you to use firearms, I strongly suggest you use them to *persuade* rather than kill. I understand you have some degree of skill in this area, Mr. McCallister. I trust I can count on your discretion."

Clay nodded. It seemed he had passed muster.

"And now," Kane continued from behind his veil of shadows, "if you two gentlemen will be kind enough to wait outside, I would like a private word with Mr. Fletcher."

By the time Clay and Loco stepped onto the sidewalk, the boy's quirky bravado had returned in full force, and it was a long five minutes before Fletch joined them on the street. "Believe we'll stay over at your hotel tonight, McCallister," he said as they walked up the hill, the boy skittering in their wake. The murky air had grown chilly, and his words came out in little

28

plumes. "We got an early start tomorrow. Lotta travelin' to do."

The big man nodded.

They walked on in silence, finally reaching a more traveled street where they were able to hail a cab.

Fletch and Loco found lodging on the third floor, just down the hall from Clay. He waited an hour before stealing noiselessly down the corridor and pausing outside their door. When he was satisfied that both men were sleeping soundly, he found the service stairs and descended to emerge in a dead-ended alley behind the building. He pulled his jacket more tightly against the damp chill and waited.

It was not long before the stillness was broken by the sound of boots softly crunching the wet gravel at the alley's entrance. Clay pulled back into the shadows of the building. A dark figure in a long duster approached, enshrouded up to the knees by swirling ground fog and silhouetted by the gaslights in the street behind him. The shadow man came closer, his footsteps echoing as he walked down the center of the alley. When he drew even with the place where Clay waited, pressed against the wall, he paused and casually reached into his breast pocket, bringing out a fancy gold cigarette case.

He extracted a ready-made and, placing it beween his lips, said, "You planning to stand there in the dark all night, Clayton?" His voice was clipped, British. He lit the cigarette, then offered the case.

McCallister stepped forward and took it, removing one for himself.

"You certainly took your sweet time getting down here," the shadow man continued. "I've been checking this alley every fifteen minutes for the last hour and a half, and I'm bloody well freezing to death."

"Sorry, Brewster," Clay said. "I had to wait. They checked in down the hall from me."

"How delightful. I must commend you on your taste in business associates, Clayton. Especially the smaller one with the big eyes and the happy feet. Charming little fellow." He smiled in an utterly insinuating fashion and tipped his hat back with a forefinger, revealing a chiseled face with an aquiline nose. A tidy crop of golden curls peeked from beneath his hat brim. "I'm assuming that you met with our Mr. Kane, and that he accepted you in all your criminal glory—or at least, he refrained from slicing you to ribbons."

"That'd be a safe bet."

"So tell me, Clay. What does the little bastard look like?"

McCallister dropped his cigarette. It disappeared into the ground fog and hissed on the damp pavement. "We're no better off on that score than we were before. I only saw his hands and heard his voice. Saw the ring, anyway."

"Damn."

They stood in silence for a moment. Then Clay spoke. "Tell J.D. he was right. Kane's lining it up just the way he figured. We're supposed to take LaCroix's daughter off the stagecoach someplace in Arizona. Two of us will stop the stage and take the girl. Two of us will be seen riding away and will lay down a set of tracks for the posse to follow. And one of us, either Fletcher or myself, is supposed to take her to the rendezvous point, wherever *that* is. I'll make it my business to be the one to transport Mrs. Lawrence."

"When and where?"

"Good question. In fact, it's such a good question that I'll let you and J.D. figure it out. Could be anywhere along the route where there's good cover."

"He didn't tell you, then."

"Just Fletch. Kane's a careful man, Brewster. He wouldn't have gotten this far if he weren't."

Brewster turned away, his lips tight, then looked back into his friend's quietly composed face. "You'll be on your own, then."

Clay allowed himself a sardonic smile. "Don't worry, Brewster. I'll take good care of her. And myself. We've known all along it'd probably go this way. You guys just take care of your end."

"At least we'll have somebody on the coach. To make certain no one gets trigger-happy."

Clay nodded. "By the way," he continued, "I ran into an old friend of ours this evening."

Brewster lifted one golden brow.

"You remember about three years ago when we broke that smuggling ring in Galveston?"

"Bodine's? Of course."

"Remember a pretty little blonde that worked in the house, the one named Rosie?"

"Ah, yes, the fair Miss Rosie . . ." Brewster grinned, his eyes twinkling mischievously. "Had I not been a happily married man, I might have been tempted to partake of her more than adequate charms."

"Well, it seems our Miss Rosie has fallen on hard times. She's working at the bar you staked out tonight. She recognized me."

Brewster stiffened. "Did she say anything?"

Clay shook his head. "No. She started to, but I . . ." He looked aside, slightly embarrassed. "She sort of fainted."

Brewster looked down at his feet, chuckling. "Fainted, did she?" He rocked back on his heels.

"Shut up, Brewster."

The chortling continued. "Just dropped dead away, I imagine." He looked up to see McCallister's pained, self-conscious face. "Did it again, didn't you?"

"It's not funny, Brewster," he muttered. "What else could I do? She recognized me. And somebody'd better get down there pretty damned fast and make sure she gets an out-of-town vacation for the next couple of weeks."

"All right, my irresistible friend," Brewster laughed, "it will be taken care of. I shall keep your shameful secret forever. I only wish to God I had a similarly deplorable gift."

McCallister stepped toward the door. "Thanks. I guess I'll see you when I see you." He put his hand on the latch, then hesitated. "By the way, tell Markheimer he does a great Swede. Guy should have gone on the stage. If I didn't know better, I'd've sworn I really *had* broken his hand during the pistol trick."

"Oh, I don't know that his thespian gifts are all *that* spectacular." Brewster pulled his hat back down and shoved his hands into the pockets of his duster. "The cast comes off next Thursday. . . ."

McCallister leaned his forehead against the door frame. "Damn." When he looked up, Charles Allen Brewster had vanished into the night.

2

Boston

"I'm sorry, Owen, but the arrangements have been made." Jessica had avoided this particular confrontation for as long as she could, and now that she'd finally found the courage to speak, she felt sick and giddy and frightened all at once. She focused on the half-finished needlepoint in her slender hands and tried to keep her voice as controlled as the fine, precise stitches. "I shall be leaving Tuesday, and I'll be back in three months. Father is expecting me, as is Rachel." She pierced the tightly stretched fabric again, drawing through pale green, silky threads and praying that she sounded more sure of herself than she felt.

"You rarely see me anyway," she continued, keeping her tone calm and even and her eyes on her needlework. "It's more than likely that you'll not even notice my absence." She was sitting in her favorite chair in the morning room, beside the wide diamond-paned window that overlooked the dark, rambling house's rose garden. Owen was standing over her, those silly little glasses perched on his nose, shaking his finger again.

"Jessica," he chided, his tone so plainly patronizing

that she wanted to slap him, "if you must insist in traipsing all over the countryside, please take some of the servants with you. At least take your personal maid, what's-her-name. That Mary Jane person."

"Miriam." Could he never get anything right? She looked up, and at the first glimpse of her husband's chubby, reddening face (puckered with an exasperation that verged on the comical), the last of the fear washed out of her.

"Pardon me?" He sniffed and adjusted his pince-nez.

"Her name is Miriam. Honestly, Owen, the woman has been with us over a year now and you still can't remember her name. And I shan't be 'traipsing all over the countryside.'" She mimicked his supercilious tone perfectly, though he failed to notice. She secured her needle at the edge of the hoop and set it aside, taking care not to tangle the bright, rich threads.

"I will be visiting Father in Denver and then my cousin Rachel in Arizona. For years, she's been begging me to come and spend time on their ranch. And now that she has been widowed . . . well, I can hardly refuse her this time. I don't think I should call that 'traipsing.'" Her fine features were set: her full lips pursed, her chin lifted. She stared down her nose at him resolutely and forged ahead.

"As to taking my maid, I've been giving it some thought, and I've come to the decision that I am a grown woman of some intelligence and resource, and that I am perfectly capable of undertaking this journey without a companion to hold my hand."

Owen clenched his moist, pudgy hands into fists and gritted his teeth. She had never before stood her ground so firmly. He took a breath and paused in an attempt to temper his anger. This new attitude of hers was most irritating. "My dear Jessica, is simply isn't done. You have absolutely no idea what difficulties you may run into. A woman traveling alone places herself in a—"

"—compromising position. I know, Owen. You've told me before. But thanks to Father and men like him, there are nice, safe railways to protect travelers such as myself from being ravaged by Indians and looted by desperados."

Owen opened his pink little mouth to interrupt, but she had built up momentum and didn't give him a chance.

"We live in a modern age, Owen. I shall be perfectly safe. I know I've never traveled alone before. I've never done *anything* alone before, and I believe it's about time that I did." She lowered her head a little, her expression softening. He was her husband, after all. "Please, Owen, allow me this one thing."

Jessica stared out the window, watching the landscape rush by, going over the conversation in her head for the hundredth time. She was still amazed that she'd stood up to him. And won. She had always deferred to Owen—outwardly, anyway—and before Owen, she had done her stepfather's bidding. And though she had sometimes been clever enough to get her own way in a roundabout fashion, she had never before been so forthright in asserting her wishes. Owen had finally, grudgingly, relented, and by the time the day of her departure arrived, he was actually pleasant, or at least as pleasant as it was possible for Owen to be.

And here she was—alone—on her way to Denver, in no one's charge but her own. That such a simple thing could be so exhilarating! She hugged herself and smiled at her own reflection as it wobbled on the rattling glass.

Jessica's mother, Margaret O'Steen Cavanaugh

LaCroix, was the auburn-haired, carefree daughter of an immigrant miner who struck it rich in the gold fields of California, and she had spent her own childhood running barefoot and wild through her father's mining camp. She was sixteen when she married Jessica's father, Sean Cavanaugh, a handsome, silver-tongued, Black Irish scamp. Two and a half years later (and six months before Jessica's birth), Sean Cavanaugh drowned in the Sacramento River. Little Jessica was still an infant when Margaret married again, this time to Samuel LaCroix, a wealthy and powerful man twenty-four years her senior.

A chubby, precocious infant, Jessica grew into a beautiful child, fair and lightly freckled like her mother, with her father's dark hair and clever mind. From her mother she also inherited a shining sense of wonder for the world around her as well as all the creatures inhabiting it.

Because they lived in town in her stepfather's big house, Jessica was denied the close proximity to nature that her mother had enjoyed during her own untamed youth; but Margaret made up for this drawback of city living by introducing her daugher, at an early age, to the wonders of the estate's gardens, kennels, and stables. Samuel LaCroix's grounds were immaculately kept, so the nature that Jessica grew to know was one carefully controlled by gardeners and groomsmen, but it was one which fascinated her nonetheless.

She remembered her mother's lullabies mingling with the drowsy purring of the marmalade cat that was her pet. This most comforting of duets consigned her to sleep each night. She remembered her mother, secretive and smiling, taking her to the stables and lifting her to look into an airy box stall filled with clean golden straw, where a newly born foal, still wet, struggled to its feet for the first time.

There were sunny summer days when she and her mother would walk through the flower gardens, Margaret pointing out the blooms, some vibrant, some subtle and sweet, reciting their rich and melodic names—amaryllis, jonquil, iris, nasturtium—and plucking blossoms for Jessie's hair and her own.

She could picture with clarity a particular day she and her mother had ridden through town in the brougham, all dressed up; going where, she could no longer recall. The streets, deep with mud and dimpled with potholes, were noisy and crowded with carriages and wagons, and they had to stop frequently while the traffic snarled and unsnarled itself. Jessie was fascinated by the hubbub and bustle of the city and was busy trying to drink in all of San Francisco in one huge gulp. So when she heard the sound of a man's angry voice raised above the normal din of street sounds she immediately poked her pink-bonneted head out the window.

"Mama!" she cried, suddenly horrified. "The horse! It's hurt, Mama!" Tears were already cutting hot paths down her cheeks as Margaret leaned past the child to see where she was pointing.

Their carriage had stopped near a treacherously steep cross street. At the top of the hill, just before the street leveled for the intersection, a horse was down. Hitched to a heavy wagon loaded with wooden kegs, it had slipped and fallen, and now lay on its side between the traces, hopelessly ensnared in its own harness. As the horse struggled in vain to stand, its driver, a burly red-faced carter, whipped it mercilessly, bellowing curses as his lash cut the groaning bay again and again.

Jessie felt her mother's hand on her arm. "Don't you move, Jessie. You stay put!" She had never before seen her mother look so angry.

"Billings, stay here," her mother called to their

37

coachman as she nimbly stepped out onto the muddy street. "Watch Jessie. But keep an eye out—I may need you!" she called as she waded purposefully through the muck.

"Yes, *ma'am!*" the driver exclaimed. Little Jessie, leaning from the window, could see his grin broaden as he watched Margaret striding—as briskly as she could through the thick mud—toward the roaring carter and his struggling mare.

They were too far away for Jessie to make out exactly all of the words they spoke, but she saw her mother stop in front of the carter and gesture angrily from him to the hapless animal and back again. By now a small crowd had gathered around the wagon, but the livid carter was not about to embarrass himself by bending to the demands of some bleeding-heart female. He furiously gestured back at her, yelled something about minding her own business, and brandished his whip in the air before he struck out at the bay again. But just before he could inflict another bloody welt on the mare, Margaret O'Steen Cavanaugh LaCroix did an amazing thing.

She lunged forward, muddy skirts flying, and ripped the lash from his hand. The carter looked up, thunderstruck, as Margaret turned the whip on *him,* striking him on the back and shoulders as he covered his head with his arms. Applause and cheers and more than a few giggles burst from the onlookers as she then grasped the whip with both hands and cracked it sharply over her knee, breaking it in two before throwing the pieces to the ground. Then she reached for her purse, pulled out a handful of coins and disdainfully threw them into the mire at the feet of the befuddled driver. Jessie watched open-mouthed as her mother, with the help of two gentlemen from the crowd, carefully calmed, untangled, and unhitched the mare, then coaxed her to her feet.

Margaret led the horse back to Jessie, who was waiting excitedly in the carriage, and tied her to the back of the brougham.

"She's going to be just fine, Jessie," she said. "You and I will see to that, won't we?" Then she threw her arm over the horse's bony withers, beaming.

And that was how she remembered her mother best: attired in mud and green velvet, plumed hat askew, arms thrown around the neck of that scrawny, battered mare—looking radiantly, amazingly beautiful.

The thin, work-worn mare, newly christened Emily, went home with them and was ensconced in a bright, roomy stall next to Margaret's favorite hunter. She soon lost her gaunt, hungry look, became fat and glossy, and was delighted to give Jessie bareback rides around the courtyard. She was an old horse when she moved into Margaret's stable, and Samuel, seeing her for the first time, pronounced that she wouldn't make it through the week. But the love and care lavished on her by Margaret and her grooms proved him wrong. She lived another nine years, and finally died peacefully in her stall, a wisp of sweet timothy hay in her mouth.

She outlived Margaret by almost eight years.

Jessie was six and a half when her mother died. The baby was born blue, someone told her later, and died in the doctor's arms even as Margaret's sightless eyes were being closed by the midwife.

The housekeeper brought the news to Jessie, telling her that she would have to be a very brave girl, because her mother had gone away.

Puzzled, she searched out her stepfather and found him in the wide, marble-floored entry hall. He was sitting on the steps at the bottom of the grand staircase, his head in his arms. Jessie put her tiny white hand on his shoulder, patting softly at his coat. His big hand reached up and covered hers, comforting her the best he could.

"But where did Mama *go?*" she asked. He looked up. She could tell he had been crying, something she had never before seen him do. "Father, don't be so sad. Mama never stays away very long. Maybe she went to get the new baby. She said we'd be getting one very soon."

Samuel reached for her and swept her tiny form into his lap, hugging her tightly. "Jessica," he said, his voice breaking, "your mother has not gone away."

"But Mrs. Fowler said—"

"Mrs. Fowler was wrong to tell you that." He ran long, slim fingers through his graying hair. "Jessica, your mother . . . your mother is dead."

Dead. She knew what dead was. Dead was the black kitten she found behind the kennels last summer. Dead was the contents of the compost heap where the stable boys buried the rats they killed. Dead was Grampa O'Steen, into whose black-draped silver casket she had looked last year. She knew what dead was.

"Father," she said, her chin quivering, "what made Mama die?"

"She . . . she was—It was the baby, Jessica. She was trying to bring your baby brother to us."

"Brother?"

Samuel coverd his face with a trembling hand. "My son, my son is dead," he sobbed. "Oh, God . . . Margaret . . ."

Jessie pulled away from her father. She stood before him, her face red and contorted. "Did the baby make Mama die?"

Samuel, weeping, could not answer.

"I'm glad!" she cried. "I'm glad the baby's dead! He

killed her! He killed my mama!"

Samuel reached for her, but she was already gone, running blindly toward her mother's stables.

Of the days and weeks that followed, she could recall only fleeting images, like faded photographs in an album: Mrs. Fowler, silently hooking the buttons on Jessie's shoes, a teardrop spattering on the shiny black leather; Billings, swollen-eyed, twisting his hat in his big chapped hands as he stood beside the brougham in the cold drizzle, waiting to drive them to the cemetery; her stepfather, tall and somber in his black suit, his eyes blank, his face devoid of expression, standing next to her as Father Stephen solemnly intoned the eulogy; the gravediggers, seen through the mist, lounging under half-denuded autumn trees, waiting to cover her mother's coffin with moist, dark earth and seal her into the ground forever.

The house itself was different. The big, high-ceilinged rooms, once bright and filled with laughter, were now silent and cold. The servants tiptoed up and down the echoing corridors, speaking in whispers, clinging to the dark-paneled walls. Samuel, suddenly old, wandered from room to room, searching for something he knew he would never find.

He could no longer bear his stepdaughter's company. Even though the once-animated child had grown pale and taciturn, her face was still her mother's. He had no comfort for her. He had none for himself.

Samuel LaCroix was the third son of a rather uninspired New Orleans cobbler and his Scots-English bride, and he grew up poor and ambitious. He left home just before his fifteenth birthday to work in the

41

offices of a struggling freight concern. A quick study, he rapidly worked his way up, mastering every facet of the business as he went.

A humorless, unexpressive man, Samuel made few friends among his peers, but impressed his superiors. He grew more ruthless with each passing year, and his investments (small at first, larger as time went on) in both the legitimate and the illicit made him a wealthy and powerful man. Before he was thirty, he owned the Overland Freight Company (now an infant railroad network) for which he had once been an errand boy, as well as a fledgling import company.

By the time he reached thirty-five, he had substantially increased his railroad holdings. The small importing company had become a large import-export house, and another half-dozen diverse concerns thrived under his stern, expert, and, by this time, quite criminal control.

For some time, Samuel had been aware that he was a man who could not love. He held no affection, no benevolence, for any thing or any person, and although he was highly respected (and frequently feared) by those with whom he associated, he had not a friend in the world, nor did he desire one. The one thing he did desire was power, and so far, he had succeeded admirably in its acquisition.

Always a handsome man, and now a wealthy one, he was considered a "good catch" by the newly blossoming upper crust of San Francisco, where he made his headquarters. But he had no time for the cosseted daughters of the nouveau riche, with their self-conscious manners and inane giggles. He was too busy making a fortune and exploring the intricacies of power to be bothered with such irrelevant nonsense.

One spring, when he was in his mid-forties, he was invited to spend the weekend at the country estate of

Patrick O'Steen. Although he disliked social situations, loathing the polite small talk and the inevitable matchmaking, he accepted. O'Steen was a man that interested him. The wily little Irishman had migrated to California along with scores of other hopefuls during the gold rush, struck a vein so rich it had become legendary, then parlayed the first fortune into a mining empire. Men such as this both fascinated and repulsed Samuel, probably because their journeys from common beginnings to wealth and power were so similar to his own. Their successes he admired, their coarse pedigrees he deplored.

For no matter how brilliant he was or how powerful he became, Samuel was still deeply ashamed of his humble start in life. His father had been a nobody, and his father's father before him. Samuel secretly pined for a lineage, a link to America's unofficial royalty—to be from a family that Mattered. And although he had built a fine mansion and surrounded it with grounds containing stately gardens, to live the life of a gentleman was not the same as actually *being* one.

He journeyed to O'Steen's that weekend with the colleague who had issued him the invitation, Clarence Villanova. Samuel's junior by more than a decade, Villanova was highly involved in many of LaCroix's enterprises. He had a particular talent for layering corporations, creating a confusing paper maze which was spectacularly efficient in washing moneys obtained from questionable enterprises. He was Samuel's second in command.

The drive from town to O'Steen's estate was not a long one. The day was fine and clear, and when they turned from the road into the long lane leading to the house, Samuel was impressed enough by the flawlessly landscaped grounds to suspend discussion in favor of sightseeing. As they rounded a gentle curve in the drive, there came into view a large manicured field fenced with pristinely whitewashed boards. Within the enclosure he could see a number of odd contraptions that appeared to be sections of different kinds of fencing, each section about twelve or fifteen feet long, of varying heights and designs. They were neatly laid out in a sort of pattern, and as he wondered what in the world O'Steen was doing with such a bizarre collection, a rider entered the far end of the enclosure.

The horse was a handsome dark bay—nearly black—thoroughbred with a splash of white on his forehead, and as he trotted through the gate, he arched his neck and pricked his ears, snorting in anticipation.

As Samuel's coach neared the arena, the horse eased into a controlled, graceful canter, making toward the first obstacle. The stallion began to pick up speed as he neared the first fence, and, just in time, launched himself into the air, his glistening body arcing, his tail flying like an ebony banner. The horse touched lightly down on the far side of the jump, then pivoted with catlike grace as his jockey urged him on to the next wall. The animal was magnificent, but it was the big hunter's rider who really captured Samuel's attention.

It was a young girl dressed in boy's clothing who piloted the thoroughbred over the difficult course, an extraordinary young girl with a billowing cloud of coppery hair who moved with the finely made horse as if she were part of him.

Samuel signaled to the driver to stop. Villanova made no comment, but arched a curious brow. Samuel stared out the carriage window for a few silent minutes before asking, "Who is she?"

"O'Steen's daughter. Margaret, I think. The local ladies consider it scandalous that she rides astride, but O'Steen doesn't seem to mind. I think he rather enjoys shocking people. He brought her up mostly out in the camps—used to take her everywhere with him before he built this place and settled in, got civilized. I've only seen her once before; she was married young. Lost her husband. I believe there is a child."

Samuel nodded. He had never experienced a feeling quite like this. He seemed compelled to watch her as she rode out the course, deriving a strangely sexual thrill from the sight of her absolute union with, yet complete control over, the horse as it leapt hurdle after hurdle, circling and crossing back and forth through the pattern of barriers.

When she finished the course, she turned the still-fresh stallion toward the lane where Samuel sat in his carriage. She smiled radiantly and raised her arm in the air, waving. Samuel felt a lump rising in his throat as he watched her abruptly wheel the horse and gallop swiftly toward the arena's enclosure fence. She sailed over the high white rails and, laughing, cantered away into the meadows.

Samuel knew he had to have her.

In the following weeks he wooed her, sending flowers, writing silly love notes, stuttering like a schoolboy in her presence. Villanova, as well as any number of Samuel's associates, was certain he had lost his mind. But the truth was that he was in love, for the first and the last time in his life. Finally he won her, and they were married within the month, Samuel beaming broadly, his eyes moist as he watched her walk down the aisle on her father's arm.

During their years together, he had kept from her the seamier details of his professional life. She had made him happier than he ever dreamt possible, and he could not have asked for a more loving, more responsive mate. She forgave him for being disappointed that she could not seem to conceive him a son, and somehow she even managed to forgive him for not loving his

45

adopted daughter, although she never understood why he did not. He was good to Jessie, in his way, but it was only Margaret to whom he could give his soul.

Margaret's love had saved him from himself, and now that she was gone, he was hollow. The child's resemblance to her mother only reminded him of his agony, and so he pushed her away. He began to work longer and longer hours at his office and to take lengthy trips away from home just to avoid seeing the child. By the time Jessie turned eight, he could no longer stand to have her in the house. Just seeing her once or twice a week as they passed in the hall was too much to bear. So he sent her away to the first in a succession of boarding schools.

When he fell in love with Margaret, he had happily given up any thoughts he might have had of marrying into the gentry. But with Jessica—who now bore his name and would someday inherit his empire—it would be different. He would send her to the finest schools, have her brought up with the best people, reading the right books, learning the proper manners. She would marry someday, and she would marry brilliantly. He would see to that. Through her, Margaret's grandchildren (and in a way, his) would obtain the social rank that was the one thing he could not buy for himself.

So Jessie lived away, boarding at a very proper convent school not far from San Francisco. Summers, she was allowed to come home to the big house in town, and Samuel would usually find a reason to be away most of the time, claiming business demands. He really saw very little of her until the summer she was fifteen.

She came home early that year, and as he had been out of town, Samuel was unaware of her presence on the property. He had taken a cab from the depot and was paying the driver when he heard noises from around the side of the big house, over toward the jumping arena he had built for Margaret so many years ago.

Angrily, he left his bags on the wide bricked drive and marched toward the sound. After Margaret's death he had ordered the ring abandoned, and the staff knew they were never to trespass within its overgrown borders. He turned the corner and stopped dead in his tracks, sucking in air.

It was Margaret.

Margaret—scandalously, beautifully astride a gleaming black horse, soaring over the jumps, riding the pattern. He clamped his eyes shut and shook his head. The horse and rider were still there, flying fluidly over the hurdles. But it was not Margaret who clung to the back of the glistening hunter. It was Jessica.

She saw him and reined in the tall thoroughbred. She smiled, waving, and rode toward him. "Father," she began, "how wonderful!"

"Just what do you think you're doing?" he demanded, sweeping his hand toward the ring.

"It's lovely, isn't it? Billings helped me cut back the brush and repair the jumps. He wouldn't do it at first, but I told him it would be all right with you. It is all right, isn't it, Father?" She was still flushed and breathless from her ride, and since he had last seen her, she had blossomed into a young woman. Except for the dark hair neatly knotted at the back of her head, she could have been her mother—Margaret, all those years ago, galloping away from him through her father's fields, laughing. Samuel left lightheaded, almost dizzy. He hadn't even known she could ride. He put one hand on the crisply whitewashed fence to steady himself.

"Where . . ." He cleared his throat. "Where did you

47

get the horse? He's not one of our carriage horses."

"Isn't he beautiful?" She patted the gelding's blue-black neck. "He belongs to Captain Forsythe. You know, Allison Forsythe's father? Allison isn't coming home this summer because she graduated and she's going to Europe for a year and then she's probably going to marry Holden Stanwyck, Jr. and live in Sacramento and he's for sale. The horse, I mean, not Holden Stanwyck, Jr." She paused to stroke the black again. "And since my birthday's next week . . . I thought that if you could see how beautiful he is, and how we cleaned up the ring and everything . . . Father, please, may I have him?" She looked at him anxiously from behind her mother's face.

Samuel could not put a name to what he was feeling as he stared into the vivid blue of his stepdaughter's—wife's eyes.

"Yes. Yes," he stuttered dumbly to Margaret's ghost. "Of course."

"Oh Father! Thank you!" She jumped down from the gelding's back and before he knew it, had slipped between the fence boards to throw her arms around him.

Falteringly, he disengaged himself. Color rose in his cheeks. "Yes, of course," he repeated. He felt immersed in treacle. "Certainly. I'll send a check. I . . ." He backed toward the house. "I must go in now, Jessica."

She knotted her fine brow and took a step toward him. "Father, are you all right? You look ill."

"No, I'm fine," he replied, regaining his composure somewhat. He took another step backward. "Just a difficult trip, that's all. I believe I'll have a rest now."

"If you're sure . . ." She cocked her head quizzically. Like Margaret.

He nodded and retreated around the corner of the house where she could not see him. He leaned heavily

48

against the brick, his hands covering his face.

What kind of monster could he be, he thought, that he would desire this child, who was as his own daughter?

The rest of the summer, Samuel physically distanced himself from Jessica. But she was accustomed to his absences and thought nothing of it. He was an important man, she knew, and the demands on his time were heavy. What she could not know was that whereas in previous years Samuel had avoided her because of the grief she provoked in him, now he avoided her because he was afraid.

Sometimes he would stand in the upstairs window, hidden from her view by the curtains, irresistibly drawn to watch her as she rode in the arena below. Time after time he would stand there, mesmerized; white-knuckled fists clenched at his sides as he felt desire for her mounting within him. And always he would turn away, shaking and pale.

He made arrangements for her to complete her education at a fashionable girl's school on the East Coast, which he chose as much for its distant setting as for its prestige. And after some thought, he sent word to her that she might take her new riding horse with her, on the condition that she promised not to ride astride in public. Not only would it make the transition to the new surroundings easier for her, but he frankly did not want the animal on the property.

It was with great relief that he watched her train pull away from the station that fall, taking her east, far away to Virginia.

The next few years saw many changes in Samuel. His

empire expanded greatly. By now he had offices in San Francisco, New Orleans, Denver, and New York, as well as London, Paris, and the Orient, and, as he liked to see to things personally, he traveled a great deal. Several times his business took him to Washington, D.C., only a few hours away from Jessie's school, but she never knew he had been so near. She wrote him long letters—one each month, like clockwork—and although he seldom answered (unless it was with a telegram in reply to something absolutely requiring a response), he sent luxurious gifts on her birthday and each Christmas.

He supplied her with a more than generous allowance and a personal maid, and he arranged for her to summer each year in Maine, with the family of one of his legitimate business associates. (This same family also oversaw, on Samuel's orders, her departure from Catholicism and her confirmation in the Episcopal church, which he perceived as more socially acceptable.) When she graduated from prep school, he put her through Vassar, and then sent her on a tour of the Continent along with two of her classmates. He was glad to foot the bill for all three girls, two maids, and a chaperone just to insure her absence for another year.

Samuel was older, now. His once jet black hair was heavily streaked with silver, and he found, much to his irritation, that he needed to wear reading glasses. He began to turn over more and more of the details of his affairs to the capable Villanova, and after great deliberation, sold the big Victorian mansion in San Francisco. He moved to Denver, where he had built an equally grand home. The climate was better for him there, the air cleaner and more crisp. He began to enjoy his new gardens.

The one thorn in his side, insofar as his business endeavors were concerned, was an upstart criminal named Nathaniel Kane. Kane, like himself, had come from nowhere and had built for himself an intricate network of criminal operations. But while Samuel had masked his illicit (and highly profitable) dealings with a solid layer of respectability, Kane made no such effort. His method was to remain relatively anonymous, drifting through the shadows of the underworld, making his presence felt rather than seen. Samuel had been aware of Kane's enterprise for some time—Kane had interfered with a project or two of his, and had even snatched one minor but lucrative deal out from under his nose. Retaliation against him was impossible, because as quickly as he surfaced and struck, he disappeared again. Kane might have begun as an irritation, but he was becoming a threat.

Kane, however, was not the only thing on Samuel's mind, for his daughter, whom he had not seen in six years, was returning from Europe.

Jessica was twenty-one now, and except for the color of her hair, was just as much Margaret as the original had been. When she swept into the new Denver house that bright summer afternoon, a wagonload of label-festooned trunks and boxes following in her wake, she greeted him with a hug.

"Father," she enthused, "how wonderful to see you again! The house is just lovely, and I can't wait to see my new rooms!"

He stiffly but politely disengaged himself. "Jessica. Welcome home. I trust you enjoyed Europe?"

"Oh, Father, it was—Oh, my! It was grand! My French is much improved, and I saw so many beautiful places! I've been boating on the Seine and I've been to the Paris Opera three times; I danced with a real baron in Vienna, and in Rome I think I saw the Pope pass by his window, and . . . Oh dear, I'm chattering like a magpie! I can tell you all about it at dinner." She spoke

51

with great animation, her eyes sparkling. Bright spots of rose glowed in her cheeks.

"Certainly. You must be tired." He bowed slightly, in the formal manner he had long ago cultivated for those times when he could not escape personally dealing with his daughter. He left the room as Jessica busied herself directing the distribution of her luggage, and closed the study door behind him. He sat at his wide mahogany desk, trembling hands flat on the blotter in front of him. It was worse this time than ever before. He waited for the erection to pass. Then he took pen and paper, and composed a wire.

Dinner was formal, as was usual in Samuel's house. The servants moved noiselessly through the huge dining room, bringing course after course of succulent foods, served on the finest silver and imported china. He preferred to dine by the light of candles rather than the gas lamps—he felt that the soft flicker of the tapers was somehow more refined then the gas jet's harsher glare. And although he rarely entertained, he insisted that the long, linen-draped table always be set for thirty. This was the time of day which Samuel set aside for himself, when he could divorce himself from the intricate spinnings of his plots and subterfuges (and lately, his growing concern over that upstart bastard, Nathaniel Kane) and simply relax and enjoy. Or gloat. For Samuel, they were interchangeable. He looked forward to these elegant solitary suppers. But tonight, dinner was excruciating.

He watched her as she sat at the far end of the long table, telling him about her trip. He barely knew what she was saying. She wore a satin gown of deep plum, lacy at the bodice and cuffs, that in the candlelight made her eyes appear almost violet. He found himself compulsively staring as she recounted her adventures, her bosom pressing against the form-fitting bodice as

52

she gestured, relating one anecdote after another. Her thick black hair was piled loosely upon her head, and the curls around her face framed her in a dark velvety cloud. Light seemed to emanate from her. Aroused almost to the point of pain, Samuel shifted continually in his high-backed chair. He wondered how she and the servants could help but notice his discomfort.

Finally, during the dessert course, he mustered the composure he needed to speak.

"Jessica," he said, interrupting one of her stories.

"Yes, Father?"

"There is something we must speak about." He folded his napkin beside his plate.

"Certainly." She smiled. Her stepfather was a man of few words, and she hung on to each one. She admired him greatly, and held him in some degree of awe. She was certain that although she had seen so little of him in her life, and although he seemed so distant, that it was just his way, and that he must love her very much. After all, he had provided her with anything and everything she could ever want: the best education, beautiful clothing, a handsome allowance, and, most recently, this extended tour of Europe. Anything he might ask of her she would surely give. "What is it, Father?"

"You are twenty-one years old now, Jessica, and I believe it is time you were married."

Although it was hardly the statement she was expecting, she was not surprised. He must think it odd that she had never expressed interest in any particular fellow, especially when so many of her friends from school were married. Some of them already had children. She, herself, had so far been more interested in pursuing an education than a mate. She tilted her head questioningly.

"I have been giving it some thought," he continued, "and I feel I have found a highly eligible suitor for you."

53

Found a suitor? She was dumbfounded. Had he really picked a husband for her already? She said nothing, waiting for him to continue.

"He comes from a most excellent Bostonian family. I was well acquainted with his late uncle. The family has extended interests in the shipping and whaling industries." He paused, taking a sip of water to steady himself. He was going to get through it, after all. "His name is Owen Lawrence. He is a widower, and childless. He lost his wife several years ago, and is just now sufficiently recovered to think of remarriage."

"I see." She sat quietly, her hands folded in her lap. "You have already arranged this with Mr. Lawrence, then."

He nodded.

"And I am to have no say in the matter?" Her voice was calm and even. She stared at her hands numbly.

"If you find him not to your liking, we can make other arrangements. But keep in mind, Jessica, that I am very much in favor of this match."

It was an order, then. Very well. It was her duty to marry and to bear children, and so far she had failed to find a mate for herself. And she owed her stepfather so much; it was ungrateful of her to have remained dependent on him for so long. He would know what was best for her. He would choose a proper husband. "When am I to meet your Mr. Lawrence, Father?" she asked.

"Within the week. I wired him this afternoon."

The train rocked and rumbled, bringing Jessica out of her reverie. She stretched her legs as well as she could in the cramped space, tensing and relaxing the muscles. In another hour they would be in Denver. She smoothed the grimy surface of the linen duster she wore over the thick mauve material of her traveling dress. It was ungainly and unquestionably hot. She found it difficult to understand how any apparel as heavy and unpleasant as this could have become so fashionable. The duster was a must—soot and dirt were an intrinsic part of travel by rail. But the heavy ensemble beneath (layers and layers of cashmere and velvet over the requisite corset and bustle) was adding insult to injury. She determined to wear something more comfortable on the second leg of her journey, from Denver to her cousin Rachel's.

The first-class car was not crowded, and she had an entire section to herself. Her past experience of extended travel by train had been limited to trips in her stepfather's private Pullmans, and it was rather exciting to be journeying in the company of strangers, although it lacked somewhat in comfort. Owen had refused to hire a car for her, saying it was far too pretentious. *(You mean expensive,* she had thought at the time. *And you want to teach me a lesson and make this as uncomfortable as possible. I imagine you'd send me by cattle car if you thought you could get away with it.)* But now she was almost glad he'd been so pigheaded. She found she enjoyed people-watching. Several seats ahead of her, two Eastern-suited gentlemen were engaged in deep discussion. Drummers, most likely, she decided. Across the aisle from them and up a little way sat a young couple, obviously very much in love. The boy sat with his arm around the girl as they spoke softly to one another, exchanging intimate smiles. Jessica wondered how it would feel to be looked at in that fashion, like something out of the poetry of which she was so fond. Owen called it her secret vice.

And perhaps it was. Her marriage to Owen was indifferent at best, and she had, over the years, convinced herself that this was the way in which intelligent, cultured people operated. Passion was something for the unwashed masses, and grand love a delusion of the middle class. But still she read the poetry: Lord Byron, the sonnets of Shakespeare, and from the Old Testament, the Song of Songs. And she wondered how it would feel to be in love, to be swept away by emotion. But it was a moot point. She was Mrs. Owen Lawrence, and such things would never be a part of her life.

Several seats behind her, across the aisle, there sat a nondescript man in a light gray suit. Of all the passengers which had come and gone as she had traveled across the continent, he was the only one who had remained since Boston. He had never spoken to her (although he had politely nodded in her direction once or twice in the dining car) and he certainly seemed harmless enough, but he bothered her somehow. He seemed to be watching her. Not that she wasn't used to being watched—she was aware that men seemed to enjoy looking at her—but this man watched in an entirely different way, one on which she couldn't quite put her finger.

Her gaze shifted back to the young lovers at the front of the car. They kissed shyly, oblivious to the other passengers. Owen would be incensed, Jessica thought, smiling. Owen was always incensed by those things he considered public displays. He was so proper he nearly squeaked.

Owen, her prospective husband, had come to visit them in Denver within the week, as her stepfather had promised. He arrived late one morning in the carriage Samuel had dispatched to the station, looking pinched and staid in his conservative Boston businessman's suit. He was of less than average height, and his light brown hair, graying at the temples, was oiled and slicked back. A pince-nez was perched on the bridge of his nose. He was forty years old, a bit thick around the middle, and appeared soft and white, as if he had never seen the sun. He also looked as if he had never smiled.

"Miss LaCroix," he said as they were introduced, nodding curtly. "This is indeed a pleasure."

"How do you do, Mr. Lawrence? I trust your journey was not too unpleasant?"

"It was very unpleasant indeed," he answered, "but having met you, I can see that any discomfort to which I have been subjected has been justified." He discreetly looked her over from head to toe, appraising swiftly. Then he turned toward Samuel and nodded again. The nod said *Yes, this one will do, thank you. I'll take her.* None of which was lost on Jessica.

So this is how the blue bloods pick their wives, she thought. *With less consideration than they would use to buy a carriage horse. At least he didn't try to check my teeth.*

What she didn't know was that she had been very carefully inspected, indeed. Her prospective groom had done some surreptitious checking, and although Samuel's criminal connections were too well buried for Owen to uncover, he had discovered that Jessica came equipped with a sizable dowry. A very sizable dowry, in fact. Upon her marriage, she would inherit more than two million dollars from her mother's estate. In addition, her father held a like amount in trust for her—the balance of her mother's money—which she would receive upon his death. And then, of course, Samuel LaCroix himself was worth a fortune. Owen's investigators had estimated it at roughly nine million dollars. In truth, he was worth much, much more.

Owen came from sturdy Brahmin stock, bearing a family name that was well-respected and, by American standards, old. His family had been a wealthy one. His great-grandfather had brought prosperity to the Lawrences with a fleet of whaling ships. His son, Owen's grandfather, had added a lucrative cargo business to the empire. Owen's father, Cyrus Lawrence, had been a lackluster manager who, even during the Civil War—when he should have been able to increase his business substantially—had not added to the family fortunes. But Cyrus had, at least, managed not to deplete them.

Owen had run them into the ground.

It was true that Lawrence Shipping and Cargo still existed, that Owen went to the office everyday, and that he had, at least in the beginning, tried to make a go of it. But his judgment was poor, his decisions bad, and his foresight nonexistent. His first wife had been from his own social strata, but had had no real money of which to speak. What little she had brought to the marriage he had depleted in a short period of time, and now he was in danger of losing the family business. Owen Lawrence was a man who could not be poor, and he knew it. So when Samuel LaCroix approached him about his daughter, she seemed like the answer to a prayer. She might come from common stock, but her money would make up for that. He was determined that he would wed her even if she had three heads and a tail.

They were married in Boston, in the newly completed Church of the Advent on Beacon Hill, with all of Boston's high society in attendance. Jessica made a breathtaking bride, and her father, giving her away, had never felt so relieved.

They honeymooned in the Hamptons, and on their wedding night, a resigned but nervous Jessica donned the prettiest nightdress in her trousseau, then climbed into the big soft hotel bed and waited. When Owen finally appeared, he had little to say to her. He merely turned out the light, climbed into her bed and stole her virginity, grunting and poking at her with his stiff little penis. Thankfully, it was over in less than five minutes, at which time he removed himself from her chambers, announcing, "Thank you, madam. Please rise early, as I plan to breakfast at half past seven."

She had cried herself to sleep.

In the two years since, their intimate life had not varied from that first encounter. Every Friday night he would come to her rooms and mount her with little ado, panting and sweating on top of her until he reached satisfaction, formally thanking her, then departing.

And this was the way it always would be.

Their lives were, for the most part, separate. She attended charity functions, played gracious hostess at Owen's occasional dinners, supervised the household staff, and, of course, she had her hobbies: she arranged flowers, did some needlepoint, and painted a few watercolors. She had given up riding at Owen's request. He himself was afraid of horses, and didn't think that a saddle was the proper place for a lady, anyway. She missed riding, but tried to make up for it in other ways.

She began to visit with Owen's cousins, Daniel and Martha Follett, who lived on a picturesque pre-Revolutionary estate not far from town. The Folletts were certainly more relaxed than their supercilious cousin, and laughter and music filled their household. Cousin Daniel was particularly fond of Jessica, and shared with her his passion for firearms. He taught her how to shoot, using clay pigeons on a makeshift range, and she grew proficient. She had promised Owen she would not ride, but he'd said nothing about just being with the animals, so she spent a great deal of time in the

Folletts' stables. They owned some excellent Morgan horses, and these she loved to visit, always bringing carrots or lumps of sugar. She also tried to paint them, but found she was not much good at it and went back to landscapes, where her lack of talent would not be so readily apparent.

As to what Owen did with his time, she had no idea. It was true that he went to the office each day, but she was uncertain as to exactly what he did there and, frankly, was not interested enough to find out. Sometimes he would not come home until very late, looking strangely excited, with a spring in his normally flatfooted step. Other nights he would not come home at all. She was curious at first, but when she asked him about his nocturnal absences, he cut her off curtly, saying, "It's none of your business, madam. You attend to your affairs, and I shall attend to mine." After that, she just didn't care. It was that much less time she had to spend with him.

As the months and then the years passed, Jessica became more and more unhappy. There were times when the thought of living out the rest of her life in the company of Owen was almost more than she could bear. She began to talk back to him. Not overtly, not rudely. She just began to question him about some of his actions, mostly relating to household affairs. They were such minor things, really, and at first she ventured her opinion quite timidly, but he responded with indignation. "Of course you don't understand why I've allocated the household funds in this manner! There is no earthly reason why you should. These things are too complicated for you to understand, Jessica. Just do as I say."

She began to keep two sets of household records: one ledger showing the actual household expenditures and one for Owen. She had never before had much of an interest in money, since it seemed to flow so freely from the fountain of her father's pocket, but now the saving of it became a game for her, a diversion from her empty life. She fired the gardener, to whom Owen paid far too much money, and found another man who did a much better job at a reasonable price. Owen never knew the difference. She also changed grocers, and did away with the butler's practice of padding the butcher's bill. She saved over three hundred dollars in one year, and was quite proud of herself. She kept the money tucked away in her bureau drawer, vaguely saving it for a rainy day. It was this little bundle of money that she tucked into her handbag just before she left for the station that last morning. She had no need to bring it along, for all her wants would be attended to. But it had become something different than money, that little packet.

It had become the symbol of her superiority to Owen.

Amid billowing clouds of steam and a great deal of rumbling and the screeching of brakes, the train arrived in the Denver station. Jessica had not expected her stepfather to meet her, and so was not surprised when she was greeted by Billings. He had brought out the four-in-hand especially for her, and he beamed broadly when she exclaimed over the four matched grays. He had brushed and polished their silvery coats until they glowed like old satin.

"Welcome home, Miss Jessica," he smiled. "It'll be quite fine to have you at the house, even if it is only for a week."

"Thank you, Billings! It's so very good to see you! I imagine that once we get away from the depot, the air will be as fresh and clear as I remember?"

"Absolutely, miss." He lifted the last of her bags onto the carriage.

"And my father, Billings, is he well?"

He opened the door and helped her in. "I believe he's well enough, miss, but he seems troubled."

She pulled the hem of her skirt into the open coach as she sat down, allowing him to close the door. "Perhaps he's nervous about my visit."

Billings smiled. "Yes, I guess he's always been a little anxious around you. But I think it's something more than that. Business troubles, maybe. Really none of my affair, you know."

He walked to the lead horse and unhooked the ground tie from its bit, carrying the heavy weight with its leather strap back with him as he climbed up into the driver's seat. "Something's preying on his mind, though."

He clucked to the horses, and they stepped out at a smart trot, carrying Jessica back to her stepfather's house.

3

It was a five-day ride from the sleepy cow town in which they detrained and unloaded their horses to the remote cabin where Fletch planned to hide the girl. High in the rocky, forested foothills, the deserted trapper's shack was built hard against the sheer outcrop of dusty pink granite which formed its rear wall. Brush and pine grew thickly all around. In front of this weathered structure was a small clearing, carpeted in a sweet-scented wildflowers and struggling grasses. Better than three times the size of the cabin itself, the clearing was mostly canopied by sycamore and soaring ponderosa pine, and at its far end stood a rusty pump that capped a sweet-watered well. Leading off to one side was a path that angled down through the trees, ending at a slant-roofed shed just big enough for their three horses.

Further down through the woods, the terrain leveled out briefly, forming a narrow valley before rising again in rock and timber. Through this valley flowed a brook both cool and clear and never deeper than five feet, its bed and banks layered in smooth, water-polished stones and pebbles. Its source was a mountain spring much farther up, and its course eventually wove down into the rugged flatland farther south.

It was along the banks of this stream, sometimes narrow and wild with white water, sometimes wide and languid, that they rode for several miles as they climbed higher and higher into the foothills to reach the cabin. Traveling single file, often crouching to avoid low-hanging boughs of cottonwood, juniper, and fragrant pine, their conversation was limited. This was just as well, as far as Clay was concerned. He was weary of Fletch's unending questions, and Loco's incessant inane and giggling chatter had set his nerves on edge.

He had finally come to the conclusion that Fletch's inquisitive manner was not founded in any genuine distrust in him or his abilities—the outlaw had decided on him as the only candidate for this job long before the interview at the Gull. He was just nosy by nature, and learned by asking questions. He was, however, more insistent, more dogged, and more personal about it that anyone Clay had ever met. Clay's background (or at least the story he was telling) seemed to fascinate Fletch, and Clay's usually general and enigmatic answers, while strengthening his cover as a hard, silent hired gun, only served to increase Fletch's innate curiosity.

Loco, on the other hand, would go through long periods of blank silence bordering on a sort of strange walking catatonia. Then suddenly he would launch into an exuberant babble, usually about some woman he had been with or some act of violence he had either heard about or performed himself. His favorite anecdotes seemed to center around perverse modes of sex or death, and at what he considered the "good parts," he would usually burst into hysterical giggles, his eyes darting wildly. Fletch reacted to this insanity as if it were completely normal: that everyone enjoyed happy little tales of physical obscenity, that it was perfectly natural to have wandering eyes and a madman's cackle. It was clear why Nathaniel Kane had specifically instructed that Loco not be the one left alone with the girl. If he were, there might soon be no one left to ransom. At least no one recognizable.

In addition to the bedrolls and saddlebags that all three men carried, Fletch toted a curious parcel. It was a box about twelve by twelve by eighteen inches, wrapped in brown paper and tied with string. Holes were poked randomly through the paper along two of its sides. He had secured it to his saddle horn with a short length of twine, and as they rode along it rested gently on his thigh, bouncing occasionally. Every once in a while, if Clay was riding closely to him, he thought he could hear a rustling, a curious muffled sound, as if something were alive in there.

As it turned out, once they reached the cabin they only stayed overnight: just long enough to rest the horses. They still had around a week, Fletch told him, before they would take the girl, giving them plenty of time to reconnoiter the kidnap site and the trail back.

Fletch was the only one of the three who was familiar with the territory, so he set out in the lead. They took a roundabout journey through the hills, the trees thinning as they descended, and on the morning of the second day they emerged close to the road. They stayed on its path, careful to leave tracks only where passing wagons and coaches would eradicate them. They rode along several miles before Fletch signaled for a stop.

"Listen, Clay," he said. They were looking down at the stage route from the crest of a hill, or rather a towering stand of rough yellow limestone which poked out of the desert landscape like an old dog's molar. They were well out in the flatlands now. There were no trees, just rocks and cactus and sage and low dusty growth and an occasional rebellious upward thrust of

65

rock much like this one. The rest of the ancient dog's teeth.

"Neither of you boys know this country like I do. So now I'm gonna show you the best way back to the shack." Fletch crouched down, rocking on his heels, and Clay did the same. Loco was below them, waiting at the base of the rise, holding the horses and talking to himself.

"I know the best way to go to lead the posse off," Fletch continued, with an air of casual but certain authority. "Know all the places that take a good track. Know where to ride so they lose the trail for a while, then find it again. Makes 'em feel like they're real smart, you know? Now, Loco and me, we're gonna take 'em the wrong way for about two day's worth, then I'm gonna run that trail right into a place that don't take *no* track, so they're gonna figure they lost us for good. By the time they finish fannin' out they'll be halfway into next week. Anyhow, me 'n' the kid're gonna mosey into a little town I know, and I'm gonna send Mr. Kane a wire and let him know it went OK on our end."

He picked up a pebble and chucked it down toward the road. "Now here's what you're gonna do," he continued. "Like I said, I'm gonna show you the best way back. There's only a coupla places you'll leave any sign, and most likely nobody'll think to look that far out, anyhow. Next, don't figure that because me and Loco'll be takin' the rescue party off on a wild goose chase, you can take your time gettin' back to the shack. You gotta get there fast."

Clay moved back off his heels and sat down in the dust. He stared out into the distance, squinting into the sun and rubbing absently at the rough stubble on his cheeks. "Why's that?"

"You know that box I brought along, the big one tied to my saddle?"

Clay nodded.

"Well, there's pigeons in it." He grinned smugly. "Homin' pigeons. Two of 'em. In case one of 'em gets shot or took by a hawk or somethin'. And you gotta get back quick with the girl and let 'em fly. They're gonna wing it straight to Mr. Kane and let him know we got the girl and she's hid. Mr. Kane likes to know just exactly what's goin' on all the time. Likes to keep right up to date."

"Isn't that an awful long way for them to fly? All the way to San Francisco?"

Fletch was still grinning. "Ain't goin' to Frisco. Mr. Kane, he moves around a lot. Birds're goin' to where he is. And the sooner you let 'em go, the sooner they get to him."

Clay looked at him. "That's real smart, Fletch. But why'd you keep them hidden until now?"

Fletch gestured toward Loco, below them. "He gets kinda strange sometimes. You prob'ly noticed that. I wasn't hidin' 'em from *you,* exactly. Just didn't want him . . . playin' with 'em. They gotta be able to fly back to Mr. Kane. I put plenty of feed and a bottle with some water in it in there for 'em before we started out so's I wouldn't have to open it up on the trail."

"That's real smart," Clay repeated.

Fletch grinned broadly. The compliment pleased him, coming from Clay. He had developed something akin to admiration for the tall, silent cowboy.

"I've been sort of curious about something, Fletch," Clay continued after a moment.

"What's that?"

"Now, don't get me wrong on this. I just wondered what contribution Loco makes to this deal."

Fletch smiled. "No, I ain't gonna take it wrong. I can see why you'd ask."

They both turned their heads toward where the kid

waited, standing with his back to them, holding the reins of all three horses. They could hear him talking to himself, occasionally making a sweeping gesture with his free hand.

"Actually, there's a good reason he's along for the ride. I'll have him show you when we get back to the shack." He stood up, Clay followed suit, and they picked their way back down the hill to the horses and the mad boy.

Fletch did know the countryside. He took them back into the hills along the route that Clay was to take with the girl. He pointed out even small patches of ground, areas to avoid, showing Clay just where to weave through the rocky, brushy areas without leaving a trace. There were a couple of areas where it was inevitable that he would leave signs that he had passed, but as Fletch had assured him, they were so far out that no one would ever come across them—and if they did, they would find only isolated areas of disturbance.

There was one particularly treacherous leg of the trip which would take him down the steep wall of a canyon. Fletch said that the only way to take it was fast, and Clay could see he was right—a horse trying to pick his way down the face would surely end up tumbling to the bottom along with a ton or two of rock. Fletch went first, and they followed his lead exactly, angling back and forth down the escarpment until they reached the canyon floor.

"That's the reason we didn't come through here on our way out," Fletch said. "Only place on the far side you can use without leavin' sign for quite a ways leadin' up to the edge. You can get down that sucker, but ain't no way you can get back up."

All along the way Clay had been figuring just how fast and how far over the uneven terrain his horse would be able to travel at top speed, carrying two

68

riders. The big liver chestnut gelding he rode had both courage and stamina that were far above average, as well as a good flash of speed. But he knew that this canyon would be as far as he could push the horse without doing him harm. He'd have to take it easy from here on out. He hoped they weren't too far from the cabin.

And they weren't. They rode the rest of the way at the same easy jog trot they'd used since daybreak, and made it back to the shack just after dark. Clay figured that with the girl, he could make it in a little over half a day.

He was thankful for Fletch's grasp of the terrain. He was certain that no one would be able to trail him. He didn't want the locals catching up with him any more than did Fletch or Loco or Mr. Nathaniel Kane.

Clarence Villanova was in the house when Jessica arrived. She was disappointed, not only because she'd never liked him very much (he was always too polite—almost courtly, in fact, a quality that in him seemed, for some reason, faintly sinister), but because his presence meant she would see her stepfather even less than the small amount of time she'd been expecting he would be able to allot to her. And she had wanted to talk to him. She had wanted to talk to him about the empty life she led married to foolish Owen, and she had wanted to ask him why: why he had given her to Owen. More than given her—it was as if he had paid Owen to take her.

This she had wanted to ask him for over a year now, ever since she overheard Owen discussing her dowry with his equally arrogant, equally pinched mother. She hadn't heard much that afternoon, just enough to hear them label her a little nobody from the provinces, and to understand just why Owen had married her.

She knew how much value her stepfather placed on the pedigrees of families like the Lawrences, but why this particular family? She wanted to ask him if he thought her so undesirable that he felt he needed to hand her over to the first available prospect. And she wanted to ask him how he ever could have considered Owen a prospect in the first place.

She wanted to ask him why he had thrown her life away.

She still loved Samuel. He was the only father she had ever known. But she could not understand why he had done this thing. If she had been more worldly and more wise, she might have been able to piece the clues together, but her education had been of the genteel sort and her vistas limited by custom. Samuel's true motivation for arranging her marriage was unimaginable to her; she had no idea that it was possible for such a thing to exist.

Samuel did not meet her when she arrived. The new housekeeper, a stranger to her, greeted her stiffly at the door and informed her that Mr. LaCroix was in conference with Mr. Villanova, and that he would see her in the morning. She spent the first night of her visit in her old rooms, sorting through her girlhood possessions and thinking about Owen.

What she really wanted was to leave him. This had become clear to her after the second day on the train. She had devoted most of her travel time to an attempt to gain perspective on her marriage, and this one desire was the single thing of which she was certain.

But to divorce him would be unthinkable—it simply was not done. And the thought of staying with him, of all the years to come of arrogance and pince-nezes and the this-is-far-too-difficuilt-for-you-to-understands and particularly the Friday night intrusions into her bed and her body: this was too much to bear.

She would talk to her father, she had thought. She would ask his permission to enter his protection once again, to move back into his house. She was bound by duty to two men—her stepfather and her husband. Her duty to her husband came first, she knew, but if Samuel were to learn how unhappy she was, perhaps he would take her back. She prayed that he would. But if he should refuse, she would at least have the summer's respite with Cousin Rachel.

The next morning, her father sent word that he had been detained once again, and she breakfasted alone on the terrace, staring at Samuel's stiff formal gardens, moving the eggs around on her plate. As he still had not appeared by luncheon, she sat alone in the great dining hall, listlessly picking at the veal. The afternoon she spent in the library, idly running her fingers over the spines of the books, pulling an occasional volume from the shelf. Not one book she looked through that afternoon had been opened before. Their spines were unbroken, uncreased, their pages as fresh, clean, and untouched as they had been the day they left the printer. Additionally, the corner of the library was stacked with unopened crates—more books Samuel would never bother to read, much less look at. They were just something else to collect. She wondered how it was possible for him to live in the same house with all these wonderful words and not take the time to read any of them.

There was a small desk in the library, and she sat down in its green leather chair, thinking to pass the afternoon with a volume of Keats she had disinterred. She tried to concentrate on the book, but when her mind insisted on wandering she abandoned it and began to look through the desk drawers in search of paper and ink, thinking that she might write to the Folletts. She found a small pot of ink and a pen in the second drawer she tried, and a sheaf of paper in the third. But the paper was not blank. On the top sheet of the stack, in Samuel's spidery handwriting, was a name written over and over again. The name was hers.

Samuel LaCroix was a troubled man. Nathaniel Kane had become a real problem, and although Samuel had so far managed to retain most of his criminal empire, the nebulous Kane and his minions had robbed him of too many pending ventures. Kane's usual method was to allow LaCroix's agents (most of whom, of course, were so far down the line that they had never heard of Samuel LaCroix or Clarence Villanova) to design whatever organization was needed for a particular operation. Then, as soon as it began to run smoothly and make money, there would be a series of mysterious disappearances in upper management, temporarily severing the lines of communication and control. And before Samuel could replace these unfortunate people, Kane would fill the gap with men of his own. When Samuel had tried to muscle him out, Kane retaliated with violence and murder.

Although there had been killings during the span of Samuel's criminal reign, they'd been few and far between. Samuel, for all his hardness and lack of conscience, drew the line at murder, or at least at having personal knowledge of it. And now he was faced with a dilemma. Kane was threatening a vital portion of his sub rosa empire—the importation and distribution of opium. Although the Chinese tongs controlled the larger share of this industry, Samuel held the reins of the most widespread organization for its dispersion throughout the United States. And connected to this enterprise was the management or ownership of hundreds of opium dens and houses of prostitution scattered throughout the country. They ranged from small-town, dollar-an-hour cathouses to large pleasure palaces where a man might find anything he desired to fill his more perverse needs. And many of the larger houses, at least those in port cities, also acted as clearing houses for smuggled goods of other kinds. Kane had pushed him into a corner and Samuel was faced with a choice—either let Kane steal his empire out from under him or go to war. He found both alternatives equally distasteful.

Villanova had arrived at the house several days previously. They had gone over and over the possibilities, and now the major-domo had nearly convinced him that they would have to fight violence with violence.

They had discussed the option of assassinating Kane, but no one knew where to find him. In fact, no one seemed to know what he looked like. The man was like a vapor, sliding under doors, doing his dirty work, then vanishing again as mysteriously as he had come. It was said that he rarely talked to anyone personally, and that if and when he did, he was always shielded by screens or shrouded by darkness. Removing Kane would have been the most expedient of cures for Samuel's woes, but it was impossible.

And now Jessica was in the house. He dreaded seeing her, and although he had had opportunities to be with her all day, and could, in fact, have easily broken away to greet her upon her arrival, he could not bring himself to do it. Villanova attributed this reluctance to an obsessive devotion to solving this crisis with Kane, but did think it a little strange that Samuel would brusquely change the subject every time he suggested that LaCroix might take a moment or two to be with his daughter.

But the time came when it could be put off no longer.

Samuel sent word to Jessica that he and Mr. Villanova would join her for the evening meal.

Villanova and her stepfather were already seated when she came down to dinner. The table was set for thirty, as usual, and the china and silver sparkled in the candlelight. According to custom, her place had been readied at the foot of the table and Samuel's at its head. Villanova was seated roughly halfway between them. She had brought five dinner dresses with her, and had chosen the light blue satin for this occasion. She wore her mother's sapphires at her throat and her ears, and she had swept her dark hair up and back, containing it in a chignon. She looked every inch the wealthy young socialite she was. She also looked quite beautiful.

Villanova rose as she entered the room, smiling in a vaguely oily fashion and bowing slightly from the waist. "Mrs. Lawrence," he said, "this is indeed a pleasure. May I say how lovely you look?"

She nodded graciously. "Thank you, Mr. Villanova." She looked toward the head of the table, and saw that Samuel had not risen, but was staring at her wordlessly. "Father?"

Still he stared. Villanova, hoping to save an awkward situation, hurriedly walked around the long table and crossed the floor to where Jessica stood, staring back at Samuel. "Father?" she repeated.

Villanova took her arm. "May I seat you, Mrs. Lawrence?" he asked.

Still her eyes were locked on Samuel's, her face full of question and hurt, his visage consumed with something Villanova had only seen there once before, long ago, when the two of them sat in a carriage on a dusty manor lane, watching a girl on a black-bay horse. Except this time, there was no gentle wonder, no softness to temper what was glaringly apparent as nearly uncontrollable lust. So this was Samuel's terrible secret. This was why he had sent the girl away all those years to school; why he had married her off so quickly the summer she returned from Europe; why he had avoided seeing her until now. And the girl had absolutely no idea—of this he was certain. He squeezed her arm gently.

The slight pressure above her elbow broke the spell. "I . . . I . . ." she stammered, surprised to see Villanova standing next to her.

"Allow me to seat you," he said again, smiling.

"Of course. Thank you." Numbly, she walked to her place, where he pulled out the chair and settled her in. What was wrong with her stepfather? Why didn't he speak to her? And he looked so strange . . . Could he be ill? But if he were, surely someone would have said something to her. She was about to inquire as to his health when he finally spoke.

"Jessica," he began, "forgive me. But you look so much like . . ." He took a sip of water. His other hand was under the table, whitely clutching the arm of his chair. "I see you are wearing your mother's sapphires. They are quite . . . quite becoming."

"Thank you, Father." That must be it. The shock of seeing her in her mother's jewelry. She knew he had loved her mother very much. "They're my favorite pieces, and I don't get a chance to wear them in Boston. Owen feels they're too pretentious."

"I'm sure that your husband would know best in such matters." He signaled to one of the maids to begin service. She looked so beautiful, so desirable. She made him feel young again, made him want to take her in his arms and . . . *Must keep in control, I must keep in control,* he thought, gripping the chair as if he could compress it into splinters.

"How was your journey?" he managed to ask. He had to make small talk, had to appear normal—no more lapses such as the one he'd had when he first saw her.

"Actually, it was as dusty and noisy as you would expect," she said. She was able to manage a smile even though she was distressed by the tone of his comment about Owen. He wasn't going to have much sympathy for her plight, she knew. "But enjoyable all the same," she added as the butler noiselessly slid a shallow bowl of broth onto her plate.

Throughout the rest of the meal, the conversation continued to be stilted and superficial. By the time they reached the main course, featuring a beautiful roast which would have been sufficient to feed twenty people (and Jessica was certain it would do just that as soon as the remains got back to the kitchen), Samuel had grown silent. Villanova bore the burden of small talk for him, asking Jessie about Boston social life and her painting. She asked him about San Francisco, where he now served as manager of Samuel's main offices, and he brought her up to date on recent developments in the city where she had spent her childhood. Twice, Jessica turned the conversation to her mother, but Villanova gently directed her to other topics. Considering that Samuel was already in obvious distress, he felt it wise to steer clear of anything which might upset him further.

Jessica was blithely unaware of the effect she was having on Samuel. As he had always acted a bit strangely in her presence, his actions tonight seemed relatively normal. If she were aware of any deviation at all, it was that he seemed more distracted than usual, and this she attributed to the stress of his business affairs.

She hoped that she'd be able to speak to him alone after dinner, even for a few minutes, but it was not to be. As soon as they finished their meal, Samuel rose stiffly and nodded his head in a curt bow.

"If you will excuse us, Jessica, Mr. Villanova and I have work to do," he said before striding, almost running, from the room.

Jessica was crestfallen. Villanova shrugged apologetically as he pulled out her chair and kissed her hand. "I'm afraid duty calls, Mrs. Lawrence," he said, and followed her stepfather, his footsteps echoing through the hall.

She stood there, staring at the doorway and rubbing absently at the hand Villanova had kissed. Then suddenly she clenched her hands into fists at her sides. She stamped her foot. "Damn," she said. "Damn, damn, damn!"

"Ma'am?" said a voice at her elbow, startling her. It was a maid, one of the Chinese girls, who was staring at her curiously. "May I get something for you?"

"No," Jessica stammered, embarrassed. "No, I . . . no, nothing, thank you."

She went to her room and slumped into the chair at her dressing table. Propping her head on one hand, she stared into the mirror. What was wrong with her, she thought, that could repulse her stepfather so? Her fingers wandered over the surface of the vanity and found her hairbrush, part of the elaborate dressing set he'd had sent her one year at Christmas. She remembered how the girls at school had marveled over the heavy silver pieces, elaborately decorated by some anonymous master craftsman. Each piece, even the delicate buttonhook, bore her monogram. The card had read, "For Jessica, from her loving father."

She threw the brush from her, sending it crashing into the wall. Then she pillowed her head in her arms and cried.

*　　*　　*

Clay finished seeing to the horses and walked back up the path from the shed. It was midmorning and the chill of the previous night had departed, leaving the air crisp but pleasant. He had taken off his jacket and held it over his shoulder, hooked on his thumb.

Fletch was waiting for him, slouched against the front of the cabin. "C'mon," he beckoned. "Got somethin' to show you."

Clay followed him through the trees, climbing uphill until they reached the little plateau above the shack. Formed by the same granite outcrop that served as the shack's rear wall, the plateau was a small, horseshoe-shaped clearing of bare rock. In its center sat Loco. He had a grip on each end of a rifle, and held it balanced on the top of his head, rocking it back and forth above his shoulders.

"You were askin' me what he did," Fletch said as they came into the clearing. He was grinning. He gestured at the boy, who stood up. "Pick somethin'," he said.

Clay looked at him. "What do you mean?"

"Pick somethin'. The farther away the better." He was still grinning.

"OK," Clay said. He slowly pivoted, gazing out into the forest. Finally he pointed to a dying ponderosa pine about two hundred yards out and lower down the hill. Where they stood, they were roughly even with its tip. "There," he said, pointing.

"Which branch?"

Clay pointed out a thick bough about twenty feet down from the top.

"Hey, kid, c'mere," Fletch called to Loco. He pointed out the branch.

"Cain't you fellers find nothin' better'n that?" the boy giggled. "My maw coulda shot *that!*"

"Just start with that one, OK?"

"'F you say so." Almost more swiftly than Clay could register, Loco dropped his arm, deftly flipping the stock away from the carriage and back again, cocking the gun even as he swung it up to his shoulder. Barely taking time to aim, he fired.

Wood chips flew from exactly the place on the limb that Clay had picked. As the boy giggled, they all watched the bough slowly dip, creaking loudly, then separate at the impact site and crash to the forest floor below.

"Pick me somethin' better, Fletch!" Loco exclaimed. His feet did a restless little jig.

Fletch did. He pointed out a second tree farther out and selected a branch, a smaller one this time. Again the boy flipped the rifle out and back and fired. The hit was clean and exact.

Over and over Fletch picked new targets, and each time Loco fired with deadly accuracy. Clay watched the boy's face as he fired. He was surprised to notice that from the time his arm began to move to cock the repeater until just after the shot was discharged, an eerie calm settled over Loco's face. He did not twitch or tremble. His eyes, otherwise never still, seemed to focus calmly, dead ahead. Even when Fletch began seeking out new, impossibly distant targets with a spyglass he pulled from his pocket, Loco did not miss.

After the kid took aim at a twig—one so far out that Clay had to observe with Fletch's spyglass—and nipped it off one inch at a time, pumping the rifle over and over, Fletch turned to Clay. "He never misses," he said with a grin.

Clay tipped his hat to the back of his head. "He's good, all right. *Damn* good. But nobody *never* misses." He was thinking about Markheimer's broken hand. "Quarter of an inch off can make a big difference."

Fletch was still smiling. "He never misses," he

repeated. "Ain't missed nothin' since he was eight years old. It's his gift. We got a lot of gifted folks in our family. His pa could whittle better'n anybody I ever saw. Couldn't never do much else, but he could carve you a bird so real you'd'a thought it was alive. We had a Cousin Elmer could sing like in one of them fancy operas. Couldn't talk until he was seven, and his ma took him to some music hall in Frisco. Anyhow, he come out singin'. 'Cept he was doin' the girl's part. After his voice changed they took him back again to hear the feller sing so's he'd quit embarrassin' 'em, singin' up so high. He was a big, strappin' fella, you know. Sang real pretty—used to make the women cry when he'd warble, and all in Eyetalian, too."

Clay just stood there. He'd heard of people like this before, but all in one family?

"Me," Fletch continued, "I ain't got no talent to speak of, 'cept maybe trackin'. Mostly, I'm just smart."

By this time the boy had used up all the ammunition he'd brought in his pockets. "I'm all outta lead, Fletch. Want I should go get some more?"

"No, Loco, that's fine. You done real good."

The kid giggled, and lifting the rifle back to the top of his head, took off down through the trees to the cabin.

"Is he that good with a handgun, too?" Clay asked.

The sandy-haired outlaw straightened and turned toward the pathway. "No," he said, his face now sober. "He's better."

When they reached the shack, Fletch spoke again. "Been meanin' to ask you . . ." he began, a little embarrassed.

Clay looked at him flatly, waiting.

"Back in Frisco. You know . . . at the tavern?"

"What about it?" *Christ,* he thought. *I thought he'd forgotten that. Don't tell me there's been something he was actually too shy to ask about!*

"That whore back there. What you done to her . . ." Fletch looked as if he felt more than a little silly asking.

"Oh, that." Clay nodded solemnly and paused for effect. "Old Indian trick."

Fletch looked at him with something akin to awe. "Not no tribe *I* ever met up with," he said, and went inside the cabin, shaking his head.

It was the day before her departure, and Jessica had seen her father only once. Villanova had dined with her two or three times, always bearing her stepfather's regrets. He had also informed her that arrangements had been made for her to take her father's private car as far as Flagstaff, where she would have to transfer to a stagecoach. The rest of the time, the servants conveyed messages that Samuel was still in conference, or that he had gone to his office in town, or that he was resting and could not be disturbed. At first, Jessie sent him notes via the servants, asking him especially to join her for tea or a walk in the garden, anything. But she finally lost hope and spent her days drifting through the house and grounds alone. There was really no other place for her to go. She had grown up in Virginia and San Francisco, and all of her friends were either there or scattered elsewhere around the country. None of her boarding school or Vassar friends had come from Denver. And as it would have been improper for her to go about the city unescorted, she really had no place to be except where she already was, a place she was not wanted.

She spent a day in the library, thumbing through different books and reverently perusing the many first editions she found, returning to the desk three times to stare at the paper filled with her name and puzzle over its meaning. Why would Samuel spend enough time thinking about her to write her name over and over like this, and then think so little of her as to completely ignore her presence when she had traveled so far, after a two-year absence, to see him? No answer came to her.

Another day was spent in the gardens. Mr. Sing, who had been her stepfather's head gardener ever since she could remember, walked the grounds with her, talking happily about his flowers and his family. Mrs. Sing saw to the supervision of Samuel's collection of Oriental antiquities—researching and cataloging them precisely. Jessica was sure that her stepfather had absolutely no idea how extensive his collection was: it was simply there. Rather, she supposed, like the collector's items in his library. Mr. Sing proudly told her that all three of his daughters were now employed as maids in the household, and that the youngest, Lin, was something of a prodigy, being, at fifteen, almost as knowledgeable about Samuel's collection as was her mother.

One afternoon she found herself in the attic, having run out of other places to investigate, and stumbled across more of her old trunks. These were the things she had kept in her rooms in the house in San Francisco—little girl things, big girl things. In one trunk she found her old riding habit, the one she'd worn the summer that Samuel had bought her Captain Forsythe's big black hunter, the horse she had named Ebony. She ran a finger lightly over the leather tops of her black riding boots, remembering fondly the afternoons she and Ebony had spent together, soaring into the air. In another trunk, she unearthed clothes she did not recognize, tiny pinafores and jumpers. She realized they were hers from a time she could barely remember. She sifted through them gently, touching the fabric, marveling at the stitchery, the tiny lace trimmings, the little child-sized pockets. In the bottom of the trunk, under the last pink party dress, she found a yellowed envelope. Curious, she slid it from its resting place and carefully opened it. Inside was a tintype, and on the tintype, with its warm, sepia tones, was a picture of her.

So startled was she that she nearly dropped it back into the trunk. In the picture, she was wearing a dated but lovely gown, probably white and quite elaborate, and her hair was somewhat different than she usually dressed it, but it was her. She looked more closely. She didn't remember posing for it, and she'd never had a dress like this. Then she turned it over in her hands and the mystery was solved. A label on the back read, "Miss Margaret O'Steen, aged 16 years. O'Leary Studios, San Francisco, California, 1858."

She turned the tintype over again. Her mother. It was true that she had memories of Margaret, but they were a child's memories. This brought her mother up to date, somehow. It made her a real flesh and blood person instead of some child's nebulous fantasy. She had never before seen a picture of Margaret. She had no way of knowing that Samuel had ordered them all destroyed after her death, and that the existence of this one was a miracle. She began to cry softly, holding it to her breast, repeating over and over, "Mama, oh Mama," rocking slowly back and forth in the attic dust.

At last her mournful weeping ceased, and she reverently tucked the little tintype into her skirt pocket, deciding that she would take it with her. Then she continued her search through the trunks, hoping to find another image of her mother.

She did not find another picture, but she found something almost better: a cache of her mother's clothes. Joyously she sorted through them—beautiful clothes, elegant clothes, most of them hopelessly out of date, but some so classically and cleverly designed that with only a few additions and alterations, Jessica could have worn them on the street tomorrow. She pulled out a few dresses that especially struck her fancy—ivory, sea green, and peach—along with a lovely, lacy nightgown and matching wrap of ecru satin, and determined to take them with her. They were her mother's, after all, and they were doing no one any good here in the attic. Samuel had probably forgotten they existed.

She carefully replaced the rest of Margaret's things and closed the trunk. Then, hugging the three gowns and the peignoir she had chosen, she virtually scampered down to her own rooms.

On her last night, Samuel once again failed to join her for dinner, and she knew he planned to avoid her tomorrow, too. She wanted to confront him, to ask him how he could treat her in such a shabby fashion. All thought of discussing her marriage had been abandoned—this, she knew, was something she would have to work out for herself. And perhaps Owen was not so bad after all. He might be priggish and condescending, but at least he talked to her sometimes, something her own father would not do.

She went to bed, but sleep would not come. She rose again and paced the floor. She had worn her mother's negligee to bed, and now she sat at the dressing table, wearing Margaret's gown, staring at Margaret's picture, sometimes putting out a finger to touch it.

She sat for quite a while like this before she returned to bed. But still she could not sleep. She rehearsed over and over in her head just what she would say to him if she had the chance to talk to him. *Why are you doing this to me? Why don't you love me? I'm your daughter and I've never done anything to displease you, so why do you hate me?* She rolled onto her side under the thick, down comforter and hugged her pillow. But her mind raced, and her eyes would not close.

Then she heard a sound in the hall. Footsteps. Samuel's footsteps. He and Villanova must have worked late, and he was just now going to his rooms. On a whim, she climbed out of bed and relit her lamp. *If the mountain won't come to Muhammad . . .* she thought.

She slipped into the wrap, and, picking up a lamp, crept out into the hallway. Down at the far end, she could see light fanning from beneath Samuel's doors. Barefoot, she padded down the length of nubby carpet and paused before the heavy double doors that would open into his chambers, setting her lamp down on one of the long narrow tables that banked the corridor. She lifted her hand to knock, then paused. He had avoided her all week—would he be terribly angry if she forced her presence upon him now? Suddenly she didn't care. She rapped on the wood with her knuckles.

"Yes, come in."

She entered. He stood with his back to her. He had taken off his suitcoat—it was folded neatly over the big bed's footboard—and was removing the gold watch chain from his vest. "Yes? What is it?" Obviously, he thought she was one of the servants.

"Father, it's Jessica." She said it softly, so as not to startle him.

But at the sound of her voice, Samuel jumped and whirled around. "What . . . what are you doing here?" he demanded loudly.

"I came because I am leaving tomorrow, and because I want to know why you have treated me so hatefully." There. It was out. Her hands were clenched into fists at her sides, her arms rigid.

Treated her hatefully? If she only knew the effort it

had cost him. Samuel moved toward his stepdaughter as if drawn to her.

Jessica stepped back, frightened by the look in his eyes, the hungry, yearning gleam.

He reached up and gripped her shoulders, pulling her toward him. Then, with an enormous effort of will, he stopped himself.

Jessica watched his eyes sweep down the length of her body, then up again, pausing at the vee of her breasts where her wrap had separated.

"Father, please . . . Father!" She whispered, tears spilling over onto her cheeks.

Abruptly, Samuel dropped his hands and turned away.

"Go," he said in the voice of a man tortured beyond endurance. "Cover yourself and get out!"

4

"What do you mean, he can't see me? He sent for me! And what's this nonsense about my wife?!" In the cavernous entry hall, Owen stood amid his baggage, shaking his fist at Villanova.

"As I told you, Mr. Lawrence, I was unaware that he had wired you." Villanova, straight and slender, stood calmly, hands clasped behind his back as the shorter, pear-shaped Owen, face puckered behind his tiny pince-nez glasses, ranted. *Obviously,* Villanova thought, *the man is an idiot. Poor lost and lovely Jessica, that she should have to live with this creature.* Owen reminded him of nothing so much as risen dough forced into a three-piece suit.

"He certainly *did* wire me!" Owen dug into his inside coat pocket and brought forth a folded sheet of paper. He thrust it in Villanova's face.

Villanova calmly plucked the telegram from Owen's grasp and read it.

STRONGLY REPEAT STRONGLY SUGGEST
YOU RETRIEVE YOUR WIFE AT ONCE
STOP
LACROIX

The date indicated that Samuel must have sent it the day after his one and only dinner with Jessica.

"Well? What's the meaning of this?" Owen demanded. "I have just spent several hideous days on a filthy, noisy train full of filthy, noisy people because of this nonsense, and now you tell me that he's not receiving? And who in thunder are you anyway?"

The taller man bowed slightly. "I am Clarence Villanova, Mr. LaCroix's chief of staff, at your service, sir. I have assumed charge during his . . . indisposition."

Owen glowered. "Chief of what staff? Of what, just exactly, are you in charge? The maids?"

"Hardly the maids, Mr. Lawrence," Villanova replied, smiling thinly. "Since the commencement of Mr. LaCroix's semiretirement, I have been president of LaCroix International, Mr. LaCroix's primary holding company. As to just what I am in charge of, Mr. Lawrence, you might say that I am in charge of everything."

"I see." Owen backed down a bit, but remained aloof. This man was, after all, a mere employee! Didn't he realize that someday, when Jessica's father died, he would be working for Owen? "But you've still failed to explain why I cannot see my father-in-law. And where is my wife?"

"As to your wife, Mrs. Lawrence departed yesterday for Arizona to visit, I believe, her cousin's ranch."

"What?" cried Owen, incensed. "She's left already? Why didn't she wait here for me?"

"I doubt that she was aware that you planned to join her. I myself was unaware that Mr. LaCroix had contacted you. It's really quite puzzling."

"And my father-in-law?"

"He is ill, Mr. Lawrence. Quite ill. He had been acting strangely throughout your wife's visit, not himself at all. The morning she was to leave, he failed to

88

come down from his rooms. By afternoon, we had become quite concerned, and the servants and I forced our way into his suite. We found him still in bed, shaken and unable, or unwilling, to speak."

"And my wife?"

"She had already departed early that morning. Billings drove her to the station at eight."

"Without saying good-bye to her father?"

"He had been able to devote little time to her during her visit, Mr. Lawrence. There have been certain pressing business matters of late. . . . I imagine she believed he would be too preoccupied to see her off, and wished to depart without disturbing him." Villanova paused. Owen was regaining his composure, he could see. What a pompous little ass Jessica's husband was. He didn't deserve her. Perhaps, someday, he could arrange for Owen to meet with an interesting accident. And perhaps Jessica could be his. Keeping it all in the family, one might say.

"Mr. LaCroix's physician is presently in attendance," he continued. "He believes that this present condition is the result of a shock of some kind. Just what that shock was, we will not know until he decides to speak. Dr. Thomas believes there is no physical reason for Mr. LaCroix's silence. We will just have to wait."

"But why? Why did he send me that telegram?" Owen demanded, pointing to the paper in Villanova's hand.

"I'm sure I don't know, Mr. Lawrence. You would have to ask him that yourself." *But I do know,* he thought. *He sent it because he wanted her out of here, not just for the present, but for good and all. He was terrified of what he might do to her. Yes, you fat little fool, he lusted after your wife, his own stepdaughter. And I think it drove him mad.* He handed the wire back to Owen.

"I'll have one of the servants make up a room for you, Mr. Lawrence." He raised his hand to shoulder level and snapped his fingers twice. A maidservant, a young Oriental girl, appeared from nowhere. "Please see that Mr. Lawrence is made comfortable, Lin. He will be staying for several days."

The girl nodded and picked up one of Owen's bags. "You will follow me, please, sir?" she said, starting toward the staircase.

Owen trailed after her, but not before he sent a withering look in Villanova's direction.

The thin man watched as Owen climbed the stairs, following Lin around the curve to the top, then across the long open second-floor landing. He thought he saw a glimmer of something rather . . . unexpected . . . on Owen's pinched face as the stuffy little man watched the young Oriental girl walking before him. Something Villanova wouldn't have believed had he not seen it himself.

That evening, after nearly two days in that curious twilight suspension, Samuel returned to the world. Dr. Thomas had told Villanova that although Samuel was mute—temporarily, he hoped—he was sure he could hear and possibly was aware of what was going on around him. It wouldn't hurt to talk to him, to try and draw him out. Perhaps a chord might be struck that would pull him back to reality, and speech.

So, after seeing to Owen, that was exactly the activity to which Villanova returned. He sat at Samuel's bedside and talked about everything he could think of. He spoke of past business ventures; Samuel's collections—the first editions, dueling pistols, and Oriental antiquities (about which he knew considerably more than did Samuel), the house and gardens. He read to him from the newspaper. He recited what little poetry he could remember from his school days. He asked Samuel questions and then answered them for him.

Finally, he said, "Samuel, I don't know if you can hear me or not. But I'm going to tell you something important. I think I know about you and Jessica. I don't know that you have actually acted on what you feel for her, but perhaps you believe the thought is as bad as the action. You don't have to tell me what you've done, Samuel, or what you've thought about doing. Just say something, anything. Come back to us."

He didn't expect an answer. He was standing at the window, talking to the dark glass and the night-filled gardens.

Samuel spoke.

He said, "Jessica." A whisper.

Villanova wheeled. He made it to the bedside in two strides and knelt beside it.

"Yes," Villanova urged, "Jessica. What about Jessica, Samuel?"

"I made her cry," Samuel continued. He looked so old, so drawn, a decade older than his sixty-seven years, withered and somehow frail in his big bed. "I didn't mean to do it, Clarence." He reached out and took Villanova's hand. "She's Margaret, you know. She's Margaret . . . and she isn't. She's . . . I've hurt her. I want to tell her I'm sorry." He squeezed Villanova's fingers and leaned toward him. "Bring her to me, Clarence. Let me tell her I'm sorry?"

Villanova rubbed brusquely at his own tearing eyes. This was a side to Samuel he had never seen before. Penitence was something he would not have expected. It seemed a day for surprises.

"She's gone, Samuel. She's gone to Rachel's. She left yesterday morning."

91

LaCroix looked frantic. "Well, we must bring her back! We must send a wire!" He paused, as if groping for a thought he had misplaced. "A wire . . . I sent a wire. Did I wire Lawrence?"

"Yes, Samuel. He arrived this afternoon. He's quite upset. Given the telegram you sent, I'm not surprised."

"You read it?"

"Yes. You told him to come and collect his wife. Immediately."

Samuel let go of Villanova's hand and pressed his fingers to his temples, as if to push the clutter from his brain.

"Another thing, Samuel. It has recently occurred to me that Kane might attempt to use Jessica to convince you to part with . . . certain holdings."

LaCroix pulled himself up on his elbows, his eyes abruptly regaining their usual piercing alertness. "This was not mentioned to me before."

Villanova waved his hands, hushing his mentor. "The possibility is somewhat remote. He's never gotten that personal before. And I didn't bring it up earlier because every mention of your daughter seemed to upset you so."

Samuel looked down at his hands.

"At any rate," Villanova continued, "I sent a man along with her. Just to be on the safe side."

LaCroix remained quiescent, staring at his thumbnails. "She doesn't know, does she?" He was asking about more than just Villanova's man.

"No, Samuel. He's just going to be another passenger along the same route. A fellow traveler. I sent Wilson Dobbs. He's a good man, and he'll watch out for her."

Samuel breathed a sigh and looked back up at his protégé. "And Rachel's?"

"I sent word to three of our people last week. They're

already signed on as ranch hands."

Samuel smiled. "You're a good man, Clarence."

Villanova returned the smile and stood up. "I know," he said, walking to the door. "I'll have some dinner brought up to you."

"Clarence?"

He paused, his hand on the latch. "Yes?"

"Would you bring it yourself? And don't tell Lawrence I'm . . . better. Not yet."

"Of course." He exited and closed the door softly behind him. How amazing it was, he thought, that with all Samuel LaCroix's power and money he was still intimidated by that pompous little prig.

She sat alone in the center of the deep couch in her stepfather's private car, her back straight, her hands folded quietly in her lap. The Pullman was incredibly luxurious. The couch upon which she sat as well as two of the five armchairs were upholstered in thick emerald green plush, tufted and buttoned, and skirted with tassels and fringe of green and gold. The remaining chairs were covered in heavy floral damask and detailed in the same manner as the couch. Paneled in rich and glossy oiled walnut, the walls matched the small conference table, and the windows, curtained in the same damask as the chairs, were etched in intricate patterns. Paintings of horses and hounds in ornate gilded frames were scattered about the sitting area. A fresco of cherubim, accented with elaborately carved moldings leafed in gold, decorated the central vault of the ceiling. Farther back, in the sleeping area of the car, the appointments were equally elegant. Even the marble washstand was fitted with valves and spigots of gold and equipped with a basin and pitcher of the finest porcelain.

Jessica was oblivious to it all. Her confusion and sorrow of the previous night had gradually passed into numbness, and she had packed, gone to the station, and boarded the train like a sleepwalker. There was nothing left for her. Nothing left but to go back to Owen at summer's end. There had only been one other door open for her, and now it was closed irrevocably.

By the time the train passed through Colorado Springs, she was beginning to function again, although druggedly. She felt like a puppet whose strings have been pulled too tightly in different directions. She could not consciously bring herself to understand Samuel's behavior. *He hates me, and he's trying to punish me, and somehow it is my fault.*

He had always been so good to her, lavished upon her every possible comfort and extravagance, and she had angered him—driven him to it. But what? What had she done? He was a good man, a fine and successful man, and surely he couldn't have acted toward her as he did unless . . . Unless what? she did not know.

I never should have come, she thought miserably, staring at her reflection in the dark glass of the window. *And you can never go back,* the singing rails seemed to say, *never go back, never go back, never . . .*

The miles blurred and the whistle stops ran together as she tortured herself with questions and recriminations to which there were no solutions, no explanations. There was only muddy, mindless, suffocating guilt.

At last, a porter tapped on the door of her car, announcing that dinner was being served. She had been unable to eat all day, but now her stomach was angrily demanding attention. Out of habit rather than vanity, she checked her hair at the big plate mirror in the sleeping area, and numbly made her way to the dining car.

She sat alone, staring out into the darkness. When the waiter came, she ordered unenthusiastically: anything would be all right, she just needed something to quiet her stomach. But when the food came, she found she was ravenous, and greedily consumed every course that was placed in front of her, from blue points to lemon ice.

She retired immediately upon returning to her car, and fell asleep wondering if perhaps the discovery that one is beneath contempt was stimulating to the appetite.

When she arose the next morning, the train was puffing its way through New Mexico. She was standing at the marble and gold vanity, splashing water on her face, when the anger finally struck her. She stood, gripping the sides of the marble sink, staring into the mirror, trembling—at first with shock at the revelation, and then in fury. She felt her fingers close around the handle of the porcelain pitcher.

With a sudden cry of rage, she dashed it against the paneled wall with all her strength. It exploded on impact, scarring the wainscoting and showering the air with shards.

"Damn you!" She screamed it at the golden taps, the damask furnishings, the ornate woodwork, the frescoed ceiling. "Damn you to hell, you filthy pig!" Then the tears came, coursing freely down her cheeks. She knelt on the shard-encrusted carpeting, unmindful of the pain as the fragments cut into her knees. She wept until she could weep no more, and then she took a bath. She scrubbed herself until her skin was red, and then scrubbed a second time.

Then she stood before the mirror, naked. She had

never done this before. She took inventory of herself, for now she was all she had. She studied herself closely: the long, even toes and narrow feet; the slim ankles; slender, gently curving calves and lean strong thighs— a legacy of her horseback days; the flat stomach and slim, almost boyish hips; the narrow waist and full breasts; the clean curve of her throat; the pale, oval, fine-featured face with its deep cobalt eyes, framed by a cloud of thick dark hair.

So this is what you wanted, my dear stepfather, she thought. *This is why you sent me away all those years. I remember now. I remember the way you acted that summer so long ago—the summer you gave me Ebony. I saw you up there in that window, you know. I thought you watched me because you were proud of the way I rode. What a stupid little fool I've been! That was when it started, wasn't it? You sent me as far away as you could after that. Not because you loved me and wanted me to have the best, and not because you hated me for doing some horrible thing, but because you wanted me. No, lusted after me. That would be a more fitting description, wouldn't it, Father? I loved you so much, and because I needed you to love me, I convinced myself that you did. All these years I have loved you and been afraid of you and done your bidding, and all the time you were afraid of me! Little me, little Jessica! All those things you sent me—what did you think about as you chose them? Did you think you would like to be my lover? My husband?*

There was a knock at the door, then the porter's muffled voice. "Breakfast is being served, ma'am."

"Thank you," she called, without taking her eyes from the mirror. "So this is what you wanted, Father," she said aloud. "Well, you shall not have it. And that stupid little fool you sold me to will never have me again, either. Oh, I'll go back to him. I haven't much

96

choice in that. But my door will be locked against him. Let him go where he goes at night and do whatever he does. I think I have an idea now. You have opened my eyes to a number of things, Samuel LaCroix, and for that I thank you. But Owen will have no heirs from me, and you shall have no grandchildren to torment." She placed a slim hand on her belly. "No. No pompous little Owens."

So this is what it feels like to take charge of one's self, she thought, smiling. *I do believe I like it.* Her eyes were hard, steely, and at this moment she was more her stepfather's daughter than she had ever been before.

She dressed and adjourned to the dining car, her head held high, her step quick and purposeful. *I'm feeling rather famished,* she thought.

About an hour before the train pulled into Flagstaff, Arizona, she noticed a familiar face. She was having her dinner, and as she glanced out the window, she saw a reflection in the glass. A man she recognized. She looked up quickly and caught a glimpse of him as he left the dining car. It was the man from the earlier train ride. The man in the light gray suit.

In Flagstaff, she left the train and went to the overland freight station, arranging to have most of her trunks hauled south by a teamster. She also picked up and paid for her stagecoach ticket to Fort Verde, where she would have to transfer to another carrier. She found a general store and made several purchases. Then she checked into the nearest hotel and waited for morning to come.

They were just over the crest of the ridge, waiting. Once again, Loco waited down below with the horses.

But this time, he busied himself filling two bags with stones. One was already full and secured with a leather thong to the horn of his saddle. The other was about halfway filled.

"Stage oughta be along any time in the next hour," Fletch was saying. "That is, if it's close to bein' on schedule."

Clay nodded. He wasn't jittery about the abduction to come, but he would be relieved when it was over. Not only to get the girl safely away, but to put some distance, at least for a while, between himself and his companions. Fletch, who had grown to trust Clay enough to relax in his presence, had come up with several new "gifted relative" stories since the morning of Loco's target practice, including an uncle who could pull his lower lip up over his nose and a third cousin who, if inspired with enough good Texas chile, could pass wind to the tune of "Believe Me, If All Those Endearing Young Charms."

Clay had had about all he could take of Fletch's family. Fortunately, the time for action was drawing near, and the sandy-haired outlaw had once again grown serious.

"Got a question for you, Fletch," Clay said.

"What's that?" He continued to look down the road, watching for the first sign of the coach's dust.

"How're you going to know it's the right stage?"

Fletch looked away from the dirt track and smiled. "I'll know."

So far, they had traveled in silence. The coach had started down the winding mountain road from Flagstaff with six passengers, an unbelievably cramped cargo. They were packed like sardines until last night's stopover, when two of their fellow travelers, a drummer and another rather thin, somberly dressed gentleman whose profession Jessica hadn't been able to guess (although she thought mortician might be close) stayed behind to wait for another connection.

Even with the lightened load, the stagecoach was as oppressive and uncomfortable as the private train car had been luxurious. The seats were hard and narrow, and transmitted, with unerring accuracy, every bump and pebble over which the coach's wheels passed. Although neither of the two remaining male passengers were smoking, the interior reeked of cheap cigars.

The coach jolted again as it hit another pothole, and Jessica grimaced. She would be black and blue before they reached the next way station. And if the road didn't kill her, the food at the rest stops would. She'd had enough stale bread, salt pork, and bad coffee to last her a lifetime. And although the light summer dress she wore, the one she had purchased in Flagstaff, was certainly cooler than her usual traveling dress would have been, it didn't provide much insulation against the jolting wooden seat.

She'd foregone the usual whalebone corset demanded by fashion (and these days, decorum), and had packed the last one gratefully away in her smallest trunk along with her hated bustle and most of her petticoats. At least, she decided, she would be comfortable—if not very chic—for the rest of the summer. Under the simple blue and white cotton dress, she wore only a lightweight chemise, one petticoat, and of course, her drawers, their elasticized eyelet cuffs stopping a few inches short of her knees. By comparison, it was an incredibly cool, easy ensemble.

But now, as the coach banged and clattered down the pocked and rutted road, she was beginning to think that those beastly bustles might actually serve a useful purpose after all.

"Here, honey, take this. I got an extra." The speaker was the other female passenger. She held out a small blue satin pillow, across which was stitched the legend "Home Sweet Home." Watching Jessica read the embroidery, she laughed coarsely and said, "I figure home is anywhere I got a place to sit down."

Jessica smiled and took the pillow, gratefully slipping it beneath her. One of the male passengers, a good-looking blond gentleman with an aquiline nose, tipped his hat and smiled as she rose slightly to adjust the cushion. The other man, ordinary looking and sober-faced, continued to stare out his window at the slowly passing landscape. It had changed, through the morning, from piney mountain green to the soft tans, dull reds, and gray-greens of the boulder and sage-strewn desert. Some of the vistas stretched for miles, and were so haunting and otherwordly that she itched to paint them and found herself wishing she'd brought along her watercolors.

"Name's Gert," the woman went on. "Gertrude Vance." She extended a clawlike hand festooned with cheap rings.

Jessica took it. "How do you do? I'm Jessica Lawrence." She had seen the woman before, at the stage depot. Jessica had arrived early, but the stage was late—not, she understood, an unusual occurrence. To fill the time, she'd been standing outside, casually watching the activity on the street. She'd seen this woman, Gert, coming out of an alley farther down the street, talking to the man from the train—the man in the light gray suit. The two spoke for only a moment and then Gert, carrying a frayed carpetbag and a bright purple hatbox, had stepped briskly up onto the sidewalk, headed for the depot where Jessica waited. The man had disappeared back into the alley.

100

"Nice to meetcha, honey. Where ya headed?" Gert continued. She spoke loudly, in an uncouth but good-natured way. Bracelets dangling from both of her wrists clanked every time she moved her hands, which was often.

"South," Jessica replied. "My cousin has a ranch northeast of Phoenix. I'm visiting for the summer." She rather wished the woman would leave her alone and let her drink in the scenery once again in peaceful silence.

But Gert had no intention of doing any such thing. "Where ya from, honey? You don't talk like you're from anywhere around here."

"Judging from the lady's accent, I should say New England, at least of late. Virginia, perhaps, with just a hint of Boston?" The speaker was the blond gentleman. His voice was neat and clipped and quite British. Jessica took an immediately liking to him.

"Why, that's exactly right!" she exclaimed. "How did you know?"

"Hobby of mine. Allow me to introduce myself. Charles Allen Brewster, at your service, ladies." He lifted his hat with a flourish and placed it back on his head, which was the only available place in the cramped vehicle for a gentleman to keep his hat. "Tragedian at liberty," he continued, his ice blue eyes twinkling, "full-time suitor to Dame Fortune."

Gert looked puzzled. "Just what the hell is that?" she asked, irritated.

Jessica laughed. "He means he's an out-of-work actor and he makes his living gambling." Brewster grinned back at her.

"Well, why the hell didn't he say so?" Gert grumbled.

Ignoring her, Brewster turned to the dour man beside him, who Jessica vaguely remembered having seen on the train. "And now that we seem to have pierced the veil of silence, who might you be, sir?"

He turned away from the window. "Huh? Oh, sorry. Dobbs. Wilson Dobbs. Salesman. Barbed wire's my line."

Brewster laughed. "Well, that explains a lot of things."

Dobbs stared at him.

"Like why you're gazing out the window so intently. Arizona is not a happy place for men in your profession, my friend, but I shouldn't think the local cattlemen would forcibly remove you from a moving stagecoach."

"No, that's not it," Dobbs said. It was obvious he had no sense of humor. "Indians. I'm watching for Indians. I heard . . . Well, I heard there were a lot of them out here. They do terrible things to white men, and they attack these stages all the time. I've heard stories that would curl your hair."

Both Jessica and Gert blanched, although Gert wore so much rouge that it was hard to tell.

Brewster retained his good spirits. He lifted his hat again, displaying neat golden ringlets. "It would appear I've already heard those stories." He turned to Jessica. "I shouldn't be bothered by it, ladies. Nowadays, the Indian problem, at least in this area, is far overrated. If you feel you need to fret over something, I suggest you worry about being shaken to death by the ungainly conveyance in which we have so ill-advisedly taken passage."

Gert looked at Jessie to translate.

"He means the stage," she explained, grinning. Dobbs had turned his attention back to the window.

Gert looked angrily at Brewster. "Why don't you say what you mean, mister?" she demanded.

He removed his hat and held it to his chest, casting his eyes down in a look of mock shame. "I'm terribly sorry, madam. I thought I had."

Fletch poked him in the ribs. "Stage comin'."

Clay rolled over, lifting his hat off his face. He'd been stretched out full length on his back, dozing. Fletch was right. He could see a small cloud of dust on the horizon, getting nearer all the time.

Fletch turned his head, calling down the hill to Loco. "Wake up, kid. She's a-comin' down the road."

Loco stood up and did a nervous skitter to one side. He was grinning wildly. "Is it the one? Is it the one, Fletch?"

Fletch had taken out his spy glass and was studying the cloud of dust, already much nearer. "Can't tell yet." He paused a moment. "No, wait. Yeah, this is the one." He collapsed the glass and tucked it into his pocket. "How 'bout that? Right on schedule: half-hour late." He stood up and motioned to Clay. They climbed down the rock toward their horses.

Clay took the reins from Loco and swung up into his saddle. Fletch did the same. "Ready?" Fletch asked, pulling his bandanna up over his face.

Clay nodded, and Fletch turned to Loco. "Now you get up that ridge in case there's trouble Clay 'n' me can't get out of. And watch they don't see no glint of sun comin' off your rifle."

The boy giggled and shuffled his feet, holding his repeater overhead at arm's length.

Clay adjusted his scarf under his eyes. "How'd you know it was the right stage?"

"Signal. Stage we want carries a purple hatbox up top." He wheeled his horse and the two men galloped away from Loco, down the far side of the ridge, parallel to the road.

Brewster was happily entertaining a delighted Jessica with stories of the London theatrical life when Dobbs lurched forward in his seat.

"Outlaws!"

Dobbs was leaning halfway out of the window, one hand gripping the frame, the other arm extended, pointing ahead.

Jessica, seated across from him, craned her head out the window. "He's right!" she exclaimed, clutching her handbag. "Two men! With guns!"

Wilson Dobbs fumbled inside his coat and brought out a revolver. But before he could level it at the outlaws, Brewster snatched it from his hand.

"Hey! What's the matter with you? Gimme that back, you sonofa—"

Brewster chucked it out the window. "Now, now, Mr. Dobbs. Better to just let them take what they want. We don't want to provoke them to violence, do we?"

Dobbs looked as if he could have killed Brewster with his bare hands. Gert looked puzzled, but concurred with the Englishman. "He's right, mister. Fellers like these can get real testy if you push 'em."

Jessica was frightened, very frightened, but at the same time strangely thrilled.

The stage slowed, and then stopped.

She heard the driver yell down to them, "Ever'body just stay calm, folks. We don't want nobody should get hurt." Then she heard, "You fellers're makin' a mistake. This stage don't carry no payroll. No mail, neither. All's I got is passengers."

Then another voice spoke, more muffled than the driver's. "That's exactly what we're lookin' for, mister.

Just toss that repeater down real easy."

There was a pause, then a dull clatter as the driver's rifle landed in the dust.

A man appeared at the door nearest Jessica, half his face covered by a red scarf. He swung the door open and motioned at them with his gun. "Everybody out," he said.

Jessica, thinking of her mother's sapphires, swiftly and discreetly tucked her handbag beneath her, under Gert Vance's pillow, before nervously climbing out of the coach and down to the dusty road. The others followed, Gert looking resigned, Brewster looking faintly amused. Dobbs was exasperated. The man holding them at gunpoint was quite tall and dark haired, and wore a fancy silver band on his hat. Jessica noticed that his eyes were a clear green. The second man, still on horseback, had lighter hair and she thought he, too, must be taller than average, although it was hard to tell with a mounted man.

The man on the horse spoke again.

"Yessir, I'd say you're carryin' just exactly what we're lookin' for." He motioned toward Jessica. "You, Miss Fancy. Step out where I can see you better."

Falteringly, Jessica stepped away from the other passengers.

"Yeah, I reckon she'll do just fine." He waved his gun at Gert, Dobbs, and Brewster. "Now, if you folks'll climb back in there, I think we can all be on our way."

Gert and Brewster obeyed, but Dobbs hesitated, half reaching out toward Jessica. Jessica heard the mounted outlaw cock his pistol. Dobbs heard it, too, and withdrew his hand. Reluctantly, he followed Gert and Brewster into the coach, closing the door behind him. "You ruffians!" he shouted. "What are you going to do with her? Who are you?"

Ignoring him, the sandy-haired outlaw turned to the

driver. "Move out," he said, and fired his pistol into the air.

With a jolt, the stage team lurched forward, hitting a gallop almost immediately and leaving Jessica and the highwaymen behind as it disappeared down the road in a billow of dust.

The outlaw with the fancy silver hatband leaned down to scoop up the driver's abandoned long gun and tossed it to his companion.

"Forty-four Rimfire," said the mounted man as he caught and swiftly appraised the firearm. "Worth keepin'."

All of her newly found strength melted away. *Oh, please, God, don't let them kill me,* was her first thought. Then she realized how foolish that was. *My father is a rich man,* she mused, *and I do believe I'm being kidnapped. They won't hurt me if they want their money. And he'll pay whatever they ask. Terribly bad form not to.* She snorted. *I hope they take him for every penny he has.*

She stuck her chin in the air. "Am I to understand that I am being abducted?"

The tall man behind the red scarf replied. "It would seem that way, Mrs. Lawrence." She was right then— they'd known all along just exactly who she was, and she thought, when he answered her, that she saw just a hint of a smile in his eyes. They really were an incredible shade of green, unlike any she'd ever seen.

The rider brought up the tall man's horse and tossed him the reins. "Saddle up," he said. "We're wastin' daylight. And tie her up." He tossed down a short length of soft cotton rope.

"I need your wrists, miss."

He tied her snugly, then hoisted her into his saddle, swinging up behind her.

They jogged down the road about half a mile before

she saw another man up ahead, just off the side of the road. He was holding the reins of a horse bearing two good-sized sacks tied in front of its saddle. As they drew closer, she could see that he was twitching, hopping from foot to foot as if his boots hurt him. Then she could hear him laughing. It was the most bizarre sound she had ever heard. Gooseflesh rose on her arms. The man behind her must have noticed her reaction, because he said quietly, "He has that effect on a lot of people."

The boy jumped up on his horse and started toward them.

The other man waved him back. "Stay on the rock, you idiot!"

"Aw, Fletch, you promised you weren't never gonna call me that no more." The boy reined in his mount and waited. She could see his eyes now, and suffered a new outbreak of shivers.

"Sorry, kid." Fletch pulled down his bandanna and settled it around his neck. "Don't need this no more."

She couldn't see him, but she felt the man behind her do the same. Then he put his free arm gently around her waist. She could feel the muscles of his chest rippling against her back as he leaned forward a bit. "You OK, miss?"

"As well as could be expected, I suppose," she said curtly. She could smell him now: leather and sweat, but not sour or bad—the scent was a bit musky, almost sweet. She decided she liked it. It made her feel rather . . . odd.

They joined the strange young man on the flat shelf of rock. The boy was quite excited. "We got her now, ain't we, Clay? We sure have got her now!"

Clay. So these were her captors. Fletch and Clay. She didn't think she cared to know the name of the other one.

They trotted on for about another quarter of a mile, then Fletch signaled a halt. "OK, here's where we part company," he said to Clay. "You know the way. Now get there fast!" He signaled to the boy, and the two of them veered away to the side, breaking into a canter as they rode from the smooth rock surface into the gravelly dirt of the desert. Clay, too, broke his horse into a lope. "Hang on, miss. I'm afraid it's going to be a little rough for a while. We've got a ways to go."

He kept to the trackless rock shelf for another half-mile or so before he cut out into the desert, and pushed the chestnut into a gallop.

He hadn't exaggerated when he said the ride would be rough. It seemed that she'd been jostling forever in front of him, pressed between his lean body, with its musky smell of leather and sweat, and the uncompromising hardness of the saddle's pommel. With her wrists bound together, it was nearly impossible to get a good grip on the saddle horn, and her precarious position in the heavy stock saddle allowed her legs no direct contact with the horse, preventing her from anticipating and compensating for its movements. She was in constant fear of being thrown to the flinty ground. The smug satisfaction she had experienced earlier at this unexpected chance to take a peculiar sort of revenge upon her stepfather had evolved into physical terror.

As the dusty desert landscape rushed endlessly past them, hours and minutes were indistinguishable. Lost in a turbulent world blurred by wind and speed, she slipped in and out of consciousness, aware only occasionally of the denim and leather-clad form behind her; his rein hand extended along her left side urging still more speed from the straining horse; his free hand to her right, gripping the saddle horn; imprisoning her jostling body in a cage of muscle and bone.

Gradually, she forced herself back to awareness, struggling to divide her environment into separate elements. The chestnut streak beneath her once again came into focus as the laboring horse. The golden mass on the saddle horn crystallized into the flesh of the outlaw's massive hand. She was able to resume control of her legs (which had been jangling, marionettelike, on either side of the saddle several inches above the stirrups), and with no small effort was able to pull her aching knees up to grip the sweating gelding's slippery pumping shoulders.

Then she looked forward, between the horse's ears, and saw the end of the world.

The edge of the cliff loomed before them, clean and sharp, nothing beyond but empty sky. A voice in her head shrieked, "Turn, you fool! Turn!" but her lips were frozen and then it was too late. They plunged over the side.

But they did not fall. There was no plummet into infinity. Instead there was a wild scramble down a steep rocky incline on the other side of the crest. At the moment they went over the edge, Jessie flew straight up out of the saddle, hair flying, legs flailing. She raised her hands to her face, half in unconscious prayer, half in the hope that to shield herself from seeing the circumstances of her own demise would somehow prevent it. As she levitated into the air (now, it seemed, in slow motion), Owen's face appeared in her mind.

Owen. White and soft and proper and pince-nezed, shaking his finger in her face. "Headstrong," he was saying, "spoiled and headstrong, and you can't possibly hope to understand—" when he melted into a picture of the room she'd had as a girl in San Francisco, white, bright, lacy and sunlit. There she sat, cross-legged on the Oriental, holding a tea party for her dolls. "Sugar or lemon, my dear Mrs. Smith?" she was asking one porcelain guest when Mrs. Fowler appeared at the door, her eyes red, saying, "Jessica, your mother has—"

She was jerked back into reality as a strong arm snatched her out of midair and back into the saddle. Madly, they zigzagged down the crumbling rock face, the horse hopping, darting, stumbling, and nearly falling. It righted itself, then as it scrambled and slid, flurries of stone and dust were sent to the bottom far below. Through it all, Clay held her firmly to him, sometimes so tightly she she feared his thick forearm would crush her ribs.

It was not until the lathered horse stopped its jolting and pitching that Jessica could see they had reached the floor of a narrow canyon over one hundred yards below the scarp from which they began the bone-bruising descent. The steaming chestnut, its liver brown coat now sweat-drenched to a deep blackberry, slowed gratefully to an easy jog-trot. As Clay reined him along the dry creek bed, Jessie realized that their relative positions atop the horse had altered.

In the confusion of that mad plummeting gallop, Clay had slid forward and down into the saddle, and she was now seated on his lap, his free arm still clasping her tightly to him. Her legs were held wide apart by the saddle's pommel, her knees instinctively gripping the outsides of the outlaw's muscular thighs. Her skirts and drawers had ridden up, exposing most of the creamy length of her thighs. The rough suede chaps he wore rubbing against her tender skin was strangely pleasurable. Her hair had given up the last of its pins and lay in a wild, dark cloud about her shoulders. Somewhere she had lost her left shoe.

Suddenly, she thought of Owen again—so correct,

110

so controlled—shaking his pudgy white finger. What would her priggish husband think if he could see her now: disheveled, disarrayed, on the lap of this burly roughneck—frankly indecent by Boston standards. Or the standards of anywhere else, for that matter.

So ludicrous was this image, so relieved was she to still be drawing breath, that she reacted in a totally unexpected manner.

She began to laugh.

Wildly. Crazily. Tears streamed down her cheeks as she roared, gasping for air. As new gales erupted, Clay reined in the horse and shook her. "What's the matter with you?" he demanded.

She couldn't stop. She began to double over.

Clay extricated himself from beneath her to dismount, and the thud when she slid off his lap and, wincing, landed back in the hard seat on her fresh bruises, elicited only further peals. And when he stood there, hands on his hips, mouth agape, staring up at her as if she were the public exhibit for Visitor's Day at the asylum, the dam burst and she was wracked with new peals of laughter, pointing at him with both index fingers, then collapsing backwards over the cantle, her head bouncing up and down on the horse's slick rump with each new convulsion.

Clay shook his head, then reached up and pulled her helplessly spasming body from the saddle. He gripped her shoulders and held her at arm's length before he shook her, hard. "Hey!" he shouted, loud enough that it echoed down the canyon. But she did not, could not stop.

"Lady," he muttered as he untied her wrists and tossed the bonds to the ground, "we really don't have time for you to be hysterical right now." She wasn't listening. She started to slip to the ground, giggling wildly. He hoisted her back up as exasperation

111

flickered across his face. He sighed and tipped back his hat. "Damn," he said. "I was trying to cut down on this."

In one sweeping gesture, he drew her to him.

Her laughter stopped abruptly as she yielded, shocked by the embrace. At first she resisted, pushing feebly on his broad chest, but he was too strong. He easily held her still-shaking body to his with one hand pressed to the small of her back as the other wove its way into the dark tangle of her hair.

Using this handful of windblown tresses for leverage, he tilted her startled, unbelieving face upward and brushed his lips against hers. "No . . ." she mumbled. "What . . . ?" Trembling and disoriented, she had lost the capacity of speech. She was vaguely aware that she was making strange, high, wordless sounds, a hysterical whimper she could not control.

"Hush," he whispered, and kissed her gently, sweetly, then again, more firmly. The kiss became more fervent as he sensed her easing from shock into submission, and he slowly but purposefully slid his hand from her back to her hip, then lower to cup her buttock through the thin fabric of her summer dress.

She felt gooseflesh emanating in prickling waves from his strong, gentle fingers. The lower half of her body felt both leaden and lighter than air, and a tinglng warmth had blossomed—surprisingly, wonderfully— between her legs. As he slid the tip of his tongue between her now-silent lips, Jessie felt herself separate completely from the world around her. His hands, his lips, the scent and taste and feel of him: these had become, quite suddenly, the boundaries of her universe.

She was vaguely aware that her own arms, once pressed against his chest in protest, had circled his neck. Her fingers combed the curls at its base, caressed

112

the muscles of his upper back and shoulders, which were so different from Owen, so strong, so powerful. So male.

She knew then that in two years of marriage to Owen, she had never been kissed, not *really* kissed, until now.

At the thought of Owen—her marriage, her duty—she faltered and tried to push away, the shrill whimper rising again in her throat. But her captor's only response was to pull her more tightly to him, his lips, his tongue becoming more insistent: advancing, retreating, teasing, tasting. The image of her husband vanished completely as she melted once again into the badman's embrace.

Her world was nothing but touch, nothing but sensation now. She felt his fingers stroke her temple, her cheek, her jaw, her neck; and once there, a subtle change of pressure upon her throat, only half-noticed as he crushed her more tightly to him. Tiny stars appeared on the inside of her closed eyelids, swimming, shimmering points of light. Against his mouth, she gasped for air. And then there was nothing.

Clay caught her deftly and swept her into his arms. Carrying her to the chestnut grazing obliviously nearby, he boosted her limp body into the saddle. She was already coming around, and looking dazed and confused, she clung dumbly to the saddle horn.

Clay did not join her on the horse. Instead, he settled his Stetson back into place and looked up at her appraisingly. He wore an expression such as one might see on the face of a man who has just repaired a complicated piece of machinery by administering a swift kick to the gearbox.

"There," he said, more or less to himself. He tugged at his ear, and looking slightly chagrined, shook his head. "Damn thing works every time."

113

Gathering up the horse's reins he added, this time directly to Jessica, "I believe I'll just walk old Chance for a while. He's already given his best for the day."

He gave the chestnut a pat on the neck and set out on foot, leading the horse and its bewildered passenger down the shadow-drenched creek bed.

5

She hadn't known it was possible to be so tired. Somewhere along the way Clay had remounted, and they had begun a seemingly endless climb through the foothills. She had begun to think she would spend the rest of her life on horseback when, finally, they entered a small clearing. It was almost dark, but through the gloom she could see a run-down cabin built up against a wall of rock, and thought with relief that there was an end of the line, after all. But he did not stop the horse. Instead, he proceeded through the little clearing, reentering the pines and following a winding, downhill path for about one hundred yards. They came out in a smaller clearing beside a weathered lean-to. Here he dismounted at last, and led the horse into the shed, Jessica still clinging to the saddle.

Inside were three narrow tie stalls, and a half-stall, which contained an ancient, shallow pile of straw which spilled out into the aisle. Farther back in the corner was a careless collection of stray boards, rusty broken traps and old scraps of discarded harness. It was upon the mound of straw that Clay placed her, after pulling her limp, drained body from the saddle.

"Wait here," he said, as if he honestly believed she

might have the strength to do otherwise. "After I see to Chance, I'll get you settled up at the cabin." He stripped the saddle and bridle from the horse, now cooled and dry, and led him into the center stall. Then he lit the kerosene lamp which hung on a nail next to the door. From the far stall, he removed a lightweight wire and wood cage containing two pigeons. He carried it outside, and returned a moment later swinging the empty cage, which he tossed into the pile of scrap behind Jessica.

What in the world is he doing? she thought as she struggled to keep her traitorous eyelids from closing.

Clay gave the horse a light rubdown, and after supplying him with fresh water and a measure of grain, turned to Jessica. She was soundly asleep on the mound of moldy straw, her cheek pressed against the rough wall of the shed.

Clay compared this tousled, dusty waif with the aloof young woman who had only this morning demanded to know if she were being abducted. Now the daughter of the mighty Samuel LaCroix lolled dead to the world, as dirty and smudged as a discarded doll. Her hair was a black, tangled nest, her dress was torn, and she was missing a shoe. Somehow, he almost preferred this version of Jessica LaCroix Lawrence to the tidier, more self-assured one.

Smiling, he scooped her into his arms and, picking up the lantern, carried her up the path.

Inside the cabin, he laid her carefully on the bed and removed her remaining shoe. She was still sleeping deeply, completely exhausted. He went out into the clearing to the pump and brought back a bucket of water for her to use in the morning. Then he stood over her bed.

She really was beautiful. The picture he had seen of her had not done her justice.

"I'm sorry about . . . earlier," he said to her un-hearing form. "It was a rotten thing to do." He reached down and pulled the tattered quilt over her, up to her chin. "Do you have any idea what's going on, Jessica Lawrence? Do you have any idea who your stepfather really is?"

He received no reply. He expected none. He stood there for another moment, then picked up the lantern. Quietly closing the door behind him, he went back down the path to spend the night with Chance in the lean-to.

When she awoke, the trapper's shack was filled with dusty light. Everything was alien, strange. She groggily tried to remember where she was. Then it came flooding back—the stage ride, the kidnapping, the ride through the desert and foothills, the green-eyed outlaw. She rubbed at her bruised fanny and grimaced.

Stiffly, she pulled herself up to a sitting position and looked around the cabin. It was small, about fifteen feet across and twelve feet deep, and had a musty, unused smell, as if it had been abandoned for many seasons. There was an ancient iron stove at one corner, not far from the washstand. Other than the bed on which she sat, the only furnishings were a small, broken-legged chest of drawers, a battered table, and three wooden chairs crusted in peeling paint. The floor was rough-sawn lumber scattered with crude, braided rugs, and the rear wall of the structure was solid rock. Light streamed randomly through spaces between the wall timbers, as well as through the gaps where they abutted the granite face. There were two four-paned windows along the front wall, one on either side of the door. A third broke the monotonous face of a side wall, near the washstand. One of the front windows was glassed and unbroken, and looked as if a recent attempt had been made to remove some of its grime.

117

The other two windows were fitted with combinations of cracked glass and translucent paper.

She was alone. Gingerly, she stood up, her sore muscles screaming, and hobbled to a front window to look for Clay. He wasn't in the clearing, either. She went back to the bed and sat slowly on its edge.

Granted, she thought, this was a convenient way to get back at her stepfather. But maybe it was going just a little too far. And just because they would get their money from Samuel, it didn't necessarily follow that they'd return her in one piece. She thought about the strange cackling boy and shivered. Of course, he might not join them here in the woods, but maybe he would. She didn't fancy spending any time with him.

She might try to escape, but where would she go, alone and on foot? She had no idea where she was, or how she had gotten there. But, maybe there was a way . . . If she could only get to the horse, she might have a chance.

She pulled herself up, making a face, and peeked out the window again. The clearing was still vacant. She opened the door a crack and peeped out, looking toward the path that led to the horse shed, then slipped out the door and furtively crossed the overgrown yard to the trees.

When she arrived at the lean-to, there was still no sign of Clay. *Where in the world could he have gotten to?* she wondered, then knitted her brow. *Wherever he is, I'll bet the horse is with him.* Her spirits fell, but she peeked inside the shed anyway.

Chance stood in his stall, contentedly munching his oats. The big chestnut turned to look at her, flicked his tail, then turned his attention back to breakfast.

Clay was still nowhere to be seen. She slid through the door and approached the horse. Quietly, efficiently, she tacked him up, groaning under her breath as she struggled with the heavy stock saddle. Then she led him outside, checking first to see that Clay hadn't come up while she was busy. He hadn't.

She led Chance to a stump, and using it as a mounting block, clambered aboard the big gelding. The stirrups were too long for her, but she didn't have time to adjust them. She gathered the reins and pressed her knees into the horse's sides.

There was no response. Chance just stood there, absently swishing his tail.

"Move!" she growled, under her breath. She kicked him this time, thumping her bare heels against his ribs once, then twice.

Nothing. The horse jerked his nose up, pulling the reins from her hands. Then he dropped his head and began to graze.

"Blast!" She leaned forward, regathered the reins and pulled Chance's muzzle away from the under-growth. "Go!" It was a shouted whisper. She kicked the horse again and smacked him across the withers with the ends of her reins.

The only movement from the horse was the stomp of one hind foot and the continued swishing of his tail.

"Blast and damn!" She raised her hand to slap him on the rump.

"'Fraid that won't do any good, miss."

She swiveled in the saddle. Clay stood not ten feet away, leaning against a tree. He was naked from the waist up, his arms folded across his chest. His shirt hung over his arm and his red suspenders dangled down to his knees. He had shaved off the stubbly beard he'd grown over the past few weeks, exposing a chiseled, strong-jawed face. He'd saved only the mustache, which was thick and full, and the same dark warm walnut as the waves on his head. He was smiling, exposing a row of strong, white teeth, and his clear green

119

eyes sparkled. He was the most handsome man she had ever seen.

Jessica opened her mouth to speak, but he beat her to it. "See, Chance is sort of a one-man horse." As if to prove his point, he said, "Go on, boy. Back to your stall."

The gelding turned around and slowly ambled past Clay and into the shed, almost scraping a bewildered Jessica from his back. Clay followed along and held out his arms, as if to help her dismount.

"I can get down myself, thank you," Jessica sniffed. She swung a leg over the gelding's neck and dropped gracefully to the ground.

Clay leaned against the partition. "That was pretty silly, anyway, you know. Where were you planning on going?"

Jessica shrugged. "Away from here."

"Any particular direction in mind?" He moved past her and began unsaddling the horse.

"No." She watched him pull the stock saddle down and sling it over the stall partition, then unbuckle Chance's bridle. The muscles in his broad back rippled smoothly as he worked. She had never before seen a partially naked man, at least this close up. Even Owen, on his weekly excursions into her bed, always wore a long white nightshirt, hitching it up only after he was beneath her covers. Clay's back was deeply tanned and muscular. Owen's, she imagined, was probably pale and doughy, like the rest of him.

Clay finished with the horse and turned to face her. "Do you know why you're here?"

"I think so. You intend to extort a great deal of money from Father, I imagine." It was difficult to keep her eyes on his face. His gaze was absolutely piercing, his green eyes looking directly, it seemed, into her soul. He made her feel naked. And it would have been too forward to stare at his chest, though she would have liked to—it was as broad and strong as she had imagined, with a T-shaped growth of thick dark curls that sprouted from his belt line. His midsection was lean and rippled like a washboard. He was one of those Greek statues she had seen in Europe come to life, sculpted not in cold marble, but in warm human flesh. She was seized with a nearly uncontrollable impulse to put her hand out and touch him. Instead, she looked at the ground.

"Well, that's pretty close," he replied. He wondered if she had any idea just how Samuel had made all that money. "Do you know much about his business?"

"I know it's all he really cares about." She looked back into those clear, bottomless eyes. Looking away from him hadn't helped. Even the sound of his voice seemed to be enticing her to touch him, to do something totally ridiculous. *Dear God, don't let him know what I'm thinking,* she prayed.

He reached into his saddlebags and pulled out a small object. He held it out to her. "Here," he said.

She held out her hand. "What is it?"

"Comb," he smiled. "You're kind of a mess. Thought you might like to get cleaned up. There's water up at the shack."

She snatched it from his hand, the spell broken. She stood there for a moment, too angry and embarrassed to speak, then finally stamped a bare foot hard on the dirt floor and marched out the door and up the path. She slammed the cabin door so loudly behind her that Chance, in his stall, started. Clay patted him on the neck.

"It's all right, boy," he said. "She'll get to like us. Maybe."

* * *

Clarence Villanova sat behind the massive desk in Samuel's private study. The room was not bright, for the heavy draperies were halfway closed. All around him were the things of Samuel's life: two Ming vases from the Oriental collection; photographs and etchings of locomotives from LaCroix's railroad line; a photo of Samuel shaking hands with President Rutherford B. Hayes; another with Chester Alan Arthur. There were no images of his stepdaughter or his wife. The darkly paneled wall behind him was filled with antique dueling pistols arranged in pairs, all highly polished, most in working order. It was the only one of Samuel's collections to be fully displayed in the house.

The desk before him was bare of its usual clutter of papers, books, and ledgers. Ony two items, two single sheets of paper, rested upon its polished surface. The first was a telegram, originating from a small town in the Verde Valley and received two hours ago. It read:

UNABLE TO PREVENT TAKING OF DAUGHTER DAY AND HALF SOUTH OF FLAGSTAFF STOP SHERIFF ALREADY LEFT WITH POSSE STOP SHALL I FORM SECOND RESCUE PARTY STOP
DOBBS

Villanova had sent a reply immediately. It read simply:

SENDING OWN RESCUE PARTY STOP YOU ARE FIRED STOP
CV

Then he had wired another man in Flagstaff, a man renowned for his tracking skills, and hired him to trail the kidnappers.

And now a second message had arrived, but this time not from Western Union. It was delivered to one of the maids by a small, nondescript boy who vanished as soon as the paper was in her hand. It read:

My Dear LaCroix,

Greetings. You are by now aware that I have taken possession of your daughter. You are also aware of those things I require from you before I will effect her release.

You have one week in which to remove your people from all contended enterprises. If, in such time, you fail to accomplish this, Mrs. Lawrence will still be returned to you; she will arrive, however, in more than one parcel.

I trust you will not be so foolish as to call in the authorities or attempt a private rescue. Should any such endeavor come to my attention, you may be sure that Mrs. Lawrence will be the one to suffer.

—N.K.—

Villanova had immediately rewired Flagstaff and called off the tracker. For now, there was nothing he could do but wait. Wait for Samuel to tell him how he wished the transfers to be handled. Samuel had rallied strongly after their talk of the other night, and during the following days had very nearly returned to his old steely self. But this morning's news had been very hard on him. For a moment, Villanova had feared he would lapse into the catatonia that had gripped him earlier.

He had sat there in the study with Villanova after Dobbs's wire arrived, smoking a cigar, staring at the cold hearth, not saying a word. There was nothing to say. He knew that it was over the moment he read the telegram, that his empire was as good as gone, and that the daughter to whom he needed to atone was in the hands of Kane's minions. He could only sit and wait for specific terms from Kane.

When the message was delivered, he had read it quietly, then set it gently on the desk. "Call off your man in Flagstaff," he'd said quietly. "I need to have words with Lawrence."

And now Samuel was in the library with Owen Lawrence. Villanova didn't envy Samuel this little talk, but he wished he could hear their conversation.

Owen was angrily pacing the floor. "I insist you call in the authorities!" he was saying. "Who knows what these ruffians will do to her! They might kill her!" *And along with her, kill my chances of collecting the rest of her inheritance,* he thought. He stopped his pacing and put his hand to his forehead. "Oh, my poor, poor Jessica," he added, for Samuel's benefit.

"I am trying to explain to you, Lawrence, that calling in the authorities would most certainly result in her immediate death. We are dealing with ruthless people." Samuel was seated at the small library desk. He looked very old and very tired. He was weary of Owen's proclamations of concern over Jessica. He knew Owen had little room for love in him, and what he reserved for his wife was directed toward her money. Samuel had always known this. He had, in fact, picked Owen for his stepdaughter not only for his pedigree, but because he knew it would be a loveless match. He had known all along what a hopeless businessman Owen was, and how badly he needed the cash that Jessica would bring to the marriage. And he knew that Jessica would find no friend, no lover, in Owen Lawrence. Somehow, he had wanted to separate her from such things, wanted to reserve those parts of her for himself, all the time knowing that to feel these things was impossible sickness, was disease. The full meaning of what he had done, the perspective on this monstrous feeling for his stepdaughter, had only become truly clear to him since that last night with her. He opened the top drawer of the desk just a little and rested his hand on the Bible he had recently placed there. *I must atone,* he thought, stroking the cover. *Repent and atone.*

"—their price?"

Samuel forced himself back to reality. "Pardon me?"

Owen glowered at him. *The old man's getting senile,* he thought. "I said that you must then intend to pay whatever they ask. To send them the money." He spoke a little louder, just in case his father-in-law was getting deaf, too.

"It isn't as simple as that, Lawrence," Samuel said softly. The Bible beneath his fingers seemed warm, as if it might burn him. "They don't want money. They want something else."

Owen straightened, his beady eyes glaring through the tiny glasses on his nose. "Well, whatever it is, give it to them!"

"This is a very complex matter, Lawrence. Rest assured that we are seeing to it as swiftly as we can, but it is going to take some time." *Just as long as it takes to ruin me,* he thought, then hated himself all the more for his selfishness.

"Not too much time, I hope." Owen stormed to the door. "I expect to see my wife returned to me within the week, unharmed. I want you to know that I hold you personally responsible for her well-being." He stalked from the room, slamming the door behind him.

"Yes. Certainly." Samuel withdrew his hand from

the drawer. His fingers could no longer stand the heat of the book he touched there. "I'm the responsible one. The responsible one."

She finally managed to tidy the rat's nest of her hair, and then she washed her face. Coffee she found in a tin on the washstand, and she brewed it in a chipped enameled pot on the little iron stove.

Her life until recently, she mused with the objectivity that comes with forced perspective, had been a syrupy sludge of guilt, self-recrimination, and surrender to circumstance—and submission to those who encouraged the first three. Things were different now, at least for the time being. Despite her captivity, she felt suddenly liberated. She had freed herself of her father that day on the train, and now she felt she was freeing herself of . . . well, of her own earlier, simpering self. She swung her bare legs up on the seat of another chair and stretched out, sipping the strong dark brew. It was as if everything was new again. The air had never smelled so sweet and crisp. She stretched sensually, like a cat. She smiled. Despite her bruises, her body had never felt so alive, so healthy. Even coffee had never tasted so good.

She was on her second cup when Clay knocked at the door.

"Thought I smelled coffee," he said. "Mind if I have a cup?"

She lifted her eyebrows. "Would I be able to stop you if I did?"

He poured himself a mug. "I suppose not." He set the pot back on the stove and leaned against the sink. "Are you still angry with me?"

She pulled her feet down off the chair. "Why should I be angry with you? What reason could I possibly have?

126

After all, what have you done except abduct me from a stagecoach, nearly kill me during that gallop through the desert, and hold me prisoner in this desolated hovel?" Her nose was in the air again. Even anger was newly enjoyable.

Clay listened calmly. "You're right," he said. "You have absolutely nothing to be angry about."

She snorted at him and turned away. The man, despite his obvious physical charms, was infuriating.

Clay sipped his coffee. "Thought you might be hungry."

She was ravenous. "I suppose," she admitted. "Maybe a little."

"Then come on," he said as he strode toward the door. "No room service around here. We'll have to catch our own."

He left so quickly that she had to scramble to catch up with him. "What do you mean, 'catch our own'?" They crossed the clearing and walked down the path to the horse shed. "You don't actually expect me to . . . to . . . *kill* something, do you?" He walked past the shed and began to follow a narrower trail leading farther into the trees. She began to hear the rush and bubble of water. "Where are you going?" she called to his back.

He stopped. She closed the distance between them to emerge at the edge of the wood, on the bank of a beautiful mountain stream. It curled here in a kind of loop, creating a wide pool, which was so clear and calm that she could see every pebble and stone on its bottom. She could also see trout circling beneath the surface a little farther downstream where the current began to rush.

"Know how to fish?" he asked, leading her toward where the water foamed and bubbled.

"No."

"Well, it's easy." He reached behind her and picked up two long, slender branches he had fashioned into poles. He handed her one. "Here," he said. "They're not very fancy, but they'll do the job."

He baited the hooks, then showed her how to flick the tip of the line over the surface of the water by snapping her wrist. They sat down on the bank, their backs to the pines, and waited.

They had fished in silence for some time when Jessica could stand it no more. It had been flitting furtively through her mind all day, and she had to have an answer.

"I . . . I was wondering about something," she said.

"Hm?" Clay was busy making short casts with the tip of his line. Jessica's had gone dead in the water and was sinking.

"About yesterday," she began. "In the canyon. When you stopped the horse and . . ." She was staring at her hands on the pole. She knew her face was turning red, but she felt compelled to finish. "I just wondered . . . I mean, about what you did."

Clay laid the homemade pole down beside him. He knitted his brow and ran a hand through his hair. He turned to face her, but found he couldn't and looked away. "I'm really sorry, but I—" He cleared his throat. "It's just something I use when . . . Well, you were hysterical, and I couldn't think of anything else. I . . . I'm sorry."

He was plainly uncomfortable, almost painfully embarrassed. He began to grind his heels into the bank.

"Oh," said Jessica. "I think I see. You needed to shut me up in a hurry. Put me in my place, I suppose." She gave her pole a yank, rescuing the bait from the bottom of the stream and began to angrily flick it back and forth on the surface of the water. "That was simply the most expedient way."

An embarrassed silence again settled over them.

Jessica had once again allowed her line to go slack, and her hook sank in the stream. Finally, Clay said, "You'd better keep that moving, or you'll never catch anything."

She looked down her nose at him. "I can't see that you've having any better luck."

He sighed. "Well, at least I'm not catching anything the *right* way. You fish about as well as you ride."

She wheeled on him. "I'll have you know I ride very well!"

Glad to get her mind away from the incident in the canyon, he egged her on. "You certainly couldn't prove it by me."

"I ride *very* well, thank you. I used to ride a great deal as a girl."

He smirked. "Sidesaddle, I suppose. Of all the silly things—"

"Astride. I rode astride. And on hunters, too!" Her lips were pursed, her brow knotted. "It's just that I am accustomed to riding alone. With my hands free. And on a *real* saddle, not that thick beast of a thing you Westerners insist on using."

"A stock saddle serves a multitude of purposes . . ." he began.

"Certainly. If you're roping cattle or something. But you'll have to admit it allows little or no leg contact with the animal. It forces you to travel *on* the horse instead of *with* him."

Clay scratched his head. "Point well taken," he admitted. Actually, he quite agreed with her. A good bit of his youth had been spent fox hunting in Maryland. But it was not something he could tak about, not in these circumstances. He was, after all, supposed to be an outlaw with no past and little future.

"I was looking at your horse," she went on, pleased

129

to have won that round. "He's not at all like the others I've seen out here."

"He's a nice one, all right," he said. Now where was she headed? She might turn out to be too observant for her own good.

"Actually," she went on, "my husband has cousins outside Boston who have a few Morgans. That's what your horse looks like to me, a Morgan. He's got that big thick neck and powerful shoulder. And a lot more knee and hock action than I'd expect to see on a ranch horse or a mustang. Except he's chestnut. I guess the only Morgans I've ever seen have been bays." She looked at him.

"You do know horses, don't you?" He grappled for a believable explanation. He couldn't tell her the truth—that the horse was from his father's breeding farm in Maryland. That wouldn't do at all. "Actually, I suppose he could be a part-bred. I won him in a poker game in St. Louis a couple of years back from an Eastern slicker. That's why I call him Chance." There. That was reasonably neat and tidy.

"Oh." The story appeased her, but something was still wrong. The cowboy was far too well-spoken, carried himself with too much of what? A cosmopolitan air, perhaps. He reminded her of Owen's cousin, Daniel Follett, who had taught her to shoot. They looked nothing alike, of course, but they both had an air of old money, of country gentlemen who don't feel they have to prove anything to anyone: men at ease in any situation. She tried to picture him in tweeds and riding breeches. The image came easily. What was he doing here in Arizona, and how had he gotten mixed up with Fletch and, especially, that young lunatic?

Her reverie was aborted by a sudden tug on her line.

"Oh! I think I've got something!"

Clay dropped his pole in the grass. "Bring it in!"

130

he cried.

She was completely out of her element. "What do I do?"

Quickly he put his arms around her, grasping the pole, bracketing her hands with his, and tried to force the struggling trout closer to the bank. It was a big one, and it was putting up a good fight. Together, they played the fish out and back, waiting for it to tire, Jessica alternately laughing and calling out useless directions.

"No! Look out! He's going the other way now!"

As she moved against his chest in her exhilaration, Clay was surprised by the degree of his excitement for her. She was supposed to be just another job, after all. But he had never had such a beautiful assignment. When she laughed, she glowed, and he could not help but glow along with her. This was a girl who was born to laugh and love and drink fully of the joys of life. He wondered just how much opportunity she'd had to do any of those things.

At last, they were able to flip the exhausted trout up on the grassy bank. By this time, they were both giggling wildly, both still gripping the pole. She turned to face him, her eyes bright and sparkling. She started to say something, and suddenly, he felt compelled to kiss her. He lowered his face to hers, but before their lips brushed, she jerked away from him, scrambled to her feet, and backed into the woods. Her bosom was heaving. In fear? In excitement? In anger? He couldn't tell.

"What were you going to do? Put me in my place again?" she spat before she turned and ran back up the path. He could not be sure, but he thought she might have been crying.

He could not have regretted the incident in the canyon any more than he did at that moment. He was

131

ashamed that he'd used that cheap trick on her, one he'd used so many times before on so many women. Because this girl was special, unique.

There was something about her, some intoxicating chemistry that made her nearly irresistible to him: those incredible sparkling blue eyes, so deep and sometimes so sad; the ripe pouting mouth that he knew had not curled into nearly enough smiles; the clean, graceful line of her throat; her delicate slender hands. He imagined her breasts, full and round, waiting for his touch; what her slim hips looked like under her skirts, and how she would move beneath him in the night. . . .

He took two steps to the stream and splashed handful after handful of water over his face and neck. It was much colder here than in the sun-warmed pool it bypassed above, and it brought him back to reality. *It's a job, McCallister,* he chided himself. *Just keep remembering it's only a job.*

Later, he appeared at the door of the cabin and presented the trout, cleaned and ready to fry. "Thought you might like some of this," he said. "You caught him, after all."

Her anger and indignation overcome by hunger, she let him in. He stoked up the old potbellied stove and before long, the shack was filled with the tantalizing aroma of frying trout. He poured two cups of coffee, then forked the fish onto tin plates. Nodding her thanks, Jessica greedily tore into her dinner. He had breaded it with seasoned flour and fried it quickly, so the outside was crisp and light and the inner flesh flaky, white, and tender. She could not remember any meal ever tasting better.

She polished off the fish, all but licking the plate before she looked up. She had been so intent on her meal that she hadn't noticed Clay, who had put his fork down and was watching her, a big grin on his face. "I must be a better cook than I thought," he said.

She blushed, but couldn't help smiling. She must have made quite a picture, wolfing down the trout as if it were her last meal on earth. She looked down at her empty plate. "It was pretty good, all right. You must be cordon bleu."

He laughed. "Not quite." He still had the better part of his own meal left, and cut it in two, sliding one of the pieces onto Jessie's plate.

"Oh, I couldn't," she said, even as she felt her salivary glands once again spring into action.

"Yes, you could." He picked up her fork and put it back in her hand. "You haven't eaten since yesterday, and I grabbed some hardtack earlier. Go ahead."

She smiled gratefully, then dove into the new portion. When she finished it, she was finally sated. She leaned back in her chair, sipping coffee.

He removed the plates, carried them to the sink, and began to wash them.

"You seem to be a man of many talents," she commented, unable to sustain any ill feeling toward him no matter how justified it was or how hard she tried. She knew that somewhere it was written that she was the one who should be washing up, but she was so comfortable, and she so enjoyed watching him as he worked (and he seemed so willing to do it), that she couldn't bring herself to move. She put her bare feet up on the seat of the chair he had just vacated. It was still warm. She laughed.

Clay turned his head, smiling. "What are you giggling about?"

"I think Owen would strongly disapprove of this situation."

He started drying the plates. "Who's Owen?" He

133

already knew, but he couldn't let her know he did.

"My husband." Actually saying his name aloud turned her smile into a scowl. She shivered and rubbed at her arms.

"What's he like?" Clay asked.

"He's not like anything," she answered. "He's just Owen." *White, pinched, pasty, priggish, secretive, overbearing, foolish little Owen. Owen, who cages me with his house and his name just as surely as propriety cages me in whalebone.* "He's just the man my father married me to." She had no idea why she had added that last bit, but there it was.

He put down the last plate and joined her at the table, turning up the lamp. It was quite dark outside by now. "Doesn't sound like a match made in heaven," he said.

"What is?" She poured herself another cup of coffee from the pot on the table. "How about you?" she asked. "Are you married?" She hadn't meant to ask that either. Words seemed to be fairly galloping from her mouth unbidden.

"No," he said.

"Why?"

"Never found the right girl, I guess," he replied. *Maybe because all along she was married to someone else,* he thought. He found himself increasingly attracted to her. What an intriguing creature she was: the beautiful daughter of one of the nation's most powerful crime lords (although he had already decided she was innocent of any knowledge of Samuel LaCroix's exploits), educated in the finest schools, married into the upper crust of Boston's finest, yet able to sit here with him in this dingy shack, her legs propped up on a chair like a housemaid, happily sipping coffee from a chipped cup. And she knew horses. And God, how he loved the sound of her laughter . . .

134

That yesterday in the canyon she had responded to that kiss with such need had surprised him at first, but the more consideration he gave it, the more sense it made. They had done some research on Owen Lawrence, and Clay knew what Jessica had only guessed at. He knew what Owen did on those nights he didn't come home. *Men with sexual proclivities like his very often have frustrated wives,* he thought. *He probably sleeps with her just often enough to keep the servants from gossiping. Poor little Jessie, all that love to give, and no one worth giving it to.* He stared into his coffee cup. Suddenly, he was very sad for her, at the same time wanting her more than he had ever wanted any other woman.

And she was watching him. *How,* she was thinking, *does a man like this get involved in a kidnapping?* He didn't belong here. He was out of place. He should be back East somewhere, riding to the hounds, or walking through the lobby of some elegant hotel, a beautiful lady on his arm. Or playing baccarat in some European casino, winning and losing hundreds or thousands with equal aplomb. He both fascinated and excited her.

She had given it some thought, and decided that maybe "the thing" he had done to her in the desert yesterday hadn't been so awful after all—at least, the part before she blacked out. When she got back to Boston, she would have that kiss and those strange, wonderful sensations to remember. It would also make it that much easier to sustain her hate for Owen. She found herself wishing that Clay would hold her again, make her feel like that again. She felt color rising in her cheeks as she remembered the surge of pleasure in her loins, and was surprised when, at the return of the memory, she began to feel some of the same warm glow between her legs. She looked up at him through her lashes. He was staring at her again. He looked rather peculiar. She couldn't read what was on his face. She only knew that it somehow increased the tingling she felt.

He stood up. "I, uh, I think I'd better get back down to the barn," he said, somewhat falteringly.

"Oh. Of course," she said, somewhat surprised at his abrupt departure. "I'll see you tomorrow."

"Right," he said, and closed the door behind him. Outside, he leaned against the cabin and looked up at the stars, waiting for his burgeoning erection to die away. Finally, he walked away, toward the lean-to. "This is going to be tougher than I thought," he mumbled aloud. "A lot tougher."

Owen was in his room. It was late and the house was quiet. He had been waiting, biding his time. It was more than he could take, watching that little Chinese girl, Lin, bustling around the house every day and not being able to touch her. He knew he would have to get out soon and find a place where he could rid himself of some of this tension. He went to the door and listened carefully. There was not a sound. Silently, he eased the door open and stole out into the hallway.

He needed a girl, needed one badly. He needed to hit her, to make her scream, to see the welts on her body. In this way, he received his ultimate satisfaction. And not just any girl would do—it had to be the right kind. Oriental girls, young ones no older than sixteen—these were his meat.

He crept down the wide staircase, a smirk on his face. Back in Boston he could have visited his usual house. They knew what he liked at Mama Sugar's, and they kept him well supplied. But Denver had places where he might find such a girl, he knew, or at least a man willing to sell one to him for the night. Not like that place he had discovered when he snuck from the house two nights earlier. He wouldn't have hurt the girl badly. There had been no need for them to throw him out into the street. The girl had looked worse off than she actually was—if only she hadn't bled so much. . . . Without thinking, he reached to touch himself, then smiled. He had grown hard just thinking about it.

When he reached the foot of the stairs, he heard a noise behind him on the ground floor, coming from Samuel's study. The door was closed, but light spilled from beneath it. Owen tiptoed closer and put his ear to the door.

It was Samuel's voice, talking. *That pig, Villanova, must be in there with him,* Owen thought. Then he realized that LaCroix was alone in the room, talking to himself.

He seemed to be praying. Not a nice clean Episcopal prayer, the kind that Owen was used to hearing, but something crazed and forlorn. He couldn't catch all of it, but the phrases that came his way were more than enlightening.

"Forgive me, Father, for I have sinned," Samuel kept repeating. Then, "lusted for my little Jessica . . . sin beyond measure . . . blackness of my heart . . . forgive . . . a sign . . . give me a sign . . . show me what to do . . . ashamed . . . forgive . . ."

Samuel continued to ramble. Owen stood up. An interesting piece of news. Most interesting. More interesting than finding a nice Chinese tart. Owen retreated quietly to his rooms to spend the night in feverish thought.

6

She had never before been in love, but whether Jessica wished it or not, she was in love now.

She awoke before dawn, and lay there, first in darkness and then in the growing light, thinking about Clay. She had gone over every word he'd said to her, every movement he'd made. She thought about his eyes and the way they bored into her soul; his strong arms and muscular torso; his clean, square jaw and the cleft in his chin; the little wrinkles at the corners of his eyes when he smiled. Even the picture of him standing at the sink, drying tin plates, was somehow almost more enticing than she could bear. She wriggled beneath her covers. Once or twice she even giggled out loud, especially when she remembered his indignation at her fishing methods. "At least I'm not catching anything the *right* way," he had muttered. How male! but coming from him, it was somehow charming rather than arrogant.

All these feelings were new to her. And the more attractive she found Clay, the more repugnant she found her life with Owen. How she wished she could wipe Owen Lawrence and Boston from her life and spend the rest of her days here in this cabin with Clay. . . .

Foolishness. Impossible foolishness. She would have to go back. There was no way around it. A divorce was completely unacceptable, and even if Owen should miraculously vanish into thin air, how could she be sure that Clay returned her feelings? He was her captor—there was no getting around it. He and those other two men had been hired to abduct her. Her father would pay the price, and she would be sent back to him, to Owen, to Boston. She probably meant no more to Clay than a cut of the ransom. But there was something in his eyes, his voice . . .

Could she be only imagining that he had some affection for her? But how could he? She was just another job to him, she imagined, just one more victim: the daughter of a rich man he'd probably never met. But maybe . . . No, it was too foolish to contemplate. With a sigh, she pulled back the covers and got to her feet.

It was midmorning by now, and there was still no sign of him. Probably fishing for breakfast, she thought, grinning as she pictured him flicking his line over the surface of the water to no avail. She added wood to the dully glowing embers in the stove and put on a pot of coffee. Then she opened the door to let in the crisp morning air.

Tacked to the outside of the door was a parcel wrapped in moist leaves. A small freshly caught and cleaned trout lay within. There was also a note. It read:

Hope you don't mind cooking your own breakfast. I'm off to scare up some small game. Be back before dinner.

—Clay

She fried the fish in no time, and although it was

139

good, she didn't think it matched the dinner he had prepared the night before. By the time she had eaten and cleaned up, it was still early, not yet noon. She looked down at her dress. The cotton frock, which had once looked so fresh and crisp, was now gray, dingy, and streaked with dirt, its pale blue stripes indistinguishable from the once-white background. The hem was torn in several places.

She fingered the rips. "Well," she said aloud, "I can't do much about these, but I can get it cleaned up a little." She ran her fingers through her hair and found it sticky and lifeless. "And me, too," she added.

She took the cake of soap she had been using at the sink and left the cabin, headed for the stream.

She was singing as she went down the path, reaching out to drag her hands along the gnarled trunks and outthrust, thick-needled branches of the pines, amazed when she realized she had never really given much thought to how wonderfully rough and organic they felt. When she reached the little clearing beside the lean-to, she stopped. Still smiling and humming, she looked around, then went in. Chance was dozing in his stall. She rubbed his neck fondly, then cast her eyes over the interior, searching. When she saw what she was looking for, she grinned and picked it up off the mound of straw on top of which it lay.

Clay's saddlebags. She opened one side, looking for the comb he had lent her before. But there was nothing here but clothing. His clothing. She pulled out a shirt and stroked it, holding it to her nose. She hesitated. *Foolishness,* she thought. *Foolish fantasy.* She stroked the fabric, then shrugged. What could it hurt? She pressed her face into the soft flannel and breathed deeply of his heady scent. At last she refolded it and reluctantly put it away, rebuckling the leather flap.

She opened the other bag. This side looked more

promising: a compass, a pocket watch; a long, wicked-looking bowie knife; tidy packets of hardtack, coffee and dried beans; a tin plate and fork; a pouch of tobacco and rolling papers; a tin box filled with sulphur matches; and so on. Then she came across something curious. A slim book met her hand as she dug through the jumble and she pulled it out. It was a volume of poetry, of Byron. Inside the front cover he had written his name: Clayton Q. McCallister IV. So he had a last name, after all. McCallister. She wondered what the *Q* stood for. And the fourth . . . another curiosity. She rolled the name on her tongue. She liked the sound of it.

She leafed through the book. Some of its pages were dog-earred, as if these few he had read over and over. What a curious thing for a desperado to carry! She knitted her brow. What in the world was going on here? She tucked the volume back thoughtfully, and resumed her search for the elusive comb.

As she ran her fingers along the inside leather, they met a slight obstruction. At first she thought it was the edge of the comb, then perhaps a seam in the cowhide. But there shouldn't have been a seam there. She pulled at it with the tip of her index finger and it parted. Curious, she slid her fingers inside the narrow opening. They met with a slim, soft-covered booklet of sorts, which she eased out of its hiding place and opened. None of the writing inside made any sense to her. It was in Clay's hand, she could tell, but it was gibberish. She turned several pages, but they were more of the same. She shook her head, trying to decipher the meaning of this new development. She opened the bag to replace it, pulling aside the tangle of items, then spied the comb. "Aha!" she said, plucking it from the hodgepodge and tucking it into her bodice. Then she began to search again for the secret compartment.

141

There was a rustling sound from outside. Clay.

Alarmed, she stuffed the notebook deep into the main compartment of the saddlebag, hurriedly rebuckled it, and dropped it back where she found it. She peeked outside.

It was only a deer, liquid-eyed and slim-legged, standing not ten feet away. The doe, seeing her, sprang up into the air and dashed back into the cover of the wood. Jessica smiled. "I guess we scared each other, didn't we?" The notebook forgotten, she made her way down to the stream.

At its edge, she removed her frock, and wading into the water in her underthings, began to scrub her dress. The water was refreshing—cool, but not cold, and she waded in almost up to her waist as she alternately soaped, then wrung out, then resoaped the dress. When she was satisfied that it was as clean as she was going to get it, she waded back to the shallows and spread it out on a smooth boulder to dry in the warm yellow sunshine. She looked down at her underthings. They, too, were in desperate need of a little soap and elbow grease. *Might as well,* she thought. *I have the whole world to myself for at least three or four hours.*

She stripped out of her underclothes, and wading out a little farther, gave them the same treatment she had given her dress, then laid them out on another rock to dry. Then, still grasping the soap and Clay's comb, she swam out to the center of the calm pool formed by the crook in the stream.

It was not deep here, and the soothing water lapped gently just under her breast bone. Holding the comb in her teeth, she began to lather her hair, being careful not to tangle it any more than necessary. Then, her hair still soapy, she combed it thoroughly, the slippery suds easing out the snarls. She leaned backward into the water and shook her head gently, allowing the lazy current to rinse the suds from her dark tresses. She watched as the residue, a hazy cloud, slowly drifted downstream, leaving the pool around her as pristine and sparkling as when she had entered.

She secured the comb in her fresh, sleek hair, and began soaping her body, slowly and luxuriously. Everything was different here in the foothills. Never before had she so enjoyed the simple act of bathing.

She was intent on lathering an arm, gliding the bar leisurely from shoulder to fingertips, when she heard a noise coming from the bank behind her. She turned toward the sound, expecting to see the little doe again.

It was Clay.

He stood there on the bank, his feet spread wide. In one hand he held a rifle, in the other, two rabbits. She had no idea how long he had been there, silently watching her. She suddenly realized that she had no cover—the water was crystalline, and he was seeing her as clearly as if she were standing before him, nude, on the dry land. But rather than flushing with embarrassment and trying to cover herself with her hands, she found that she was paralyzed, and that her breath was coming in rapid, shallow pants. She could not speak. She could only look into his eyes, which were locked on hers.

He was not smiling now. He looked very serious—almost frightening in his intensity—but she could not take her eyes away. She watched him with the rapt intensity of a cobra charmed by a fakir. Without taking his eyes from hers, he put down the rifle, then the rabbits. Then, slowly, he began to undress.

First he tugged off his shirt, then his boots and Levi's, then his underthings. He stood there on the bank, completely naked, and more symmetrically, perfectly beautiful than any human or animal she had ever seen. Wordlessly, he waded into the water and

143

came toward her.

He stopped only inches away. For the first time, his eyes dropped from hers. Slowly, his gaze shifted downward and came to rest on her breasts, buoyant in the water. He reached for her hand, which still clutched the soap, and plucking the bar from her fingers, tossed it hard over his shoulder. She heard a little thump as it landed far away on the bank.

His hands were under the water now, lightly touching her forearms. She felt his fingers gliding up to her shoulders, sending shivers through her limbs. She was mesmerized by his eyes. She wanted to climb inside him, to fall endlessly into those green, green eyes.

"Jessie," he whispered, enfolding her in his arms. He kissed her sweetly, gently, at first only brushing her lips with his. Her arms were around his neck now, her elbows resting lightly on his wide shoulders, her fingers stroking the soft hair at the nape of his neck and caressing his temples. As his kisses became longer and more insistent, she felt her lips part to admit the flickering tip of his tongue. Her nipples, gently abraded by the coarse, wet curls of his chest, sent spiraling shivers racing through her tingling body and she could feel his manhood pressing stiffly against the flatness of her belly. As they began to kiss more deeply, Owen and Boston were farther away than the moon—they had ceased to exist.

Gently, Clay withdrew his lips from hers, and began to kiss the line of her jaw, then her throat, each touch of his lips branding her flesh with prickles of excitement. She realized vaguely that he had circled her waist with one arm, and, with the other under her buttocks, was slowly lifting her buoyant form upward in the water. He kissed her damp skin as she emerged, making tiny circles on her tingling flesh with his tongue, flicking away the beads of water, until he reached her breast.

144

Easily holding her halfway out of the water, he tenderly took one swollen nipple into his warm, moist mouth, sucking gently, swirling it with his tongue. Jessica gasped and dug into his shoulders with her nails, her eyes screwed shut against anything that might intrude on this indescribable new ecstasy.

He released her nipple, kissing the tip lightly in farewell, then turned his attention to the other breast. He traced soft circles around its rosy peak with his tongue, then took it between his lips, first drawing on it, almost nursing; then using his teeth to nip gently, teasingly. It felt as if there were a silver wire, vibrating with heat and desire, running from her breast to the center of her belly, and just when she thought she could stand no more, he pulled away, and began to lower her deeper into the water, kissing his way up her throat until her face was level with his.

He looked into her eyes, his gaze intense, riveting. He was breathing harder now, and she could see his nostrils flare slightly with every breath. "Jessie," he said again, then kissed her once more, his sweet tongue probing within her mouth. As she clung to him, lost in his embrace, she felt his hand slide down between their bodies and gently touch her at the juncture of her legs; lightly at first, just grazing the dark delta, then with more pressure. He slid his hand gently between her legs, and began to move it slowly, rhythmically. As she hugged his neck tighter their kisses grew more fervent, and she felt him tentatively slip first one, then two of his fingers deep inside her.

She was burning now, despite the cool water in which they were immersed. *Don't ever let this stop,* she thought. *Please let this go on forever!* She heard herself moaning and whispering his name as his fingers slipped free of her. She wanted to take his hand and put it back, but he was already running it down her thigh, pulling her leg up to curl around his waist. Then he reached between them again, and pushed the slick, bulbous tip of his erect manhood against her, poised at her threshold. He was very big, bigger than she had imagined was possible, and as he eased the tip inside her, she gasped.

He stopped immediately, holding her steady. "Are you all right, Jessie?" he whispered. "Am I hurting you?" His face was contorted with concern as well as desire.

In answer, she kissed him passionately, hugging him to her with all of her strength and twisting her fingers into his hair.

He reached beneath the water again and lifted her other leg until it, too, curled around his waist, her ankles locking behind his back. Now he penetrated her very slowly, very deeply, supporting her bottom with one hand, her back with the other, until he was completely embedded within her. The sensation of him inside her, of the completeness and rightness of their union, was overwhelming. Tears began to spill down her cheeks.

"Jessie? Jessie," he panted, "I'm sorry, I *am* hurting you!"

She shook her head, the tears still flowing. "No," she wept, "I'm just so happy! I . . . I never knew . . ."

He smiled and gripped her tighter, tenderly brushing her eyelids with his lips and kissing the tears from her cheeks. Then, tasting her lips again, he began to move within her slowly, deliberately: cradling her in his arms as he rocked her up and down in the clear water. She felt her hips and pelvis responding to his movements as incredible spiraling surges of pleasure emanated from their conjunction.

As he advanced, retreated, then advanced again, rapture washed through her in ever-increasing, ever-intensifying waves. Every cell of her body seemed charged with a supernatural electricity, building and building even when she thought there was nowhere else to go, and then suddenly, every atom of her being exploded.

Lights swirled behind her eyelids. She felt as if flames traveled along her limbs, their tongues flicking into every pore. She heard herself calling his name over and over as her body twisted and jerked, completely beyond her power to control it. Her head was swimming, and she feared she would lose consciousness. Then Clay's hand cupped the back of her lolling head, forcing her to open her eyes and look at him.

"Don't leave me now, Jessie," he whispered hoarsely. She tightened her grip around his neck, and felt him plunge deeply into her once, twice, then three times, his already swollen member seeming to suddenly grow even larger inside her. Then he jerked spasmodically, gasping for air, hugging her tightly to him, and she felt him spew his seed deep within her body. As he clutched her, lost in the throes of his own climax, she rained kisses upon his face, his hair.

At last, he could speak again. "Jessie, Jessie," he whispered, pressing his cheek to hers. He began to lift her up, to slide himself from within her.

"No," she said softly. "Stay inside me, please. Just a little longer."

He nestled her back down and lightly ran his fingers over her forehead. "I love you, Jessie," he said, and kissed her as sweetly as anyone has ever been kissed.

Later that evening, Fletch and Loco were less pleasantly occupied. They made camp as the sun surrendered to the horizon in a brilliant blaze of color. They paid it no attention except to curse the passing of

147

the light.

And now the desert all around was subdued, otherworldly. The moon, nearly full, picked out soft gray highlights on the sage and looming cactus. There was no color to define their environment—only silver and shadow and the slither of the creeping and gliding things that hunt by night.

Fletch stirred the pot of beans hanging over the little campfire. They were almost done. Loco plopped down beside him in the circle of light.

"Aw, I'm sick of beans. I mean, I'm really sick of 'em, Fletch. I don't know why we couldn't 'a got us some decent grub while we was in town this mornin'," he whined.

"I already told you about a dozen times, kid, we didn't have time to go sit down in no restaurant. We gotta get back north and check to see everything's all right." He sat back on his heels, and retrieved his tin cup from a flat rock at the fire's edge. The coffee was still steaming, but finally cool enough to drink. "Besides, there's nothin' wrong with beans and hardtack. When we get up to the cabin, you can shoot some fresh game."

Somewhere farther out in the desert, a coyote howled. Loco licked at his lips. "Wish that som-bitch would come in a little closer. I hear coyotes makes good eatin'." He rubbed absently at his kneecaps, his eyes dancing. "When you gonna tell me what Mr. Kane said in his telegram, huh, Fletch?"

He stirred the beans again. He was fairly sick of them, too. "Now, don't pester me about it, Loco. You know how you get." He mashed a bean against the side of the pot, spreading it into a paste. "Gimme yer plate. Beans're done."

"Must be good, if'n you won't tell me right off." The

boy began to giggle shrilly, then put both hands over his own mouth as if to push the sound back inside. "You can tell me, Fletch, honest. Is it good? Is it real good?"

Fletch handed him his dinner, then bent back over the fire to serve himself, his sandy hair reflecting gold in the firelight. He sat back down, cross-legged, and looked at the boy. He was sitting there in the dust, arms hugging his shins, his untouched plate balanced on his knees, looking expectantly at his cousin. He was managing to hold very still.

"Oh, all right," Fletch said.

Loco jerked suddenly, a huge grin on his face, nearly spilling his plate into the dirt. Fletch calmly shot a hand out and grabbed it before it could spatter onto the ground, as if he had done this a hundred times before. He handed the plate back.

"See?" he said. "I ain't even told you yet, and you're gettin' all . . . Well, you know." He shoved a forkful of beans into his mouth. God, he was sick to death of beans. The coyote howled again. Maybe the kid wasn't so far off: maybe coyote did taste—

"Aw, Fletch, c'mon. I waited all day. I didn't hardly ask you none at all!"

"Just every five minutes."

He shook his head solemnly. "Uh-uh. Not no every five minutes." He picked thoughtfully at a rip in his trousers. "Every ten, maybe. 'Sides, I think I already know what he said, but you gotta tell me. It ain't the same 'less'n you tell me."

Fletch sighed and, resigned, put his plate down. "All right," he said wearily. "I'll tell you, but you got to promise not to start in, all right? Promise?"

Loco grinned crazily, his head shaking, his fingers drumming an exotic twisted tune on his knees. "I

149

promise, Fletch!" He made a sign on his chest. "Cross my heart and hope to die."

"OK. Mr. Kane wired back and he said—"

"He said we don't need her no more, didn't he, Fletch? That's what he said, ain't it?" He was breathing hard now, his grin extended from ear to ear, his yellow bird's eyes doing a St. Vitus' dance in their sockets. "Ain't that it, Fletch? You gotta tell me if that's it! It ain't the same if'n you don't tell me!"

Fletch let out a weary sigh. "Jesus, I'm tryin' to. Just calm down, Ed. Remember what you promised."

Loco nodded. When Fletch called him by his real name, it meant he was serious.

"It's all gotta be a ritual with you, don't it?" The boy looked perplexed, so Fletch just went on with it. "Mr. Kane said we was to get back up there and wait two days. That's the day after tomorrow. He's sendin' Gert Vance up to tell us—"

"Aw, Gert don't know where that place is," Loco interjected. "*I* didn't even know where that place was 'til you showed me." Insofar as it was possible for Loco to look indignant, he did.

"She knows it, I reckon. Her brother built it, long time ago. She's the one told *me* about it." He didn't mention to Loco the rumor that Gert Vance was the only person who had ever actually seen Nathaniel Kane. The only living person, anyhow. Yes, Gert Vance knew a lot of things. She was a scary old broad, if you asked him.

Loco was rocking from his rear to his boots and back again, his arms wrapped around his legs. "She did, huh? Jeez, Fletch, nobody never tells me nothin'."

"You ain't exactly confidence *inspirin'*, Ed." Fletch took another swallow of coffee. It was getting cold now. He reached for the pot to warm it up. "Now you gonna quit askin' me about Gert so's I can finish tellin' you?"

The boy nodded his head, his shock of white hair flopping in his eyes.

"He said Gert'll let us know what we're supposed to do with the girl. 'Tween you and me I don't think there's much chance he's gonna want her back, but we gotta wait to find out."

Loco commenced a mad titter, than slapped his hands over his mouth again until he had himself reasonably under control. "I kin have her, can't I, huh, Fletch? I kin have her to do with, can't I?"

"I reckon you can if he don't need her back. But we got to wait for Gert, to make sure. And kid, if you do get to keep her, just don't let it get . . . Well, just don't get so carried away this time, OK? It like to made me sick what you done that last time."

Loco was oblivious, lost in his own little world. "Gonna do 'er good, I am," he muttered. He picked up the plate and began shoving beans in his mouth. "Yessir, gonna do her good," he mumbled gleefully as he chewed. "Let 'er go ahead and holler, holler all she wants. Gonna do 'er good . . ."

"You promised me, kid, you promised me you wasn't gonna start in." But Loco didn't hear him. Fletch leaned back against a rock, sighed, and pulled his hat down over his eyes. Now he'd have to listen to this all night and all day tomorrow, too, until they got back up to the shack.

He didn't tell the kid that he had been nearly certain from the start that Kane wasn't going to want that girl back under any circumstances. As far as Fletch could figure—and he could actually figure pretty well—Kane hated that little gal's daddy pretty bad. And with Kane, that'd mean he'd hate her, too. Enough to want her

151

dead regardless of the ransom being paid or not. Enough to not much care how she died, just so long as she did. Be it a day or a week or a month, he was only going to keep her alive long enough to hedge his bets.

He didn't tell the kid any of that. Had he done so, Loco would have jumped on his horse tonight and ridden it to death to get back up to the shack.

It was not yet dawn, and Jessie had not slept. Clay drowsed beside her. She watched her hand, fingers woven through the forest of dark curls on his chest, rise and fall as he breathed. Her head rested on his shoulder, and he slept with his arm protectively encircling her. She couldn't sleep. She was afraid that if she were to doze off, he would vanish forever into the land of her dreams.

She smiled, watching his chest move easily up and down. He was so beautiful, and he did love her, she was sure. It was as if all the poetry in the world, all the finest literature, all the words she had lingered over and drunk of so deeply were nothing to compare with the emotions newly born in her heart, her mind, her body.

And how wonderful it was to lie here next to him, naked, as he slept, flesh touching flesh. It was so decadent, so indecent—and somehow, so right.

Yes, he loved her. He loved her exceedingly well. She broke out in warm gooseflesh each time she thought of that encounter in the stream. It was as if she had been asleep for twenty-four years, and his touch, like the kiss of a fairy-tale prince, had brought her to awareness, to life.

He had held her, there in the stream, after he loved her, stroking her hair and saying her name over and over. *Jessie, Jessie . . .*

No one had called her Jessie since her mother died. Later, as they lay in the sunshine on the grassy bank, she had told him about her mother and what she remembered about her; about finding the picture in her stepfather's attic; about the trunks of Margaret's dresses. She almost told him about what had happened between her and Samuel later that same night, but found she was too ashamed.

It was late spring here in the hills. The banks of the stream were patched with wildflowers of yellow and purple, and the clean, sweet air was filled with the music of birds. Lying in the shelter of Clay's arms, her bare skin warmed by his, the fragrant grasses tickling at the backs of her knees, she felt fresh and new and unabashedly alive—as if her own flesh were an integral part of the untamed nature surrounding her.

"'For, lo, the winter is past,'" she quoted softly, staring into the clear blue sky above, "'the rain is over and gone . . .'"

"'The flowers appear on the earth,'" he continued for her, smiling. "'The time of the singing of birds is come, and the voice of the turtle is heard in our land . . .'"

He stroked her drying hair as he whispered to her from the Song of Songs, looking into her eyes, and then he fell silent, taking her into his arms again; and he made love to her there in the warm wind-touched grass, so slowly and so sweetly that when she called out his name in the throes of that ultimate bliss, she thought she would die from happiness.

Afterward, they slept, drowsing naked on the bank until the sun began to set, taking its warmth away to the west. Then they had risen and dressed and walked, arm in arm, back to the little cabin.

Jessie watched as he readied the meal and set the pot

of stew on the stove. She stood at the edge of the table, staring at him. She wanted him again, so badly she could taste it. Shocked by her own brazenness, she was afraid to approach him, but there was no need for her to.

He looked into her eyes and, reading the desire there, came toward her wordlessly; first pulling her almost roughly against him, then lifting her off the floor and laying her down on the table on her back. He slid her toward him, so that her hips rested just at the table's edge, then reached up under her skirts and pulled down her drawers, sliding them over her legs and feet, then tossing them to the bed. She found she was breathing in little gasps, her bosom rising and falling rapidly as she watched him remove his suspenders and unbutton his trousers, letting them fall to the floor. He was fully aroused, and the sight of him added to her own excitement.

He smiled down at her as he stood between her legs, and lifted them up until she could lock her ankles behind his neck, her white petticoat falling in a pool about her waist. Then he slid her even farther off the table, supporting her hips with one hand, the other softly stroking her inner thigh. "Watch, Jessie," he said, showing her with his eyes where he wanted her to look.

And she had. Although she hadn't thought it was possible to be any more flushed with desire than she already was, the sight of his slow and deliberate penetration pushed her to the brink of rapture. her head began to swim, and she gripped the sides of the table as the cadence of his thrusts quickened. The ceiling began to spin above her as she received him again and again, her body awash with sensation, her spirit drowning in passion. With a bone-jarring jolt she burst—screaming—into a pleasure so exquisite as to be nearly unbearable. Not once, not twice, but three times she swam in that sea of ecstasy before Clay collapsed, spent and exhausted, upon her.

That night they had gone to bed, Clay undressing her slowly in the silver moonlight. He joined her under the covers and lay there quietly beside her, stroking her hair, her arm.

"Stay with me, Jessie."

She stared at the ceiling. "You don't know what you're asking."

"You could leave him." He rubbed at his forehead, then pinched the bridge of his nose. He looked at her profile, her features set and determined as she stared into the darkness. "No, I don't suppose you can. You'll go back to him and pick up where you left off. Business as usual."

She turned on him. "You know it isn't like that. It's not like that at all. What could you understand of duty, living the way you do?" Her eyes were hard, angry.

"Duty!" he snorted. "Damn your duty!" He pulled his arm from her and sat up.

"It's easy for you to say that. We come from different worlds. I don't know anything about you!" she wept, her anger turning to tears of frustration. "Nothing, except that you're an outlaw, a kidnapper!"

He brushed the salt from her face with his thumb. "You know I love you, Jess. Is anything else so important right now?" He lay back down beside her.

"Maybe not for today, or tomorrow, but yes—in the long run, there is something more important."

He sighed. "They've really done a job on you, haven't they, Jessica LaCroix Lawrence?" He rolled onto his side and looked down at her. "If I weren't an . . . if I were someone else—"

"Don't you see, it wouldn't make any difference?" she broke in. "I have to go back. I don't have any choice. I haven't that luxury."

He lowered his head and kissed her temple. His eyes glistened with tears that mirrored her own, for he, too, came from that world, and he knew the demands it made upon those who dwelt in the shadow of its rigid codes.

She reached for him, and they made love again, tenderly, lingeringly, moving slowly under the tattered quilt.

And now it was nearly dawn. Clay slept soundly beside her, his breathing deep and regular.

In hours since he had fallen asleep, she had evolved through several planes of emotion, attempting to create order out of chaos and sort her way through the confused maze of her feelings. First she passed through joy, the most fleeting. On its heels came sorrow; sorrow that it would soon be over; that the ransom would be paid and she would be sent back to her own world, back to Owen. Then misery turned to anger—anger at a world that insisted on such rigid conformity to stupid rules and codes of conduct. Anger at Clay, because he had entered her life in the role of villain, kidnapper, and criminal, and then revealed himself to be in complete opposition to any definition she would have put to those titles. Anger at herself for loving him.

At last, logic replaced that bitter wrath. She found that she no longer felt any hate for her stepfather. She could understand, now, some of his long-repressed lust. And although she could not completely forgive

156

him, she could feel pity for him, and even, in a strange way, gratitude: gratitude that he was a rich enough man that someone would want to abduct his daughter—and hire Clay McCallister to do it.

It was true she knew nothing about her lover except that he cared for her. The mystery enshrouding him continued to grow, rather than dispel. Who was this rough, rugged badman who had carried her away from the stagecoach, who also carried a tattered volume of Byron in his saddlebags, recited the poetry of Solomon, and caressed her as gently as one might stroke a hummingbird? And what about the curious notebook she'd unearthed, filled with nonsensical scribblings? Then there were his two compatriots . . .

She shivered as an image of the boy took shape in her mind. No matter how she tried, she couldn't put him together with Clay. The puzzle pieces were all there, she suspected, but she could not make them fit. Perhaps they didn't need to.

It was a curious, twisted stroke of chance that had led her to Clay, and she knew he could not be a part of the pattern of her life, nor she of his, no matter how much she loved him. But she could take the small amount of time that fate had allotted her, and with him, construct the memories of her future, tucking each neatly into her heart and mind to be taken out and cherished in later years. She didn't know how much time they had left. It might be a day or a week. But she knew that whatever the fates allowed her, she would gather with gratitude, and without question.

She lay there, waiting for the sun to bring the singing of the birds and the voice of the turtle.

Far away in Denver, her husband also lay awake.

157

Owen Lawrence had been a busy man, an attentive man. Listening at keyholes, he was finding, came quite naturally to him. And what he had learned while practicing this newly acquired skill might very well make him an exceptionally wealthy man.

That first, accidental session at Samuel's study door on the previous night had produced the knowledge of his father-in-law's growing mental instability. This, in itself, was a fascinating tidbit. The mighty Samuel LaCroix driven mad by his lust for his own step-daughter! The possibilities for manipulation were infinite. He had tossed them in his head as one might toss a salad, reaching for one bright bit of leaf after another as they rose and fell in the air, searching for the perfect morsel.

But tonight's intentional eavesdropping had imbued him with information even more monumental: information that required immediate attention.

He had crept once again down the wide stair after the servants had retired, and made his way to the study door. He knew that neither LaCroix or Villanova had gone to their rooms—he had been watching.

He was correct in assuming they would both still be in the study. Light shone faintly under the door, and he could hear the murmur of voices. Stealthily, he crept closer and peeped through the keyhole.

Samuel, white and drawn, sat behind his desk. Clarence Villanova was pacing up and down, his hands locked behind his back.

"I can't see how we can move any faster, Samuel," Villanova was saying. "The same mechanisms that insulate the two of us also serve to deprive us of any hope of immediate action. There are just too many channels to go through, too many people, too much paper. I fear that I have done my job too well." He

158

halted, facing the hearth. A small fire had been set against the evening chill, and it cast a dull orange glow on his trousers and shoes.

"Then you believe there's no hope?"

Villanova's face was filled with pain. "Kane will surely realize within the next twenty-four hours that we cannot meet his demands in the time allowed. I believe he has known all along that we could not." He paused, gathering himself. "Samuel, I know how excruciating all of this is for you. But please try to think clearly. He is going to kill Jessica. He has planned to kill her all along. She may already—"

"No!" Samuel banged his fists on the desk, his face contorted in rage and grief. "No, she is not dead! She cannot be! I have to see her, to talk to her . . . I . . ." He covered his face with his fingers, pressing at the parchmentlike skin.

Villanova spoke again, quietly, firmly. "Samuel, I'm sorry, but this is something you must face. She's gone, and it's highly possible that we will never see her again. Please, let me halt the changeovers I've already instigated. Don't give Kane a gift for murdering your daughter."

"No." Samuel's voice was controlled now, restrained. "We will not give up. I can't and you *must* not. Perhaps we can't turn over the ransom in time, but we can send people in, find her, bring her out!"

"You know that's impossible, Samuel. You're grasping at straws. The marshal's posse lost the trail halfway to the Superstitions. It just stopped. And there's no telling where she might be now. She could be anywhere. That is, if she's still alive."

Samuel moaned, rubbing at his eyes. "She's alive, I tell you! She has to be!" He sat up, stiffly erect, and put his hands flat on the desk top. He stared not at

Villanova, but straight ahead, at the door. On the other side of the keyhole, Owen shuddered involuntarily.

"It is true," Samuel continued tonelessly, "that finding her now, ourselves, would be a miracle. You are right about that. But I tell you that I will not fail her again. I have already done too much of that."

He turned to face Villanova. "There will be no changes now. You will continue what you have begun, and proceed with all possible speed. I don't care what it costs me—give him the filthy opium, the damned houses, everything! I don't care—give it all to him. Just get my Jessica back."

Owen pulled away from the keyhole, clutching at the knob to steady himself. So that was it! The wily old bastard! All these years . . . He heard footsteps approaching from inside the study and quickly hid himself around the corner.

It was Villanova. Owen watched as he emerged, closed the door behind him, and vanished into the darkness at the top of the stairs. He waited a few moments for Villanova to get safely settled in his room, then started for the stairway himself. As he crept up it, he could again hear Samuel's voice, lost in lunatic prayer.

And this is what Owen had decided:

His father-in-law was a criminal, obviously a very successful one. He didn't know how much money Samuel was worth, but it must be many times more than he had ever imagined. And now Samuel was going mad.

Jessica was in the hands of this Kane person, and it was doubtful that she would live much longer. Regardless of Samuel's wealth, Jessica still had the rest of her mother's fortune, which she would inherit upon her stepfather's demise, and which Owen would receive

MORE PASSION AND ADVENTURE AWAIT... YOUR TRIP TO A BIG ADVENTUROUS WORLD BEGINS WHEN YOU ACCEPT YOUR FIRST 4 NOVELS ABSOLUTELY *FREE* (AN $18.00 VALUE)

Accept your Free gift and start to experience more of the passion and adventure you like in a historical romance novel. Each Zebra novel is filled with proud men, spirited women and tempestuous love that you'll remember long after you turn the last page.

Zebra Historical Romances are the finest novels of their kind. They are written by authors who really know how to weave tales of romance and adventure in the historical settings you love. You'll feel like you've actually gone back in time with the thrilling stories that each Zebra novel offers.

GET YOUR FREE GIFT WITH THE START OF YOUR HOME SUBSCRIPTION

Our readers tell us that these books sell out very fast in book stores and often they miss the newest titles. So Zebra has made arrangements for you to receive the four newest novels published each month.

You'll be guaranteed that you'll never miss a title, and home delivery is so convenient. And to show you just how easy it is to get Zebra Historical Romances, we'll send you your first 4 books absolutely FREE! Our gift to you just for trying our home subscription service.

BIG SAVINGS AND FREE HOME DELIVERY

Each month, you'll receive the four newest titles as soon as they are published. You'll probably receive them even before the bookstores do. What's more, you may preview these exciting novels free for 10 days. If you like them as much as we think you will, just pay the low preferred subscriber's price of just $3.75 each. *You'll save $3.00 each month off the publisher's price.* AND, your savings are even greater because there are never any shipping, handling or other hidden charges—FREE Home Delivery. Of course you can return any shipment within 10 days for full credit, no questions asked. There is no minimum number of books you must buy.

4 FREE BOOKS

TO GET YOUR 4 FREE BOOKS WORTH $18.00 — MAIL IN THE FREE BOOK CERTIFICATE T O D A Y

Fill in the Free Book Certificate below, and we'll send your FREE BOOKS to you as soon as we receive it.

If the certificate is missing below, write to: Zebra Home Subscription Service, Inc., P.O. Box 5214, 120 Brighton Road, Clifton, New Jersey 07015-5214.

FREE BOOK CERTIFICATE

4 FREE BOOKS

ZEBRA HOME SUBSCRIPTION SERVICE, INC.

YES! Please start my subscription to Zebra Historical Romances and send me my first 4 books absolutely FREE. I understand that each month I may preview four new Zebra Historical Romances free for 10 days. If I'm not satisfied with them, I may return the four books within 10 days and owe nothing. Otherwise, I will pay the low preferred subscriber's price of just $3.75 each; a total of $15.00, *a savings off the publisher's price of $3.00*. I may return any shipment and I may cancel this subscription at any time. There is no obligation to buy any shipment and there are no shipping, handling or other hidden charges. Regardless of what I decide, the four free books are mine to keep.

NAME

ADDRESS   APT

CITY   STATE   ZIP
(   )
TELEPHONE

SIGNATURE   (If under 18, parent or guardian must sign)

Terms, offer and prices subject to change without notice. Subscription subject to acceptance by Zebra Books. Zebra Books reserves the right to reject any order or cancel any subscription.   039102

upon hers: but only if Samuel preceded her in death. Should Jessica die first, he would be left empty-handed.

He mulled this over, and came to a conclusion. Jessica would surely not survive the week, and with her would die his chances at claiming not only the other two and a half million dollars Samuel held for her, but the old man's fortune as well.

Samuel would have to predecease her. And Owen thought he just might have a way to arrange that.

He put his hands on his hips. "Jessica Lawson Lawrence!" he chided. "All of the Eastern seaboard would plunge into seizures if they could see you there, naked as a jaybird. Have you no sh—" She burst out laughing . . . and pulled it

7

Jessie had fallen asleep after all. And when she awoke, Clay was still there beside her, head propped on his hand, watching her, smiling.

"Well. Morning, lazybones," he grinned cheerfully. "It's almost noon. You must've been worn out."

Blushing, she laughed and shoved against his chest, toppling him to the floor. "And whose fault is that?"

He shook his head in a feigned reprimand. "Women," he muttered. "A little knowledge is a dangerous thing . . . Personally, I never slept better. You, my dear," he grinned, brushing the tip of her nose with his forefinger, "take a lot out of a fella. I'm lucky I'm not permanently crippled. And now I suppose you want some breakfast."

Jessie giggled, then rolled her eyes toward the ceiling, swirling the tip of her index finger into her chin. "Hmm . . . Depends on what the kitchen is serving this morning."

"First course!" he announced, getting to his knees and pulling her toward him. The covers fell to the bed as he kissed her playfully. Then he stood up, bare as the day he was born. A grinning Jessie, resting on her heels, watched him from the mattress.

He put his hands on his hips. "Jessica LaCroix Lawrence!" he chided. "All of the Eastern seaboard would plunge into seizures if they could see you sitting there, naked as a jaybird! Have you no shame?"

She burst out laughing and pulled the quilt up around her. "I don't think I'd talk if I were you!"

He looked down at himself and shook his head. "You've got a point there," he confessed happily. "But then, I've always *wanted* to plunge the entire Eastern seaboard into seizures." He found his britches and pulled them on, then tossed a few sticks of wood into the stove. "I guess we're stuck with leftover rabbit stew. OK with you?"

"Perfect," she replied, wondering if anyone else in the history of the planet had ever felt as gloriously right and bright as she did this morning. "Absolutely, beautifully perfect. Leftover rabbit stew is my favorite breakfast in the whole, entire world!" She fairly leapt from the bed, whirling in her quilt sarong, then stopped suddenly and tried to look serious. "You are going to make coffee, too, aren't you? And bacon? And biscuits? And marmalade? And eggs and ham? And fresh fruit? And—"

Laughing, he grabbed for her and gave her a playful swat on the fanny, then threw her over his shoulder and plopped her down on the table top. He picked up her drawers and gravely presented them.

"Madam," he intoned, utterly solemn except for those twinkling green eyes, "all diners shall be suitably clad in *my* establishment! And no back talk from the patrons!"

They polished off the stew, devouring it ravenously and washing it down with a pot of fresh, hot coffee. Throughout the meal they chattered happily, and Jessie marveled at how easily it all came with him. He was like the best part of her, a part she had never

163

known existed, but for which she had somehow always yearned. She soaked up every movement he made, every word he said, storing them away greedily.

"I'm afraid I've been neglecting old Chance," he said after they had scraped the last edible drop of rich, salty stew from the pot. "Poor fella's going to get awfully stiff if I don't get him out for some exercise. Thought I'd have a little look-see, too. You want to come along?"

She shook her head, suddenly shy. "I'd like to," she answered, "but I'm a little, um . . ." She stared at the floor, her cheeks burning, ". . . tender."

He laughed, and reached for her chin, tipping up her head to kiss her. "I'm not a bit surprised," he teased. "You're turning into a shameless hussy, Jess. And I wouldn't have you any other way." He brushed his lips against her forehead, then opened the door.

"I'll be gone an hour, maybe two, no longer. OK?"

She nodded. "You just don't want to help with the dishes."

"Smart girl," he grinned, and walked out into the sunshine.

The branch slapped Fletch in the face, stinging him with pine needles. He shoved it out of the way and picked a stray bit of green out of his mouth. "Goddammit, kid, I think you're swingin' 'em at me on purpose! Just hold up and let me take the point!"

Loco reined in the thin bay and allowed Fletch to pass him on the narrow bank. "Sorry, Fletch," he said. He actually did look sorry. "I was just thinkin', that's all."

"Well, for Christ's sake, don't tell me what about. I'm tired of hearin' it," he growled. "First you're sick of beans 'n hardtack. Then you're gonna do this to the girl or that to the girl, 'n then you're sick of beans again. I already heard it all about four dozen times." They started forward again.

"But this is a new one, Fletch, honest it is!" the boy insisted. "I was just thinkin', you know? I heared once about the Indians doin' it . . . You think maybe I could make me a tobacco pouch outta her—"

"God*damn* it! Just shut up! I mean it now, Ed!"

Loco sank into silence again. Fletch, grateful for any respite, didn't attempt to instigate any further conversation until about an hour later.

By then they were fairly close to the cabin. Fletch reined in his horse and Loco rode up beside him.

"You know your way from here?" he asked.

"Reckon." The boy looked relatively calm. Fletch studied him for a minute.

"I guess it'll be OK," he said, more or less to himself. Then, "You go on up ahead to the shack and let Clay know we're here. I'm gonna go on up the ridge"—he pointed to a crest of trees not too far distant—"and see if I can't get us some fresh meat, deer maybe."

"Sure, Fletch, you bet!" Loco's animation returned in full force. He kicked his horse on up the bank.

"You stay away from that gal with anything sharp, you hear me?" Fletch called after him. "She's gotta stay alive until at least tomorrow evenin'! You hear me, Ed?"

"I hear ya," the boy answered, punctuating the reply with a crazy laugh as he disappeared into the trees.

Fletch shook his head. "I ain't never again gonna promise nobody's Ma I'll look after him, even if she *is* kin." He headed off toward the ridge.

Jessie stood at the washstand, humming as she lackadaisically sloshed soapy water over the breakfast dishes. She was in no hurry. Clay had only been gone a half-hour or so, and she had plenty of time to kill. She had recently been struck with an attack of nesting instinct—foolish, she knew. But she couldn't help thinking that maybe if there was new glass in the windows, and maybe some nice yellow curtains, that—

She heard the door swing open and she smiled automatically. "Back so soon?" she asked, turning toward him.

But it wasn't Clay. It was the boy from the road, the boy with the crazy eyes. He was standing there, tapping one foot, grinning rabidly.

"How come you ain't trussed up." he demanded, the tapping foot going into double time.

Jessie clutched at the dishrag. "I . . . Where would I go?" she sputtered. *Dear God,* she prayed, *let Clay come back soon, right now.*

"Makes sense," he admitted, pulling up a chair. "Washin' dishes, huh?" His eyes darted independently around the room. "Didn't know rich gals knew how to do that." He took off his hat and set it on the table beside him. His hair, matted to his scalp, was completely white. Jessica shuddered.

"Don't let me stop ya, rich gal. You jus' go right ahead and do yer work. An' I'll watch to see yer doin' it right." He propped his feet up and leaned back.

Jessie was frozen. She could only stand there, staring at him.

He rocked the chair forward again. The thud when its front legs hit the floor jolted her out of her paralysis.

"I said git to work!" he shouted, his eyes widening.

She began to scrub at the plates earnestly, clattering them in the basin, and he leaned back again, giggling. "Just needs a firm hand, all you gals. That's all."

She continued to soap the dishes, staring out the window. *Oh please come back oh please come back oh*

166

please come back oh please . . .

"So where's Clay?"

Her head jerked. His voice was like a nail on a chalkboard. "He went out. He'll be back any minute now." She kept her eyes on the soapy water, her flesh crawling. She could feel him staring at her. She scrubbed at the chipped enamel until she thought she would rub it off.

"Ain't them dishes done yet?" he demanded.

She heard his chair scrape the floor. *Oh please stay over there please don't come near me dear God don't let him touch me.* "Y-yes," she stuttered. "Yes, they're done now. All finished." She stacked them up on the sideboard and dried her hands.

"Coffee!" he barked, slapping the table.

"It's all—"

"I said make me some coffee! Ain't had no decent coffee in days, no decent grub, neither." His fingers were beating a distorted rhythm on the table top.

"There's no water," she began.

"Well, go get some. You too fancy to fetch me some water?" Abruptly, he got to his feet and took a step toward her.

"No! I mean, no, I'll get it. I'll go out to the pump and get it. Right now!" She picked up the bucket and started outside.

He followed her. "Reckon I'll jus' keep an eye on you, Little Miss Rich Gal. Wouldn't want you takin' a hike out into them woods. Wouldn't want you gettin' lost." He seemed to find the thought quite amusing, and burst into a fit of giggles.

Jessie crossed the yard, Loco following, and began to pump water into the heavy wooden bucket. He stood about ten feet behind her, watching her skirt swish as she struggled with the rusty handle.

She filled the bucket at last, picked it up, and turned

167

back toward the cabin. But he would not let her pass. She tried to walk around him, but he stepped in front of her. She moved to the other side. Again, he cut her off.

"Been thinkin'," he grinned. "Been thinkin' yer kinda purty fer a rich girl. Been thinkin' maybe you 'n' me could have us a little fun while we's waitin' fer the others."

"Clay—," she faltered, "Clay will be here any minute now."

"Aw, I don't think so." He shifted from foot to foot. "I think he's prob'ly off huntin' somewheres, same as Fletch. I don't think he's gonna be back fer a real long time, ain't that right? So how's about you give Ol' Ed a great big kiss, girly-girl?"

As he reached for her she swung out with her free arm to slap him, but he caught it before it could land. He held it tightly, high in the air; his yellow eyes were bright and wild. "That's good! That's real good! I likes me a gal with some fight in 'er!" He reached for her shoulder.

She jerked backward, dropping the bucket. It landed hard on his instep.

"*Holy Jesus!*" he cried, releasing her arm and hopping in a little circle, whooping in pain.

Jessie ran.

She darted across the clearing blindly, with no good plan of escape except to hide in the trees or make it to the lean-to, to find someplace to curl into a safe invisible ball until Clay came back. She could hear Loco behind her, still whooping, but now with manic glee.

The edge of the wood was three strides away, then two, then one, and she threw herself toward the dark beckoning wall of trunks. But just as she reached the first piñon pine, a shot rang out and a branch neatly severed from above crashed down upon her shoulder, ripping her dress and leaving behind a searing pain and a raw jagged line of beading blood.

She cried out in pain and terror, flailing at the sharp twigs that attached the fallen branch to her hair like some nightmare ornament.

"Ol' Ed, he never misses," he shouted from the center of the clearing. "That's me, yessir and yes ma'am and pass the biscuits! Never misses nothin'!" He threw back his head as he waved his six-gun at her, laughing crazily, his feet shuffling into a perverted jig. He began to move toward her.

She yanked at the last twigs, and the branch—along with more than a few strands of her hair—pulled free. Even before it landed on the forest floor, she was gone, jumping blindly into the trees like a terrified house cat.

She had not gone ten feet before another shot sang into the air: a heavier limb severed with a scream from a ponderosa in her path and crashed to the ground before her, cutting off her line of escape. She wheeled abruptly, darting to her right, deeper into the wood.

A third shot.

Another bough, a big one, descended upon her. It scraped her cheek and gouged another ragged gash in her bodice and her flesh before it landed on her bare feet.

She could hear him giggling insanely, much nearer now. "Jus' keep on runnin' rich gal!" he called. "Ain't had this much fun in a coon's age! An' after you and me finish playin' hide-'n-go-seek, Ol' Ed, he's gonna give you a gen-u-ine treat!"

Somehow, Jessica managed to organize her fevered brain long enough to realized that she'd never make it going through the trees: not barefoot, and certainly not with this lunatic sharpshooter so close behind her— closer with every breath she took.

She pivoted and headed for the lean-to: running,

darting, weaving as fast as her sore and bleeding feet would carry her to the path. She came out of the trees not more than twenty feet from the shed and made it in four strides, ducking inside, hoping to barricade herself within.

She slammed the door behind her and pulled down the flimsy crossbar, praying it would hold.

It didn't.

First he was outside and then he was inside, with barely a heartbeat in between. He had simply shoved his way through the rotting wood.

"That's real good, honey," he slavered. "I likes me a gal with spirit!" He started toward her slowly, a horrible, ghoulish smirk on his face. "You bite? You scratch? You claw?" He grinned wider to show his stained teeth. "You like to get your titties bit?"

Where was Clay? Why wasn't he here to save her? It suddenly dawned on her that he might not come: that nobody would save her unless she saved herself. She looked desperately for a weapon and spotted one meager ray of hope: a pitchfork, its rusty tines resting against the wall near the straw mound.

But before she could reach for it, Loco was upon her.

He shot out his hand and grabbed the already-tattered shoulder of her dress, ripping it down to her waist. She covered herself with her arms and back up another step, toward the matted mound of straw in the corner, toward her only salvation. Loco had proved—in no uncertain terms—that he was faster than he looked, and she doubted she could claim the pitchfork and use it before he reacted, but she had to try.

Loco laughed maniacally. "Yeah, you got *nice* titties, all right. I'm gonna leave me a few marks on you today, I reckon! Gonna do you good, real good!" He took another step closer to her, breathing hard.

She was nearly backed into the corner. Loco was

three steps away, his Colt reholstered. The fork was very close to her now, an arm's length away, and with the gun no longer pointed at her, it was now or not at all.

Without warning, she whirled and grabbed the pitchfork, jabbing as hard as she could in Loco's direction. But before she could pierce his grimy flesh with the rusty metal, another explosion—magnified to thunderous proportions in the confines of the lean-to—blew the tines neatly from the handle and threw them across the shed, into an empty stall.

In a fury born of total desperation, she raised the handle overhead in a last-ditch effort to club him, beat him, hurt him so badly that he would die. And oh, how she wanted him to die—to be dead and gone and to leave her alone.

But before she could bring the wooden pole down on his skull, Loco fired once, twice, the slugs smashing into the stick on the long end, and again between her clenched fists. Splinters exploded above her head, leaving her holding a short, useless stick of wood in each hand.

Smiling at her insanely, a tiny line of spittle at one corner of his crooked grin, he tucked the six-gun back into its holster. "Now, don't you go tryin' to poke Ol' Ed, rich gal."

He caught her wrist, his hand like a vise. "Use yer fingernails, use yer teeth! I'm gonna use mine!" As if to underscore his complete superiority, he unbuckled his gunbelt and tossed it to the side, smiling that madman's smile all the while.

Twisting her wrist, he bent her arm backward over her shoulder, abruptly forcing her to the floor. Her head, already sore and bleeding, cracked against something hard, something that made a crunching sound at the impact and stabbed cruelly into her scalp.

Tiny points of light danced before her eyes then fled as quickly as they had come.

"That's right, sugar-pie," he grunted from above. "Let's jus' you'n' me get comf'terble here."

He was on top of her now, and she could smell his stench, like rotted meat. He shoved a knee between her legs, prying them apart, and began pulling at her skirts. She heard them rip sickeningly, then rip again.

He had been farther up in the hills, letting Chance work out some of the kinks in a wide meadow—a legacy of enterprising beavers—when he heard the report of a rifle. He'd headed for the sound, which had come from the ridge to the west. He was nearly halfway there when he met Fletch coming down through the trees. A young buck slung in front of the outlaw's saddle explained the shot he'd heard. Fletch waved in greeting and trotted up to join him.

"Back early," Clay said, disappointed to see him.

"Yeah, we come back the short way." They started toward the cabin. "Lost that posse slicker'n shit. They're prob'ly still out there, tryin' to figure out where we 'vap'rated to." He ducked to avoid a low-hanging branch. "You 'n' the girl gettin' along OK?"

Clay nodded. "No problem." They rode on a bit farther. "What happens now?"

"We gotta wait 'til tomorrow to find out. Mr. Kane, he's gonna send somebody up—Gert Vance. You seen her when we stopped the coach. She's gonna let us know where to take the girl next. That is, if he *wants* her moved." Fletch shrugged.

Clay's spine turned to ice. "Guess that'd mean he doesn't need her back," he ventured, hoping he was wrong.

"Yeah." Fletch reached down and jerked on the dead

172

buck's nubby antlers, pulling it over farther to one side. "'Bout to lose the damn thing," he muttered. "Promised the kid I'd bring in some fresh meat."

Clay was careful to keep his face blank, void of expression. "Where *is* the kid?"

"Sent him up to the shack a spell back. Thought you'd be up there." He shifted the deer back a little the other way. "There, that's better."

As he spoke, the distant echo of three spaced revolver shots pierced the forest calm, and instantly, Fletch realized that he'd allowed—worse, *created*—the one situation Kane had specifically threatened against: Loco was alone with the girl.

"Shit!" he spat, giving his horse a savage kick. *Mr. Kane's not gonna like this,* he thought, then realizing what a vast understatement that was, urged his mount to travel faster as he shoved the deer off to one side, leaving it in his wake.

A frantic Clay was already ahead of him, pushing Chance into a jolting trot, the fastest he could travel as he weaved through the trees. All he could think of was Jessie alone down there with that monster.

Three additional shots sounded in rapid succession, and Fletch shouted to him, "Loco likes playin' with 'em, but he never stops to reload. He'll be gettin' down to business any time now. We gotta stop him before . . ." He lashed his horse across the withers in frustration. "Shit! Kane's gonna string our innards from Deadwood to Dixie!"

Fletch didn't much care what happened to the girl: it was his own certain and excruciating fate that terrified him now. The girl's life itself didn't matter so much, because he was certain Kane was going to have her killed anyway, but he'd want her killed when he said and not one minute before—Mr. Nathaniel Kane was a real goddamn stickler for details. Fletch knew that if

Kane's precious schedule got messed up it would be his fault because he was supposed to be in charge up here.

And he would pay for it in the way that only Kane could collect—he would be methodically, mercilessly tracked and hunted. He also knew that when Kane's assassins caught up with him, whether it be next week or next year, his final screams would find no sympathetic ear. He'd seen the handiwork of Ralphy "The Cutter" Briscoe and "The Reverend Doctor" John English, and if Fletch was certain of only one thing in the world, it was that he didn't want to die like that.

So he had to get to Loco—had to stop him before he finished with her. From grisly experience, Fletch was more than aware of what efficient use his cousin could make of the fifteen minutes it would take to get back down to the cabin. He prayed that Loco would "do" the girl twice before he got to the part with the knife: that might give them time to get her away from him alive. She'd be beat up pretty bad, he knew, and brewing up a good case of the clap, but she might still be breathing.

If it were possible, Clay was even more frantic. *Dear God, Jess, why did I ever leave you alone? What's that filthy son of a bitch doing to you?* he asked himself, afraid to admit he knew the answer all too well. He cursed under his breath as he bent low to avoid another juniper bough. Any obstacle slowing his pace was worthy of damnation.

He could picture Loc's dirty claws touching her, doing unspeakable things, desecrating her pale and perfect body, the body she had so willingly and trustingly offered to him and which he had so joyously accepted. He was torn between the hope that she was still alive, that he could save her, and the certain, chilling knowledge that it might be better if one of those shots he'd heard had found home—abruptly and permanently placing Jessica beyond the possibility of further pain.

She heard a final rip as Loco shredded his way through her drawers. *So this is rape,* she thought dully. He was going to rape her, and then he was going to kill her or worse. She prayed he'd kill her.

She did not fight him now. There was no fight left in her; it, and her hope, had shattered along with the wooden pitchfork handle his bullets had splintered in her hands. As Loco ripped away what little remained of the front of her bodice, she pressed her free hand against the ache at the back of her head, and in doing so, felt leather.

Both his knees were between her legs now, spreading them wide, and he stared at her there, saliva beading at the corners of his mouth. "Yessir, gonna have us a good time," he muttered, looking back at her face. He still held her wrist with one hand, and now, with the other, began to unbuckle his belt. She stared into his eyes, trying to remember something—something about leather that was important.

Loco fumbled with the buttons of his trousers, cackling wildly. His pants dropped down around his knees.

Think, I have to think! And then she remembered—a flash of pictures in her head. Clay's saddlebag! Never taking her eyes from Loco's, she slid her fingers to the buckle. It was sticky with blood where its prong had stabbed her scalp. *Please, don't be the side with the shirts . . .*

Loco put out his free hand and touched her between her legs. "Coochie coo!" he cackled as she fought a nearly irresistible urge to vomit.

The buckle came loose, and she slipped her hand

under the flap, never taking her eyes from the boy's distorted face.

His hand clutched his filthy, encrusted organ. "This is fer you, rich gal!" He flopped on top of her, brutally kicking her legs even farther apart. She could feel his hand between her thighs as he clumsily tried to position himself.

Her fingers searched and sifted. *Please, God!*

His face was inches from hers, his foul breath wafting over her face. "Now, you jus' go ahead an' pitch as big a fit as you want, rich gal. Yer gonna like it better if'n you fight. Ol' Ed, he's gonna make you feel like the goddamn Queen a' Sheba."

Her fingers touched the bone grip of Clay's Bowie knife.

He shifted again, fumbling between her legs. Then, satisfied he was ready, he looked into her eyes. "Yer really gonna enjoy this, girly-girl."

"More than you'll ever know," Samuel's daughter said flatly, and in one smooth, premeditated motion, brought the knife arcing from its hiding place. With more strength than she knew she had, she buried it deep in his back.

At last, the clearing came into sight. As they thundered down through the last of the pines, both men were half-crazed with fear, each for his own reason.

"Check the shed!" Clay shouted as he reined Chance toward the cabin.

Fletch nodded and galloped across the clearing.

Clay leapt from his still-moving horse and ran to the cabin. It was empty. "Jessie!" he cried. "Jessie, where are you!"

He hurried outside and scanned the forest at the edge

of the yard. Nothing. Just a bucket turned on its side in a circle of mud.

Then he heard Fletch's roar coming from the lean-to.

She was pulling herself from beneath the corpse when Fletch burst in through the remains of the door. She was crying now, her half-naked body dirty and smeared with Loco's blood.

At first he just stood there, stunned, uncomprehending. Jessie looked up at him, her torso free at last, frantically trying to push Loco off her legs.

Suddenly his eyes widened and he took in a huge gulp of air. "Fuckin' bitch!" he screamed. "Goddamn filthy bitch!"

With herculean effort, she freed her legs and pulled on the knife, still embedded in Loco's back. It wouldn't budge.

Fletch came toward her, his hands outstretched, his fingers like talons.

Jessie grabbed at the closest object—the saddlebags. With all her might, she swung them at his face then dropped immediately to crouch over Loco again, to tug furiously at the knife's bone handle.

But Fletch's reflexes were fast, and he simply reached out and caught them. Unconsciously clutching the leather pouches, he advanced, his face distorted with malice and fury.

He would not have killed her—he would never have gone so mad as to do that and bring the full-blown and terrible wrath of Nathaniel Kane down upon his own head—but he was going to catch the naked, teasing, little whore and beat the holy living hell out of her. And maybe he'd just fuck her himself—bend the bitch over the feed bin and give her one for Loco, right up her lily-white ass. And when the time did come to kill her, he'd make Kane's executioners look like choir boys.

He took another step forward.

She pulled once more at the knife, then abandoned it. It was hopelessly wedged in the boy's back, lodged between his ribs. She backed away from Fletch, cowering; her knees were bent, bloody strips of tattered cloth trailed from her waist and her shoulder; her hair was wild and hanging in her eyes. There was nowhere else to go. She felt the mound of straw behind her and stepped up on it, edging backward until she was pressed against the wall.

"Filthy bitch," Fletch repeated, this time hissing it through his teeth. He was one stride away. He looked down at the body of his cousin, then back at her, his eyes narrowing.

"Jessie!"

Suddenly, Clay was behind him. He reached for Fletch's shoulder and spun him around. Fletch swung at him with the saddlebags, but Clay ducked and landed a fist in Fletch's midsection that knocked him back into a stall divider. In the far stall, Loco's bay reared and kicked out.

Fletch recovered his balance quickly and, flinging the saddlebags aside, lowered his head and threw himself at Clay, ramming him hard into a post just as the bags hit the wall, their contents flying into the air.

As he slammed into the pillar, Clay's head snapped back, bouncing his skull hard on the wood. He slumped to the floor, unconscious. When Clay hit the post, Fletch was knocked backward, careening into a partition. He, too, slid downward.

But while Clay was stunned, Fletch was only momentarily discomforted. Shaking his head, he put out a hand to push himself up. His fingers touched paper. He looked down and picked it up, suddenly transfixed.

178

It was Clay's notebook, the one Jessie had discovered and then neglected to slide back into its hiding place. He stood there, staring at it as Clay groaned senseless at his feet. So engrossed was he that he took no heed of Jessica, frantically searching the pile of rubble in the corner for something, anything, she might use as a weapon.

Abruptly, Fletch threw the book to the floor and glared down at Clay. His face was red with fury, his fists clenched and trembling.

"Pinkerton," he sneered. "Son of a bitchin' Pinkerton spy!" He drew his pistol, leveling it at Clay's head. Slowly, deliberately, he pulled back the hammer. "Son of a bitch," he snarled. "How'd you ever get past me? I must be gettin'—"

The timber smashed into the side of his head, splintering on impact in Jessie's hands. Fletch crumpled to the floor, blood welling from his scalp and ear, the revolver falling from his limp fingers.

She stepped over him and crouched beside Clay. He was returning to consciousness, but disoriented. She took his face in her hands. "Clay!" she shouted at him. "Clay! Get up! Can you hear me?" She had to get him up, had to get him out of there, had to get them both away from this terrible place.

He mumbled nonsensically, his head lolling. She reached under his arm and began to haul him up. "Clay!" she demanded. "Stand up! Listen to me, stand up!"

After some struggle, she got him to his feet, then outside and up the path, stumbling into trees as she swayed under his weight, nearly falling to her knees several times; talking to him constantly, trying to bring him back to his senses.

Finally they were in the cabin. She lowered him onto a chair, then brought in water and began bathing his forehead; talking, still talking. "Clay, do you know who I am? Clay, it's me, it's Jessie. Do you know where you are? Can you hear me?"

"Jess?" he gasped, "What . . ." He put his hand out to grip the edge of the table. "Jessie?"

"Yes," she whispered, his face in her hands. "Yes, it's Jessie. Clay, do you know where you are?"

"Cabin?" He looked around, still clutching the table. "Yes." Then his eyes focused on her—blood spattered, clad in filthy rags—and it began to come back to him: Loco, dead in the aisle of the lean-to. He took her arm. "Are you . . . Did he hurt you, Jess?"

"No," she said, stroking his forehead, then added flatly, "I killed him."

He put his arms around her and hugged her, his forehead pressed to her bosom. "God, I'm so sorry. Tomorrow . . . They shouldn't have come back 'til tomorrow. That sick little monster—if he had . . ."

She stroked his hair.

After a moment, he pulled away from her, as if he had suddenly remembered something important. "Fletch," he said. "What happened to Fletch?"

"I hit with with a board. He was going to kill you. I threw your saddlebag at him, and there was a little book . . . He called you a Pinkerton spy, and he was going to shoot you. So I . . ." She cupped his head in her hands and tilted it up, looking deep into his eyes. "You are, aren't you? I knew you couldn't be one of—"

"Is he dead?" Clay demanded, struggling to his feet.

She stared at him.

He grabbed her by the shoulders. "Jessie, is he dead?"

"I don't know! Clay, what's—"

"Jesus." He ran stumbling out the door toward the horse shed, Jessie following in his wake. She caught up with him at the bottom of the path. He was standing in the lean-to's doorway. She couldn't follow him farther, couldn't go back in there.

"He's gone," he grimaced. "Damn!"

She stood there, staring at him.

In three strides, he came out and grabbed her by the arm, dragging her into the shed. "Can you ride?"

She couldn't answer. She gaped at him, completely befuddled.

He shook her, hard. "Jessie, are you all right to ride? Answer me!"

She managed to force her head up and down in a nod.

He let go of her arm and began hurriedly gathering up his scattered belongings from the floor, stuffing them back in his saddlebags, then went to Loco's corpse and yanked the knife from it. The body rose from the floor when he pulled on the blade, then thudded softly down again into the pool of congealing blood. Jessie turned away, covering her mouth with her hands as her stomach lurched.

Clay rifled through his saddlebags, then spun her around, shoving trousers and a shirt into her hands. "Here, put these on."

She took them, looking down at herself. She was nearly naked. Only a strip of the left side of her bodice was still intact. The rest of it hung in rags from her waist. All that remained of her skirts and undergarment were bloody shreds and tatters.

He had moved into the far stall and was saddling Loco's horse. He nodded toward the corpse. "Get his boots off."

She stared at him numbly, clutching the clothes to her chest.

Shoving the bay out of his path, he crossed over to her and took her shoulders again. He took a deep breath before he spoke.

"Listen, Jess. Something very bad just happened here. And when something very bad happens, sometimes you get all pumped up just so you can get through it. Then when it's over, the pump goes away and you feel like you can't move, like maybe you're never going to move again. That's how you feel right now. But I'm telling you that you've *got* to move and *keep* moving and think about it later."

She was staring at the body, at the boots.

He shook her again. "Jess! You can't ride without them. I have to stop Fletch before he can get to a telegraph and I can't leave you here." His fingers were digging into her shoulders. "Do you understand?"

Finally, she did. She nodded, then moved to the corpse. She began to pry Loco out of his boots.

It was too dark to go any farther. Traveling as fast as Fletch was, he wasn't taking the time to disguise his trail, and Clay and Jessie had followed him easily. Besides, he was heading just where Clay thought he would—to the nearest telegraph.

But the moon that night was blanketed with clouds, and traveling any later into the darkness would have been folly. They made camp.

Jessie was exhausted, but she needed to talk. There'd been no time for words since they left the foothills. Riding hard, they had covered miles of rough ground, Clay in the lead, Jessie bringing up the rear on Loco's bay.

"I'm afraid there's not much for dinner," Clay apologized, handing her a scrap of hardtack. "At least we'll have some coffee in a minute." He poked at the little fire he'd built. A scorched pot sat heating on one of the flat rocks ringing the flames.

She tore into the jerky. It was tasteless and it seemed

182

one could never chew it enough, but she devoured it greedily. When her rumbling stomach had at last been mollified, she took a cup of steaming coffee from Clay and leaned back against a rock. She watched his chiseled profile in the firelight, his face enigmatic as he stared out into the darkness beyond.

"When are you going to tell me?" she asked.

He turned toward her, his face set.

"When are you going to tell me what's going on?" she repeated. "I think I have a right to know."

He rubbed at his forehead. "Jess, it's all pretty complicated."

"Perhaps. But in the past fews days I've been abducted and attacked and today I stabbed a man, and I want you to tell me why all this is happening." Her voice was calm and steady. "There is more to this than a simple abduction. Pinkerton agents don't show up in advance for those, I'm sure. So yes, I don't doubt that it's complicated. Simple explanations are for why the postman is late or why the milliner sent the wrong hat or why Cook burned the roast. Not for why I had to kill a man." Her face was expressionless, her eyes intent, piercing.

He knew he would have to tell her. Maybe not everything, but even what he could tell her would hurt. He didn't relish the idea. "How much do you know about your stepfather's business?" he began.

"Didn't we have this conversation once before? I told you. I know that he's successful. Very successful." She stated this with some degree of pride, then added, "His business is everything to him. But what does that have to do with anything?"

"I mean, do you know what sort of business he's involved in?" She wasn't making it any easier.

"Everyone knows that," she replied, amazed that he would think she wouldn't. "He has railroad interests and freighting interests," she recited, "and then an importing company and, oh, I don't know. I suppose lots of other things, too."

"It's the 'lots of other things' we're concerned about, Jess." He tried to think of the best way to proceed. "Some of his business activities aren't, well, they're not exactly above board." That was probably the understatement of the century.

She shook her head. "I don't understand what you're saying."

"I'm saying, Jess, that Samuel LaCroix is mixed up in some things that . . . things that aren't too nice. And that another man, a man named Nathaniel Kane, wants to take over those businesses. And Kane is the man that had you kidnapped to force your stepfather into moving out of the way."

"What things? What could Father possibly have done . . . He's a rich man! He wouldn't have to stoop to—"

He reached out and took her arm. "Jessie, how do you think he got so rich? It's been going on for years; we think since long before you were born. He's just always covered his tracks so well that we could never prove it, never trace anything directly to him."

"Well then, how—"

He took her by both shoulders now. She looked as if she were going to cry. "Trust me, Jess, it's true. We've been trying to get him for years, and this Kane, too. This was our chance to stop them both, to really drive a wedge in."

"But I don't understand, what could he possibly have been doing—" She did start to cry now. She wasn't quite certain why she should feel so badly about this man who had reared her from a distance, then lusted after her. But he was, after all, the only father she had ever known, the man who had lavished her not,

184

perhaps, with attention and love, but who had at least given her a fine education in a time when women were not deemed worthy of that opportunity; the man who had sent her beautiful presents, gorgeous clothes; who had seen that her every need was filled, her every wish granted. He was the man her mother had loved.

Clay pulled her closer to him in the firelight. "Are you sure you want to know, Jessie?"

He felt her nod against his chest.

"All right. It's mostly drugs—opium, mainly. That's the beginning. Then there are the houses—"

She looked up, shocked. "You mean—I've heard stories about those places. Where men go in and smoke opium and just lie there smoking more and more until they don't care about anything else, and they starve themselves to death? But I always thought that it was only the Chinese that—"

"A lot of people think that, and a lot of people are wrong. And the houses I'm talking about . . . Some of them are, I guess, what you'd think of as opium dens, but mostly they're . . ." She was still staring at him. *All right,* he thought, *I might as well get it over with.* "They're houses of prostitution, Jessie. Whorehouses. He has them all over the country."

She pushed away. "No!" she shouted angrily. "That's not possible!"

He took her shoulders and held her firmly at arm's length. "Yes, it is possible, and it's true. There are little dives with two or three over-the-hill hookers, and big palaces with gambling salons and bars and restaurants and high-class ladies, and every sort of place in between—"

"No!"

He shook her. "Yes! You wanted to know, Jessie, so listen! Every kind of illicit operation you can imagine is run out of those places. Smuggling, extortion, murder

185

for hire, you name it. But as bad as Sam LaCroix is, Nathaniel Kane is worse. He makes your stepfather look like a humanitarian. And he's the one that arranged all this."

She saw the conviction in his eyes and stopped fighting. It was true, then.

"We've known Kane was planning something like this for over a year now. He more than likely had one of his people in your house in Boston."

"In my house?" She was aghast.

"And I'm certain he had a man on you all the way out from Boston."

It began to come together. "The man in gray! There was a man in a light gray suit. He was in the same car all the way out!"

"We had people on you too, just in case Kane decided to take you earlier than expected. But I doubt that you would have noticed them."

"No, there was no one else, he was the only one who—"

"We wouldn't be foolish enough to use the same operative for the entire journey. Kane's man would have spotted him. There were several."

She shuffled through the faces from the train: the endless stream of drummers, farmers, couples, businessmen, pilgrims—any of them might have been Pinkertons, she supposed. "The woman on the stage with me. In Flagstaff I saw her talking to the man in the gray suit. Was she one of—"

"Kane's people? Yes, I'm sure she was. I don't think that purple hatbox on top of the stage belonged to that drummer or Brewster. It was the signal to let Fletch know it was the right coach."

She pushed away again, but this time she managed to smile. "Mr. Brewster? Is he one of you, too?"

Clay nodded. "'Fraid so. You sound like you

enjoyed his company."

The smile broke into a grin. "He's quite a dandy, isn't he? Yes, I liked him very much."

"Not *too* much, I hope," he frowned.

Jessie burst out laughing.

"Well, I'm relieved to see you find *some* humor in this." He leaned forward and poked at the fire again. When a cloud of sparks billowed, he added a few sticks of kindling.

"He must be a very good friend of yours," she smiled. "I think I can see that. You're very different, but in a strange way, quite alike, too."

"Yeah, I suppose. Guess I never gave it all that much thought." He leaned back again and put his arm around her, giving her a little squeeze. "You going to be all right? I mean, about . . ."

She put her hand on his knee and stared into the fire. "It'll take some getting used to. I guess I've always known there was something wrong. I just didn't . . . I just didn't put it together. Is my . . . Is Owen involved in any of this?"

"As far as we can tell, no. I don't think he knows anything about it." *He doesn't even know he's one of his father-in-law's best customers,* he thought.

The thought of Owen was chilling. She changed the subject. "I promised myself I wasn't going to ask you any questions about yourself, but maybe you'd answer just one for me?"

He nodded. "If I can."

"I never could quite believe that you were like . . . like the other two. You're a gentleman." She smiled. "A gentleman spy. Where does someone like you come from?"

He rubbed her arm. "That's easy enough. I grew up in Maryland. Went to school there, too, then finished up in England, at Oxford. My father's alma mater.

187

That's where I ran into Brewster. I got involved with the Pinkertons sort of by accident while I was still in England, and well, I just stuck with them after I came home.

"And you were right about Chance. I made up that stuff about the poker game. He's from my father's breeding farm. Dad has mostly English Thoroughbreds, but the Morgans are his hobby. Anything else you want to know?"

She smiled wearily, half-asleep. "Yes, there are a lot of things I'd like to know. But I think I'm better off stopping here."

"I understand," he said, and held her quietly until she drifted off to sleep.

Several miles ahead, Fletch was still moving, picking his way through the darkness. *Make time, gotta make time,* he thought. *Goddamn Pinkertons! How could I have been so stupid!*

He had to wire Kane, had to wire him that Pinkertons were on the case, and had to do it before Gert Vance saw what was up at the cabin and reported it. After that it would be too late, and no excuse or information he could offer would call off Kane's hounds.

He was running blind, pushing the horse mercilessly through a night made moonless by the clouds. But his luck was not to hold. Without warning, the sorrel dropped from beneath him and he went flying, landing on his shoulder in the red dust.

He pulled himself up, cursing and rubbing his arm. The horse lay in a shadowy heap behind him, struggling to rise.

"Aw, shit," he muttered and went to it. He was right. One of its front legs was broken just below the knee.

"Goddamn chuckholes," he hissed, and took out his revolver.

He aimed the barrel at the animal's head, then hesitated. "Sorry, fella," he said. "Too much noise." He reholstered the gun, then pulled the horse over far enough to one side that it could raise itself. It stood there pitifully on three legs.

He stripped it of everything he could carry—saddlebags, pack roll, rifle—then, as an afterthought, pulled off the sorrel's saddle and bridle.

He patted the horse's neck. "Reckon they'll find you in the morning. Guess you might's well be comf'terble 'til then." He picked up his gear and walked away.

The horse hobbled a few steps after him, then gave up. Standing silently, it watched Fletch disappear into the night.

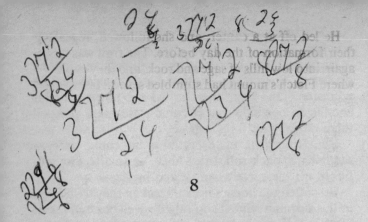

8

She awoke to the heady smell of fresh coffee. Clay waved the steaming cup under her nose. "Time to get up, Jess. It's almost dawn."

She propped herself on an elbow, accepted the brew, and tried to orient herself. Sometime during the night Clay had moved her to a blanket beside the fire and pillowed her head on Loco's saddle. Although it was certainly more conducive to rest than sleeping sitting up under Clay's arm, she had never been so stiff and sore. She rolled her head and tried to stretch her back. It only made matters worse.

Clay stood over her, grinning.

She looked up, her face knotted with discomfort. "This is the last time I stay in this hotel," she grimaced groggily.

"Yeah," he agreed, helping her up. "The mattresses are lousy." He kicked at a stone, then shrugged. "You'll get rid of those kinks after you move around a little. Go ahead and finish your coffee while I saddle the horses. We need to be moving out."

So much for romance, she thought, and by the time he was ready to break camp, she had downed two cups of coffee and another chunk of hardtack.

He led off at a canter, and she followed, repeating their formation of the day before. The trail was rising again into low hills of sage and rock, and they could see where Fletch's mount had stumbled several times in the darkness.

After two hours after they left their campsite, they found Fletch's horse, standing quietly on his three good legs, waiting patiently. They dismounted, and Jessie held their horses while Clay went to the sorrel, speaking softly and holding out his hand. He bent and gently picked up the horse's leg.

"He's had it, Jess," he said, shaking his head. He drew his pistol. "Turn around and hold onto those reins, tight."

She obeyed, screwing her eyes shut. When the shot came, followed by a sickening thud, she steadied Chance and the bay, concentrating on soothing them rather than what she knew she would see if she were to look over her shoulder.

Clay touched her arm. "Are you OK?"

She handed him Chance's reins. "Of course I'm not OK. I haven't been OK since yesterday morning. I'm getting *used* to not being OK," she muttered as he gave her a boost into the saddle. She averted her eyes when they passed the dead sorrel.

They traveled more slowly now, at an easy jog trot. They hadn't gone too far before Clay slowed and waited for her to catch up with him. "He's not going to be very far off, Jess. He's been on foot all night and he's probably found a good place to hole up and wait for us to ride into range. I want you to stay behind me a ways, and if you hear anything that even sounds like it *might* be a shot, dive off that horse and find some cover." He was all business now, much like he'd been back at the shed when he discovered Fletch was missing. Jessie didn't speak, just nodded at him to let him know that

191

she had understood, then dropped her horse back about twenty paces behind him.

They were entering an area studded with looming red rocks, rocks the color of rust and blood that jutted high above the desert floor like the half-buried bodies of some ancient race of stone giants. Under any other circumstances, Jessie thought, she would have considered the majestic landscape hauntingly beautiful. But now, knowing that Fletch might be hiding somewhere, anywhere in the rocks, his rifle aimed at either of their heads, the vista's prehistoric grandeur left her merely nervous and frightened. Her eyes constantly darted from one crag to the next. Was he there to the left? Was there movement ahead? Was it Fletch, or the scuffling movement of a coyote that raised that puff of dust? *Too jumpy,* she thought. *I'm too jumpy. Clay will know, Clay will see long before I do. . . .*

But Clay didn't. She saw his hat fly from his head, silver band flashing, just before she heard the shot. He dove off his horse, rifle in hand, and shouting at her to do the same, scrambled behind a pile of boulders.

She was close to a good-sized outcrop of rock. She kicked the bay in the ribs and piloted him, in one leap, to its shelter. Sliding deftly from the saddle, she jerked Loco's rifle from the boot. As quickly as she could, she ripped the saddlebags off the skittering gelding and dumped them into the dirt beside her. She pawed through the jumble and found two boxes of cartridges that would fit Loco's long gun. She checked the chamber. It was full, ready to go, and silently, she thanked both God and Cousin Daniel that she knew, at least, which end of the rifle to point.

"Jess!" Clay was ahead of her, and to her right. She could see him, crouched behind a pile of rocks. His cover was not as good as hers. "Are you all right?"

"Yes!" she called. "Where is he?"

Clay motioned to the top of a towering rise of dull red rock about two hundred and fifty yards ahead. Its face was pocked with wind-hewn caves and, a hundred feet over the desert floor, its rusty crest rose and fell like blunt sharks' teeth.

He saw the rifle in her hands. "Can you shoot that thing?" he shouted.

She nodded, and cranked the carriage away from the stock and back again.

"I'll be damned," Clay muttered under his breath, then shouted, "Up there! Watch for the flash of light when the sun hits his barrel, and aim for it."

And then she saw it, just before she heard a bullet sing off a rock just over Clay's head, followed by the gun's report. She began to fire toward the vee in the rocks where she'd seen the glint of Fletch's gun.

Before she knew it she had emptied the rifle and was rummaging behind her in the dust for a box of cartridges. Clay was yelling something at her. She ducked down and looked around the edge of the bank of rock, reloading as she moved.

"Can you cover me?" he was shouting. "Jess!"

In answer, she screamed, "Go!" and began emptying the repeater once again toward Fletch's lair. When next she looked for Clay, he was gone.

She crammed another load of cartridges into the magazine as a hail of bullets spattered into the rocks all around her, sending stinging bits of stone shrapnel flying in all directions. But she rose again, mindlessly delivering cartridge after cartridge to that crevice in the rock, trying to pretend it was lined with Cousin Daniel's empty bottles and clay pots.

She had no idea how long she had been firing, reloading, then firing again. She had emptied the first box of shells and was well into the second when she felt a hand on her arm.

She screamed and spun around, pointing the repeater.

Clay jumped back with his hands in the air. "Jesus! It's me!" When she slumped over, lowering the gun, he came forward and took it from her unprotesting hands. "I yelled at you before, but you didn't hear me."

She leaned back against the rock, then slid down into the dirt. "Is he . . . ?"

Clay shook his head. "He's alive. Got him trussed up over there." He indicated a mound of yellow boulders far to her right. She strained to see, and there was Fletch, his hands and feet tied, leaning against the rocks. His shirt was stained with blood, and his head hung low on his chest.

"I got back up behind him. You were keeping him too busy to notice me until it was too late." He sat down next to her. "Who taught you to shoot?"

"My cousin . . . well, actually, my husband's cousin. With bottles and things."

"He's a good teacher." He pointed his finger toward the rock castle where Fletch had waited for them. "You winged him once in the shoulder."

"Oh." There wasn't anything else to say. She felt as if someone had let all the air out of her.

Clay stood up and whistled for Chance, who obediently trotted up to him. He looked down at Jessie, limp and dejected. "You're having one hell of a week, aren't you, honey?" He knelt on one knee and lifted her chin. "I'm going to go have a little talk with Fletch, OK? You just stay put, and here—" He reached into the pile of Loco's belongings and pulled out a battered flask. He unscrewed the top and sniffed at it. Good Kentucky bourbon. At least the kid had taste in something. "—drink some of this."

Numbly, she took it from his hand and lifted it to her

lips. He had mounted and started away toward Fletch when he heard her cough and sputter. He smiled and shook his head. "A little at a time," he called over his shoulder, never breaking stride.

"This ought to keep out the cougars and such," Clay said as he fitted the last stone into place. "At least the little ones . . ."

"That's real goddamn comfortin', McCallister." Fletch's voice was muffled by the wall of stones Clay had stacked across the mouth of the tiny, weather-hewn cave. It was just tall enough for the outlaw to sit up straight, and just deep enough that he could stretch out his long legs.

He was still tied. Clay's rope bound his ankles together, and his hands were secured behind his back. His shoulder had been seen to and bandaged after Clay determined that Jessie's bullet had passed cleanly through the muscle. And Clay had provided him with a canteen of water, a packet of hardtack, and a small, fairly dull pocketknife taken from Fletch's own saddlebags.

Clay crouched on the ledge outside Fletch's prison, a pockmark in the sloping backside of that same stand of red rock in which the outlaw had made his final stand against them. It was the best of several possible solutions to the problem of what to do with Fletch.

By rights, he should haul the outlaw back up to Flagstaff and turn him in—he was, after all, guilty of any number of crimes. But there were only two horses, and his first priority was to get Jessie to safety with all possible speed. Dragging Fletch along would only slow them down. He supposed he could just put a gun to Fletch's head and dispatch him the same way he'd dispatched the luckless desperado's horse earlier that morning, but he didn't have it in his heart to commit such a cold-blooded act. And he knew that turning Fletch in to the law in Flagstaff—or anywhere, for that matter—was the same as killing him here: Kane's people would get to him, and he'd be dead long before he came to trial.

He tipped back his hat. "Now, the way I figure it, Fletch, it'll take you at least until morning to saw your way through those ropes with that little knife. It's not what I'd call sharp, and I reckon that adding that to a shoulder that's got to be hurting like hell, you're not going to be sawing away too fast."

"You're a real goddamn comedian, McCallister," Fletch growled sarcastically from within the cave. "Are all you Pinkerton boys so funny?"

"Pretty much," Clay mused. "Guess it all depends on your sense of humor . . ." He looked toward the west, gauging that they had about an hour before dusk, then raised his voice again so that Fletch could hear him through the rocks. "Now, you're going to be able to take down these stones pretty easy—just start at the top and work your way down. But I wouldn't recommend doing that until after sunrise. I left you a full canteen and enough grub to keep you for a day's walk. When you get out, just head due east, and you'll come to a Wells Fargo way-station. You can buy a horse there—I put your money in the same pack as your hardtack."

"Why the hell are you doin' this, Pinkerton? Why don't you just finish me off?"

"Imagine you'd prefer that, wouldn't you? Your boss isn't going to be very happy about this little problem, is he, Fletch?" *Course, neither is mine,* Clay thought, *but at least J.D. hasn't turned to disembowelment as a form of reprimand. Yet.*

"My guess is that your friend Gert has already been up to the shack by now," he continued. "Already found

196

Loco, dead in the lean-to with his britches half-off. And already high-tailed it back toward civilization and the nearest telegraph office. I don't need to kill you, Fletch. You're already a dead man."

"You're all heart, you sonofabitch," Fletch spat. "I'll get you for this! I'll find you, and I'll—"

"I don't think you're going to do any such thing, my friend," Clay cut in. "I think you're smart enough to realize that by the time you get out of here, Kane will have already signed your death warrant. He's got to figure one of three or four things: one, you decided to go into business for yourself once you found out how rich the girl's old man really is; two, you got cold feet and switched to the other side; three, you decided the girl was just too pretty to give back and you ran off with her; or maybe you killed her after what she did to your cousin. Maybe you and Loco fought over her and you won. I'll bet your Mr. Kane can even come up with a few more options. And I'll lay money that none of them'll be in your favor.

"In fact, the way I see it, the most generous interpretation of what Gert found up there is that you just plain fouled up. Kinda like your pal Drago—if you get my drift."

Fletch didn't answer. There was nothing for him to say. Everything Clay had just said he'd thought a hundred times himself.

"My suggestion, Fletch," Clay went on, "is that you get yourself out of the country just as fast as you can. I hear South America's nice this time of year. You speak any Spanish?"

There was still no answer.

"I'm certain you'll see the wisdom in this. That's why I left you the knife."

"I'll come back someday, McCallister," the outlaw growled from behind the pile-rock barrier, "and I'll

197

find you. You can count on it. You can believe that more than you can believe the sun'll come up every mornin'."

"Right now, Fletch," Clay said as he stood up and brushed fine dust, the color of dried blood, from his knees, "what I believe is that you're smart enough to get your butt out of here first thing in the morning, get yourself a horse, and head south real goddamn fast."

He started back down the rock toward Jessie.

He hadn't asked her to help with Fletch's temporary entombment, and she had not offered, electing to stay in the shadow of the rocks, sipping sporadically at Loco's dented flask. At first the whiskey had given her comfort, and by now she was floating in her own little world.

When Clay joined her in the shade, she was humming softly to herself, intently studying a dark splotch on the ground between her knees. Clay watched her as she picked up a rock. She was still staring at the same dark spot on the ground. It seemed to be moving slowly.

A gleeful look came into her eyes. "Son of a—" She smashed the rock down hard "—bitch!" then peeked beneath it. The dark spot was wider than before, and using the same stone, she pushed it away from her, flipping it into a pile of similar brown objects between her feet.

Clay pushed back his hat, grinning. "What on God's earth are you doing?" He looked at her little stack of smashed things, then suddenly reached down, grabbed her by the arm and hauled her up. She hung there, limply, a lopsided smile on her face.

"Jessie, those are scorpions!" He was horrified. She

198

must have been sitting in the middle of a nest of them.

"Oh, hello!" She dangled from his grasp. "Are we all finished? Gonna go track down some more des'prados now?"

"No. We're not going anywhere. Jessie, did any of those things sting you?" He looked at her baggy trousers and shirt. In her condition, she could have a couple dozen of the little bastards crawling around in there with her and never know the difference.

"They look just like little lobsters, don't they, Clay? Here, wait, I saw a real good one a minute ago . . ." She swung away from him, back toward the shade.

"No, that's fine, Jess, I've seen them before. Now let's just make sure you haven't started a collection of—" He looked down and saw movement in one of her trouser cuffs. *Damn it!* He began tearing at the rope she had used as a belt, frantically trying to dislodge the knot. She was singing again, slumped forward over his shoulder as he bent to his work.

"Whaaat a friend we have in Jeeesus," she sang, brightly and with gusto, "Aaall our sins and griefs to bear . . ."

The knot came free and he ripped the rope out of its loops.

"Whaaat a priv-a-ledge to caaarry . . ."

He shoved the pants down to her knees, then stood up, lifting her off the ground, her waist bent over his shoulder.

"Evvv'ry thing to God in prayer!"

He ripped them off over her feet and threw them to one side, then began to tug at her boots.

"You know, I know all the verses to this," she chirped brightly. She started in again. "O, what peace we often forrrfeit . . ."

He got the boots off and began to search her bottom

199

and the backs of her legs for fresh wounds. There were none that he could see, and he pulled her down from his shoulder and carried her a few feet farther away from the nest before he sat down and began to check the fronts of her legs.

"O, what needless pain we bear . . ."

Her legs looked all right. He began tearing at the buttons of her baggy shirt. He jerked it off of her.

"Hey, Clay. Did you know that rhymes? Hey, Clay," she repeated. "Hey, Clay . . ."

"The hymn, Jess." There were no sting marks on her back, her front. He checked beneath her arms, her breasts, sifted his fingers through her hair. The marks from her battle with Loco were still there: a long meandering gash on her shoulder and arm; another, shorter cut just above her right breast; a raw red scrape on her cheek. The fact that they were not infected, that they were healing, did not detract from his frustration and guilt. But her cuts were mending, her bruises yellowing, beginning to fade, and for that, at least, he could be thankful.

"Aaall because we do not caaarry—Did I do that part already?" She shrugged and lifted her voice again. "Evvv'ry thing to God in prayer . . ." She rubbed at her bare arms. "Did it get cooler?" She looked down at herself, then up at him.

Quite seriously, she said, "Clay, I really don't think that this is either the proper time or place for—"

He burst out laughing, then stood up. "Jess, you must have an angel sitting on your shoulder." He picked up the discarded shirt and began to shake it vigorously, checking it inside and out before handing it back to her. She took it from him, stared at it as if it were an object totally foreign to her, then looked at him quizzically.

"Oh, here," he laughed, and helped her into it, and then to her feet. The shirt hung down almost to her knees. "I guess you're decent enough for now."

"OK!" she sparkled, and sat down quite abruptly. "Oops!" she said. "Didn't mean to do that! Not very Vassar . . . A lady must always cross her limbs!" she pronounced, and swung her long bare legs out in front of her in the dust. She daintily crossed her ankles, smiled primly up at him, then collapsed straight backwards, unconscious.

Clay shook his head and walked back to her pile of flattened scorpions. He found the flask, and after giving it a kick to make sure nothing poisonous had taken up residence beneath, picked it up. It was neatly stoppered, and completely empty.

When she woke, it was dark and her head was pounding. Clay stood over her, a damp cloth in his hand.

"Here," he said, applying it to her forehead. "This'll help some."

She put her hands to the cloth and lowered her head. "Oh, my," she moaned. "Oh, my goodness . . ."

"Want some coffee?" How could he possibly sound so bright when she felt so wretched?

She shook her head. The movement was more painful than she had thought possible.

"Didn't think so." She felt him pressing something into her hand, a fresh flask. "Here," he said, "drink this. A little hair of the dog. Found it in Fletch's pack roll."

She raised it to her lips. The stench of the whiskey was overpowering, but she took a sip anyway. The throb in her temples eased just a little. "Thank you," she whispered.

201

She looked up.

They were in the pines again. All around, she could see their outlines, black against the gray night sky. There was a faint sound of water over pebbles, and she knew that he had made their camp not far from a small stream.

"How did we get here?" she asked, taking another sip of the bourbon. Then she pulled back the blanket in which she was wrapped. "What happened to my pants!?"

"In answer to your first question, I packed you up here. We're only a couple of miles up from where we found Fletch. I wanted to get into the trees for the night." He poured himself another mug of coffee, borrowing her flask momentarily to add a dollop of whiskey to his cup. "Now, about your britches . . ."

He told her about her afternoon in the scorpion nest, leaving her shivering. She started to take another sip of Fletch's bourbon, but he took the flask from her, pouring a shot into a tin cup and topping it off with coffee. "I think you'd better start mixing that, Jess."

She found the mixture delightful, better than either coffee or whiskey alone, and drank it as quickly as its heat would permit. About halfway through the cup, she realized that something else smelled wonderful. She focused on the fire, and saw a rabbit roasting.

"It'll be ready in a few minutes," he said. "You think you can eat?"

"Absolutely," she grinned. "It smells divine!"

When the hare was cooked, they ate it hungrily under the clear, starlit sky. Jessie licked her fingers and wished there could have been more. A rabbit, say, the size of a small hog, would have been more in order. Her

202

headache was completely gone now, and she felt relaxed and warm, despite the crisp mountain air. Even Clay had discarded his tense businesslike manner and had slipped into the same quiet charm and unstudied ease he had exhibited at the cabin before Fletch and Loco's return.

At one point, she'd gathered the courage to confess to him that it was her fault Fletch had discovered his true identity—that she'd found the code book and neglected to tuck it back into its hiding place. To her amazement, he wasn't angry with her. In fact, he didn't even seem upset. "Water under the bridge, Jess," he said. "Don't worry about it."

They laughed and talked, their voices low as they held hands and stared into the campfire's glow. The whiskey and the meal had calmed and warmed them, and they were relaxed, too, by the knowledge that both Fletch and Loco were out of the way; and that for tonight, at least, they were safe and alone and together. As they talked, Clay paused occasionally to drop a kiss on her temple or her cheek, and the tone of his voice was as deep and seductive as any physical caress. She wondered how to tell him that she wanted him, that she needed him tonight.

Then he reached behind the log against which they leaned. With a grin, he produced a bandanna full of wild berries.

"Found these up the hill while you were still asleep," he smiled, offering them. "Thought you might like some dessert."

She picked out one perfect berry, rolling it thoughtfully in her fingers. Then she held it before his lips. "Only if you'll join me."

Obligingly, he opened his mouth, and she plopped the morsel inside. He took her hand and kissed the pads of her fingers, then her palm. "I think dessert can wait a little while, don't you Jess?"

She nodded, and reached out to him.

He unbuttoned her too-big shirt and slipped it from her shoulders, kissing the hurt places, the cuts, the bruises, as if by the touch of his lips he could take away the marks upon her body and the pain she had suffered.

And when she moaned softly and whispered his name, he made love to her there in the firelight, on a blanketed bed made soft by a mattress of fragrant pine, moving deeply within her with such strength and tenderness that she wept for happiness.

Later, woven together in a tangle of legs and arms, they nibbled on the berries and counted the stars. Finally, Jessie had the courage to ask.

"You'll have to take me back now, won't you?"

She felt him stiffen.

"I do have to take you back, Jess. But you don't have to stay."

She shook her head, turning away from him.

"But it's different now," he insisted. "You know I'm not one of them. We're alike, Jessie, you and I. We need to be together. You could leave your husband, and—"

"No. No, it's more complicated than that, and you know it." She turned to face him, looking deeply into his eyes. "It's my duty—"

"Duty! There you go again with duty! What duty can you possibly owe—"

"I made a vow. I've already broken it in part, I know, but perhaps no more than Owen. It's true that I don't love him. I never did. But I'm legally and morally bound to go back to him. Can you understand that?" She was pleading, now.

204

"Dammit, why can't you just leave it all behind?" he demanded angrily. "All the rules? All the codes? Forget what a lot of people who don't give a damn about you anyway are going to think! I love you, Jessie! Can you understand that?"

She sat up, clutching the blanket to her. "Of course I can understand! I love you, too. I love you more than I ever thought it was possible to love anybody. I love you so much that everytime I think about going back to Owen I want to be sick!"

He sat up, too, and put his arms around her. "Then why, Jessie?"

"Because I have to," she sobbed. "I have no choice. Because there can't be a divorce, and because I can't live with you without marriage. It's not just other people—it's me! I'm just not built that way."

He knew she was right—she was too deeply conditioned to be any other way. Still, he had to try once more. "But you can make love with me?" he asked, trying to make her see the dichotomy of her stand.

"It's a terrible sin, I know—but Clay, oh Clay, I've got to store it all up somehow—remember it all, take in every bit and scrap I can, because these few days of you, they'll have to last me for the rest of my life. Please, Clay. If you love me, you won't ask me again." She buried her head in his chest, her tears spilling freely. "God, I love you so much, and all I seem to do is get you all wet."

He drew her back down upon the pine mattress and loved her again, this time passionately, wildly, almost fiercely. And in the end she invoked his name along with the Deity's.

*   *   *

Owen handed his fare up to the driver and stepped out of the cab. Although the hour was late, there was still life on the street, and the windows and doorways of the bars and brothels glowed with dim, artificial light.

He'd decided on a plan of action concerning Samuel: a nearly perfect plan. And tonight he'd snuck out of the big house to celebrate. He looked up and down the street and rubbed his hands together. Where to start? he wondered. Waiting somewhere was a little jewel of the Orient with his name on her. If not, perhaps he could put it there—in welts.

A hand touched his arm.

Startled, he spun around. "What—"

It was a fair-haired man wearing a long duster. The front was unbuttoned, revealing a tailored, dark blue suit. He was far too well dressed for the neighborhood. "Excuse me, Mr. Lawrence?" The voice was oddly cadenced. An Englishman.

Owen shook his arm free—not much of an effort, since the Englishman did not hold it tightly. "I beg your pardon, sir," he said brusquely. "I don't believe—"

"Allow me to introduce myself, Mr. Lawrence," the Englishman went on, coolly. He reached into his breast pocket and pulled out a slim wallet. He opened it and held it in front of Owen's face. The engraved card read, "Pinkerton's National Detective Agency." In the center of the card was a picture of an eye, beneath which was written the legend, "We Never Sleep." He snapped it shut and returned it to his pocket. "Charles Allen Brewster, Mr. Lawrence. I wonder if I might have a few moments of your time."

Owen stared at him. Pinkertons! Surely Samuel had not hired detectives, not with his fingers in so many illicit pies. "I don't understand why—"

Brewster took his arm and piloted him toward a

206

tavern. "It's about your wife, Mr. Lawrence."

They found a quiet table in the corner. "Mr. Brewster, I don't see what—"

A consumptive-looking man with a dirty bar towel tucked into his belt materialized at the table. "What'll it be?" he asked with an air of detached contempt.

"I don't care for—" Owen began.

"He'll have an ale," Brewster broke in. "That is, a beer. We'll *both* have a beer."

The man was only gone a moment before two smudged mugs were slid onto the damp wooden slab between them. Brewster shoved a few coins onto the table, never taking his eyes off of Owen's face. "Now, Mr. Lawrence," he began, once they were alone, "I believe you were going to say that you didn't see what business this was of mine, or for that matter, the Pinkerton agency."

Owen frowned. "I wasn't going to say any such thing."

Brewster raised a brow.

"Well, all right, I was," Owen admitted testily. "And what business is it of yours anyway? Who hired you? It takes money to hire the Pinkertons. I didn't send for you, and I'm certain that my father-in-law didn't either."

"Who engaged the agency is of no consequence, Mr. Lawrence. What is important is that you understand that the safety of your wife is of the utmost importance to us."

Owen absently twirled the grimy beer mug between his fingers, then seeing how filthy it was, took out a monogrammed handkerchief and wiped at his hands. He waited for Brewster to continue.

"It goes without saying, Mr. Lawrence, that I would appreciate your silence as concerns our meeting here tonight."

Owen nodded. "What exactly do you want from me, Mr. Brewster? I can't see what I could possibly say that would be helpful to you. I'm as much in the dark about this dreadful thing as everyone else."

I doubt that, my slimy friend, Brewster thought. *You know more than you're letting on.* "First of all," he began, "we know that a message was delivered to the house four days ago, presumably from Mrs. Lawrence's abductors. Have there been any other communications since that time?"

"None of which I am aware. But then, my father-in-law is not prone to take me into his confidence." He thumped his fingers on the table.

"Have you discussed the matter with him at all?"

Owen tilted his head back and stared down his nose, his most imperious look. "Well, *certainly* it has been discussed! This is, after all, a grave and urgent matter. We are all highly concerned with the well-being of my dear wife. To the best of my knowledge, her father is acting with all possible speed to effect her release from these scoundrels." He snorted superciliously.

"I see." Brewster was unaffected by his tone. If anything, it only made the pasty little man seem even more repugnant—if that were possible. "Do you believe that Mr. LaCroix will, indeed, be able to meet their demands? In time, that is?"

Owen looked away from him, toward the wall. *The wheels are turning,* Brewster thought. *What's he up to now?*

Finally, Owen faced him again. Although his features were calm, his eyes seemed unnaturally bright.

"I *am* worried about something, Mr. Brewster, if I

might take you into my confidence?" he began.

Here we go, Brewster thought. He shifted slightly, getting more comfortable. He felt that Owen was about to be highly entertaining and possibly enlightening. "Certainly," he said.

"Two nights ago, I happened to accidentally over-hear a certain conversation between my father-in-law and Mr. Clarence Villanova, a gentleman in his employ." He paused, waiting for a prompt from the Englishman.

Brewster nodded slightly and leaned forward on his elbows.

"I . . . My eavesdropping was unavoidable, I can assure you." He looked a little flustered.

"I'm certain it was, Mr. Lawrence. Please do go on."

"Yes. Certainly. Well, I'm not sure that I understood everything that was said, you see. But the gist of it was that this Mr. Kane, the scoundrel that has abducted my poor Jessica—" He managed a pitiful look.

Nice touch, Brewster thought.

"—is making demands that are nearly impossible to meet in the time he has alloted. This is taking a tremendous toll on my poor father-in-law. If he believes that he will not be able to ransom Jessica in time, well, I just don't now what he'll do." He wrung his hands in a fairly convincing parody of torment. "He loves her so, you see, as do we all."

"There, there, Mr. Lawrence." Brewster reached across the table and patted his shoulder. *Too bad you're such a disgusting little creature, my friend,* Brewster mused. *With a little training, we might have made a passable actor out of you. Something in the low, melodramatic line, perhaps . . . Yes, you've got something up your tailored sleeve, all right—hedging your bets, somehow.*

209

"I know this is very difficult for you," the detective said, "but again, let me tell you that we are doing everything possible to ensure your wife's continued good health."

"Then you know where she is? You can guarantee her safety?" Owen attempted to look hopeful, and succeeded fairly well.

"Not precisely, Mr. Lawrence. I'm afraid that in circumstances such as these, there are few absolutes." Was that a glimmer of satisfaction he saw in Owen's eyes?

"I see." Jessica's husband pushed away from the table, signaling the end of the interview. Brewster rose with him.

They walked out into the street. "By the way," Brewster added as they parted, "if I were you, I think I should stay out of neighborhoods such as this. Quite dangerous, you know." He couldn't resist.

"Oh, yes, certainly," Owen huffed. "I don't know the city well, you see. Just had to get out and clear my head. Thought I'd get some air. Don't know why the damned driver brought me here. . . ."

"Quite understandable, I'm sure." Brewster smiled ingratiatingly. "The town is rife with unscrupulous cabbies." One was approaching as he spoke, and he held out an arm, hailing it. He saw Owen safely inside and gave the driver Samuel's address. "Now see that you take him straight there," he lectured the befuddled driver. "This gentleman has already suffered once this evening at the hands of one of your compatriots." He clapped the horse on the rump and watched the cab clatter down the street, Owen tucked neatly inside.

Brewster waited a few minutes for another cab to come along. He signaled it to stop and, tersely giving the driver instructions, was off.

As Owen bumped down the street in the privacy of his hansom, he smiled and rubbed his hands together almost gleefully. Perfect. It was perfect. All thought of an Oriental evening paled next to this most opportune encounter. It didn't matter one whit who had hired this Brewster fellow. And it didn't sound as if even the Pinkertons, with all their might, were terribly sure that they could return Jessica alive. What really mattered, the single most important thing, was that someone knew. Someone knew that Samuel was distraught. That he might do something . . . serious. *And that I am terribly concerned for the welfare of my beloved father-in-law,* he thought, chuckling out loud.

"You say somethin', mister?" the cabbie called down to him.

"No, nothing," he shouted back. "Drive on."

Brewster went to his hotel and mounted the stairs. But he did not go immediately to his own room. He stopped one flight down, and tapped at a door.

It opened a crack. A spectacled man peered out and recognizing him, motioned him inside. A second man, bearlike and darkly bearded, was seated in an overstuffed chair, smoking a cigar and sifting through a monumental stack of papers. They were strewn over his lap and the reading table next to him, and spilled into a sea of white on the floor all around. He looked up and nodded. "Evening, Brewster. Go all right?"

Brewster pulled up a chair. "It was . . . interesting, J.D."

The man sighed and tossed his papers to the floor. They spread out in a jagged fan upon the already covered carpet. He chomped down on his cigar. "Damn paperwork." He motioned toward the spectacled man who had answered the door. "Johnson! See if you can't make some sense out of this."

The little man with the glasses nodded nervously. "Yessir, Mr. James." He scurried over and scooped up the scattered sheets, then scuttled into the next room, closing the door behind him.

J.D. James shook his head. "Jumpy little thing, isn't he? Gives me the creeps sometimes. Acts like he's scared to death of me. Don't know why." He motioned toward a cut-glass decanter sitting on a side table. "Get us a drink, there, Brewster. Paper shuffling gives me a tremendous thirst."

The Englishman happily complied, pouring a small drink for himself and a double shot for J.D.

"So how's that pretty little wife of yours? Damn near broke my heart when she married you and left the stage. Sang like a nightingale, she did."

"Now, don't wax maudlin on me, J.D." He handed the glass to the bearded man. "And my darling Ann is perfectly fine, thank you. I'm certain she'd send her regards if she knew I were seeing you."

"Thinks of me fondly, does she?" He swallowed the whiskey in one gulp, then grimaced. "Dammit, I said a *drink!*" He got up and went to the decanter himself, this time filling his glass nearly to the brim.

"I don't know that *fondly* is exactly the word I should have chosen, J.D. Engraved upon her . . . uh . . . memory would be more appropriate," Brewster grinned. "You're not supposed to make a habit out of pinching the leading lady, you know. You should reserve that dubious privilege for the chorus girls."

"Aw, hell. Keeps 'em in their place." He took a swallow of whiskey. "No offense meant, of course, Brewster."

"None taken, J.D. Now, about this Lawrence

212

business tonight . . ."

Briefly, he recapped his conversation with Owen. "I've got a very nervous feeling about this."

"You mean about the husband. Yes, I'd agree with you there. He's up to something, all right. Doesn't seem to want the wife back, and something funny going on there with the father. Don't see what we can do about it if we don't know exactly what it is, though. Next to digging out Kane, it's small potatoes."

"It's not just that." Brewster leaned back in his chair and clasped his hands in front of him. "It's something else. Something's been bothering me since yesterday—J.D., I want to go back down to Arizona."

The big man smacked his glass down on the reading table beside him. "Now, that's a gigantic piece of tomfoolery if I ever heard one! What the hell are you going to do down there? Far as we know, everything's going along according to plan. Kane's moving as expected, and we haven't heard a peep out of your friend McCallister. Far as I know, Kane hasn't had a word from his boys either. Just the way it should be."

Brewster sighed. "I know that, J.D. But I've got this feeling . . . I'm convinced something is wrong. I can't give you a concrete reason for it."

J.D. shook his head and stroked his beard thoughtfully. "You're going no matter what I say, aren't you?"

"I'm afraid so."

"Well, all right, dammit!" he roared. "Fine! Go on ahead!" He got up and poured himself another drink, then spoke again, this time more softly. "I remember another time you had one of those nervous feelings. You and McCallister sure pulled my chestnuts out of the fire that time."

He lowered himself back into his overstuffed chair. "Well, go on! Get out of here! I suppose we can wire

213

you on the train if anything breaks that you need to know about."

Grinning, Brewster picked up his hat and headed for the door. "You were going to send me all along, weren't you?" He closed it behind him just as J.D.'s glass sang off the frame. He could hear J.D. bellowing through the door.

"Johnson, get in here, dammit! What're you doing in there, taking a nap? We've got to finish this damn paperwork!"

Two hours later, Brewster was bedded down in an upper berth on a first-class Pullman, steaming south over the rails.

9

It was late afternoon when Clay and Jessica rode into Flagstaff. Clay took her to a hotel in Old Town, far from the hotel she'd stayed in only eight days before, and where she might be recognized. He secured two rooms for them, registering himself under the name John Clayton and Jessica as his sister, Justine. The desk clerk eyed Jessie's baggy men's clothing, lifting a curious eyebrow as Clay hurried her upstairs.

"I have to send a few wires and see to the horses," he said brusquely, all business again. "I won't be too long. I'll see if I can't find you something more suitable for town, too. Oh, and don't answer the door for anyone." Before she could answer, he was gone, turning the key in the lock behind him.

She sank into the room's only chair, a hideously upholstered monstrosity with a complaining spring, and fell immediately asleep.

The next thing of which she was aware was Clay's hand on her shoulder, gently shaking her.

"Jess?" he whispered. "Wake up, Jess."

Her eyelids fluttered. It was dark now, and he had lit a lamp and pulled the curtains. "What time?" she asked groggily.

"It's still early," he said. "Not quite seven. I brought you some clothes. Hope they fit." He indicated a few bundles on the bed. "I also ordered some hot water for a bath. Thought you might like one."

There was a knock at the door. "Speak of the devil," he smiled. He peeked outside, then admitted a young, lank-haired lad who bore two buckets of steaming water and proceeded to pour them into an iron tub in the room's corner. The tub looked brand new. It was enameled with an ornate pattern of flowers and cherubim, and was totally out of place in contrast to the rest of the furnishings.

The first boy departed just as another entered with two additional steaming pails. As he poured them into the tub, the first boy entered again, tipping a fifth bucket into the bath and leaving the sixth on the floor. He brushed his hair out of his eyes. "Fer rinsin', ma'am," he announced solemnly, and picking up the empty pail, he sauntered, stoop-shouldered, out of the room.

When he was gone, Clay went to the door. "I'm going to go get cleaned up myself. I'll be back in about two hours to take you to dinner. Think you can be ready by then? The kitchen won't serve us any later than that."

She nodded, eyeing the steaming tub. It looked incredibly inviting, almost hypnotically so. "Two hours? That's fine. Thank—"

He was gone.

Eagerly, she stripped out of Clay's trail-dusty clothes and lowered herself into the cast-iron tub. The water was almost hotter than she could bear, but delicious all the same. She sat for quite a while immersed in the warmth, the vapors wafting over and enveloping her, before she took the bar of soap in hand and began to scrub in earnest.

By the time the bathwater grew tepid she had

finished and dried herself and wrapped her hair in an extra towel. Then she opened Clay's packages.

He had thought of everything. A lovely blue dress, simple, with a square neckline; underclothes, stockings, and shoes. In another, smaller parcel, she found a comb, a brush, even a packet of hairpins.

Smiling, she dressed, then stood in front of the mirror. The clothes were a perfect fit. How could he have known . . . ? She blushed when she realized that by this time he would certainly know every curve and contour of her body, probably better than she herself did. She took the brush in hand, and began to work at her hair, bending from the waist and brushing it forward, shaking and brushing it dry. Then she pulled it up and began to arrange it.

Clay was true to his word, and appeared at exactly the appointed time.

"Are you hungry?" he asked after letting himself in.

She stared at him, open-mouthed. He, too, was newly scrubbed and outfitted. He wore a dark gray double-breasted suit with a silk cravat of smoky gray and deep emerald which made his green eyes seem even more brilliant. He was freshly shaved, his mustache neatly tidied, and his hair was trimmed and slicked.

"You . . ." she finally stuttered, "you look—"

"So do you," he cut in, smiling. "Sorry the clothes aren't a little more up-to-date, but they were the best I could find. Oh, yes . . ." He paused as he dug into his pocket. "I thought you might like these." He handed her a tiny paper packet. "They're only glass, but they do match your eyes."

"Thank you," she smiled, folding back the paper. They were earrings, simple and silver: delicate little flowers no bigger than the tip of the nail of her little finger. There was a tiny bead of deep clear-blue glass in each center. "They're lovely, Clay! Thank you!" She went to the mirror and put them on, then gleefully whirled about. "What do you think?"

He looked at her, suddenly very sad. "They ought to be sapphires."

She took his hands. "I already have sapphires," she said, looking up at him through her lashes. "And I like these better."

He stood there a moment, holding her small hands in his, then seemed to collect himself. "C'mon," he grinned. "Let's eat before they close down the kitchen. I don't know about you, but I'm looking forward to a meal I didn't have to shoot for myself!"

Downstairs, the clerk stopped them and handed Clay a telegram. "'Nother wire just came in for you, Mr. Clayton. You expecting many more of these?" He looked a little disgruntled.

"Hard to tell," Clay answered. He dipped two fingers into his pocket, then pressed a coin into the desk clerk's hand. "I'd appreciate it if you could personally see that any others that arrive are brought straight to me?"

The clerk looked down at the coin in his palm, suddenly brightening. "Yes, certainly, sir," he beamed. "I'll take care of it myself!"

Clay nodded graciously, then took Jessica's arm and piloted her toward the small dining room, seating her at a corner table. He pulled out the chair opposite her and sat down, his back to the wall. He had a clear view of the room and both its doorways.

"I had to order in advance," he explained as a white-aproned waitress brought a tray. "Hope you don't mind."

"No, not at all!" The serving girl began to slide plates down in front of her. There was a thick slab of roast beef, pink and juicy and smothered in grilled onions; green peas and fried potatoes were heaped along the side. Another dish was ladled full of thick, chunky applesauce sprinkled with cinnamon and sugar, and there was a basket, lined with a red checkered cloth and containing a warm and fragrant loaf of bread. This was accompanied by a pot of rich, freshly churned butter and another of honey.

"I think I must have died and gone to heaven!" she exclaimed as she eagerly tore into her dinner.

Clay grinned at her, and after glancing at the newest telegram he followed suit, waiting until the pace of her eating slowed before he spoke.

"I've had some wires," he began.

"Oh, that reminds me," Jessica interrupted. "I need to let Father and—I need to let them know I'm all right."

"Not yet, Jess."

She furrowed her brow.

"I'm sorry, Jessie, but it's too early. No one can know that anything has changed. If you tell your stepfather, Kane will know. It's vital that both he and your stepfather believe that you're still in the hands of Kane's men."

"Oh." She put down her knife and fork. "What do we do now?"

"We wait. There's another agent already on his way here. Your friend Brewster."

She brightened at the mention of Brewster's name. Clay scowled a little. "You don't have to be so happy about it."

She laughed. "You don't have to be so jealous, either."

"Well . . ." he growled. He took a bite of the crusty bread and leaned back, chewing with annoyance. "You'll be happy to know he'll be in Flagstaff tomorrow."

She looked up, her brows knotted. "So soon? But . . . but I thought we'd have at least . . ." She stared back down at her plate, her appetite gone.

"So did I." He pushed his plate away and rested his arms on the table. "So did I."

Later, he walked her back to her door. They stood there uncomfortably, not knowing what to say, what to do. Words were somehow not adequate, but at last Clay broke the uneasy silence.

"Good night, Jess," he whispered, pulling her just close enough to brush his lips against her forehead. He reached behind her and opened the door, backing her into the room. Then he stepped away and gently closed the door between them.

She stood there, staring at the door for several minutes, then crossed her little room and sat down in the ugly chair. There was a lot of thinking to do.

It was close to midnight before she got to her feet. All her options were closed, her life planned out for her. But she had this one night left, one night before the constraints of society and her own rigid code would once again bind her. She smoothed her skirts, took a deep breath, and peeked out into the corridor. It was dark, empty.

Silently, she crossed the hall and tapped lightly on Clay's door. It was several moments before he answered. She could hear him mumbling as he turned the key. "Damn J.D., sending telegrams in the middle of the night."

The door opened a few inches. He looked up sleepily, holding out his hand for the wire. Instead, Jessie placed her hand in his. Silently, he led her into the darkened room, laid aside the cocked pistol he'd held behind the door, and turned the key in the lock behind her.

She put her arms around his neck. "I had to come, Clay. It's our last night together. I couldn't spend it alone." She stood on tiptoes to kiss him and he bent down to meet her, taking her in his arms as carefully as if she were a delicate bloom. Their lips brushed gently in the darkness, then he buried his face in her hair, using one hand to release it from its prison of pins. Within seconds it was free, cascading about her shoulders and down her back.

"Oh, Jess, what am I going to do without you?" he whispered, his voice breaking as he kissed her throat.

"Don't think about it, love," she answered softly. "Just think about tonight." She hugged him more tightly as his lips reached the neckline of her dress, then returned to her waiting mouth. "Just think about here and now," she whispered as his lips closed over hers, kissing her with a passion both sweet and sorrowful.

He lifted her then, and carried her to the bed, sitting her on its edge and kneeling before her. He kissed the palms of her hands, then slowly and carefully began to undo the row of tiny buttons running down the front of her bodice. He did not speak.

She lightly touched his face, his hair, memorizing him with her fingers: the high cheekbones, the strong muscled jaw, the down at his temples, the wide forehead and dark, thick brows. All these things she would remember. She would recall them more easily than she could recall her own countenance. And she knew she would see him on every stranger's face, and in the darkness of her lonely chambers each night for the rest of her life. A tear fell from the corner of her eye, spattering on his fingers as they freed the last button.

He looked up, and she could see that his eyes, too, were moist. And he seemed so sad—so sad that it nearly broke her already desperately wounded heart to look at him. He raised his fingers to brush the moisture from her cheek. "Oh, Jess . . ." he whispered, ready to form a question, a final plea.

But she silenced him, gently laying her fingers upon his lips. "No," she said. "Just love me. Love me enough to last forever."

He took her shoulders and pulled her toward him. "I already do," he breathed, then kissed her deeply and with abiding sorrow.

Her arms had circled his neck as they kissed, but he gently pulled them down so he could slip the dress from her shoulders. Never breaking contact with his seeking mouth, she again raised her arms as he slipped free the ribbon that secured her camisole and slid both his hands inside to cup her full breasts.

She opened her mouth wider, flicking her tongue against his as his hands slipped to her sides, his thumbs gently kneading her taut nipples.

Then they were standing, she was not certain how, and she felt him slide her dress and petticoats down over her hips to the floor, then slip his hand beneath the elastic waist of her drawers to stroke her buttocks gently, sensuously. And somehow, the drawers joined the pool of clothing about her feet.

She breathed his name, and he pulled away from her, standing erect as he pushed the straps of the camisole over her shoulders. It fluttered to the floor and she stood before him, naked save for the little silver earrings he had given her. He looked at her for what seemed like a very long time, then slowly began to remove his own undergarments.

When he reached the last button, she stepped forward and began to peel them off of him, kissing all the newly bare places as she went. First came his shoulders and torso: she brushed her lips against the smooth skin covering the muscles of his arms and buried her face in the curls on his chest as she whispered his name over and over, circling his nipples with her tongue and inhaling deeply of his scent.

She pressed her face to his hard belly, then stroked his column with her cheek, brushing her lips up and down along the raised underside as his underclothes joined the array of discarded clothing on the rug.

She was on her knees before him now, and she pressed her forehead to his belly, slowly running her hands up his sides from his knees to his chest. He took her hands then and raised her, guiding her to the bed. She let herself be led, for her eyes could not leave his: starlit, crystalline green.

Solemnly, he laid her down upon the crisp, fresh sheets, then stretched out beside her. He did not kiss her now, but rested on his side, silently stroking her throat, her arms, her breasts and belly, intently watching his hands move over her pale skin, for he, too, was committing every pore to memory.

And as he touched her, waves of warm shivers spread through her, as if her flesh were a pool of still water and his hand a polished stone skimming its surface.

She reached for him, to kiss him, but instead he bent his head to her breast, taking the nipple into the warmth of his mouth. He drew her tightly to him as he suckled, and she pressed her cheek into his hair, stroking him, soothing him as if it were a child who nursed at her bosom.

As they lay there, Clay's gentle, hungry lips and tongue drawing at her swollen nipple as her tears mingled with the soft curls of his head, she once again felt that silver cord within her, linking her breast to her solar plexus and reverberating with an intense pleasure that vibrated every nerve in her body. Stronger and stronger became the shivering of that silver thread, until she felt she would explode. She felt her body arch, as if she could press her nipple, now incendiary with sensation, farther into his mouth, and he responded by pulling at it more intently, nipping

223

with his teeth, suckling, then nipping again as he slowly slid his hand down her body, pausing to rub languid circles on her belly while his fingertips teased the edge of the dark thatch at its base, then slipping it deftly between her legs.

She spread her thighs slightly to accommodate him, whispering his name and drawing in air in ragged gasps. He cupped her there, tenderly but firmly, and slid a finger within. He pressed gently, rocking his hand but once before every nerve in her body seemed to burst in an explosion of molten metal, sending out spinning droplets of fiery liquid silver in skyrocket patterns. Clutching at him blindly as her body jerked out of control, she was only vaguely aware of his hand covering her mouth as she called out his name over and over.

At last she lay quietly in his arms, stroking his face and chest, kissing his shoulder. He turned her head toward his, and as he began to kiss her again, more and more passionately, she found her own excitement returning in full measure. While he probed her mouth with his tongue and caressed the length of her body his his expert, sorcerer's hands, she explored the finely tuned muscles of his arms, his shoulders, his back, committing each hard swell and tendon to memory, delighting in the feel of his tempered strength as he moved his hands over her.

He began to work his way down her torso, kissing and caressing what seemed like every square inch of her body—rubbing, kneading, stroking with his fingers, his lips never ceasing to pleasure her: nipping here, kissing there. His tongue made tiny circles around her navel, then darted inside, nearly driving her mad with want.

Then lower and lower still he moved, until she could feel his hot breath on the dark cloud at the juncture of her legs. Gently, he parted her thighs and moved between them, and then she felt him kiss her, caressing her so intimately and so expertly and with such ardor that it seemed the earth had ceased to turn on its axis. Her body began to writhe again, but all she could say was a weakly whispered, "Please . . ."

And so he mounted her, sliding slowly, easily inside her, filling her completely. She raised her knees, pulling them up to hug his torso as he lay upon her, his weight resting on his elbows, and he kissed her lips again, sweetly, poignantly.

Then, leaning to one side, he reached back, trailing his fingers along the underside of her raised leg, and pulled it even farther forward, hooking his elbow behind her knee. As he repeated the process on the other side, she felt him push even deeper inside her, deeper than she had thought possible.

He kissed her again, then slowly began to move within her: long, lazy strokes, pulling almost completely from her and pausing, hovering, teasing until she wanted to scream; then entering again—slowly, unfalteringly, and so completely that each time he reached the point of deepest penetration she sucked in air through her clenched teeth in an attempt to cage her feverish cries of pleasure.

There was magic in him, in her. She might have been mated with the thunder god himself, for thunder and lightning pounded within her, her senses reverberating with the electricity of their joining. The roaring of the storm was in her ears, and an impossible aurora waved, misty and magical, before her eyes.

Still he plunged within her, Thor reincarnated, she the willing anvil upon which his thunderbolts were forged. Her nails branded him as her fingers dug into his shoulders, then dropped to clutch and tear at the sheets. Her head whipped back and forth, fueled by the electric frenzy of their passion.

She began to contract her throbbing pelvic muscles, as if by doing so she could pull him more deeply inside her, envelop him completely. And as she did, she heard him gasp, felt him grow even larger, pushing her over the edge and into the whirling maelstrom. She twisted and bucked beneath him, jamming her knuckles into her own mouth to stifle her screams as lightning—blinding, bedazzling, purifying—shot through her. She thought the room beyond her tightly closed eyes must be brighter than day, illuminated by the fulmination of their ecstasy.

As Clay jolted one last, thunderous time, spilling his seed deep within her, she felt her own pounding muscles contract again, as if to coax his essence even farther inside her, high into her womb.

He released her legs and hovered over her, propped on his elbows, his head lowered and resting between her breasts. He gave a soft kiss to each, sweeping his tongue over the nipples as she slid her legs along his slick, sweat-drenched sides, then down to the mattress.

She realized then that she was crying, and when he looked up, his face, too, was streaked with tears.

"Damn you, Jess," he wept. "Damn your duty . . ."

She pulled his head to her shoulder, and they mourned together, softly crying and rocking; their only succor beyond their grasp. . . .

She waited until he was asleep, then soundlessly slipped from his arms, dressed, and crept back to her own room to wait for the dawn.

It was a pale and shrunken Samuel who sat beside the big, dark desk. Owen stood facing the fireplace, his hands clasped behind him, his smile hidden from the older man. Yes, it was perfect. The old man was ripe.

226

He wouldn't have to dirty his hands with this at all.

With no small effort, he turned his smile into a grimace of concern and frustration, adding more than a dash of righteous indignation. He turned around.

"You're telling me there's nothing you can do," he scowled.

Samuel wrung his hands. He was less than a shadow of his former self, wasted and ghostly. He had aged decades in the past week. The last two days had been especially hard on him, as he had finally become convinced of the truth: he could not save his daughter; he could not make anything up to her; she, and along with her, any hope of his own salvation, was lost.

He had begun talking to Margaret at night. He could not sleep, and he would sit in his big bed in the darkness, begging first her forgiveness, then God's. He pleaded with them to grant him mercy, to forgive his sins of lust, of denial, and now, of impotence. For it was at last clear to him that for once in his life, the one time that mattered the most, there was nothing he could do. And for this, he could not forgive himself.

Not only was it a sin against his stepchild as well as his dead wife and his God, what was nearly worse was that it was a sin against that which he held almost more holy: the inflexible rules of the society he so admired and by which he so longed to be accepted.

And there was Owen: ever present in the house with his pince-nez, his tidy suits, his sniffs of disapproval and looks of disdain. Owen, always there to remind him (never in words but only by his attitude, as was proper) that he was failing in his duty. And duty was everything.

Villanova had tried to talk sense to him, tried to pry Samuel's mind away from his failings, to return him to his former razor sharpness. But even he, who perhaps loved Samuel more than any other person, could not

227

pull him from the mire of self-recrimination into which he had sunk.

And now it was too late to save any of it. His empire was falling apart before his eyes, but not fast enough to placate Kane, whom Samuel alternately saw as a mocking incarnation of Satan and then an avenging and righteous God coming in fire to punish him for his grievous failings. And this Kane, be he menacing demon or vengeful angel, would soon be sending him scraps of his beautiful Jessica—bits and pieces arriving day by day in the morning mail along with the handbills and correspondence and . . .

At last he looked up at Owen, standing before him like an icon of decency, a pillar of virtue, all things good and right and proper. Tremulously, he whispered, "No, there is nothing." He could not bear his son-in-law's unspoken condemnation.

"I see." Owen allowed those two small words to carry a meaning more ominous than any paragraph of remonstration he might have uttered. He turned away once more. *Very delicate situation,* he thought. *Mustn't try to push. Just guide, ever so gently.* He rocked a little on his heels, then spoke again. "What do you intend to do now?"

"I don't know, I . . ." Samuel ran thin white fingers through his sparse hair. It had been coming away in handfuls the past few days. "I have prayed," he ended lamely.

"So have I," Owen added, his voice grim. "It seems our prayers are not answered." *At least yours haven't been* . . .

Samuel looked at his hands, filled with silver strands of his own hair. Soon there would be nothing left. "I don't know what else to do, Lawrence. I just don't know . . ."

"It seems to me that there is only one option," Owen

continued, careful to modulate his voice. He dared not look around. It had to be perfect. "One option open for a gentleman, that is." Slowly, he turned his head and allowed his gaze to fall not on Samuel, but on the wall behind him; on the collection of dueling pistols so carefully mounted there. He paused for a moment, making sure Samuel would fully understand the gravity of his suggestion, then dropped his eyes.

"It is late," he murmured, finally breaking the silence. He still dared not look at his father-in-law. "If you will excuse me, I believe I will retire." He turned and walked stiffly to the door, closing it softly behind him before he allowed the sneer of satisfaction to bloom on his face.

He climbed the stairs and went to his chamber, walking slowly, smugly. Never had he been so physically excited by mere words.

He had not been in his rooms for more than a few minutes before he heard the shot.

He had to change his trousers before he could go back downstairs.

10

He'd sent a note the next morning with her breakfast tray, asking her to stay in her room. He had a few things to take care of, he'd said—the boy would bring her meals.

It was easy enough to comply—easier to be physically separated from him than to see him, be near him and make small talk with him, knowing that he could never again be hers to touch, to hold, to love. She had to start putting it all behind her now, mentally consigning him to a place called Past, erasing him from the place called Present.

But now it was two in the afternoon, and she was nearly mad with boredom. She'd read the local paper—every article, every advertisement—three times over. And it wouldn't really be going *out,* would it, to just slip down the stairs to the lobby? To see if the desk clerk might have a book or even an older newspaper? She needed something, anything, to take her mind from the sluggish passage of minutes.

She went to the door and unlocked it, peeking out into the hallway. It was empty. She silently relatched the door and stood a moment, her hand on the knob. *Unduly protective,* she thought. *He's just being unduly protective. After all, Fletch is long gone, and the other one*— She shuddered involuntarily, her stomach lurching as the unbidden image of a grinning, slobbering Loco, kneeling over her on the filthy lean-to floor, sprang into her mind. —*the other one's dead.* Surely there was no worse peril in the world than that, and it was erased, gone forever.

She squared her shoulders. *What a ninny I am!* she chided herself. *Afraid to go down a simple flight of stairs and ask a perfectly nice man for something to read!*

She slipped out the door and headed for the lobby.

Downstairs, Clay sat alone in the dining room, drinking a cup of coffee. He'd just come in, and was going over the most recent wires from J.D. and Brewster.

J.D.'s was more of the same, telling him he'd bollixed it up. But he could tell by the wording—he knew J.D. too well by now—that his immediate superior (whom Brewster affectionately called—behind his back, of course—"the Woolly Mammoth") was not angry with him so much as with an operation gone awry. And he knew that if J.D. was venting his more than adequate spleen now, he'd be calmed down by the time they met face to face in Denver.

He tucked the slim codebook, along with J.D.'s wire, into his vest pocket and turned his attention to Brewster's message. It, like its author, was to the point if not necessarily concise. He didn't need his notebook to decipher this one. He and Brewster communicated in their own special language, built on confidences, secrets, and inside jokes they'd shared since Oxford. The wire was, of course, addressed to John Clayton, in care of the hotel. It read:

UNDERSTAND YOU PASSED PRIMARY

COURSES BUT FAILED DANCING AND
ELOCUTION STOP FATHER ANNOYED
BUT WILL NOT CUT OFF YOUR ALLOW-
ANCE STOP YOUR CHEQUE IS IN THE
MAIL STOP EXPECT DELIVERY AS PRO-
MISED STOP (signed) UNCLE CHARLES

Clay smiled. Only Brewster would refer to Loco and
Fletch as "dancing" and "elocution." And the wire
confirmed his appraisal of the extent of J.D.'s wrath—
he was just blowing off steam. The wire also told him
that Brewster was on schedule. He checked his pocket
watch. Brewster's train would be pulling into the
station in about forty-five minutes.

He took another sip of coffee and glanced absently
toward the lobby. He sat forward abruptly. Jessie was
standing at the desk, chatting with the clerk!

He leapt to his feet, his leg banging into the table and
sloshing coffee onto the saucer and tablecloth. *Damn!*

Rubbing at his thigh, he crossed the deserted dining
room and went to her side. She was smiling, accepting a
newspaper from the obviously smitten man at the desk.

Clay took her elbow firmly, smiled politely at the
clerk and hissed, "Sister dear, what are you doing
downstairs? I thought you were going to stay in your
room today."

Surprised, she stuttered, "I—I was so bored, I . . ."
She gestured toward the reading matter in her hand.
Clay was smiling, yes, but it was for the benefit of the
desk clerk alone. She could tell he was very, very angry
with her, and she suddenly felt a little afraid of him.

Still gripping her arm, Clay nodded toward the desk
clerk. "Thank you for your kindness, sir," he said, and
steered Jessie up the stairs and to her room.

Unobserved and standing behind them in the half-
light shadows near the doorway was an older woman

232

dressed in last year's fashion. She was overrouged, rather coarse looking, and adorned with cheap jewelry; and she'd been observing the couple at the front desk with more than idle curiosity.

She stepped into the tunnel of light streaming through the open door. The desk clerk look up. "Afternoon, Miz Vincent. Want yer key?"

"Not just now, thanks," she said. "I just remembered another errand I have to run." She turned, accompanied by the clatter of too many bangle bracelets, and, stepping out onto the bright sidewalk, marched purposefully down the street.

Ten minutes later, a smiling Gert Vance was feverishly scribbling out a message in the Western Union office.

Outside, night was falling. Jessica had drawn the curtains and was wading through her newest tabloid for the second time.

Clay had been furious with her, true, but she knew it was only because he feared for her safety. And he was right—she *had* done a foolish thing. He'd scolded her, nearly shouting, but then he'd softened, and when he departed to meet Brewster at the station he'd left her with a kiss that made her knees clatter.

Again, she put her mind to creating a distance between them. It had to be done. She had to be strong.

The Margaret in her wanted to chuck it all, to run away with Clay—to be with him forever, and let the rest of the world be damned. Her Margaret side would have stayed with him in a shack in the middle of the desert, dressed in rags, with nothing to live on but love: she would have given up anything and everything for him.

The part of her that was her stepfather hammered at

her, *Wrong, wrong, it's wrong* ... The Samuel side was pomp and ceremony and suffocation. It was structure and order and what she had been taught was right.

There was a battle, but there was never really any question as to the outcome. Samuel's side won easily.

Margaret had only had her daughter for six short years. Samuel (or more precisely, his hand-picked legions of clergy and educators) had molded her for eighteen. Margaret's daughter had surfaced and lived briefly, gloriously, for a few short days in the foothills with Clay; and true, there had always been and would always be a bit of Margaret in Jessica. But now Samuel's daughter was taking control again.

There was a tap at the door and the muffled sound of Clay's voice. Smiling in spite of the mental discipline she was in the process of mustering, she turned the key.

Brewster was there with him. They both stood solemnly in the corridor, hats in their hands, awkwardly silent. Jessica looked anxiously from Clay to Brewster and back again, the smile gone from her lips. Something was terribly wrong.

Brewster spoke first. "Good evening, Mrs. Lawrence." He attempted a grin and failed. Both men stepped into the room.

She turned to Clay, who met her eyes sadly for a moment, then looked away almost guiltily. She turned to Brewster. "What is it?" she asked. "What's wrong?"

Clay took her elbow, guiding her toward the edge of her bed. "Sit down, Jess."

She did. "What is it?" she repeated, shifting her gaze from one man to the other.

"Jess," Clay began as he sat down next to her and took her hand in his, "it's your stepfather."

"What? What about Father?" *Dear God in heaven,* she wondered, *what else could there possibly be?*

Clay gripped her hand more tightly. Brewster stared at the floor.

"Tell me!" she demanded. She suddenly felt very cold, as if she were being enveloped in dark, suffocating ice.

Clay cleared his throat. "He . . . I can't think of an easy way to put this." He looked away, but she tugged at his hand almost imperceptibly. His eyes came back to meet hers. "He took his own life. He's dead, Jessie."

She just sat there, numbly staring back at him, her blue eyes wide but tearless. "Why?" she finally stuttered. "Why would he . . . ?"

"We're not certain, Mr. Lawrence," Brewster explained softly, when he saw his friend could not. "He didn't leave a note. It's possible he did what he did because of the strain of . . . of, well, present circumstances." He twisted his hat in his hands. It was unusual for him to be at a loss for words. He had been the bearer of bad news before and so had his long-time comrade, but never had he seen Clay so crippled by any situation.

Clay had said nothing about his relationship with the girl, but by now Brewster knew him well enough to read him better than most men. Knew him well enough to realize that this girl was the one for whom Clay had been searching for years. And now that he'd found her, she was not only another man's wife, but the daughter of one of the blackguards they'd been sent to ensnare: a blackguard who had died because they'd allowed the net to settle too firmly around his lair.

"I'm deeply sorry, Mrs. Lawrence," he finished lamely. "We're all deeply sorry."

"Yes." She didn't cry. She stared at her knees, suddenly fascinated by the tiny print in the fabric of her skirt. "I see."

Clay and Brewster exchanged nervous, worried glances.

There was an uncomfortable silence before Brewster could steel himself to continue. "Because of your stepfather's . . . untimely death, there is no longer any need for you to remain incommunicado." Jessica nodded slightly. "I checked," he continued, "and your private car was sitting on a side railing down by the depot. They're hooking it up now. We're leaving in just under an hour for Denver." He looked at Clay questioningly, but his friend's eyes were locked on Jessica's profile. She still stared at her lap, her eyes veiled.

Clay put an arm around her. "Jess?" he whispered. "Do you understand?"

She nodded without looking up. "I'll be ready." Her voice was soft, barely more than a whisper. Her face was devoid of emotion.

Brewster took a step away, toward the door. The lady is going into shock, he thought. Or perhaps she was more her father's daughter than Clay had realized. "By the way," he added as Clay reluctantly rose to join him, "I located your trunks. They were still stacked in the freight office, waiting for a teamster. I took the liberty of having them transferred to your car."

"Yes." She rose stiffly. "Thank you, Mr. Brewster. You are very kind." She extended her hand quite formally, as if he were an unwelcome guest who had brought the wrong bottle of wine. He grasped her cold fingers, pressing them briefly before he opened the door. He saw that her eyes were steely, not the eyes of the girl he'd met on the stage, the girl who'd opened the door to him minutes before. Whether true nature or immediate circumstance had fostered this alteration, he could not tell. More likely, he surmised, a combination of both.

The transformation had not escaped Clay. Her expression and her attitude were foreign to him—but then, he had not seen her face at the instant she'd held his knife in her hand, piercing first the air, then Loco's heart.

He wrinkled his brow and touched her face. "Jessie, are you—"

Almost absently, she brushed his hand away. "Fine. I'll be fine."

He hesitated, unaware of Brewster's inquisitively arched brow. "Are you sure?" he asked gently. Why didn't she cry? Why didn't she get angry? Why didn't she do *something?* And why did she look so cold—her eyes were like hard blue ice.

She turned away. "Yes," Samuel's daughter said evenly, standing with one foot in the mountains of Northern Arizona and the other in Boston. The Boston side was pulling harder and harder.

Clay backed away, feeling as if he had been dismissed.

Which, of course, he had been.

Heavy damask drapes were pulled against the rushing blackness outside. They hung in thick, continually shivering folds as the train steamed east toward the New Mexico border. Jessica sat alone in back, in the sleeping chamber. The door between her bedroom and the car's parlor was open a crack, and she could hear the murmur of voices: Clay and Brewster.

She had bathed and changed her clothes, resurrecting her largest, most fashionable bustle and strapping herself once again into the attire of "civilized" America with whalebone. She hadn't anything black with her, so she donned the darkest dress, the closest thing to mourning clothes she had: a velvet gown of deep ultramarine, with double-frill epaulets of the same black Chantilly lace that ringed her cuffs and covered

237

the narrow ice blue satin undervest. Her dark hair was piled softly upon her head, with wispy ringlets surrounding her face and brushing the back of her neck, and she carried a handpainted Chinese fan. At her ears, she still wore Clay's tiny silver flowers.

She looked very, very elegant.

There was a tap at the door. It was Clay, his voice muffled, telling her the porter was on his way with a late supper. She rose and passed through into the salon.

Brewster was seated at the table. Clay, engaged in conversation, stood with his back to her, so Brewster saw her first. He stopped in mid-sentence and stared, a grin of undisguised appreciation blooming on his naturally mischievous face. Puzzled, Clay followed his gaze, slowly turning to face her.

He had never seen her like this. She was beautiful, yes—this he already knew. But there she stood, pale and regal in a fabulous gown which had most likely cost more than the home office would pay him this year. For the first time, his inheritance, the family estate in Maryland, had concrete value to him—he could easily keep her in clothes like this, too, if only she would let him. For an instant, the rocking car evaporated, and he saw her in the drawing room at home, at Turtle Creek; she would be talking about the morning's hunt and warming a brandy for him between her slim hands, and he would go to her and take her into his arms and—

The sound of Brewster's voice shattered the illusion, bringing him back to the harsh reality of the clattering train, and where it was headed . . . and why.

"You were going to walk the train, Clayton," Brewster was saying. They were taking turns patrolling, once an hour. The danger to Jessica at present was probably nil, but there was no reason to take chances.

With noticeable difficulty, Clay turned away and exited, nearly bumping into a tray-laden porter who stood outside the platform door, his knuckles poised to tap at the glass.

The first porter was followed by another, this one bearing two trays, and together they set the table for three and began to serve the first course. Brewster seated Jessica, then took his place across from her. "We've no need to wait for Clayton," he smiled. "He'll catch us up in no time, once he returns."

He turned to the porters, who stood silently to one side, waiting to serve the second course. He reached into his pocket, pulled forth a few coins, and handed them to the white-coated men. "Thank you, gentlemen," he said, "but I believe we can serve ourselves. You might want to come back in a couple of hours. To collect the rubble."

Pocketing their tips, they nodded and silently left, leaving Jessica and Brewster alone to face a mountain of food. Brewster opened a bottle of wine—three had arrived along with their dinner—and poured a bit into his own glass. He tasted it and, pronouncing it passable, filled her glass and then his own. "Should have been left to breathe for a half-hour or so," he confided, a twinkle in his eye, "but then, you can't expect them to know everything."

He raised his glass, indicating that she should follow suit. She did so, still mute, and after clinking it halfheartedly against his ("To fine food and charming company in which to enjoy it," had been his toast), she took a polite sip, set down the glass and proceeded to stare into the bowl of oxtail soup steaming on her plate. The coldness had passed from her eyes, he noted, and had been replaced by an empty stillness. *Are you alive in there, Jessica Lawrence,* he wondered, *or has this finished you off for good and all?* There had to be a way

239

to bring her out of it.

He wished Ann were along. She was always much better in such situations than was he. He thought Ann would like this girl very much. It bothered him just a little that his wife was so taken with Clayton, but he knew that if she were here (along with all of her incessant matchmaker's guile), that she'd surely figure out a way not only to bring Jessica out of her funk, but to manage, somehow, to create a way for the lovers to stay together.

But the artful Ann was two thousand miles away in Chicago, and he was here and he needed to do *something*. He reached into his pocket and brought out his watch.

"Would you like to see a picture of my wife?" he asked. He was certain she wouldn't care in the slightest one way or the other, but at least it might start the conversational ball rolling and bring Jessica back from wherever she was. He opened the case and handed it to her.

Listlessly, she took it and looked at the inside lid. Mounted there was a cunningly painted miniature of a smiling, doe-eyed woman, as blond as Brewster, her grin subdued but just as infectious as his. She looked somehow familiar.

"That's my Ann," Brewster glowed. "Beautiful, isn't she?"

"She's lovely," Jessica agreed, finally speaking. "I can't help but think I've seen her before." She squinted at the tiny portrait. "She looks familiar."

"Entirely possible," Brewster said proudly. "Would it be of assistance if I told you her maiden name was Ann Halliday?"

The memory came rushing back; the petite fair-haired woman far away on the concert hall stage, producing such exquisite, wonderful sounds that

Jessica had been riveted to her seat. Even the usually disdainful Owen had been impressed.

The set line of her lips curled into a smile. "Oh, she's wonderful! I heard her sing last year when she came out of retirement to do a limited tour of the East Coast! And she's your wife?" She handed the pocket watch with its tiny portrait back to Brewster.

"She is indeed, though the Lord only knows how I ever talked her into it," he grinned.

"Oh, I doubt that you had too much trouble," she smiled, and without realizing it, began to eat her soup.

They continued through the meal alone, making small talk. Jessica learned that Brewster and Ann were expecting a child late in the fall, and that he planned to take a leave of absence from field work and, as he put it, "push papers in the home office" so that he would be with his wife when the baby came. He did not bring up Clay's name, nor did he make any reference to him—he could see she was so sick at heart that any reminder might send her back into silence.

Midway through the dessert course, he got up to rummage through his valise. He pulled out a pen and paper, and scribbled a few words. Then he produced her handbag.

"You left this on the stagecoach," he said, tucking the paper inside and handing it to her.

She opened the purse and touched the folded sheet, looking at him for an explanation.

"That's our address in Chicago, my wife's and mine. If you should care to write, or if you should want to contact—" He broke off as her fingers tightened on the paper. "Well, I just thought that you and Ann should be great friends," he finished lamely. *I'm no bloody good at this,* he thought. *No bloody good at all.*

Just then she looked up to see Clay's tall figure silhouetted on the door's frosted and etched glass

241

panel. She knew she couldn't face him. Quickly, she got to her feet and excused herself, leaving a bewildered Brewster alone to greet his sorrowful associate.

It was just as well, as Clay was no more up to being in the same room with her, unable to hold her, than was she to be with him.

Alone in her sleeping chamber, Jessica sat down on the side of the bed and twisted open the silver clasp of her bag. She unfolded the sheet of paper and read the address, then carefully replaced it. She had forgotten all about the handbag she'd left behind, and now she slowly searched through it. Her mother's sapphires, still snug in their velvet case, were within, as was the tintype of Margaret, safe and unscratched. And something else.

She pulled out the envelope and lifted the flap, pulling out the neat packet of bills, three hundred dollars worth, that she had so carefully saved from the household money. *My little symbol of superiority,* she thought, berating herself for ever having been so naive. *It doesn't matter. None of it matters. Because in the end they always win, the Owens of the world. They win because they're the ones who make the rules by which we all have to play.*

The packet in her hand, she turned the latch on the car's back door, opened it, and stepped out on the little observation platform. She stood there a moment, watching the rails beneath her rush away as the train steamed through the desert.

Then slowly, one, two, three bills at a time, she held the money out in her hand, allowing the wind to take it until it was all gone, fluttering into the desolate New Mexico night.

"Thank God," Owen Lawrence was murmuring into

the doughy hands he held pressed over his face, not so much in joy and relief as to hide his diasppointment. What a shame she hadn't joined her father, say, the next day—just long enough afterward to land the entire estate firmly in his own grasping hands. Oh, well. It was probably too much to hope for. *For what we have received,* he mused, *may we be truly grateful . . .*

"Thank God she's alive!"

The charade was not lost on J.D. James, who was, as much as Brewster and McCallister, a seasoned professional: he knew a phony when he saw one. It was nearly the same act he'd seen Lawrence put on earlier today at the funeral, joy and sorrow interchangeable. But it was none of his business. His business, at least with this nasty little man, would be complete as soon as the wife was returned.

He had bigger fish to fry. No so big as he would have liked, for Nathaniel Kane had disappeared into thin air: either fled the country or pulled one of his usual and totally frustrating disappearing acts. J.D. sometimes wondered if the man were flesh at all—he was as elusive as smoke. LaCroix's suicide had wreaked havoc with the intricately plotted operation; and the network of agents patiently standing by in cities across the nation, waiting for the word to move in, found themselves immersed in chaos.

In the finely woven fabric of Samuel's empire, some people had received word of the turnover, and others, being farther away from the center of the weave, had not. There'd been no time to gather the clean evidence that would enable them to charge and convict the higher-ups in Samuel's organization, let alone LaCroix or Villanova. They could have taken Kane, had they been able to find the sonofabitch—he was substantially nearer, in the hierarchy of things, to his own operatives, and now the Pinkertons could prove it. But how, J.D. wondered, do you convict a phantom?

Kane's men had been deserted by their leader, and, deprived of orders and instructions, they were taking care of their own interests, some moving in to grab what they could, others vanishing completely.

The Pinkertons were salvaging what they were able, but they were only making seizures and arrests on the lowest level, nothing more than tokens, really. There was no denying that it was a snarled disaster that would take months, even years, to straighten out.

J.D. knew full well that sooner or later, Kane would resurface in some new guise and begin again, and that Villanova would most certainly reweave his web. Samuel LaCroix's impenetrable armor of paper, that which shielded him in death as in life, was Villanova's handiwork. There was no doubt in his mind that Villanova would rise again, and probably higher even than the late Mr. LaCroix, because Villanova was, by far, the more ruthless of the two.

And, at least for now, there was nothing J.D. or anyone else could do about it. The whole thing gave him indigestion.

So here he sat, in Samuel LaCroix's monster of a house, talking to this pompous little nitwit who was pretending to be overcome with emotion at the news that his wife lived and was coming home to him. He felt in need of a drink. A very large drink.

He waited for Owen to finish with the melodramatics and start asking the questions he knew would follow. He didn't have too long to wait.

Owen looked up, sniffling and rubbing at his nose with a silk handkerchief. "It is joyous news you have brought me tonight, Mr. James. I cannot thank you enough."

"Please don't try, Mr. Lawrence," he replied. And he

244

meant it. A little of this snot-nosed prig went a long way.

"I cannot help but wonder," Owen went on, "just how the Pinkertons came to be involved in this matter. As I told you, I was approached by your Mr. Brewster, but he told me nothing. Perhaps you could enlighten me?"

"I'm afraid I'm not at liberty to disclose any further information, Mr. Lawrence, other than to tell you that the agency was engaged by an interested third party, a party pursuing a related case." What was he supposed to tell him? That Uncle Sam was after his father-in-law, but that God got him before the government did? Wouldn't do at all. Christ, he could use a whiskey . . .

"I see." Owen tucked his handkerchief neatly into his pocket. "When can I expect to see my dear wife again?"

Don't you mean your dear rich *wife?* J.D. thought sarcastically. With difficulty, he tempered his tone of voice before speaking. "I should say tomorrow evening, sir, if the train's running on time. If it's all the same to you, I'll be back here then, to meet her and my men." *Little bastard doesn't even want to know if she's in one piece.*

"Certainly, certainly." Owen stood up, signaling an end to the interview. As anxious to leave as Owen was to see him go, J.D. got to his feet, instantly dwarfing Owen with his towering bulk.

"I will be expecting you, then," Owen said as they walked out into the grand entry hall. Owen grabbed for his hand and shook it, much to J.D.'s chagrin. He extricated himself as quickly as possible, then slapped his hat on his head and strode out, looking very much like an irritated grizzly bear in a bowler and topcoat.

Once the door had closed behind him, he scraped his palm against his pant leg, half expecting to leave behind a shiny trail of slime.

Inside, Owen returned to Samuel's study—his study now. He sat behind Samuel's desk (his desk) and smirked. All right, she was alive. But was it really so important? She would stay in line; hadn't she always? She would take care of his house, maybe even give him an heir someday. And he supposed that he really had to have a wife, for propriety's sake. This was probably all for the best; it would save him, at least, from having to find another.

He tugged at a thick silk cord hanging down the wall behind the desk, and a few minutes later Mrs. Sing appeared. For some reason he had not seen her daughter Lin for several days now. He could not know that she had gone to her mother, terrified by the way Miss Jessica's husband stared at her, begging that she not have to go near him again.

"Yes, Mr. Lawrence?" she asked in her neat, precise English. "What may I do for you?"

Owen looked up, irritated that she was not her daughter. "Tell Villanova I want to see him," he ordered.

Mrs. Sing nodded, her slender face placid. "Certainly." But she made no move to leave the room.

Owen furrowed his brow. "Well? What is it?" he growled.

"We are wondering," Mrs. Sing intoned softly, "if you and Mrs. Lawrence intend to remain in Denver now that Mr. Samuel is with his ancestors."

Owen sat back in his chair, irritated. "You are very forward, Mrs. Sing."

"Perhaps so, sir, and I hope you will forgive my boldness. But it is a question in the minds of many of the staff. We only wish to know whether the household is to remain intact, or if we should begin to make other plans. Many of us accompanied Mr. Samuel here from

San Francisco, you see. There is a great feeling of loyalty to the family. To Mr. Samuel and Miss Jessica . . ." She might as well have added *but not to you.*

"I see." He leaned forward again. "Frankly, Mrs. Sing, I have not yet made up my mind. You will be advised as soon as I come to a decision." Actually, he had a pretty good idea of just what he wanted to do, but he wasn't going to give a servant the satisfaction of having a direct question answered. These people had to be kept in their place.

"By the way, Mrs. Sing, you may spread the word among the servants that I have just received word that my dear wife will be coming home to us tomorrow evening." That would keep them busy for a while.

The normally enigmatic Mrs. Sing abruptly broke into a close-lipped smile: for her, the height of rejoicing. "That is very good news, sir, very good indeed. Everyone will be most happy."

Owen did not return her smile. He waved his hand, saying, "And now, if you will get Mr. Villanova?"

"Of course." She bowed her head and slipped silently from the room.

Ten minutes later, Villanova was seated across from him.

"I suppose the maid has already told you the good news about Mrs. Lawrence," Owen began.

"Yes, and I am delighted. In fact, it is the reason I was detained. Mr. and Mrs. Sing and I enjoyed a toast to her safe return. By the way, Lawrence, I should hardly call Mrs. Sing a maid. She's rather a brilliant woman. Samuel thought very highly of her."

"A servant, nonetheless, not to mention a foreigner," Owen replied, getting in a last word before changing the subject. "I wish to speak to you about the disbursement of my father-in-law's estate."

247

"There has not yet been a reading of the will."
Villanova sat back and crossed his legs, then reached
into his pocket for a cigar. Samuel's humidor sat on the
desk in front of Owen, but he doubted that Owen
would be gracious enough to offer. "I don't see how we
can discuss the disbursal of assets before we know how
Samuel has assigned them."

Owen glared at him. He had ceased any attempt to
mask his dislike of Samuel's major-domo. He could
not stand the man; he was always so cool, so collected,
so in charge. And he was a filthy little nobody. They
were *all* filthy little nobodies! He wanted to hear a little
reverence in their tones when they addressed him—
didn't they know who he was? He had this gnawing feeling
of being, well, patronized, and he wouldn't stand for it
much longer—he'd fire them all, by God, and bring in
people who knew their places and stayed in them!

"I'm well aware of that, Mr. Villanova," he snorted.
"But I think it goes without saying that the bulk of the
estate will go to me. I . . . my wife, that is . . ."

Villanova blew a puff of cigar smoke in Owen's
general direction. His face was as calm as a pool of still
water on a windless day, never betraying the seething
anger and hatred beneath. Villanova was as far from a
fool as it was possible to be, and he had suspected from
the start that somehow, Jessica's filthy high hat of a
husband had a decisive hand in Samuel's suicide—
almost enough to call it murder. He could not have
borne more malice toward Owen if he had killed
Villanova's own father, for Samuel had been more of a
friend, a confidante, and a parent to him than had his
own sire.

He had loved Samuel.

"I'm certain you're accurate in your assumption,
Lawrence," he said, once again leaving off the
"Mister"—he knew how it aggravated the plump little

248

Bostonian. "However, while I have no knowledge as to the amounts of any bequests, Samuel did tell me he'd made provisions for the staff and myself, along with several charities. Those provisions, especially in the case of staff who have been with him for some years, such as Billings and the Sing family being rather sizable. The precise extent of his generosity will have to remain a mystery until the will is read. And that must wait until Mrs. Lawrence arrives."

Damn! Villanova was doing it to him again. And, of course, he was right. But as soon as LaCroix's attorney read the blasted will, he was going to give Mr. Clarence Villanova his walking papers. And then he was going to sell everything, get rid of it all: the big Denver house (Denver! Who could possibly want to live in the middle of nowhere!), the railroad, the export company, everything. He wanted none of his father-in-law's business responsibilities. What he wanted was the money, enough money to last him forever, and the next generation beyond him if that little broodmare daughter of Samuel's would produce an heir for him.

He plunged ahead. If he could get the answer to one simple question, it would at least give him a starting point. "Point well taken, Mr. Villanova. But can you give me—understand, I only require a rough estimate—some idea of the size of my father-in-law's estate?" There. It was a direct enough question. He'd have to answer that. Owen sat back, smugly folding his arms across his chest.

Villanova took another puff at his cigar. "No," he said. "I'm afraid I can't."

Owen shot forward, rocking Samuel's heavy leather chair. "I warn you, sir, don't be impudent with me!" He smacked a pudgy fist on the desktop. "I have every right to that information! Who are you to deny it to me?"

Villanova calmly relieved his cigar of its ash, rolling the tip in the crystal tray beside his chair. He wished Samuel were here to see the pink-faced, nearly hysterical creature behind his desk, this fat, avaricious cretin: the symbol for the societal status poor Samuel had so tragically admired and tried to emulate.

"Certainly you are within your rights, Lawrence." He could see Owen grinding his teeth at the omitted "Mister." Good. "But you must understand the accounting problems here. Samuel's assets are far-flung, to say the least. To gather that information and come up with a final tally will more than likely take a team of accountants several weeks. Possibly months."

Owen's face, which had, in the space of only a few moments gone from white to pink, was now working toward dark, livid red. Villanova wondered . . . if he waited long enough, would it explode, like something left too long on the stove?

"But-but-," Owen sputtered, "you must have *some* idea!"

Villanova rose and went to the door. "No, Lawrence. I'm afraid not." He was delighted to see Owen's complexion move toward burgundy, and not an unattractive shade, either. He stepped through the door and closed it behind him. *Well,* he thought as he climbed the stairs, *that was entertaining. Maybe Lawrence does have his uses, after all.*

It was Clay's turn to walk the train again. He'd made his way all the way to the front, or at least as far as it was possible to go without climbing up top. He'd checked the first-class Pullmans. Their sleeping berths were made up and occupied, their curtains snugly closed while passengers snored or tossed in upper or lower berths.

The second and third-class cars were relatively quiet, too. These travelers, not so fortunate as their first-class companions, made do with upright slumber, and they were twisted into strange, contorted shapes on the hard, narrow seats. They looked painfully uncomfortable, but most of them were managing to sleep. Clay could commiserate with them, for rare was the opportunity for an active agent to ride first class unless demanded by his cover or permitted by his own pocketbook.

He even checked the deserted dining car, and the kitchen and staff cars as well. All was quiet, at least as quiet as it was possible to be within those rushing, rocking cars. The train was asleep.

And now he made his way back, stepping quietly over more than a few outstretched legs in second and third class, then outside to cross to the first of the two sleeping cars, toward the rear of the train. Things were as they should be. There would be no trouble.

Walking through the last of the first-class sleepers, he did not see the drapes shielding the upper berth at 14A part slightly as he passed. And so he did not notice the eyes that followed him down the aisle. Nor did he hear the faint jangle of bracelets from within.

11

Morning.

She'd slept late—no surprise, since she'd spent most of the night tossing and turning, staring through the darkness at the walls and ceiling of her chamber. Now the sun was well up and light flooded into the interior of the car. She was thankful they had allowed her to sleep. It subtracted from the time she had to be conscious of her plight. It lessened the time that she had to function, to think.

So far, she had clung to the privacy of her room like a life preserver and had, by the grace of God, been able to avoid being in the same room with Clay. She hoped she would be able to make it through today, and tomorrow, the final, most difficult day, without caving in.

By the time she washed at the basin and donned her clothes, Brewster was tapping at her door.

"You've been rattling around in there for quite a while, now, my dear," he said from the next room. "Might a fellow suppose that you're nearly decent and ready for some breakfast? Or should I say lunch?" His tone was light and teasing.

She *was* hungry. She just hoped Brewster was out

there alone—she knew she couldn't stand to face Clay. Her resolve was stronger by now, but not so strong that the sight of him would not bring on that awful ache of yearning.

But she didn't have to ask Brewster—he was one step ahead of her.

"I hope you don't mind dining alone with me once more," he added tactfully. "My partner is out patrolling again, and I seem to have ordered a great many sandwiches and a lovely bottle of wine. Please don't force me to devour such a gargantuan repast by myself."

Jessica smiled and shook her head. She had developed quite a soft spot in her heart for the dashing blond Englishman. "All right, Mr. Brewster." She laughed softly in spite of herself. "Thank you. I'll be right out."

She gave a final tug to her overvest, reached back to make certain her bustle was sitting exactly right, and joined him in the salon.

They chattered amiably throughout luncheon, snacking on the trimmed sandwiches he'd especially ordered from the kitchen, and making their way through a bottle of very good rosé.

They had finished their meal and pushed away from the table when they heard the outer door open and saw Clay's silhouette loom on the inner door's frosted glass panel. Immediately, Jessica rose.

"If you will excuse me, Mr. Brewster?" she asked, a worried, almost frantic look seizing her features.

The Englishman understood. He inclined his head in the faintest sort of bow. "Of course, Mrs. Lawrence," he said graciously.

She slipped back into her room just as Clay entered the parlor.

He saw just the flash of her disappearing skirts as she

shut the door behind her, and he stood there, staring at the closed door, looking like a whipped puppy.

Brewster shook his head. *This,* he thought, with a certain degree of disgust, *is pathetic. I hope I wasn't this bad with Ann.* Then he realized that he had been, nearly; and somewhat chagrined, stepped into the breach.

"Everything all right out there?" he asked.

Clay nodded. "The same."

Brewster crossed the slightly swaying room, his shoes sinking into the plush carpeting. He reached into his inside pocket and withdrew his cigarette case. "What say you and I have a smoke outside?" he suggested. His voice was much more chipper than he felt. "I could use a breath of fresh air and cinders. The noise out there will probably do me good, too."

"What? Oh, sure."

"That was a joke, Clayton." Brewster put a hand on his friend's shoulder and aimed him toward the door. "Although obviously not a very good one."

"Right. Sure. Sorry, Brewster. Guess I'm just a little distracted."

They went back through the door by which Clay had just entered, out to the connecting platform.

A little less than an hour later, when the train slowed and ground to a halt for one of the many stops it had made (and would continue to make before it brought Jessica and her party to Denver) a man boarded the train. He was an ordinary man, and as he waited on the platform there in Santa Fe, he did not stand out among his fellow travelers. He was not someone to spark either interest or comment, let alone a personage one would file into one's memory.

His face would not have been familiar to Clay, nor

to Brewster. But if Jessica had been on the platform, or if she had left her Pullman and walked forward into first class, she would have remembered him, and been afraid.

He was the man in the light gray suit.

His name was Ralphy "The Cutter" Briscoe, and he was on this particular train to do some work. He took his seat and kept to himself, politely but undeniably letting the fat woman and her daughter seated opposite him know, with a curt nod, that he was not interested in conversation of any sort. He buried his nose in a newspaper, and he remained in this position for over an hour.

At that time, a woman in black, her heavy veil indicating the depth of her grief, passed by him, clattering faintly as she walked. She exited the car in the direction of the front of the train, and a few minutes later the man in the light gray suit put down his paper, pulled a cigarette case from his pocket, nodded formally to the fat woman and her daughter, and exited in the same direction.

The widow was standing to one side on the little railed platform between the cars when he walked out. The wind tore at her dull black skirts and plastered the dense veil to one side of her obscured face.

Ralphy Briscoe slid the silver case back into his pocket without withdrawing a cigarette.

"How many?" he asked over the roar of steel on steel as the rails passed swiftly under the speeding train. He could see them whizzing by on either side of the coupling, in the space between the platform on which they stood and the edge of the next car's tiny deck.

"Two men. A blond fancy-pants Englishman and a big man, dark headed. And the girl." Though the veil was thick, her words came through clearly.

"When?"

"Tonight. The men take turns walkin' the train every hour. You can set your watch by 'em. We'll take the first one out between cars when he's doin' his rounds. Sooner or later the second one will have to come out to find out what's happened to the first. We'll take him, and then the girl will be easy."

"Suppose you have this all mapped out?"

The veiled woman nodded. "We've got to wait 'til late, when most everybody's asleep. The best place is between our car and theirs, when he's on his way back."

Ralphy frowned. "Too close to the other bodyguard for my taste. Why not take him right here?"

"Night porter. He'll be movin' between cars every once in a while, hard to tell when. But he won't have any business back there. Nothin' beyond but the girl's private car."

The Cutter nodded.

"I got the Baby with me—" She patted at her handbag, also black, and he knew that inside she had her favorite derringer. "—but I don't want to have to use her. Too much noise. Want to keep this as smooth and easy as possible."

The train was rounding a curve, and a gust of wind lifted her veil. She snatched at it with a clawlike hand, but not before it fluttered up to expose a portion of her lined and painted face.

"We'll wait for them to do the two a.m. check. Most everybody should be asleep by then. After whichever one it is passes through to the front of the train, I'll meetcha on the rear platform. I'll be there to cover ya just in case. But I'm expectin' this to be neat and clean. Don't disappoint me, Ralphy. Just slit his throat and give him a shove off the side. Keep it simple. And when the second one sticks his head out to see what's keepin' his partner, he gets the same."

"Not much sport in it, Gert." He stared back down at

256

the rails. The wooden crossties were blurred by speed into invisibility.

"Can't see there was all that much sport in what ya done to Drago last month, either."

Ralphy shrugged. "It's a job, I reckon."

Gert nodded. "We do this right, we can be off the train at the first stop in the morning. Be hours before anybody figures out anything's wrong."

"Nice and neat?"

"Nice and neat."

The man in the light gray suit went back into first class and returned to his seat. Gert Vance walked forward to the dining car and ordered a cup of tea and some biscuits.

Nice and neat, she thought smugly, and beneath her veil, smiled.

He was having the nicest dream.

He was home with Ann, and she was fluttering those long, sweeping lashes at him as she sat on his lap in the parlor. The fire was lit, and it was late at night, and he was thinking that he might just take her right here in the drawing room. She stroked his cheek and whispered something in his ear, and he smiled at her and suddenly her clothes just vanished, leaving her naked in his lap. He cupped his hand over the familiar plumpness of her breast, and—

"Wake up, Brewster!" Clay was shaking him.

Groggy—and more than a little disgruntled—he opened his eyes. The vibrating parlor was dimly lighted by one shivering lamp, turned down low.

"Wake up, will you? It's two o'clock. I have to walk the train."

Brewster, stretched out on the divan, yawned and pulled himself up to a sitting position. "Your timing is impeccable, Clayton," he croaked, the sleep still heavy in his voice. "When we finish with this little journey, I am going to treat myself to a full two hours of blissfully uninterrupted slumber."

Clay walked to the door. "Very funny, Charles. Just stay awake for the next twenty minutes or so, will you?" He let himself out, closing the door softly behind him.

He headed toward the front of the train, passing through the swaying cars with their cargo of sleeping passengers. Everything was quiet, correct. But as he started back, he began to get that funny tingling in his spine that told him something was wrong. *Just nerves,* he told himself. *And not enough sleep.*

Just the same, he was particularly observant on the way back. But still, everything seemed in its place. There was nothing out of the ordinary except that funny feeling he couldn't shake. He wondered if Brewster was feeling anything similar; he, too, usually had a good sense of, well, of *wrongness.* And Clay couldn't shake the gnawing feeling that something wasn't right.

Gert Vance and Ralphy "The Cutter" Briscoe took up their positions on the two tiny platforms that connected the first-class car and Jessica's Pullman.

Gert, minus her heavy veil, stood on the private car's balcony, far to the side. She was pressed against the railing, her black widow's garb making her nearly invisible in the night. Ralphy waited on the opposite platform: kitty-corner from Gert and next to the door through which their victim would walk into the snare.

In Gert's hand was a tiny derringer, the "Baby" that was her insurance. In Ralphy's was a finely honed stiletto, slim and deadly. Over his gray suit he had donned a linen duster. It could be tossed over the side of the train along with the bodies after he had finished his work. There was no sense in getting blood all over a perfectly good suit.

They did not speak to one another. They knew their jobs. They waited.

Clay entered the last first-class car. As with the one before it, all the privacy curtains were closed. A foot or an arm poked through here and there to dangle into the aisle. The car was filled with the snores of strangers and the occasional murmured dreamer's mumble. Quiet, calm, right . . . but not right.

He shook his head. The job was getting to him. *She* was getting to him. Correction—she had already gotten to him. This was something entirely different.

He opened the back door of the compartment and walked out into the night air.

A hand, an arm, snaked around his left shoulder, his neck, pulling him back and to the right, jerking his chin into the air. The corner of his eye registered the glint of metal coming toward him—arcing swiftly, from the right.

Instinctively, he threw his weight backward against his attacker, at the same time leaning left, into the restraining arm.

The ploy, quicker than half a heartbeat, saved his life.

The knife sliced into his flesh, but not his throat, its intended target. He felt and heard the sickening scrape as it skittered across his collarbone and sliced across the tender flesh above his right breast. The pain was immediate and excruciating, but there was no time to hesitate.

Clay shot his right hand up and out to clamp around the wrist of his attacker's knife hand, preventing—just in time—a penetration of his midsection.

Instantly he repeated the first move, throwing all his weight backward, slamming the faceless man into the rear wall of the car. Then he pivoted, twisting his own body down and to the side, swinging his opponent out and away, hoping he would drop the knife which was still dangerously close.

But his adversary was quick and skillful. He moved with Clay's lunge rather than fighting against it, and instead of losing his balance and his weapon, retained both. He landed in front of Clay with the grace of a cat, and despite Clay's grip on his knife hand, he smiled briefly, grimly, into the Pinkerton's eyes.

Gert watched from the opposite platform as the two men struggled, trading positions in the blink of an eye. Ralphy was the best there was in a knife fight, but the big man was strong. Ralphy was struggling, trying to push the knife home despite the iron grip that the big man still held on his wrist. The Pinkerton's blood looked black in the moonlight, and as they struggled, she could catch glimpses of the dark stain that was spreading rapidly on his shirt. *He can't keep this up,* she thought, and waited for him to weaken, for The Cutter's blade to slice downward.

Inside, Brewster was sitting up straight on the divan, staring at his forearms. The golden hairs there were standing on end. *Something is wrong,* he thought. *Something is terribly wrong.*

When the feeling first came over him, his immediate instinct was to head up front and find Clay. But Jessica could not be left alone, expecially if he was right and something was amiss.

He rubbed at his arms, then rose and went to the opposite side of the parlor. He stood against the wall, where he would see anyone entering before they saw him, and pulling a pistol from the holster he wore beneath his shoulder, waited.

He was weakening, and he was in trouble. His shoulder thudded and he knew his shirt was sticky with blood, but still he struggled. The two men skittered this way and that on the swaying platform: participants in a macabre and deadly dance. Both their right arms were raised high overhead as each sought to turn the blade away from himself and toward the other. The knife flashed silver in the starlight as first one man gained advantage, then lost it to his opponent.

The Cutter's left hand was at his throat, the thumb digging cruelly into his windpipe, and Clay's attempts to pry the viselike fingers away were in vain. His air was being cut off, and the loss of blood from the slash across his chest was making him weaker by the second.

He dropped his hand from the assailant's grip on his throat, and balling it into a fist, pulled it back. With his last burst of energy, he punched as hard as he could, landing the blow in his opponent's side. With intense satisfaction, he felt bone give way, and knew he had broken some ribs when Ralphy grunted and momentarily eased his grip on Clay's throat.

Gulping blessed air, Clay immediately recoiled his arm and landed a second punch on the same spot. He felt his attacker's body give and raise up a fraction as the man groaned again. And this time, when Clay pushed hard at his knife hand and felt it give, he knew he was in control.

Quickly, he drove home a third blow, at the same time twisting to the side, smashing The Cutter's knife hand against the wall of the car. The blade clattered to the platform, bounced once, and dropped into the

261

darkness beneath the train. Clay turned again as Ralphy's left hand released his throat and dropped to administer a punch to Clay's midsection.

The blow was well placed and strong, but Clay had been ready for it—Ralphy's punch met a hard, tensed wall of muscle. Now Clay twisted to the side again, still holding The Cutter's empty knife hand high in the air. He landed three rapid punches to the assassin's rib cage, turning with him as the blows drove him in a tight little circle, the last bars of the dance. Just as he landed the third, and knew that the man was beaten, he saw starlight reflected on a gun barrel on the opposite platform.

For the first time, he realized that they were not alone. He saw the barrel come up, and abruptly he twisted again, pulling Ralphy between himself and the pistol.

Gert's bullet caught The Cutter low in the center of his back, severing his spine, and he slumped forward against Clay. Gert immediately leapt to the center of the opposite platform and raised the derringer again. With only one shot left, she took careful aim at Clay's head as he struggled under the weight of the dying Ralphy. But just as she fired, he shoved with all his might, half pushing, half throwing the limp body across the space between the cars.

Ralphy landed with a thud against Gert, toppling her backward against the door of Jessica's car. Her second shot went wild as both she and the luckless Ralphy landed in the arms of a surprised Brewster, who had come running, pistol in hand, at the sound of the first shot.

Gert let out a shriek and with a strength born of outrage, pushed the body of her dying comrade away. As Ralphy tumbled and slid between the cars to be ground under relentless iron wheels, Gert wrenched away from Brewster in an attempt to hurdle Clay—who had slumped to the floor of the other deck—and retreat toward the front of the train.

But Clay, freed of Ralphy, had at last been able to reach into his coat and pull out his own pistol. He now held it outstretched, pointed directly at Gert Vance's heart.

She stopped dead in her tracks, her talon fingers curled into bony fists, and backed toward the outside guard rail. She shot a withering glance at Brewster, whose gun was also leveled in her direction. For the first time, she spoke.

"You bastards gonna shoot me?" she asked huskily, her nose in the air, a sneer on her painted face.

Clay, bleeding heavily, was up on his knees. "You'd like that, wouldn't you? Better than facing up to a jury. Or your boss. But you're out of luck. We're taking you in."

She threw back her head and laughed coarsely, clamping her hands on her hips. "Like hell!" she shouted, and without further ado, disappeared over the side rail.

Brewster leapt torward the railing in an attempt to catch her, but his fingers touched only the fleeting hem of her dress as she went over the side. He stood there for a moment, looking back into the gloom before he went to Clay.

"Another typical case of death before dishonor, I should imagine," he grunted as he helped Clay to his feet. "I hope you realize you're getting blood all over my favorite shirt," he added, taking care to jostle Clay's right shoulder as little as possible.

"These people don't seem to take much to the idea of failure," Clay groaned.

Brewster pulled him upright and, supporting him, crossed the gap between the cars. "I thought she took it a little hard myself," he said, and managed to get Clay as far as the divan before the tall man, covered in his own blood, blacked out.

When he regained consciousness, his ruined shirt was gone, and there was a clean white bandage strapped across his chest. He moved to pull himself up, and groaned when a pain shot through his shoulder.

Brewster, seated across the parlor and smoking a cigarette, smiled. "I shouldn't try to wiggle about too much, Clayton. You'll spoil all my nice needlework."

Clay, his face screwed into a grimace, eased back down on the divan. "Christ, Brewster, you didn't sew me up again, did you? Couldn't you have found a *real* doctor?"

The Englishman leaned forward in his chair. "I take a certain degree of umbrage at that statement, McCallister," he grinned. "You know perfectly well I stitch better than most any veterinarian. Besides," he added, leaning back again, "I'm free."

Clay nodded. "Guess I can't argue with that." He took in Brewster's blood-stained shirt, now dried to a dark rusty brown. "All that mine?"

"I'm afraid so. Haven't had time to change yet. Just finished you up. You have excellent timing, by the way. I so hate it when you lads wake up in the middle of it all and start screaming—makes it difficult to keep the stitches even."

He stubbed out his cigarette and got to his feet. "Believe I'll change now. But first . . ." He went to the small service cupboard, opened it, and drew out a bottle. He removed the cork and tipped out half a tumbler of dark liquid, then handed the glass to Clay.

"Stashed a bottle of port away in there—for medicinal purposes only, you understand. And you seem as deserving a case as any."

"I hate port," Clay grumbled.

"Drink it anyway. Good for you." Brewster stripped to the waist and tossed his stained clothing into the wastebasket on top of Clay's blood saturated shirt. He opened his valise, then pulled out and donned a fresh shirt and vest. "You ought to be glad J.D.'s not here. You wouldn't get away with just a glass of port. He'd force-feed you a fifth of whiskey and a suckling pig. For your own good, of course."

Clay tipped back the glass and made himself swallow a mouthful of the too-sweet (for his taste, anyway) fluid. It was not long before he was suffused with the beginnings of a warm glow, and the pain in his shoulder did seem to ease, but he still wished Brewster had thought to stash away a bottle of good bourbon.

"I want you to do me a favor, Charles." He had emptied the glass now, and gingerly turned to set it on the little table next to the couch.

"Absolutely." Brewster lit a cigarette and offered it to his friend. When Clay gratefully accepted, he lit another for himself. "What's on your mind?"

"I'd appreciate it if you didn't mention this to . . . to Mrs. Lawrence." He was intently studying the orange glow on the end of his ready-made, avoiding Brewster's eyes, as he had every time he had discussed her with his partner.

Brewster sat down and propped his feet up. "If you like. I won't say a word. Any particular reason?"

"I . . . I just think it might upset her. That's all."

You just don't want to stoop to a sympathy ploy, my friend, Brewster thought. *I suppose I can understand that. Lord, these colonists are bullheaded.* "All right, Clayton," he said, smiling. "By the way, you'll be pleased to know that your shoulder wasn't nearly so nasty as it looked—or felt, I imagine. Bled a lot, but it

265

wasn't deep. You ought to be your old sober-sided self in a couple of days."

"Just in time to get the stitches ripped out?"

Brewster grinned wickedly. "Precisely. Now get some sleep. I'll stand watch the rest of the night."

Clay slept until the morning, but he did not sleep soundly, for he dreamt through the night of Jessie, and life without her.

12

And now she was just an hour away.

An hour away from the real world of Denver, of Owen, and of her father's house; an hour away from the final grim reality of her life as it had been before and would be from now on. She had spent the last days steeling herself to face her future.

This morning, repacking her trunks and gathering her things, she had found a shard of porcelain on the floor, tucked back against the baseboard: a last fragment of the pitcher she'd smashed so many days ago, when the train was headed the other way, toward a peaceful summer south of the Verde Valley. She leaned against the side of her bed, turning the shiny sliver over and over in her fingers.

It had been a cathartic moment, true, that divorcement of her life from her stepfather's and her resignation to return to her loveless marriage. But how much simpler that resolve had been to muster when the only thing she had to leave behind was the hollow memory of Samuel's love: the exchange of one empty life for another.

There was so much to leave behind now, so much just beyond the reach of her hesitant, duty-bound grasp. If she had been another woman living in another time, it would have been easy, so easy, to desert Owen or divorce him, to run to Clay free of guilt or shame.

But she was a child of the Victorian Age, firmly catechized in all its protocol and ceremonies, and indoctrinated in its prim and rigid formalities. And according to those rituals and rules by which she had been so starchily reared, there were no options. It was as if she had been brainwashed into dutifully walking over the edge of the cliff to fall to the sea below, simply because all the other lemmings were convinced it was the proper thing to do.

And she could not see beyond her conditioning. It surrounded her like a thick wall—too high to see over, let alone scale.

None of these things occurred to her. She was so much a part of them (and they so much a part of her) that they were not recognizable as outside influences. She only knew that her heart was broken, and that in an hour she would say good-bye to Clay forever. And along with him, she would say good-bye to herself.

She looked at her hand as it held the porcelain shard. Tiny wounds were there, scabbed over and healing now. She curled her fingers into a fist, and saw the perfect tattoo of her teeth where she had bitten down on her own hand that last time, to keep from crying out. It would leave a scar, she knew: a ring of white marks to remind her, always, of her passion and her infidelity.

And now, they were an hour away from Denver. She stood at the back door of the car, staring out its window, preferring to see where she had been rather than where she was going.

There was a tap at the door.

"Yes, come in." It would be Brewster, coming to tell her they were almost there. As if she hadn't been painfully aware of the minutes and hours slipping away from her.

"Jess?" It was Clay. She felt her knees turn to water and put out a hand to steady herself against the car's vibrating paneled wall. She turned to face him, knowing the sight of him would bring on a nearly physical pain. But she was unable to stop herself.

They stood for a moment, Jessie gripping the ridge of wainscoting as she trembled; Clay across the chamber, his back to the door, his eyes reflecting the infinite sadness in hers. At last he pierced the silence.

"We'll be there in an hour, they tell me." His voice broke slightly.

"Yes, I know. I . . . I'm ready. Packed, I mean. I . . ." She lowered her eyes as a tear welled, lodging first in her sooty lashes, then falling to splash on her bodice, making a dark round stain. She felt his hand on her shoulder, but she could not bring herself to look up, to look into his eyes. She knew that if she did, she would be lost in them forever; and that as she tumbled there, she would lose her soul.

He cradled the side of her face in his hand. "Look at me, Jess," he begged. The pain in his voice brought on a new torrent of tears, a silent weeping she was helpless to control, but still she did not raise her eyes, even when he turned her face toward his.

"Jess, please . . ." A whispered plea.

"No," she wept through shuttered lids, "no, I can't . . . we can't . . . Don't you see, Clay? It's all real again." Her voice cracked, frail and fragile with tears.

"You're wrong, Jessie, you're so wrong. Back there, you and I together—that was real, that was the way it's supposed to be for us." He gripped her shoulder more tightly, as if he could squeeze the truth into her, or the conditioning out. Then he drew her to him, hugging her to his chest in hopelessness. She would not bend, would not and could not desert that code which was her touchstone, all she had ever known. He knew he could force her, make her come with him. But if he did, a part of her would hate him forever, and through the years, that part would grow and grow until it would overshadow the rest. No, he would not make her hate him.

"Jessie, beautiful Jess," he whispered, stroking her brow as her salty tears marked his lapel. "I guess our turtledove has stopped singing, after all."

Her arms came around him then, hugging his waist tightly as her sobs became audible. "Oh, Clay," she wept, "the rest of my life is winter . . ." And then she could say no more.

They stood there quite a while, locked in each other's arms in that rattling, rumbling Pullman, and there was, for that space of time, nothing in the world except their love and their sorrow.

Billings met them at the station. His cap clutched in his big hostler's hands, he came toward them through the crowd of travelers and greeters milling through the trainside billows of steam.

"Miss Jessica!" he blurted, barely keeping back the tears, and reached a hand out to her. "Thank God you're with us again! All of us . . . we all . . . we're so sorry about Mr. . . . your father."

She looked at him as he stood there beneath the gaslights, and she remembered his grin, so many years ago, as he watched her mother flog that surly carter; how carefully he'd led old Emily around the courtyard with her astride, feeling, at six years old, like Scheherazade; the tears on his weathered face at her mother's funeral; his reservation, then his final bemused resignation when he helped her clear the

270

brush from Margaret's old riding ring; and the genuine pride and respect she'd seen on his face when he'd watched her clear the jumps. Suddenly, holding his hand was not enough. She threw her arms around his neck and hugged him.

"Thank you, Billings," she whispered in his ear. "Thank you for everything."

He blushed, a little flustered, as she stepped away and smiled at him sadly. He smiled back, rubbing at his eyes, then settled his cap on his head. "I . . . I brought the grays out for you, miss," he ventured, as a porter loaded the last of her trunks onto a handcart.

"That was very thoughtful, Billings," she said kindly, then indicated her companions with a gesture. "This is Mr. McCallister and Mr. Brewster. They're with the Pinkerton Agency, and they'll be coming along to the house with us."

Billings nodded first at the tall, solemn-faced Clay, standing soberly a few feet behind Jessica, eyeing the crowd; and then (with some curiosity) at Brewster, who leaned against the luggage cart on one elbow, his hat tipped back rakishly, not looking a bit like any picture he might have previously had of a Pinkerton.

There were too many trunks and valises to fit into the brougham, so Jessica picked the few she'd need tonight. Billings left the rest inside the station under watchful eyes until he could send a boy for them.

The teams of four grays stepping out smartly, they made their way to Samuel's house.

When they arrived, J.D. James was waiting in the mammoth entry hall. That he'd been pacing was evident by the line of cigar ash he'd shed on the marble floor.

"About time you boys got here," he barked. He stepped forward testily, but when he saw Jessica, his scowl turned into a smile of appreciation.

"Mrs. Lawrence, I presume," he grinned, kissing her

hand with a graceful flourish that surprised her, coming from one of such massive proportions. "Delighted to meet you, my dear! Delighted to see you in such fine fettle! J.D. James of the Pinkerton's, at your service." He bowed slightly as Clay looked on in disbelief. Brewster, who'd seen J.D.'s demeanor in Ann's presence, grinned and shook his head. As always, J.D. was bigger than life.

"How do you do, Mr. James," Jessica said, somewhat taken aback by this unexpectedly theatrical greeting.

"Much better, now that I see you safe and sound," he replied, finally letting go of her hand. "I trust these two rowdies have treated you well?"

She nodded. "Yes, thank you, they—"

Just then, Villanova emerged from the study, followed shortly by a primly smiling Mrs. Sing, who materialized from the general direction of the kitchen.

"You are here at last, Mrs. Lawrence!" Villanova effused, kissing the hand that J.D. had just released. "I can't begin to tell you how happy I am—we all are—to have you safely home and out of the hands of those ruffians!"

"Thank you, Mr. Villanova," she replied. She could never remember seeing him so enthusiastic. Mrs. Sing was waiting quietly in the background, and Jessica disengaged herself as politely as she could from her father's associate. She walked between him and J.D., crossing the hall to the slim Oriental woman. She held out her hands and Mrs. Sing squeezed them as her calm brow clenched into an unaccustomed knot.

"Oh, Miss Jessica," she began before she started to cry, "what will we do now that Mr. Samuel is . . ."

Jessica put her arm around the slender, usually dignified woman, comforting her. "We will carry on, Mrs. Sing," she murmured. "He would want us to carry on." The words were hollow and hackneyed, she knew, but they were all she had.

Mrs. Sing nodded and straightened, collecting herself. "Yes," she agreed. "You are right." She folded her hands neatly before her as her face eased once again into its usual calm, unreadable mask. "The rest of the staff would like to greet you, also. They are waiting belowstairs. May I assemble them?"

Jessica was about to grant her permission, but J.D., overhearing, broke in. "If you don't mind, ma'am," he said, addressing Mrs. Sing, "I'd like to put that off a while."

"Certainly, sir," she replied, then turned to Jessica. "I will be near, should you need anything."

Jessica gave her a tired, grateful smile. "Thank you, Mrs. Sing. And I will see everyone later, I promise."

She nodded. "Mr. Lawrence will be down presently," she added, almost as an afterthought, before she departed in the direction of the kitchen, presumably to spread the news of Jessica's safe arrival.

Villanova spoke up. "Perhaps we can all await Mrs. Lawrence's husband in the study," he suggested. "I'm certain we shall all be more comfortable there."

"Dandy suggestion, Villanova," J.D. admitted grudgingly, and flicked yet another spray of cigar ash on the polished floor. As ruthless and dangerous as he knew this Villanova character was, he had to admire the fellow's brain. And he was certainly preferable to that idiot, Owen Lawrence. How the devil had that little prig managed to land the vision in velvet he'd just met? An arranged marriage for certain, but why the hell would LaCroix have settled on Lawrence? Didn't make any sense at all. *Oh, well. Guess it doesn't have to. None of my goddamned business anyway,* he thought.

Clay pulled him aside and spoke a few quiet, terse words.

J.D. listened intently, then looked to Villanova. "If you don't mind," he grumbled, "we'll join you in a minute. I'd like to have a word with McCallister, here." He waved a hand toward Clay.

Villanova bowed slightly, ushering Jessica and a grinning Brewster into the study. Brewster, drinking in every overdone detail of the architecture, took her arm. "My dear Mrs. Lawrence," he whispered in her ear, "I never realized you'd been reared in such unbridled nouveau grandeur!"

Jessica almost laughed in spite of herself—she'd never given it much thought before, but he was right: her father's house was probably as ridiculously close to a palace as you could get without actually being the very recently installed king of something or other. And Brewster was unabashedly gawking, a big silly smile on his face as he took it all in.

"Keep wondering where all the velvet ropes are," he teased as he steered her along in Villanova's wake. "The ones they put up to keep the commoners from lying about on the upholstery."

Villanova closed the study door behind them, and as Brewster released her elbow to get a closer look at Samuel's collection of dueling pistols, Jessica turned to the thin, dark-haired man.

"I suppose the funeral service has already been held," she stated flatly.

"Yes," Villanova replied, "it was yesterday afternoon." By the break in his voice and his physical attitude, she could see he was genuinely grief-stricken. He really had cared for her stepfather, after all. She was somehow touched by this and put a hand on his sleeve to comfort him, in much the same manner as she had once tried to ease Samuel's sorrow upon the death of her mother.

Villanova was quite moved by her gesture. He

274

covered her hand with his in the same way Samuel had done all those years ago, and looked into her eyes, misinterpreting the pain he saw there. "His death, Mrs. Lawrence . . . I want you to know that his death will not—" Just then the door opened, and Owen Lawrence entered the room.

He sniffed haughtily at Villanova, making note of his hand as it slipped from atop Jessica's. Brewster, investigating the bric-a-brac, had worked his way around the room by now, and he leaned casually against the wall next to the door and behind Owen. He had a good view—*front row center,* he thought—for the reunion.

Jessica's face betrayed no emotion. She simply stood her ground, and after what seemed like a long silence, said simply, "Owen." Flatly, matter-of-factly, with less inflection that she would have said *rock* or *chair.*

Haltingly, Owen moved toward her, awkwardly taking her into his arms. "My very dear Jessica," he said as he embraced her.

This is all for our benefit, Brewster realized instantaneously. *If we weren't here, he'd probably say something like, "So nice to have you back, madam, and my socks need darning." How sad. How very, very sad.*

Jessica stood stiffly in her husband's arms, resigned to the situation. Staring down at the carpet as she endured his halfhearted embrace, she didn't see J.D. and Clay enter the room.

Clay stopped dead in his tracks, shocked and angered at the sight of her in another man's arms, husband or not. And without thinking, he began to move forward, his hand outstretched as if to take Owen Lawrence by the shoulder and toss him into the next county.

But Brewster had seen it coming and grasped his arm, staying him and bringing him back to the reality

275

of the situation. None of this was lost on J.D., who arched a bushy brow curiously; or Villanova, who filed it away for future reference in a mental folder marked *Pinkerton Bodyguards—Overzealousness of Same.*

Owen, apparently feeling he'd embraced his wife long enough to satisfy decorum, released her and turned to face the three Pinkerton men, leaving her swaying forlornly in the center of the room. He addressed J.D. "Mr. James, I cannot thank you enough for returning my dear wife. I am more grateful than you will ever know." He reached for the agent's massive hand and shook it with limp enthusiasm.

"Line of duty, Mr. Lawrence," J.D. growled. He pointed his thumb at Brewster. "Believe you know my man Charles Brewster."

Before Owen could put out his hand, the Englishman stepped back, crossing his arms casually, and leaned back against the wall, resuming his former posture. "We've met," he said, nodding.

"Yes, certainly," Owen stuttered, a little uncertain as to whether he had or had not been rebuffed.

"And this is Clay McCallister," J.D. continued gruffly, putting his hand on Clay's shoulder. "Brewster and McCallister here are a couple of the best damn men I've got." Then, remembering Jessica was still in the room, he added, "Pardon me, ma'am, hope I didn't offend you."

"No, not . . . not at all."

She sank into a big leather wing chair. Seeing the two of them together—one representing the love, the freedom, and the ecstasy of her recent and all too short past, and the other, the inevitable living death of her future—was more than she could bear. She studied her hands weakly, feeling as if she might faint, and hoping that if she did, she would never regain consciousness.

J.D. took no notice and plowed ahead with his

introductions. "This is the gent who's largely responsible for getting Mrs. Lawrence back to you in one piece," he continued, still gripping Clay's shoulder with huge fingers.

Owen presented his hand and Clay took it automatically, numbly. He felt Owen's chubby palm pressed into his. He was vaguely aware that he was being thanked profusely, that he had mumbled something in reply, and that Owen's hand was then gone from his. More than anything else, he wanted to be away from here, away from the disgusting creature to whom he was surrendering the only woman he had ever loved. He knew that if he did not leave soon, he wouldn't be able to restrain himself from reaching out and throttling the pasty little wretch.

Jessica continued to stare at her hands. She could hear Owen's insipid babbling, then the low, rich tone of Clay's voice, then Owen's again, made all the more squeaky and repulsive by comparison. She felt the tears welling up in her eyes, then saw them spatter on her primly folded hands, run between her fingers, and coat her wedding ring with hot, wet salt.

Then something white fluttered near. Villanova stood above her, offering a linen handkerchief, pressing it into her hands.

"Thank you," she whispered, and took it gratefully. She rubbed at her eyes, patted her glistening face and hands, and slowly raised her eyes to steal one last glimpse of Clay: one final image to last forever.

But when she looked up, he was gone.

"Madam," Owen was saying, "I'm certain you must be tired after your long journey. I suggest you go upstairs and lie down. We can discuss the reading of the will later."

*   *   *

Villanova saw them to the door.

"Think you folks ought to know," J.D. said, "that another attempt was made upon Mrs. Lawrence's life yesterday on the train. We'd be happy to send a man on home with her, if she and her husband wish. You might want to pass that along to the husband." Actually, it was something that *he* should be passing along to Lawrence, but somehow, he felt the information would have more weight in Villanova's hands. He reached into his coat pocket for a fresh cigar.

"You know where I'm staying. If you don't, Lawrence does. In any case, we'll keep a man with her at least until they leave for Boston."

"Thank you for your concern, Mr. James," Villanova replied, "but I believe . . . If it's all the same to you, sir, I think I should prefer to handle the matter privately."

Well, that doesn't come as any big hoorah of a surprise, J.D. thought, neatly clipping off the tip of his cigar with a silver snip he pulled from his pocket. It fell to the marble floor and joined the ash he'd deposited there earlier this evening.

"As you wish, Mr. Villanova," he growled, "As you wish."

The three agents stood in the dark outside Samuel's grand house.

"I don't know about you boys," J.D. pronounced, "but I need a drink. And dinner. A big dinner." He chewed at his cigar as he stared down the bricked drive. Billings was just bringing up the brougham. "Hell of a hacienda, isn't it?" he rumbled, waving toward the looming facade of Samuel's mansion.

"It only serves to prove, J.D.," Brewster observed, "that there's big money in sin. I've been meaning to ask

278

you . . . Why is it that the bad guys make all the money and we just get shot at and stabbed? I'm somewhat disgruntled that this was never pointed out to me before I signed on with the organization . . ."

"You're a real goddamned card, Brewster," J.D. grumbled crankily. The carriage stopped in the drive before them. "I'm going back to the hotel, and I don't give a damn what you do. I've never seen two more pathetic people. Especially you, McCallister. What the hell's wrong with you, anyway? You haven't made one smart-ass remark all night!" Without bothering to wait for an answer, he hoisted himself into the carriage, leaving the door ajar behind him.

"You boys want a lift or not? Speak up if you do— I've got two tons of paperwork and a rack of lamb waiting for me. And that damned fool Johnson can't do anything unless I'm there to aim him at it."

Brewster glanced at Clay, standing stonily beside him, and decided his friend wasn't in the mood for any more of J.D.'s expansiveness just at the moment. He reached out and closed the carriage door, clicking the latch into place.

"Thank you for the offer, J.D., but we've been sitting on our collective hindquarters far too much over the past days. Bit of a stroll right now might fill the bill."

J.D. leaned back, signaling to Billings that he was ready to go. "Brewster, I want to see you first thing in the morning! And be careful—too much exercise is bad for the constitution!" he shouted as the brougham pulled away and disappeared down the drive.

Clay and Brewster followed slowly on foot.

Brewster tried to make conversation.

"How's the shoulder?" he asked.

"Tolerable." Clay was in no mood for chatter, and Brewster decided to let it rest for a while. He lit a cigarette for himself, then offered the case to Clay, who declined.

They walked on into the night.

There had been rain. The paving stones underfoot were shiny and dark, and their boots crunched stray pebbles and grit into the hard damp surface.

They had gone almost a mile before the Englishman spoke again. "I don't suppose we'll be staying around here long. J.D. will more than likely assign us to the clean-up in San Francisco."

Clay was walking with his head down and his hands in his pockets.

"What? Oh. Yes, he is." Just then they walked under a street lamp, and Clay paused, requesting a cigarette. Brewster handed him the case.

"Was that among the topics of your little discussion in the hallway, then? To what else did our illustrious leader make you privy?"

As Clay lit the ready-made, the match reflecting in his clear green eyes, which Brewster could now see were rimmed with red. He looked as if he'd been on a three-week bender.

He exhaled a cloud of smoke. "You're staying here until Jess—the Lawrences—leave for Boston. I'm getting out tonight. I've got just enough time to collect Chance and give him a little workout before I load him into another freight car."

Brewster tipped back his hat. "You're in a frightful hurry to leave, my friend. You'll hurt my feelings."

The taller man started walking again, and Brewster moved alongside him. "I've got to . . . I just need to be by myself for a while, Charlie. I got in over my head this time. It's Jessie—Mrs. Lawrence . . . You see—"

Brewster stopped in his tracks, grabbing Clay's arm and pulling him up short. "Honestly, Clayton, you must really take me for an idiot."

Clay looked at the ground. "That obvious, is it?"

"Glaringly, my boy. So what are you going to do about it?"

Clay flicked the last third of his cigarette to the pavement and met his friend's concerned gaze. "Nothing I *can* do. Nothing anyone can do. So I guess I'll just do as I'm told for the time being."

Brewster knitted his brow and stared off into the distance. The expression on Clay's face had become too painful for him to look upon. He had tried to put himself in his friend's place, to imagine how he would feel if he had to stand by and see Ann taken by another man, but it was too dreadful even to contemplate. "And after that?"

"I don't know. Ask me again in ten or twenty years. Maybe I'll know by then." Clay rammed his hands back into his pockets and looked down the street. "I guess this is where we part company. I can find a hack down the way that'll take me back to the depot."

Brewster nodded. "Right," he said. "Guess I'll see you when I see you." There was nothing more he could say. He stood for a while, watching his colleague's back disappear into the gloom.

"You finally kissed the wrong girl, didn't you, you poor bloody bastard?" he said under his breath, then turned on his heel and headed toward the hotel alone.

Owen and Jessica, as well as the servants, had retired for the evening, and Villanova was alone in the study. He removed paper and ink from the center drawer and composed a wire. He could not send it directly to the one for whom it was intended, but he knew it would arrive eventually and with all due speed, though it might well pass through two or three hands before it reached its ultimate destination.

It read:

HAVE TAKEN CHARGE STOP HAVE NONE OF LACROIX'S RETICENCE STOP TOUCH THE GIRL AGAIN AND YOU WILL DEAL WITH ME STOP (signed) VILLANOVA

13

July

Out of some strange and nameless twilight he came for her in a dream both sweet and savage, erasing those already vague barriers between conscious and unconscious, between reality and madness. Her own longing was mirrored in his eyes. Familiar, welcome magic was in his touch.

She was lost in him, tumbling uncontrollably in the frenzied heat of passion. First he was above her, his cadence creating a hypnotic, almost audible meter as she joyously writhed beneath his weight. Then he was below, his body hard and slick between her legs, guiding her in that same relentless rhythm, her hips as twisting and greedy as his.

His hands were everywhere, the hands of a wizard—stroking, caressing, bewitching her flesh. He breathed words into her ear, words that told her he would never leave her, he would always love her: that she would always be his and that no other man would ever possess her. And the rhythm, the never-ceasing pounding . . .

She was lost in his enchantment—there was no bed, no room, no house, no world. There was only Clay: the welcome heat of his feverish skin, and his kisses—tender at first then intense, bruising. They drank deeply of each other, immersed in liquid flame that burned not with pain, but with an intense and all-consuming passion.

She hovered there, balanced on the brink of the precipice, the cells of her body shivering and jumping like beads of water dancing on hot iron as he loved her, branded her body with his lust and his words as no other man ever had or ever would.

And then she erupted, screaming into ecstasy, ripping at the bedclothes, crying out again and again with wordless, primal shrieks; and the pounding, the pounding . . .

. . . became sharper, defined. Sound. Knuckles against wood. Voices?

She opened her eyes. Voices? One voice: Mrs. Sanders.

"Mrs. Lawrence! Mrs. Lawrence!" It was clearer now. The room took shape around her. Boston. She was in her bed in Boston. Fists beat upon her door. "Mrs. Lawrence, let me in! Are you all right? Please, Mrs. Lawrence!"

"Yes," she managed to croak. She put out a hand to raise herself, and touched damp linen. Her sheets were soaked. She put a hand to her brow, and her fingers came away wet. Outside, rain drummed in torrents against the window glass, and she could hear a distant roll of thunder.

"Are you all right, ma'am?" came Mrs. Sander's voice, calmer now, but still concerned. "You cried out."

"I'm sorry to have disturbed you. Please go back to bed, Mrs. Sanders. It was only a dream." *Only a dream,* she thought as she heard the housekeeper's footsteps fade away. *Only a dream.*

She sat up, lit the lamp beside her bed and brushed

the sodden strands of hair away from her face. She turned the lamp down to shed a dim pool of light over the night table, then slid open the drawer. She withdrew something shiny and golden: a locket.

Turning it over in her hands, she leaned back into the pillows and remembered. . . .

She and Owen had departed that next day for Boston. The will had been read early in the morning at Owen's anxious insistence, and Samuel's instructions had been very much as she had imagined. Owen was disappointed—almost angry, she thought—when the bequests to the family retainers had been so generous, but Jessica had been pleased. Her stepfather had left enough money to Billings and the Sings, as well as his erstwhile cook, Mrs. Lemke, for them to retire and live quite comfortably for the rest of their lives. He'd even left a goodly amount in trust for the higher education of the Sings' daughters.

Villanova was taken care of quite nicely, also. He had been named executor of the estate, and was to administer its disbursal. He himself had been bequeathed sole ownership of Samuel's import/export firm and all its subsidiaries. Owen was livid.

Insofar as Jessica was concerned, Margaret's money was, of course, released to her: all two and a half million—close to three million now because of Samuel's judicious investments on her behalf. The railroad interests were hers, as well as numerous bonds and stocks, and part or sole ownerships in a number of small and intermediate-sized companies manufacturing everything from corsets to artillery.

And, of course, the house and all its contents came to her.

She had never known how much there was, nor how

diverse were her father's interests. It was almost too much for her to assimilate, and afterward, Villanova had taken her aside in the study. He told her that while he knew it must be confusing to her, it might simplify things if she knew that her assets now roughly totaled seventeen million dollars. Counting her mother's money, it was over twenty.

"Give or take a million," he said.

She stood there, her mouth ajar. The figure was beyond her comprehension.

"Mrs. Lawrence, I want you to know that once the accounting process is completed I shall abide by your wishes and your wishes alone, regardless of your husband's desires. When the time comes for a decision to be made, be assured that you will have the final say." At this point he had cleared his throat and looked toward the door to make certain they were not being overheard.

"Frankly, Mrs. Lawrence, I hope you will forgive my bluntness, but I do not care for your husband."

Jessica understood perfectly, not caring for him herself. But she said nothing, simply nodding.

"I believe your father would have wished his business enterprises to progress undisturbed," the slender man continued, "but, as I say, it will be up to you. Should you take that course, I can promise that your yearly income will be more than you can possibly begin to spend, and that your assets will continue to expand."

"I have one question, Mr. Villanova," she stated. "I understand that my father—and you, also, I would assume—were involved in some rather, shall we say . . . undesirable enterprises? The sorts of things that a lady is loathe to mention?" She looked at him flatly, a steely glint in her eyes, and for just a fraction of a moment, he thought he was standing there with Samuel.

He hadn't realized she knew about Samuel's other interests. The Pinkertons—they must have told her what they suspected but could not prove. (And would not be able to prove. He had taken care of that.)

He chose his words carefully before he spoke. "I can promise you, Mrs. Lawrence, that any enterprise you choose to retain will be pristine—strictly above board—so long as I control it in your name. I know it is what Samuel would have wished."

"Very well." There was really nothing to think over. Villanova was a brilliant man, and although he was surely as much a criminal as had been her stepfather, he was infinitely more trustworthy than was her husband. She thought of how many people might be put out of work if she were to sell everything, as she knew Owen would want to do. And she could not possibly begin to take over their supervision herself. Villanova would look after her interests, and very well too, if only out of respect for Samuel's memory. In this, she decided, she could trust him.

"I don't feel we have any need to wait, Mr. Villanova," she said, straightening. "I believe I can tell you right now that I wish you to take over for me and continue in that position, providing things are run on the up and up. Do we have an understanding?"

"We do, indeed, Mrs. Lawrence." He reached for her hand, squeezing it first, then kissing it. She was in his camp now. "As far as your recent . . . unpleasantness is concerned, please have no further fears. I have seen to the matter myself, and you will not be bothered by . . . by any more vulgar people, if you understand my meaning."

Owen appeared in the doorway, his nose in the air, tiny pince-nez glasses perched precariously. "It seems to me, Mr. Villanova," he sniffed, "that every time I walk into this room I find you holding my wife's hand."

287

Jessica pulled away and glared at her husband. "Oh, don't be such an ass, Owen," she blurted before stalking from the room.

Both men stared after her, flabbergasted.

The train ride back to Boston had been uneventful, although its circumstances were somewhat curious. Apparently Owen had decided that while it was too pretentious and expensive for his wife to travel west by private car, it was only fitting and proper that they journey home together in the private Pullman.

"Very well, Owen," she'd said, never looking up from her packing. She was putting away all the dresses she'd brought with her. Mrs. Sing had managed to find her three very nice dresses in proper mourning black, each a perfect fit, and she would wear these until she arrived in Massachusetts.

"I must admit I prefer the comfort of the private car," she continued, matter-of-factly, "but I am telling you now that while I will share the parlor with you if I must, I shall sleep alone." She carried on folding clothes.

Owen stiffly rose to his full height, hardly a towering figure. "Madam," he demanded, "am I to understand that you would deny me my rights as your husband?"

She closed the latch on one of the big cases and started on the next one. "That is absolutely correct."

"Why," Owen sputtered, "why, I could divorce you for that, madam!" He was far more incensed at the indignity of having to spend another long journey sleeping in a first-class berth than in being deprived of what little pleasure he took in his wife's body.

"Fine," Jessica continued, rearranging garments, smoothing wrinkles, never looking up. "Divorce me, Owen. Divorce my money."

He fell silent, and without seeing it, she knew his doughy face was turning pinker and pinker. She let him stew a few minutes before making a suggestion. "You may not realize it, Owen, but we now own several private cars, not just one. I don't suppose we should have any difficulty convincing the powers that be to connect a pair of cars instead of a single. Unless, of course, you would prefer an upper berth."

There was no further discussion on the matter. They took two cars, Jessica insisting that hers be the last hooked to the train. ("I will not have a stream of porters parading through my chambers every time you order a snack from the dining car," she had declared.) She brought along a box of books from Samuel's library, and spent those long days on the train reading. She found she was not up to perusing anything too sentimental or romantic, so she delved deeply into adventure novels, rereading *The Adventures of Tom Sawyer* and Bret Harte's *Outcasts of Poker Flat* among others.

And when at last they arrived in Boston, she immediately made arrangements to spend the following weekend in the country with Daniel and Martha Follett.

Once there, she had thrown caution to the wind and ridden—ridden astride—in direct opposition to Owen's expressed wishes. She talked Cousin Daniel into saddling a strong Morgan gelding for her.

"Not a sidesaddle!" she'd exclaimed when he led the bay out the first time. "A real saddle, please, Daniel? I intend to take some jumps today!"

Daniel looked at her as if she had lost her mind, but retacked the horse for her anyway, being too much of a gentleman to argue. She had spent a glorious afternoon chasing through the hills; leaping ditches, rails, and hedges on the sturdy gelding. When she returned later in the day, flushed from her ride, a worried Martha had taken her aside.

"Jessica dear, please! What are people going to think? What is Owen going to say? If he finds out, he might not let you come again! Besides, you might have been hurt!" Martha was obviously and genuinely distressed. Not only did she and Daniel look forward to Jessica's company, but she was the most enthusiastically rapt audience they had yet come across for their piano and violin duets.

She smiled at Martha's last comment, in her mind contrasting a few easy three-foot jumps (over neatly trimmed hedges and tidy stone walls) to plummeting down the sheer face of a canyon wall. Her grin widened, much to Martha's dismay.

"Jessica!" she cried, "what's come over you?"

But Jessica had only laughed and hugged her. "Oh, don't worry, Martha, Owen won't stop me doing anything anymore." *Almost anything,* she'd thought, thinking of the one thing she wanted above all others, and could never have.

In town, there was little to do. She drifted aimlessly through the house and the gardens, trying to come up with some grand idea, some perfect project to take up all her time and her thoughts, but so far, none had been forthcoming.

Her personal maid, Miriam, had vanished not long after Jessica and Owen's departure from Denver. Mrs. Sanders told her that the girl had simply gone out to do some marketing one day, and had never come back, nor had she sent for her things. It was all quite a mystery, Mrs. Sanders said. The police had been called in, but couldn't find a clue, and the staff was buzzing with the rumor that she'd run off with some man. Jessica, who now realized that Miriam had been one of Nathaniel Kane's minions, did nothing to deprive them of their happily sordid speculations.

She had stopped crying now. At first, she had wept every night and sporadically during the days, often bursting into tears with little or no provocation. But now she was gaining more and more control, and kept her sorrow buried, channeling it into a deep and abiding hatred for everything smacking of Owen.

At least she hadn't been forced to endure too much of his company since their return. She had informed him, in no uncertain terms, that from now on he was not welcome in her chambers for any reason (save possibly the house burning down), and that her door would be locked. He had taken it fairly well, all things considered. He seemed to be finding his recreation elsewhere, as he had spent more nights away from home than he had in his own rooms. Jessica could not have been more delighted.

And there was something else that gave her secret delight. Her menses had not yet come, and she was beginning to feel woozy in the mornings. She prayed that what she suspected was true—perhaps she would never have Clay, but she could bear his child, the product of their love. She hoped it would be a boy, and that he would grow up as fine and strong and handsome as his father.

Then yesterday, a parcel had come for her. She'd been out in the garden, sitting in a wicker lawn chair and staring abstractedly into the distance, when Mrs. Sanders jarred her out of her reverie. Materializing at Jessica's elbow, the housekeeper held out a small package wrapped in brown paper and tied with string.

"Postman brought this, missus," she announced, handing it over and asking if Mrs. Lawrence might not like some lemonade. Mrs. Lawrence had admitted that, yes, lemonade would be lovely, thank you, and Mrs. Sanders had gone off to fetch it.

There was no return address on the package, but she recognized the handwriting that spelled her name. A wave of shivers raced up her spine as she carefully removed the twine and peeled back the paper.

Inside was a little flat box, which she opened with trembling fingers. There was no note, no message of any kind. But wrapped safely in cotton was a slim, shimmering locket on a long, fine chain, both flawlessly crafted in brushed gold. Carefully, she opened it. On the left hand side was an etching, tiny and precisely detailed, of a turtledove. And on the right was engraved the notation *Song of Songs 2:10-13.* Below that, the single initial *C.*

She didn't have to look up the verses. She knew them by heart. She clutched the locket to her bosom and whispered the words, her eyes welling with the tears she thought she had left behind.

"'For, lo,'" she whispered, "'the winter is past, the rain is over and gone; the flowers appear on the earth; the time of the singing of birds is come, and the voice of the turtle is heard in our land . . .'"

When Mrs. Sanders returned with the lemonade, she found her mistress weeping helplessly, collapsed in a weak, black-skirted bundle on the lawn.

And now this dream: her belly still thrummed with sweet aftershocks. His memory had come to her like an incubus, finding her a willing victim for its insistent and welcome demands. She slipped out of bed, stripped off the soaked nightdress and donned a fresh one, pausing to stand before the rain-streaked window and stare down at the dark wet garden before climbing back into bed.

Again, she picked up his gift. She passed the delicate chain over her head, lifting her long hair to let the clasp rest against the back of her neck, and dropped the locket down the front of her gown. It nestled between her breasts, over her heart.

Only then did she turn out the light and ease back into the cool, dry sheets on the other side of the mattress. She spent the rest of the night in a deep and dreamless sleep.

On the other side of town, in a far less fashionable district than that in which his wife lay slumbering, Owen Lawrence had found shelter from the storm. Outside it was raining hard and the streets were full of water, but here it was warm and dry.

He came here often. It was one of his favorite haunts, and they kept him in mind when they brought in the new girls. There was always someone new and young and fresh for him every couple of months. He paid Mama Sugar a great deal of money to keep him in girls and to keep her mouth shut. He kept her on a retainer, in the same way he did his firm's attorney. All he had to do was drop by, and he would be accommodated at any time of the night or day.

And they had promised him a new girl tonight: fourteen years old, Mama Sugar had said, and a virgin. His mouth had been watering all day. There were other places he frequented on his nightly haunts, but Mama Sugar's house (which he visited several times a week) held the cream of the crop.

He stood in the parlor, rocking on his heels, an anticipatory smirk on his round face. The place was empty tonight, the plush and neatly kept parlor completely deserted except for Owen. Probably due to the inclement weather, he decided. Mama Sugar must have even gone so far as to give her girls the night off, as none were in evidence. The street outside had been empty, too, of anything except torrents of rain. But he knew the madam would have everything ready for him. Not even a hurricane could keep him away from a new girl, and Mama Sugar would know that.

Double doors slid open. He stepped forward, expecting Mama Sugar, her huge white, barely covered bosoms extending over her fat belly like giant bags of aspic, smiling a big painted smile and ready to usher him to the back room.

But it was not she. Instead, it was the new bouncer, Big Roy Dean. Big Roy had been in the house the last two times Owen had visited, and the tall blond man frightened him just a little. When he'd asked Mama Sugar why she'd hired him, she shrugged and looked away.

"Ah didn't hire him, Mistah Lawrence," she'd explained in her syrupy drawl. "He was jist sent down."

It took a while for Owen to realize that this had to mean that Mama Sugar was not the sole proprietor of her establishment. She must have higher-ups to whom she had to answer. It was curious, but not really very important. What *was* important was that Mama Sugar always found what he wanted, and let him do exactly as he pleased.

Big Roy stood in the doorway, scowling at him. "Mama Sugar's busy," he said, staring at Owen with his cold gray eyes. There was no reason for it, but Owen suddenly felt chilled.

"What's that to me?" he blurted. "If she's been detained, I'm perfectly able to find the way to my room." He did, indeed, have his own room at Mama Sugar's. It was the primary luxury he had afforded himself after marrying Jessica's money. He paid enough for its use, and it was certainly unfit for use by any of the madam's other clients. It was all his.

Big Roy shoved the pocket doors all the way open

294

and stood under the arch, his arms outstretched and his hands clamped to the moulding on either side, his body formed into a huge and menacing T. He scowled, looking Owen up and down before dropping his hands to his sides.

"OK," he growled, then stepped to one side. "She said the girl's back there already."

Owen stepped forward to pass him, hoping to scurry by quickly; the bouncer was making him more nervous by the minute. But as he passed Big Roy, he felt a huge restraining hand on his shoulder.

Owen stopped short.

"Mama Sugar's a little too free with you for my mind, Mr. Lawrence. You take it easy on that girl, you hear me?" His eyes were as cold and as hard as new tombstones.

Owen could not answer. His lips and tongue seemed to be frozen. He felt himself nod slowly, jerkily.

Big Roy released his arm and walked away, dismissing him.

It was a moment before Owen began to breathe again. And then, the bouncer out of sight, he began to grow angry. *What nerve,* he stormed. *What unmitigated* gall *that creature had to try and intimidate Owen Lawrence!* Obviously he had no idea of the amount of money Owen paid to this establishment each and every month like clockwork (never a tardy payment!) for young girls, clean girls, and the privilege of doing whatever he damn well pleased with them!

He would speak to Mama Sugar again, and firmly. He'd find out just who in the hell had "sent down" this Mr. Big Roy Dean, and he'd by God and Merry Christmas go over everybody's head and have the impertinent sonofabitch fired! Flogged through the streets! Oh, for the days when one could have a scoundrel drawn and quartered!

He'd worked up quite a head of steam by the time he got to the end of the long, narrow hallway and put his hand out to touch the last door. His room was far in the back, where the noise would not disturb the other customers. He took a deep breath, smiled and turned the knob.

The gas was turned down low, as it always was when he entered. He liked to turn it up slowly, especially with a new girl, exquisitely drawing out those first few moments of discovery. He removed his coat and collar, hanging them primly on hooks near the door, then put his fingers on the gas jet's valve and twisted slightly.

The room—his room—was windowless and free of decoration. The walls were whitewashed plaster, flecked here and there by rusty stains. And, as always, the room was stripped nearly bare of furnishings. There was no couch, no bed, no wardrobe, chest, or chiffonier. There was only a long slim table along one wall, covered with shadowy, indiscernible objects, and a single armchair which sat in one corner, facing out into the center of the chamber. He twisted the valve a bit farther.

He could see her outline now in the dimness. Yes, she had been prepared for him. She was there in the middle of the room, her hands high over her head and bound together. She was suspended from the high ceiling by an iron chain that hooked to the thongs encircling her slender wrists.

Owen licked his lips and rubbed at his trousers. Yes, it was going to be a good night. Gradually, savoring every moment, he turned the gas jet up until the room was full of light, and walked toward the girl. Her back was to him, her head hanging down. He scowled, hoping Mama Sugar hadn't doped her too much: a great part of his pleasure would come from the expression on her face and the sounds she would make.

He reached out and turned her toward him. It was easy; she was a tiny thing, and most of her slight weight was taken by the chain suspending her. Long straight blue-black hair hung down, obscuring her face. He put out his hand to tip up her chin, but paused. He looked down at her slender body, already stripped naked for him, and dropped his fingers to her small high breasts. Lightly, he scraped the edge of his nail across one nipple. When he saw it contract and harden in response, he smiled. She was conscious enough.

He raised her chin and pushed the sleek shiny hair from her features. It was revealed to him, golden and oval, and she moaned pitifully—the whimper of a caged animal who has given up all hope of freedom—as she opened her black, almond-shaped eyes. They were dilated with the drug, but she was not so far gone that she could not feel terror and hopelessness. A tear welled from one eye and cascaded down Owen's fingers.

Immediately he dropped her head, which sagged again upon her breast, and pulled a handkerchief from his pocket, scrubbing the last trace of moisture from his hand.

"Too soon for tears, my little jewel," he pronounced, speaking aloud for the first time. "We've not yet begun.

"Now I want you to know," he continued as he crossed the room toward the narrow table, "that I will do nothing to seriously hurt you. You may even grow to enjoy my little visits—to look forward to them, as I shall look forward to visiting you." He ran his fingers over the array of equipment there, randomly stroking devices of leather and metal and ivory and wood until his fingers met the implement of choice.

It was about two feet long and multilashed, with each leather thong ending in a small lead bead. The lashes were stained a dark, rusty brown. It was his favorite.

With his free hand, he slowly unbuttoned his trousers and slipped his fingers inside, touching himself. A smile spread on his face. Yes, it was going to be a very good night, indeed. He decided to forgo the formalities—there would be no need to sit in his chair and stare at her, anticipate her, using his hands to prime himself before he began. Maybe later, the second or third time. But not now.

"Do you speak any English, dear?" he said, and raising the cat-o'-nine-tails, stepped toward her.

The girl was wonderful, the best Mama Sugar had ever found for him. Her thin shrieks and garbled pleas were music to his ears. He had barely touched her with the whip before she began to cry out, and he was just about ready, he thought. Just about ready to cast aside the whip and drop his trousers; spread her legs as she hung there and impale her—just once, and very hard— and end her days of maidenhood.

But first, just one more row of neat, hard welts . . . He raised the lash once more and the terrified girl screamed again, shrilly. Owen grinned a mad, adrenaline laced grin and brought the leather down.

But it did not strike flesh.

A hand, massive and broad knuckled, came out of nowhere to catch his wrist, forcing him to drop the lash. He jumped back, startled, but Big Roy Dean held him fast. He saw Mama Sugar scurry into the room and past them, her immense breasts shuddering beneath her rumpled, dirty kimono as she trotted toward the weeping girl.

"What's the meaning of this!" Owen demanded,

simultaneously shocked, outraged, and terribly embarrassed.

"Outta my hands, Mistah Lawrence," she mumbled, avoiding his eyes as she untied the now hysterical girl and lowered her to the floor. "Nothin' Ah kin do about it."

Big Roy jerked him to one side. The bouncer's grip on his wrist was cutting off his circulation, and he was losing the feeling in his hand. But as frightened as he was, Owen was still livid with the outrage of being subjected to such unprecedented indignity.

"Let go of me, you fool!" he shouted with more command than he knew he possessed.

Amazingly, Big Roy did let him go, although he stood his ground and looked not the least intimidated. However, Owen felt he had won the point. Seething, he stooped to retrieve his cat-o'-nine-tails, now spattered with fresh blood.

"Get her outta here and get her cleaned up!" Big Roy barked at the harried and obviously frightened madam.

"And you!" He turned on Owen, now pink-faced, clutching his lash, and on the verge of a tantrum. "You get yer hand outta yer pants and yer ass outta this house!"

That did it. Owen, mad with embarrassment and indignation, raised the flail with the intent to whip a little respect into the filthy uncouth lout.

It was the worst and last mistake he would ever make.

Big Roy caught his arm again, wrenching the flail from his clenched fingers and throwing it to the floor. Owen watched the whip's course as it flew through the air, then slowly raised his widening, now horrified eyes to meet Big Roy's cold gray gaze. Big Roy was smiling.

"Thanks, Mr. Lawrence," he hissed. "That was just about all the excuse I needed." Still gripping Owen's arm, he lifted the little man off his feet and flung him high against the wall. He let go at the last moment, and Owen crashed into the plaster full force, sliding to the floor. He landed on his hands and knees, more terrified than he'd thought humanly possible.

Coat and collar forgotten, he scrambled out into the corridor and made for the street door as fast as his short shaking legs would carry him, stumbling and careening into walls. Behind him came Big Roy, his face set into a grim smile; striding purposefully, single-mindedly after him.

Owen made it to the front door, mindless with fear, scratching and clawing at the knob until he finally managed to turn it and shove the door open. He could hear Big Roy's steady bootsteps coming up behind him. *Sweet Judas Priest,* shrieked an alien, frantic voice inside his skull, *has the whole world gone mad?* He lurched out into the night.

The street was deserted, sheeted with rain. There was no one to help him. He slipped and fell in the mud, got up and fell again. He was weeping with fear, his hysterical cries rendered mute by the crashing thunder. Then he felt Big Roy's hand at the back of his sodden shirt.

His bladder emptied as Big Roy effortlessly lifted him into the air and tossed him into a deep puddle in the pitted road. Owen flailed blindly as the bouncer crouched over him, one knee on his flabby chest. The next to the last thing he saw was the cold, flinty glint of gray eyes, glaring at him through the pouring rain.

The last thing was the huge palm of Big Roy's hand as it pushed his face beneath the muddy water.

*   *   *

Big Roy waited for quite a while after the last bubbles rose before he released his grip. He gave Owen's chest a final shove with his knee, then stood up. The storm showed no sign of lessening, and water coursed over him, rinsing away the last spatters of mud he'd picked up as Owen struggled.

He looked down at the body stoically. "Well," he muttered as he ran broad fingers through the soaking cap of yellow hair plastered to his forehead, "guess that oughta square me with Villanova. Didn't look forward to it much, but after meetin' ya, it got to be a real pleasure."

He gave one last hard kick to the dead man's rib cage, then walked back up the street to Mama Sugar's.

It was a little after ten the next morning when they came to the house to tell her. She was out in the garden again, sipping at a cool glass of iced tea, taking advantage of the sunshine before the fullness of the afternoon heat arrived. She had been quite ill earlier in the morning, but by now had fully recovered, and was wondering if she should attempt another watercolor of the summer blooms. Somehow, all those she had begun since her return had turned into looming red rocks and desert sage.

She heard voices at the far end of the wide, manicured lawn, at the top of the slope near the house, and looked up to see Mrs. Sanders bustling toward her, two gentlemen in her wake. Mrs. Sanders looked quite upset. As they drew nearer, she recognized one of the men as Duane Moore, from her husband's offices. She had met Mr. Moore and his wife on several occasions. Both of them were churchy, stuffy sort of people. The other man, slim, dark, and very tall, was a stranger to her.

Jessica rose to greet them.

Mrs. Sanders reached her first. "Mrs. Lawrence," she puffed, "these two men say they have to talk to you." She lowered her voice. "They said it was urgent. They wouldn't wait for me to announce them proper."

"It's all right, Mrs. Sanders," Jessica said. "Thank you." She turned toward the callers as the stalwart housekeeper marched back up the hill toward the house.

"Good morning, gentlemen. Mr. Moore." She nodded toward Owen's business associate, then indicated his companion. "I don't believe I am acquainted with this gentleman. If you are looking for my husband, I'm afraid he's not presently at home."

Mr. Moore, a darkly bearded bookish sort, spoke. "I know that, Mrs. Lawrence. It . . . it was you we wanted to see." He looked quite nervous and upset. Jessica waited patiently for him to continue.

"Please, Mrs. Lawrence, won't you sit down?" He took a step toward her, as if to take her arm and guide her back to her chair, but she stepped away and seated herself primly, looking from one man to the next.

Mr. Moore cleared his throat. "This . . . this is Inspector Stevens, Mrs. Lawrence," he faltered, gesturing at the tall dark man. "He is with the Boston police. He . . . we . . ."

Staring quizzically at Mr. Moore, Jessica put her hand out to Inspector Stevens. "How do you do, sir?" she said politely. "To what do I owe your visit? Have you come with news of our runaway maid?"

Stevens, dressed in a dark business suit (not like a policeman at all, she thought), stood very straight, holding his hat behind his back with both hands. "I wouldn't know anything about that, ma'am." He cleared his throat. "I'm afraid I have some unhappy news for you, Mrs. Lawrence," he began. His gentle voice was in direct opposition to his starched and somewhat threatening demeanor. "It's about your husband."

Her fingers clutched at the wicker arm of her chair. "I don't understand," she said, in a calm voice that belied the icy prickles she felt working their way up her spine. "What has happened? Has there been an accident?"

The inspector sat down in the chair next to hers. Mr. Moore had turned away, and was staring at his black hat as he turned it over and over in front of him.

Stevens put his hand over hers as it gripped the chair's arm. This beautiful young woman was already dressed in black—her father had recently passed away, Moore had told him on the way over. And now he had to add this to her burden of misery. He looked into her deep blue eyes and took a breath. He hated this part of his job.

"Mrs. Lawrence, I'm sorry to be the one to tell you this, but I'm afraid your husband has met with a terrible misfortune."

She stared at him blankly, her knuckles whitening beneath his comforting fingers. She opened her mouth, and for a moment no sound came out. Then finally, she managed, "What—?"

From experience, Stevens knew it was better just to plunge ahead and get it over with, no matter how difficult. He did. "As you know, we had a very hard rain last night. Many of the streets were in near-flood condition. We're not yet certain as to the exact circumstances, but it appears that your husband was the victim of robbery. There is every indication that the thieves knocked him senseless and left him in the street. He must have fallen into a pool of water." He refrained from telling her that her husband's body had been found in one of the seedier parts of town. There was no need to add to her grief.

"He was drowned, Mrs. Lawrence. We found his coat about a block away. His money was gone, but we did find a business card, and got in touch with Mr. Moore." He looked toward the businessman, who stepped forward, nodding sympathetically.

Jessica pulled her fingers from beneath Stevens's and covered her face with her hands, falling back into the chair's cushions. The sun suddenly felt very hot.

"Oh dear!" she heard Mr. Moore blurt. "Oh dear! She's going to swoon! My wife always does this before she swoons! I'll get the housekeeper!"

She was vaguely aware of the sound of his retreating footsteps as he trotted toward the house, and then everything swam into darkness.

The next thing of which she was aware was a spinning of colors in her head and a burning sensation. She swatted at something in front of her face: Mrs. Sanders's hand, holding the smelling salts.

She coughed, rubbing at her eyes, and sat up. Three faces hovered over hers, huge and looming. "I'm all right," she choked, "I'm fine." *Just get away from me, all of you,* she wanted to scream.

The faces pulled back and assumed normal proportions. She was still in the garden. She couldn't have been out for more than a minute or two.

"Would you like me to contact your church, Mrs. Lawrence?" Moore offered. "Perhaps they could send—"

She cut him off. There would be no clergy, not now. "No thank you, Mr. Moore. Please do not trouble yourself." Then, as an afterthought, she added, "But perhaps you could see to the . . . the arrangements for me? I'm afraid I shouldn't know where to start."

The businessman brightened, relieved to have something to do. "Certainly, ma'am. I'll take care of

304

everything. You won't be bothered with any of the details."

Inspector Stevens stood up. "If you're all right now, Mrs. Lawrence, I'll be taking my leave. But I'd like to say once more how sorry I am."

"You're very kind, Inspector," Jessica said, laying her left hand over her heart. "Very kind. And if you will excuse me, also, Mr. Moore, I think I should like to be alone for a time. I'm sure you understand."

Moore nodded and touched her right hand, as it rested on the arm of the chair. "Of course, of course. The Lord moves in mysterious ways, Mrs. Lawrence."

"Indeed he does, Mr. Moore. Indeed he does."

She watched them tread back up the lawn and disappear around the side of the house, guided by Mrs. Sanders. When they were gone, she lifted her hand from the fabric of her bodice and slipped her fingers beneath the collar. She drew forth the locket, warm from its resting place at her bosom, where it had been pressed by her hand.

She held it to her lips as she turned to face the west. "Mysterious ways, indeed," she whispered.

14

August

And here she was again: in the same private Pullman, rattling along the tracks through the darkness. But this time it was different. This time she was free, and on her way to Clay. She could only pray that he would still want her as much as she did him. She rubbed absently at her ring finger, now naked of any ornament. Her first act upon entering the car had been to slip Owen's ring from her hand and drop it into the bottom of one of the dresser drawers.

She had written the Pinkerton National Detective Agency and had received a terse, businesslike letter in reply: they were very sorry, they said, but they were not at liberty to disclose the location of any persons or persons who might or might not be in their employ, and so on.

She understood. It had been foolish of her to think that they might give her any information—they had the lives of their agents to protect. And they certainly would have no way of knowing why she wanted to contact him—she could not have written such things in a letter that would, more than likely, be opened and responded to by some harried, nameless clerk.

And then she had remembered Brewster, and resurrecting her handbag, found his address and wrote to him in Chicago. The mails were slow, but at last she received a reply, not from Brewster, but from his wife.

My dear Mrs. Lawrence,

You are probably surprised to receive this letter from me and not my husband. He is away at present, and I must confess that when the postman brought your letter (on scented stationery of a variety undeniably feminine), it was less than twenty-four hours before I was forced by my curious (and somewhat wicked) nature to open it myself. I was pleased to see that it was from you, and not another infatuated chorus girl. Not that Charles pursues them, you understand—he is just so naturally charming that they seem to gravitate to him.

My husband has spoken of you often in relation to a job of work he undertook recently, and more often in relation to his great friend Clay McCallister, whose whereabouts you desire to know. I am sorry to tell you that I do not have that information. Most of the time, I do not even know my own husband's whereabouts while he is working. However, he is due to return within the next few days (or so I am told), and I shall pass your letter along to him at the first opportunity.

The letter, written in a beautiful and flowery hand, went on for several pages, finally ending,

Once again, please let your heart rest in the knowledge that I am certain my husband will do everything in his power to put you in touch with our friend Clayton. I do hope to meet you someday, as Charles tells me (repeatedly, I might add) that we should be great friends, and I am sure he is right. He usually is.

Until such time I remain

> Very truly yours,
> Ann (Halliday) Brewster

And Ann was true to her word. Within a week, there was a telegram from Brewster, composed in typical Brewster style:

FEAR NOT STOP CAVALRY ON ITS WAY STOP ARRIVING BOSTON 14 AUGUST STOP BE PREPARED TO TRAVEL STOP TRUST YOU HAVE GUEST ROOM STOP (signed) BREWSTER

He arrived on her doorstep that afternoon, blond and impish and full of mystery, and she had never been so happy to see anyone in her life.

"My dear Mrs. Lawrence," he'd grinned as he patted her hand, "don't ask so many questions! Just pack your bags and be ready to leave tomorrow morning. I've made all the arrangements."

Throughout dinner and the evening, he had avoided her questions about Clay, continually telling her not to worry, to rest easy, and then changing the subject (always) to Ann. By the evening's end, she knew more about his wife than she did about herself, but she still knew nothing of Clay.

When it was time to retire, she finally got a hint, though not much more than that, of what was to come.

"Can you be ready to leave by eight, my dear?" he'd asked, mellowed somewhat by a bottle of excellent brandy she'd resurrected from Owen's wine cellar.

"Hope you don't mind," he continued, "but I told a little lie in your name today. Told the powers that be at the depot that I was your agent, and that you had ordered your Pullman hooked up behind the first engine headed south in the morning."

South, she'd thought. *He's in the South. How far in the South? Virginia? The Carolinas? Georgia? Was he on assignment?*

Brewster poured himself another brandy. "He's packed it up, you see. He's gone home to Turtle Creek."

Jessica, standing in the doorway, put a hand out to lean against the wall. "Turtle Creek?"

"In Maryland." He swirled the dark fragrant liquid in the crystal snifter cupped in his hand. "And that's all you're getting from me tonight, young lady." His grin was broad, if somewhat lopsided. "Lord, I love a mystery."

She shook her head. He had this all staged in his mind, like a play, and she wasn't going to get anything more from him tonight. She was glad she'd joined him for the first glass of Napoleon. It was her only chance at a good night's sleep.

With a certain reluctance, she excused herself and went up to her rooms, leaving him to his brandy and cigarettes and plotting.

The next morning they were headed south. After the initial flurry of activity subsided and they were clear of the station, Brewster (who miraculously seemed none the worse for having polished off better than half a bottle of Napoleon the night before) happily slouched in one of the drawing room's deep chairs.

"Couldn't get us an express," he admitted, "so I'm afraid there'll be a bit of stopping and starting involved. But we ought to be there by midday

309

tomorrow." He looked around at the plush fittings, the paintings, the frescoed ceiling. "I'll have to get one of these for myself someday. Only way to travel. By the way, I told another lie. Told them I was your bodyguard. Hope you don't mind if I sleep on your couch tonight. Unfortunately, the Company's not paying the freight for this trip." He looked a little uncomfortable, and Jessica put him at ease immediately.

"Mr. Brewster," she smiled, "I am so indebted to your for your kindness. If you wish, you can take the bedroom and *I'll* take the divan." *And if things work out, I'll give you the bloody Pullman,* she mused.

He grinned at her. "No need to go quite *that* far, Mrs. Lawrence. But would you do me the great favor of dropping the 'Mister'? Even my wife calls me Brewster half the time."

"Only if you will call me Jessica." If she never again heard anyone call her Mrs. Lawrence, it would be too soon.

"All right, Jessica. You have a bargain." He crossed his arms in front of him happily and stuck his legs out into the center of the room.

"Does he . . . does Clay know we're coming?" she ventured.

"He knows *I'm* coming. I'm saving you for a surprise."

"Oh." She looked down at her hands, suddenly unsure. "But what . . . what if he doesn't want—"

"Oh, I shouldn't worry. He'll want to see you." *And that,* he thought, *is more than likely the greatest understatement of my illustrious career.*

"Last night you said he quit the Pinkertons. Why?"

"He told me he decided he was too old for our particular line of endeavor. That's what he *told* me. But my guess is that it had more than a little to do with you, Jessica."

She raised a brow.

"His . . . time with you. I imagine it made him think about, well, a great number of things to which he hadn't previously given much consideration. Things he'd taken for granted. And one of those was Turtle Creek." He pulled out his cigarette case. "May I?"

"Please do," she said. *And please do continue,* she thought.

He lit a cigarette before he went on. "Turtle Creek's been in the McCallister family for generations. And his father, the Captain, has always been disappointed that Clayton never evinced any interest in taking it over. He's an only child, you know."

"No, I didn't know that." When Brewster looked at her inquisitively, she added, "I'm afraid I don't know much of anything. You see, the time we had together was so brief, and . . ."

He could well imagine. "No need to explain, Jessica," he cut in, waving his hand. "The upshot is that our Clayton had a sudden yen to go home and pick up the familial reins, as it were. It's just as well. He didn't have the heart for a life of intrigue anymore. Anyway, I call it intrigue. Ann calls it 'big boys playing at very dangerous little boy games.' I guess Clay finally took her words to heart."

And now it was night. Nearly morning, in fact. Brewster was out front, snoring, snuggled cozily on the parlor couch, and she was tossing and turning in her bed, plagued by an endless stream of what-ifs. What if he had changed his mind? What if he should see her in a different light now that she wasn't a part of some

311

glamorous espionage? What if he didn't want the baby? Even the rails sang it as they rolled south: what if, what if, what if, what if . . .

Clay did not meet them at the station. "I didn't tell him when I'd be coming, only that I would be," Brewster grinned mischievously. "I imagine he could use a surprise."

I just hope this is the one he wants, she thought, and stepped down to the platform.

After making arrangements about Jessica's Pullman, Brewster hired a buggy and they set off. About an hour later, he turned off the dusty country road into a sycamore-lined lane. Massive granite markers were set on either side of the entrance, the words "Turtle Creek" engraved deeply in each. Jessica had clenched and unclenched her hands so many times that they were nearly bloodless.

Hardly unaware of her agitation, Brewster remarked, "I shouldn't be nervous, my dear. If anyone should be anxious, it should be yours truly. Clayton will most likely have me drawn and quartered for not alerting him in time to hire a brass band for your welcome."

But it didn't help. She was still riddled with doubts. It was all too important, more important than anything ever had been or ever would be.

Through the tall trees that bordered and canopied the winding estate road, she could see horses— beautiful English Thoroughbreds, fat and sleek— grazing in the fields. Some of the mares had foals at their sides. Then the drive turned toward the right, and the trees parted, revealing a huge three-story brick house, its front lined with towering white pillars. Brewster reined in the horse and helped Jessica down from the buggy.

As she straightened her skirts, a tall, handsome, older gentleman came striding around the side of the mansion. He was quite distinguished in a casual sort of way, and looked very much as she would have imagined Clay might appear in thirty years.

When he recognized Brewster, he grinned and waved. "Brewster, you scalawag!" he called, marching toward them. "Clay told me you were coming down to see us! Good to see you, boy, good to see you!" He threw his arms around Jessica's affable escort and hugged him as a man might greet his own son.

"By God, you're looking well! And how's that little wife of yours? When are you going to bring her down to visit me again? It's still the talk of the county, you know—the great Ann Halliday, singing in the parlor at Turtle Creek."

And then he turned to Jessica, dressed in black and standing nervously nearby. He stepped away from Brewster, his eyes widening in appreciation. "And who might this vision be?" he asked.

"Captain McCallister, I should like you to meet Mrs. Jessica Lawrence, a good friend of both mine and Clayton's."

The captain reached for her hand and kissed it gallantly. "Charmed, absolutely charmed, Mrs. Lawrence," he glowed. He shot a glance at Brewster, as if to ask, *Is this the one? Is she the reason?*

Brewster nodded almost imperceptibly.

"It's a pleasure to welcome you to Turtle Creek, madam. A genuine pleasure. Perhaps you'd like to see a bit of the place?"

"Y-Yes," Jessica stuttered, taken somewhat aback. "Certainly. It's beautiful! I'd love to see it all, as soon as—" *As soon as I've seen Clay,* she was going to say.

"Wonderful!" the captain enthused, cutting her off.

"Hey! Geordie!"

A towheaded boy of about fifteen was coming around the drive on foot. At the captain's shout, he looked up, grinning, and came trotting toward them. "Yessir?" he asked somewhat breathlessly as he looked from the captain to Brewster to Jessica, then back again at the captain.

"Geordie, this is Mrs. Lawrence, and she'd like to see the loafing paddocks."

"Oh, really, Mr.—I mean Captain McCallister, I really should—"

"Nonsense, my dear!" he beamed. "You just follow Geordie, here. They're very interesting, the loafing paddocks. Your friend Brewster and I, we'll just wait for you. Take your time, now, and don't give us a second thought."

She looked to Brewster for assistance. He would know how badly she wanted to see Clay—and only Clay—at this moment. But he was no help. He only grinned that infuriating grin at her and waved her away. "Go along now, Jessica. You'll have plenty of time for other things later."

She felt a tug at her sleeve. "This way, ma'am," the boy said, and reluctantly she followed him, turning back every few steps to look at Brewster and the captain, now immersed in some story or other as they walked into the great house.

The lane they followed wound downhill through the trees, and emerged in a large clearing that was the site of not just a stable, but a complex of outbuildings.

"Them's the main stables," the lad said proudly, pointing to a long low white building on their left. "Thirty box stalls in there. And down the hill's the foalin' barn and the yearling shed."

The yearling shed was far from the structure one would have surmised from its title: it was a long sturdy building of stone, probably original to the estate, with its own set of whitewashed paddocks.

Geordie waved toward the left. "Over here's the stallion barn, and the hay barn, of course. 'N down here's the trainin' barn." They were a little farther down the hill now. "For the two 'n three year olds. Trainin' track's over farther to the east."

It was all incredibly impressive. She hadn't had any idea Clay came from all of this. But where was he? She wanted to get this tour over with and get back to the house, to Clay. She had to find out if he still—

"Loafin' paddocks are down this way, miss," the boy said, leading her around the curve, toward the other side of the training barn.

Yes, she thought, *All right, let's look at them and get back to—*

Just then, they turned the corner, and she saw him.

He was in the nearest of the six paddocks, working a tall chestnut filly on the end of a longe line, teasing her into a smooth, effortless trot as she circled him. He was hatless and wearing a light blue wash shirt. His tight tan riding breeches were tucked into scuffed leather boots, knee high and flat heeled. There was a riding crop stuck into the top of the right boot, and its business end rubbed against his thigh as he worked the filly. His dark walnut hair glinted in the soft Maryland sun, and she could hear him talking gently to the young mare, clucking to her, gaining her trust.

He looked incredibly handsome. He looked just as she had always imagined he should.

Then he saw her. He stopped and stared, unable to move or speak as the filly continued trotting around him in slow, wide circles. At last he broke the spell. Never taking his eyes from hers, he called to the boy. "Geordie! This filly's finished for today. Put her away for me, will you?"

The boy opened the gate and relieved him of the lead line. "I thought you was going to work her for another half-hour, Mr. Clay," he said as the filly slowed to a halt.

"Changed my mind, Geordie," he answered, his eyes still locked to Jessica's, as he crossed the ring toward her. He stopped a few feet away, still staring at her as if she were a mirage.

She saw him take in the locket he'd sent her, now worn boldly over the bosom of her gown instead of hidden within, and then her left hand, where only a thin white line remained to mark the place where her wedding ring had rested. Then his eyes came back to meet hers.

Finally, she answered his unspoken question. "Owen's dead," she said flatly, then, "I didn't know if I should . . . if you'd want me to . . ."

He still did not speak. She managed to pull her eyes away from his and looked down. "Brewster brought me," she finished lamely.

She felt his hand on her arm.

"Come on," he said, and walked her down along the edge of the paddock fences and past another grove of trees. She couldn't tell if he was happy or angry or irritated. He had that businesslike look on his face again, the one with which she was all too familiar.

Then the trees ended, and they were approaching another house, not so grand or so new as the main house, but beautiful just the same. He opened the door and led her through a reception hall and into the front parlor.

The wide, high-ceilinged room was finely but comfortably furnished, and looked warm and casually homey. It reminded her of a much grander version of Martha and Daniel Follett's house; it felt as if generations of people had laughed here, loved here, had been happy here. Through the front window she could see glimpses, between the trunks of oaks and sycamores, of white-fenced paddocks. A rabbit, completely fearless, had hopped out of the wood and onto the lawn to nibble at the closely cropped clover growing there. It was peaceful here. It was a home.

"It's the original house," she heard him say.

"Someone lives here," she said, at a loss for conversation. What was he thinking? If he didn't want her, why didn't he just say so instead of giving her a polite tour?

"I live here," he whispered, suddenly very close behind her. "And I want you to live here with me."

She turned to him, tears of joy suddenly coursing down her cheeks, and held out her arms. He pulled her against him.

"Jess, Jess," he murmured as he stroked her hair, "you're the best part of me." He kissed her, hugging her as if he would never let her go, and then she felt his fingers searching out the pins in her hair, freeing it to fall in a dark tumble about her shoulders. "I love you, Jessie," he whispered, and covered her face and throat with kisses.

And then he began to undress her, slowly and with great satisfaction, cursing under his breath when he came to the corset with its whalebone staves. Finally, it came off, and he held it out between his fingers as he lifted her chemise to tickle her bare stomach with his lips. He looked up at her comically and asked, "You don't really enjoy wearing these, do you?"

She laughed, standing there half-naked in the parlor. "No, I detest them!"

"Good," he said, and tossed it aside. "Because we're going to burn every last damned one of them. It takes too long to get you out of them for my taste."

Slowly, he stripped her of the rest of her garments,

easing the chemise from her shoulders and covering her breasts with warm, welcoming kisses; pulling her underdrawers down and off; relieving her of her garters, stockings, and shoes; until she stood before him, surrounded by the scattered and rumpled islands of her clothing, completely naked except for the simple gold locket resting between her breasts.

He put his arms around her and hugged her to him, pressing her newly bare skin against his still-clothed body. "I love you, Clay," she whispered and she circled his neck with her arms. "I love you more than my own life. I'll stay with you as long as you want me."

He pressed his lips to hers, then swept her into his arms as if she were weightless and carried her to the stairs. Up he climbed, pausing every few steps to lower his head to kiss her lips or nibble at the smooth curve of her throat.

"Christ, Jessie," he muttered, halfway up the staircase, "I hope I can make it to the bedroom," then lifted her to press his lips into the vee between her breasts.

But they did make it to his bedroom, and he laid her down on the quilt, then stood over her as he undressed himself. When he was naked, she held out her hand to him, and he joined her, making love to her very slowly, with a joy and fervor that were nearly religious in their depth and devotion.

Later, she awoke from a light, satiated doze to see him standing at the window. He had pulled his breeches back on, and stood with his wide back to her, watching the sun go down. Noiselessly, she reached to the floor and scooped up his blue shirt, pulling it around her like a knee-length kimono before she joined him.

He smiled and pulled her to him, with her back against his chest so that she could enjoy the view. Crossing his arms beneath her breasts, he nuzzled at her ear.

"Jessie McCallister," he whispered. "Do you like the sound of that?" He raised one hand to tip her chin to the side and up so that he could look into her deep blue eyes. "I hope so, because you're going to be hearing it for the rest of your life." He bent to kiss her upturned face, and hugged her more tightly to him.

She had never felt so warm and happy, so genuinely and perfectly right. Through the window, she watched the dying sun turn the distant woods into a riot of color as a flock of birds—doves, she thought—rose from the trees in a flurry of black silhouettes. Closer, in the rolling pastures, the last, low rays made halos of orange and gold around the mares grazing peacefully in the fields of Turtle Creek.

"It's so beautiful." She felt she could stand like this forever, safe and warm, with his arms around her.

"You should see it in the spring," he whispered. "It's my favorite season here. Everything's fresh and misty and pale green, and from this window you can see the new foals kicking up their heels at their mothers' sides." He gave her a little hug.

"Turtle Creek has been in our family for four generations now. I really never appreciated that until . . ." He tightened his arms again, giving her a little hug. "You and I, Jessie, we'll have sons and daughters to carry it on into the future."

Staring out into the orange glow, she smiled. "Sooner than you think," she said softly.

He took her face in his hand again and tilted it back. He was grinning. "Jess?"

"Around the first of March, I should imagine," she smiled. No sight was more welcome than the undisguised delight on his face.

He kissed her, then slid his hands inside her shirt. It fell open, and he laid his big tanned hand against her still-flat belly. He held her like that for a moment, then turned her to face him.

"I love you, Jessie," he whispered. "I love you both." Then he slipped the shirt from her shoulders. It fluttered to the floor with a whisper, leaving her clothed only in the warm golden glow of the setting sun.

She reached up and, with her fingertips, gently traced the thin pink scar that started above his breast and ran up and outward over his collarbone. "Where did you get this?" she asked, knitting her fine brow.

He smiled and took her hand, kissing her fingertips. "I'll tell you all about it later. Right now, I'd rather show you something else."

"Don't you think we should go back up to the main house?" She smiled. "Brewster and your father will be waiting for us."

"They can wait a little longer." He grinned and, lifting her into his arms, carried Margaret's daughter back to bed.